WILDEST HUNGER

ALSO BY LAURA LAAKSO

WILDEST HUNGER

Laura Laakso

Wilde Investigations 4

2022
Louise Walters Books

Wildest Hunger
by Laura Laakso

A catalogue card for this book is available from the British Library.

Produced and published in 2022
by Louise Walters Books

ISBN 9781916112384
eISBN 9781916112391

Typeset in PT Serif 11pt by Blot Publishing

Printed and bound by Clays Ltd, Elcograf S.p.A.

louisewaltersbooks.co.uk

info@louisewaltersbooks.co.uk

Louise Walters Books
Northamptonshire
UK

For you, the reader, for asking what happens next.

CONTENTS

FRIDAY

1

RIPPLES

The map of Old London rustles in the breeze, its edge catching on the brim of my tourist hat. Through the gap between them, I watch as a group of Mages strides across the square. Their destination is the marble-clad Guildhall behind me, the administrative centre of Old London and the place where the High Council of Mages has been meeting for centuries. The Mages' cloaks, marking them as Council members, flutter in their wake. A light breeze blows their scent towards me.

Hidden behind my disguise, I allow the forked tongue of a snake to sample the air: two West Mages and a South Mage.

No Leeches.

My task of vetting the High Council of Mages is almost complete, and so far I have found no one masquerading as a Mage. With every name I tick off my list, I am wondering more and more whether Gideor Braeman was the solitary exception. But Lord Wellaim Ellensthorne as the Speaker is paying a premium fee for my services and I have every reason to be thorough.

A glance at my watch shows that the Council meeting has begun. Anyone in attendance will have arrived already. Time for me to leave.

I am straightening the map to fold it when running footsteps draw my attention back to the square. A young man in the earthy green cloak of an East Mage is hurrying towards the Guildhall. Right before he passes by, his scent reaches me, sour and strange. Even without resorting to the power in my blood, my brain gives him a category: a Leech.

The map rustles while my body shudders and adrenaline floods my veins. I want to call upon the claws of a lynx and the teeth of a bear to defend myself, although they would be of no use against a Leech. It has been nearly two months since Jans broke into my flat, and yet the sour tang of a Leech is enough to send my pulse tripping and for bile to rise in my throat. I search my memory for a name: Gerreint Lloid. He is one of the newer members of the Council and one I thought was high risk. I was right.

Aside from the initial tremor in my hands, I force my demeanour to remain neutral as I turn away and fold the map. It will not do for a PI to show their emotions. In Old London, someone is always watching. As I leave the square, I hesitate by a bin, but opt to keep my disguise. I have not yet finished vetting the Circle of Shamans. The tourist outfit may come in handy.

When my calves begin to ache and my knee jars, I realise I have been rushing to reach my car. A glance over my shoulder shows nothing out of the ordinary. Why should there be, when the Leech did not notice me in his haste to get to the meeting? Yet my breathing only evens when I close the car door and lock it behind me.

Scrolling through the contacts on my phone, I select one. When the call connects, I skip all niceties.

'Mr Whyte, I found a Leech.'

Once home, I hurry through my damp office and up the stairs. Lady Bergamon is due to visit and I want to make sure the house is tidy. When I open the door to the lounge, Sinta trots to greet me. She comes halfway across the room before squatting. I pick up a clean rag from a pile by the fireplace and lay it on the puddle. Scooping her up, I open the lounge window and climb out. She reaches to lick my chin.

How strange to come home to find I have been missed so much.

I set Sinta down. She spends a long while sniffing at the individual blades of grass before the few remaining leaves clinging to a blackcurrant bush arrest her attention. She bounds across the small lawn and leaps at the leaves. In the past month, she has grown. Her wobbly bat-ears still look disproportionate, but her body has lengthened. She is beginning to look more like the corgi she is rather than a ball of fluff with giant ears. Her attention span remains that of a puppy, and she soon loses interest in the leaves. She also seems to have no interest in going to the toilet now she is outside.

Back in the lounge, I have time to clean up after Sinta and set the kettle to boil before the doorbell rings. Sinta howls and I silence her with a finger on her nose. She tries to follow me down the stairs, and closing the door in front of her earns me another howl.

Lady Bergamon is dressed in a heavy wool cloak, and her white hair is just visible under the fur-trimmed hood. I catch a few notes of 'Santa Baby' from a passing car. I step aside to let Lady Bergamon in, and she sets down her basket while she unclasps the cloak and hands it to me. She watches me with a smile as I hang the cloak on my coat-stand. Her face is thinner than I recall, almost gaunt, and her aura has an uneven feel to it. When she draws me into a hug, her strength surprises me. She has not yet recovered from the attack on her garden, but at least she appears to be on the mend. I let my relief show in my smile.

'How are your hands?' she asks.

I flex them and they twinge. The burn of Baneacre's rot is still fresh in my memory. It has been nearly three weeks since Lady Bergamon declared the healing had progressed far enough that I no longer needed to visit her every day. Between her herbs and magic, the cold iron tokens, and the antibiotics, the Fey infection has subsided. Like the knife wound on my side, the burns that covered my hands have faded to silvery scar tissue. The healing skin is tight, but a huge improvement on the weeping sores.

'A little tender, but much better.'

'That will ease over time,' Lady Bergamon says as she follows me upstairs. 'Fey magic is tricky. Any lingering effects from the wolfsbane?'

'None, thanks to you and Wishearth.'

'Good.'

As soon as we step into the lounge, Sinta rushes to Lady Bergamon. Sinta's expression is one of adoration, which I thought was reserved for Funja and Wishearth. Although she and Lady Bergamon have never met, Sinta is smitten.

'Wishearth told me you'd adopted a puppy.' Lady Bergamon strokes Sinta, who squirms and whimpers. 'He was quite taken with her.'

'From what I gathered, Wishearth conspired with Funja to make sure Sinta came to me.'

'You could share your life with someone far worse.'

'Sinta is quickly showing that to be true.' I smile as I head towards the kitchen. 'Tea?'

'Please.' Lady Bergamon follows me. 'I have your father's medicine.'

'Thanks. When I go to the conclave, I'll bring back the last batch of bottles.'

'That would be helpful, otherwise I shall be required to drink more wine.'

We share a laugh while I prepare a pot of tea and place mugs and a plate of custard creams on the table. I study Lady Bergamon as she pours milk into her tea; the only sounds in the room are the clink of our spoons and Sinta gnawing on a calf hoof. The lines around Lady Bergamon's eyes and mouth are deeper than when we first met, and in them, I read a tale of pain and regret. When she catches me staring, there is fatigue in her eyes.

'How are you?' I ask.

'Time is the greatest healer of all,' she says with forced brightness. When I offer no response, she busies herself with selecting a biscuit, which she dunks in her tea. 'Truth be told, I haven't been sleeping well. The worst part of all is that I know I'll soon feel better.'

I wait for her to continue, but when she says nothing further, I shake my head. 'I don't understand.'

'The guilt I now feel, the sorrow, the anger at having been so helpless will fade until I will struggle to remember why I was so sad.'

'How much of your life do you remember?'

It was not what I intended to ask. I cover my uncertainty by lifting the mug to my lips while I wait to see whether my question has offended her.

'I remember a great deal, especially major events. But names and faces fade over time. My plants help with that.'

'You can store memories in your plants?'

Lady Bergamon laughs, and the sound is the rustle of silver birch leaves in a gentle breeze. 'Nothing like that. But scent has a great ability to unlock lost memories. I find natural smells far more potent than any others.'

As I dip my chin, my mind conjures recalled scents of heathered hills, fog-clad lakes, and fresh kills.

'And I imagine many of your memories are connected to the natural world.'

'Indeed,' she says.

I want to ask her again what she is. Last time the subject came up, she admitted to not being a Plant Shaman, but said nothing further. I have an inkling of what the truth might be, but I am hesitant to present my theories to her.

Lady Bergamon pets Sinta, who responds by rolling over. She is rewarded with long fingers tickling her belly. One of her back paws beats a rhythm of pleasure against the table leg.

'It's good you have company. We could all do with an occasional break from solitude.' Lady Bergamon straightens in her seat.

'Are you lonely in your house and your garden?' I had not intended to blurt out this question either, and as soon as I do, I fear I have overstepped the boundaries of our friendship.

A smile lifts the fatigue from her face as she regards me. 'I have my plants and Bradán for company. With visits from you and Wishearth, what else would I need?'

Her words prompt an image of Bradán roaming her garden, protecting both their domain and his lover from intruders. Only, he could not stop the decay Baneacre inflicted, nor could he reverse the spell on Lady

Bergamon. Does a Fey feel guilt like we mortals do? How long before he forgets?

But, I soon realise that she did not answer my question. I do not push the matter further. If she wants to confide in me, I trust she will.

Lady Bergamon finishes her tea and sets down the mug. 'I shan't keep you any longer. You have a long drive ahead of you, and the work of a gardener is never finished.'

She helps me carry the crockery back to the kitchen, empties her basket, and tops up my jar of pain-relieving tea. As we head downstairs, I tell her what has been occupying a part of my mind during her visit.

'I found another Leech in the Council.'

Lady Bergamon twists to look at me, fingertips resting against the staircase wall. 'Did they spot you?'

'No. He was in a rush to get to the Council meeting.'

She turns to continue down, but not before I see the tight compression of her lips. Once I have helped her don the cloak, she presses a kiss on my cheek.

'You must take care, my dear. A Leech is a dangerous creature at the best of times, and with influence among the Council and the threat of exposure, there's no telling what he'll do.'

'I'll be careful,' I say, smiling to try to dispel her unease. 'Besides, I'm fleeing the city for a few days.'

'No bad thing, I believe.' Lady Bergamon picks up her basket. 'Do call around when you're back if you have a spare moment. And bring Sinta with you.'

I promise to do so and we say our goodbyes. Leaning against the doorframe, I watch her ascend the stairs to the street until the chill of the day forces me to shut the door.

9

The sound of my phone ringing causes me to rush upstairs, ignoring the ominous crunch from my left knee. Sinta is barking at the window, and I shush her as I pick up the phone. It is Detective Inspector Jamie Manning. I hesitate, conscious of how distant he has been of late. We have not spoken since the case involving Baneacre was wrapped up more than a month ago and I told him everything I'd held back during the investigation.

I answer the call.

'Hi, Yannia,' he says, and my awkwardness is mirrored in his tone.

'Hello, Jamie. What can I do for you?'

'I was hoping to ask your opinion on some crime scene photos that have found their way to me. Another police force asked me to consult on the case, given my expertise in magical crimes. The photos are baffling, but you're the expert on all things natural.'

'Are they urgent?' I ask as I transfer my father's medicine into a canvas bag. Despite the paper wrapping, the bottles clunk against each other.

'Not terribly. If you could give me your thoughts sometime in the next couple of days, that would be great.'

'Sure. I'm heading up north for a brief visit to the conclave, but I should be back tomorrow evening.'

'Everything all right with your family?' Some of the formal edge in Jamie's voice gives way to curiosity.

'Fine. I just need to drop something off and make an appearance.'

I have never told Jamie who my father is, nor about the promises that bind me. Now is not the time to enlighten him.

'Right. I'll email those photos to you now. Call me when you're ready to share your thoughts.'

Some of the awkwardness returns when Jamie says goodbye, and I am relieved to slip the phone in my back pocket. While my laptop boots, I pack my rucksack and check I have the medication I need. The email arrives as I am feeding Sinta. It contains nothing but Jamie's standard email signature and a zipped folder. I start the download while I pack the car. Although there is no urgency with the photos, I click on the first to discover what kind of crime scene Jamie needs my help with.

It is a death, possibly a murder. The field and the body barely register as my eyes are drawn to the tracks around the body. I stare at the photo until Sinta leaping on a squeaky toy pheasant pulls me from my preoccupation and I close the laptop lid. With the laptop under one arm and Sinta under the other, I leave. Sinta takes her place on the front seat with the certainty born out of two previous car journeys, and I fasten her harness to the belt. Even as I pet her and start the car, my mind's image of the photo never fades.

2

CONFIDANT

It is dark when I reach the conclave lands. Moonlight casts pools of paleness between the skeletal limbs of the trees. Sinta looks confused when I set her down next to the car without clipping on her lead. She sniffs the carpet of crunchy leaves and soon finds the courage to venture to the mud-caked tyres of the vehicle next to mine. I leave her to her explorations while I unload the car. Her low growl alerts me to the fact that we are no longer alone.

A figure moves beneath a sycamore tree, indistinguishable in the darkness. Without sharpening my sight, I know it is Dearon, and my heart clenches. The sentries must answer to him now.

Despite knowing he is there, I call upon the power thrumming through the forest and my senses are restored to what the Wild Folk consider normal. What used to be as natural as breathing now requires careful balance. The last time I allowed myself to be swept away by my new ability to view the world, I witnessed Karrion withering before my eyes. It is not an experience I wish to repeat with Dearon. But the more I tread the tightrope between using all of my senses and seeing the rot of all things, the more I will learn to control it.

Dearon's expression remains hidden among the shadows as he approaches. I lock the car, shoulder my bags, and wonder how best to greet him. Our recent telephone conversations have thawed the ice between us, but I find myself on uneven ground.

When Sinta and I circle the Jeep, Dearon stops. Sinta scampers forward, her gait unsteady, until she stands between me and him. She growls again.

'What's that?'

Anger chases away a flash of disappointment. '*She* is a corgi puppy. My corgi puppy.'

'You bought a dog?'

'Something like that.' I cross my arms. 'I thought it would be nice to share my home with someone.'

Dearon opens his mouth and closes it again. Even if I cannot see the tight press of his lips, the anger coming off him in waves washes over me.

It seems nothing has changed.

A crashing sound approaching from the woods signals the second half of the welcoming committee. Ollie leaps out of the darkness, missing Dearon by an inch, and comes to an abrupt halt when he spots Sinta. His whole back end is shivering as he eases forward, one paw at a time. Sinta pulls her ears back. When Ollie is close enough, she launches herself at him with all the ferocity a small ball of fluff can muster. He nearly somersaults backwards in his haste to get away, and Sinta returns to my side, tail and ears up.

Dearon laughs. 'I can see why you picked her.'

'It was more the other way round.'

Crouching, Dearon offers his hand to Sinta. His magic unfurls, gently encouraging her. Sinta looks at me and takes a hesitant step. A brief sniff is all Dearon gets before she turns away. Ollie has been observing all this from behind Dearon's legs, and his whining increases. After giving Sinta a reassuring pat, I open my arms.

'Go on, then.'

Ollie leaps and lands against me with a thump. He dances on his hind legs to lick at my chin. I laugh, trying to keep him away, but this only encourages him further.

'You'd think I'd been gone years rather than a month.'

'Time has no meaning to dogs,' Dearon says, while Ollie stands in front of me, tail wagging. 'You were here and then you were gone. That's all he knows.'

Shifting my focus from Ollie to Dearon, I find his expression inscrutable. Does he think the same way? As much as we embrace the wild instincts, they sit side by side with our human awareness of the world.

Before I have a chance to say anything, Ollie becomes impatient and leaps up again. In doing so, he steps on Sinta's paw, and she responds with an outraged bark. I rest a finger on her nose.

'Enough now, Sinta.'

'I take it you're here to deliver the Elderman's tonic.'

'Yes.'

I mentioned the visit when we last spoke, though I see no reason to remind him of that. The prospect of another argument settles a blanket of fatigue over me, and I adjust my grip on the bags.

'You're just in time for the evening gathering.'

Every evening, the conclave comes together around the fire to share a meal and mugs of tea. As valued as the communal meal is, even more important is the sharing of songs and stories. That is how the wisdom of our ancestors is passed on through countless generations. We recall the ways of old, dream of how our lives used to be, and continue an unbroken line of tradition. The honouring of the old ways is part of what makes us Wild Folk, and every aspect of our lives is steeped in tradition. It is what has seen us flourishing through the centuries and millennia, while the country around has been transformed time and time again. It is also why we are so resistant to change.

As much as I am the rebel of the conclave, trying to encourage different ways of looking at the world in the others is like banging my head against Hadrian's Wall.

The last time I sat around the fire with the rest of the conclave was over a year ago. I doubt they will be as welcoming now. This winter has been the first time I have returned since I chose exile. Both visits can be described as fleeting at best; at worst, I have fled back to Old London as quickly as I could. Until I return to stay, I will not be welcomed with open arms.

But there will come a time when I must return, even though Lady Bergamon's medicine will prolong my father's life and delay Dearon becoming the Elderman.

The silence has gone on for too long, and I force a smile as I nod. Sinta stays by my side as we choose the path that will take us to the heart of the conclave, but soon she finds the courage to venture further from me. An owl's hoot brings her scampering back, as does the snap of a branch and the rustle of leaves. For Sinta's first time in a forest, I am glad she gets to experience the unspoilt landscape of the conclave.

Once the glow of the fire ahead is visible, I call Sinta back to me and pick her up.

'Would you mind holding Sinta while I see my father?'

'Are you trying to hide the puppy from him?'

'I'm sure he knows by now, but that doesn't mean I wish to invite a discussion on the subject.'

Perhaps it is my weary tone that discourages a reply; Dearon takes Sinta from me. She twists in his hold to watch me, and I give her a quick stroke between the ears.

'I won't be long.'

My father is asleep in the main room. His face is less gaunt than before, and it looks like he has gained a pound or two. A wild hope surges through me. Could Lady Bergamon's medicine be turning the tide instead of just slowing it?

I hand the bottles to the healer and replace them with the empty ones. There is little for us to say to one another, and I continue down the corridor to my bedroom. Nothing has changed, or so I think until the scent of lavender reaches my nose. A small dried blossom is resting on my pillow, and I twirl it between my fingers. Did Dearon do this? If so, why?

Returning the sprig to the pillow, I leave through the window. Most of the conclave has convened around the fires, and the nearer I get, the more hesitant my steps become. I feel unwelcome, though no one has so much as glanced my way. These are my people, my kind, and yet I am not certain I am theirs. The old mould has been broken, and I have left the pieces behind.

Dearon walks through the gathered crowd and beckons me forward.

'You must be hungry.'

Near the benches forming a circle around the fire is a table stacked with clay bowls and wooden spoons. Two men heft an iron pot of stew onto it, and a breadboard piled high with dark crusty bread follows. The conclave members form a queue, but rather than approach the food, they turn to Dearon.

The subtle sign of obeisance tells me everything I need to know about who leads the conclave in all but name.

With a dip of his chin, Dearon takes two of the bowls, Sinta tucked into the crook of his left arm. He offers one of them to me and helps himself to the food. I join the back of the queue, and some of the tension in the clearing lifts. When Dearon turns with a full bowl, he frowns, but says nothing.

Once everyone has food, we take our places around the fire. The benches are covered in hides, and I drape a woollen blanket over my shoulders. Dearon passes Sinta to me, and she curls up on my lap. Warmth seeps through the clay bowl and into my fingers. All around us, there is a steady murmur of conversations, but Dearon and I eat in silence. The stew is hot and filling. If it and the bread lack a bit of seasoning, no one complains. The food here serves a purpose rather than aiming for culinary heights.

After the meal, empty bowls give way to mugs of tea. The children of the conclave – all six of them – are sitting on a lower bench. Next to them are the seven teenagers. They all turn when Greoff, one of the Elders, steps up to the fire.

'Who will begin tonight?' he asks.

One of the teenagers, a girl I think is fourteen, stands and clears her throat. She recites a poem about earthworms, beetles, and spiders. I smile. How often did I debate the meaning of the rhymes with Dearon when we were younger? When I argued that earthworms were weird, he brought up slugs, and the conversation was sidetracked.

When the girl finishes, someone else stands to sing about the midwinter and the pause before new life begins. And so it goes. Different members of the conclave relate memories or life lessons, sing songs passed down through the generations. As much as the daily lessons teach us how to survive in the wilderness, the evening gatherings tell us what it means to be Wild Folk.

There is a lull in the storytelling when the mugs of tea are refilled. Dearon rises and turns to me.

'Yannia, do you have any wisdom from your travels you'd like to share with us?'

A hush spreads around the benches. I hesitate, but pass the sleeping puppy to Dearon and pick up my mug. Taking a sip gives me time to gather my thoughts until I find a place to begin.

I tell the story of a Wild Folk in the Unseen Lands. Although I preface it with a reference to our past, when the Fair Folk were still frequent visitors to our world, it is my own experiences I relay. I speak of Kelpies, mushroom circles, and dark hounds. I caution against games of wit, challenging the Fey, but most of all, my story is a warning against striking bargains without understanding the true cost of the agreement. My words may, at times, be hesitant, my narrative rusty, but from the faces around the fire, I see that the gravity of my tale has captured many people.

After I have returned to my seat, my thoughts are drawn to the Fey hounds and to the photos Jamie emailed me, and I lose the thread of the storytelling. I am not certain how long I have stared at the flames before Dearon nudges me with his knee.

'You're distracted.'

'I guess I am. Sorry.'

'Do you want to talk about it?'

My first instinct is to say no, but I realise I do want to share this with Dearon. I nod. He glances towards my father's cabin, and I nod again. We both stand. The story in progress falters as people turn to us. I am grateful for the darkness that hides my heating cheeks. Dearon takes my mug and heads for the pantry shed. I fold up the blankets and murmur a goodnight to the nearest people.

Ollie has been lying on the edge of the light and now sidles to greet me. Ushering him away from the leftover food, I set Sinta down and coax her to follow me. By the time we reach my window, Dearon is already waiting. As I open it, I think back to the many occasions when we slipped in and out of each other's rooms this way, and I smile, despite myself. When Dearon passes Sinta to me, I see the corners of his mouth are also lifting.

Dearon lights a candle on the table while I get my laptop. It is still on and the folder containing the photos is open.

'A detective friend emailed me these photos and asked for my thoughts on them. I'm assuming he meant on the tracks around the body.'

'Show me.'

I pass the laptop to Dearon and open the first photo. As he takes in the details, his expression darkens in much the same way as I imagine mine did earlier today.

The photo shows a woman's body in a field of autumn-sown wheat. She is dressed for jogging, and splashes of mud speckle her neon orange trainers and matching leggings. White earbuds lie next to her head, the wires partly trampled into the soil. Wide eyes and bloodied forearms speak of a struggle.

Animals have got to the body. The blood-spattered seedlings and torn throat indicate they may have contributed to the cause of death. A little of the woman's torso is visible beneath the gore, shredded clothes, and coils of intestines. The animals have done what comes naturally to predators and opened the chest cavity to reach the internal organs. Without the autopsy results, it is impossible to say what has been eaten and what remains. Wide slashes across the woman's thighs have exposed the bone, and there are chunks of flesh missing.

As before, my eyes are drawn to the tracks around the body. Dearon frowns and leans closer to the screen.

'You can zoom in, if you want,' I say, and point to the buttons below the photo.

His movements are uncoordinated as he struggles to use the touchpad. I say nothing while I try to recall the last time I saw Dearon doing something he is not good at. Nothing springs to mind. Although I grow impatient, I let him use the touchpad until the cursor moves a little more smoothly across the screen.

Dearon studies each photo with close attention while I resist the temptation to drum my fingers on my knee. When he has finally returned to the first one, he points to the bottom left corner.

'Those are from some sort of canid.' He zooms in. 'Make that a wolf.'

'That would be my guess too, though it's impossible to say for certain from the photo.'

He moves the cursor around the photo as he speaks. 'There's a bear, a fox, a lynx, a weasel, an eagle, a wolverine, a wild cat, and a buzzard. Too many animals for such an unspoilt carcass.'

'Not to mention it doesn't look like she died in the wilderness.' I turn to Dearon. 'But you left one out.'

The cursor moves to cover the print of a hand-sewn boot. Our eyes meet.

'Wild Folk.'

SATURDAY

3

BALANCE OF POWER

A whimpering wakes me. I roll out of bed, open the window, and lift Sinta out with practised ease. In the pre-dawn greyness, the trees are indistinct and the forest holds a mysterious quality that tempts me to explore the familiar landscape anew. The temperature has dropped during the night, and the frosty air is sharp in my lungs. I remain leaning against the windowframe, letting the scents of the forest and the conclave welcome me home until Sinta whimpers again.

Once I have fed her and dressed, we leave by the window. My father is likely to be awake, and I want to delay the inevitable conversation I will have with him. Ollie lopes around the corner of the cabin, but his greeting is more restrained with Sinta staring at him, hackles up. Dearon soon follows with two mugs of tea.

'Let's take a walk,' he says, and motions towards the forest.

We follow a path away from the cabins and through a copse of oaks. My senses sharpen until the darkness no longer hinders me. As I crouch to tie my shoelace, I admire the patterns of frost on the fallen leaves. Beyond the trees, the meadow is grey and frozen solid. Sinta trots forward to investigate, and she sneezes. Ollie leaps past her and flushes out a rabbit, which darts away from him.

He gives chase, but the rabbit ducks into a hole and he is left whimpering his frustration.

'I couldn't sleep last night,' Dearon says, breaking the silence.

'The photos?' I finish my tea.

'Yes. I keep trying to think of reasons why one of us would have left their footprints by a body.'

'We're not even sure it was one of us,' I say.

'Who else could it be?'

'A hardcore historical re-enactor?' At a puzzled glance from Dearon, I shake my head. 'The point is, there could be people other than Wild Folk out there who wear handmade boots. Or they could have been wearing plastic booties over their shoes to try to disguise their footprints.'

'That seems unlikely.'

'More unlikely than one of us being at a kill site?'

'It wasn't just the boot print. All those animal prints at a carcass that had barely been disturbed. It doesn't make any sense. Not unless they weren't made by animals at all.'

Calling Sinta away from a shallow stream, I stop, hands on my hips. 'Are you seriously suggesting that one of us killed that woman and ate parts of her?'

Dearon presses his toes against a boulder on the raised bank, arms crossed. The contours of his frown reflect my unease. Of all the laws and traditions that govern our existence, one stands above all others: it is forbidden to consume the flesh of humankind. By absolute obedience to that law, we have survived through the centuries. Strangers – human and magical people – have at times encroached upon our lands, threatened us, and driven us to the last remaining wild places, but by choosing not to hunt their kind, we have ensured a truce rather than persecution.

But beneath the laws that govern our existence, the oldest of the dream memories I have accessed suggests that eating human flesh may not have always been a taboo. Those fragmented images are never spoken of, never mentioned during the evening gatherings. Instead, the Elders impress control upon us from an early age, even before we come to our powers. We learn to recognise the wild instincts and to channel the predatory hunger in ways that ensure the safety of the people straying onto our lands, and ensures our continued existence.

'I don't know,' he says after a while. 'But whatever happened cannot be ignored.'

'I'll let Jamie know our thoughts and leave him to decide what he wants to do.'

'Jamie is the human?'

I nod.

'No.' Dearon shakes his head. 'This matter concerns the Wild Folk, not humans. It is not up to them to investigate our kind.'

Resisting the urge to roll my eyes, I pick up Sinta and leap across the stream. A splash of a boot landing in the mud indicates Dearon has done likewise.

'It's too late for that now,' I say, pushing past coils of brambles. A thorn catches the back of my hand and redness wells in the wound. I lick the cut and savour the rich taste of blood. My stomach growls. 'The police are already conducting an investigation. Given that Jamie called me to ask my thoughts, I'm guessing they're treating the death as suspicious.'

'Nevertheless, this is no business of theirs.'

I nuzzle the top of Sinta's head while I try to rein in

my temper, and then I set her down. 'And what do you propose we do? Travel the length of the country in the hopes that we stumble upon one of us feeding on a corpse? We don't even know where the woman from the photos died and how long ago it was. If a Wild Folk is responsible, they could be anywhere by now.'

'You can find out where the body was discovered.'

'Jamie called me to ask for advice, not to volunteer the particulars of the case.'

'Then give him a list of the animal tracks we identified in the photos and ask for information in return.'

'No. Jamie's human, not stupid. He'll notice I've omitted commenting on the boot print and want to know why. I'm not going to lie to him.'

'Then what do you propose? Telling a human that we think a Wild Folk may have killed that woman will put every conclave in Britain in danger.'

'I trust Jamie not to shout this from the rooftops. There may be an alternative. My PI business has an agreement in place with New Scotland Yard, which allows me to be a paid consultant on select cases. I can ask Jamie to clear me and Karrion to assist them. If it turns out the killer was one of us, hopefully I can do some damage control as part of my investigation.'

'A Bird Shaman investigating Wild Folk is not a big step up from humans.'

I whirl around and glare at Dearon. He takes a step back.

'You'll find that Karrion is more than capable, and he's discreet. I'm lucky to have someone like him assisting me.'

'That doesn't mean I want him poking his beak into Wild Folk business. Our kind should be the ones conducting the investigation.'

'I didn't realise my race had changed while I've been living and working in Old London.'

'Of course it hasn't. My concern is contacting other conclaves for aid and information.'

'So? I know how to get in touch with the conclaves.'

Dearon crouches to inspect deer tracks, but not before I see embarrassment mixed with frustration in his expression.

'What?' I ask, sensing I will not like his answer.

Sinta jumps up against Dearon's side, her coat clumpy from the frost. He busies himself by stroking her back and her legs, until Ollie gets jealous and nudges him from the other side. Dearon rises and both dogs follow him.

'What is it?' I ask again, my tone sharper than before.

'People talk, Yannia.'

'About what?'

'About you. About how you left the conclave and turned your back on our way of life. About how you're not fully Wild Folk anymore.'

'Living in the city doesn't change my blood or the source of my power.'

'A wolf once crawled out of the shadows, mesmerised by the dance of flames, and laid his head in the dirt next to a human. That wolf became a dog.'

Heat floods my cheeks. 'Do you really think that expanding my world beyond our lands and connecting with people other than Wild Folk and Shamans will domesticate me? That I will become a docile creature bereft of the power of the Wild? That the magic in my blood will simply fade away?'

'It's what people think is happening to you.' Dearon refuses to meet my eyes.

My temper flares anew and the words fly off my lips.

27

'Surely you're hoping for that. I'll be easier to control if I've been tamed by others.'

Dearon whirls around, his fists clenched, and it is my turn to take a step back. He will not hit me, of that I am certain, but his fury is a blast of heat. His aura expands with his temper, and the edges of my magic sting and blister where they touch his power. Drawing my shoulders back, I stand my ground against the oncoming storm.

A low growl draws our attention to the ground. Sinta is standing between us, tail stiff and ears drawn back as she snarls at Dearon with all the ferocity of a fourteen-week-old puppy. Although there is little Sinta can do, her actions break the tension. The press of Dearon's aura against mine eases. He turns, rubbing his face with the hand not holding his empty mug. When he speaks, his words are so low I need to call upon my magic to hear him.

'If you think I prefer you tame and docile, you're a fool.'

An angry retort rises to my lips, but I have no chance to voice my objections before Dearon continues.

'I'm merely recounting the rumours I've heard. People are concerned about the future of the conclave, concerned that you are setting a dangerous precedent. Human tribes fade away because the young leave to find a life elsewhere. We Wild Folk are more than our connection to nature; we thrive because we live as cohesive communities. It's the pack, the herd, the flock, the pod, that makes us who we are. We cannot thrive alone.'

'I'm doing just fine,' I mutter, but the words lack the earlier heat. A spot at the centre of my forehead throbs, and I rub it until a sliver of ice runs down my spine. 'There have been many times in our history when we've had to change in order to prosper. This could be one of those times.'

Dearon rolls his shoulders, but the tension in his back remains. 'Perhaps. Though one of us breaking the oldest law is bad news. I'm simply offering an explanation as to why the other conclaves may be reluctant to aid your enquiries.'

'I'm going to receive a much warmer reception than the human police could ever hope for.'

'That may not be enough.'

'Then what do you suggest?' I ask, tired of his hedging. A breath of frost caresses my cheek, and the scent is sharp. It reminds me briefly of Ilana, but I push the thought aside.

'I could help you.'

'You could what?'

'As I said, this is a matter that should be handled by our kind. All the conclaves will extend their hospitality to your father's successor.'

It is my turn to crouch to inspect tracks while I try to keep the incredulity off my face. 'And what possible use could you be to the investigation here?'

'I wasn't proposing to stay here.'

I stand up, abandoning all attempts to keep my feelings hidden. 'Let me get this straight: having just criticised me for my choice of leaving the conclave, you're now going to do the same?'

The sun rises above the frozen landscape, gilding the trees in a golden shroud. I angle my face towards it. Although the light is bright through my eyelids, I cannot feel the warmth. Perhaps the winter sun is too weak for that; perhaps the invisible mark of the Winter Queen insulates me against anything from the domain of the Summer King.

'Only temporarily. It is common for the Eldermen to

travel between the conclaves and resolve issues without involving outside authorities.'

'Yes, but I can see two problems with that proposal: one, you're not the Elderman; two, if the human police allow me to investigate this death, I won't be doing it in the Wild Folk lands. I'm returning to Old London until I have solid leads to follow.'

'I may not be the Elderman yet, but I am his representative among the other conclaves.'

I cover a snort by laughing. 'And as his representative, do you really think the Elderman is going to let you go to Old London with me?'

'Yes, I believe he will.'

'This is crazy,' I say as we step back into the woods where the cabins are. 'You have no experience with police procedures or murder investigations.'

'Was that not the case with you when you first settled in Old London?'

His comment hits the mark, and I flinch. 'Fine. If the Elderman agrees to your plan, I'll ring Jamie and ask him to let me consult on the case.'

Dearon nods. 'Good.'

We speak no more while we return to the heart of the conclave. Everyone else has risen during our walk and the fire pit becomes the centre of activity. Men and women are engaged in the dozens of tasks that make up the life at the conclave: cooking, cleaning, chopping firewood, sewing, repairing tools and huts, preparing herbal salves and teas. Some adults have a couple of children or teenagers with them. A large portion of the learning at the conclave happens by copying the Elders.

The people we pass acknowledge Dearon's presence with the briefest of glances. While I wash our mugs in the pantry shed, Dearon stops to speak to Greoff, who has stretched a deer hide across a frame and is scraping it clean. When I return, we continue to my father's cabin. Sinta tries to follow us in, but I tell her to wait outside.

My father is awake. The healer looks up when we enter and, without being asked to do so, leaves. My father is propped up against pillows and he twists his head. His expression does not change.

'Yannia. Our healer told me you brought more medicine.'

'Yes.' I kneel by the cot while Dearon remains standing by the fireplace. 'You were asleep and I didn't want to wake you.'

'It would have been no matter. You brought a dog with you.'

'A puppy, yes.'

'Is it wise, having a dog in the city?'

'I think it's better to be alive and in the city than unwanted and dead in the countryside.'

My father says nothing, but Dearon's face registers surprise. I never did tell him Sinta's story.

'Just so long as you appreciate that any dog here must serve a purpose.'

I bite my tongue before I point out there are ways for a dog to be helpful that have nothing to do with hunting or tracking. Antagonising the Elderman will achieve little, especially when Dearon wants something from him.

'Our bargain still stands,' my father says into the silence that has settled between us. I nod, though I had assumed that to be the case without seeking the confirmation.

'There's something Dearon needs to discuss with you,' I say, and push myself up. My knees ache from the hard floorboards.

'Go on.'

Dearon steps forward and kneels by the cot. 'A matter has arisen outside our borders. I would investigate it with Yannia.'

The Elderman's hand twitches towards the door. 'Leave us.'

It takes me a few seconds to realise he is talking to me. Dearon fixes his eyes on the floorboards.

'Fine,' I say. The door bangs shut behind me with a little more force than necessary.

The dogs rush to greet me, and I push aside my anger. They are the distraction I need. I pick up strips of dried meat from the pantry shed and continue Sinta's basic training. Ollie joins in, mostly to claim his share of the treats, and what he lacks in attention span, he more than makes up for with enthusiasm. By the time I spot Dearon at the far side of the clearing, my mood has improved.

He makes his way to me, pausing to exchange a few words with someone or to rest his hand on the head of a pointer. Although he keeps his expression neutral, he moves with an edge of confidence I learned to recognise as satisfaction when we were younger. Ducking his head, he speaks close to my ear.

'I have permission to leave.'

'Great,' I say, and my lack of enthusiasm colours my voice. 'I'll call Jamie.'

We head further from the fire while I reach for my phone. I select Jamie's number and listen to it ringing until it becomes clear he is not going to answer. It is so unlike him, I am tempted to redial straight away. Instead, I return the phone to my back pocket.

'No answer. He must be busy.'

'You can call him again when we're on our way.'

Dearon's tone sparks the embers of anger in me, but I stay silent. He has made up his mind and nothing I say will change it. We share the same stubborn streak; I have known as much for a long time. It is one of the reasons we clash so often.

With no way of persuading him otherwise, I nod. Dearon is coming with me to Old London.

4

A TRAIL OF MEMORIES

I remove my Bluetooth earpiece. We have been driving for three hours and Jamie is still not answering his phone. Next to me, Dearon is staring out of the window with an unreadable expression. The silence in the car is more comfortable than when we were driving to the conclave from Old London two months ago, but the prospect of a long journey with neither of us speaking sends a shudder of anxiety through me.

In the past, being quiet in Dearon's company was never a problem. Have I adopted some of Old London's small-talk habits, or is it Dearon that concerns me? If we remain silent, will the words we never speak become loud enough that we'll catch an echo of them?

To distract myself, I ask a question that has been on my mind a great deal in the past couple of months.

'What was my mother like?'

Dearon turns to me, frowning. 'Surely you must remember? You weren't that young when she died.'

'Of course I do. But I remember her being my mum. What I'd like to know is what she was like as a person.'

He watches the road long enough that my mind jumps to all sorts of conclusions. But when I glance to my left, he is smiling.

'She was kind and funny, but what I remember clearest is her smile. It could lift the heaviest shadows, and she used it as a shield and a mask.'

'What do you mean?'

'It hid her pain. She used it to dazzle anyone who was concerned about her. Long after we could smell the sickness in her breath, she kept the agony of the disease locked behind the radiance of her smile.'

I recall how she was always ready with a laugh and kind words for me. She struck a stark contrast with my father's dour countenance. Were it not for the fact that I know their mating was arranged, I would wonder what my mother ever saw in the Elderman.

'One thing she couldn't hide was her concern for you,' Dearon continues when I say nothing.

'What do you mean?' I ask again.

'When you danced through the woods and by the fire, I watched her stare at the way your knees and elbows bent back. I believe she saw something of your illness long before the pain began. But just as our herbal medicines couldn't cure the disease eating her from the inside, they did precious little for you.'

We have never discussed my Ehlers-Danlos Syndrome, not really, but once again, Dearon shows he is more perceptive than I have given him credit for. Emboldened by this, I drop my guard a little.

'Perhaps that's why she left me a car and her savings. She knew I'd need human medication to manage my condition.'

'It wouldn't surprise me. As much as she was the heart of the conclave, you were *her* heart.'

'I thought the Elderman was the heart of the conclave.'

Dearon's smile takes on an edge of sadness. 'Your

father's role is to ensure we survive, but it was your mother who allowed us to thrive.'

When I offer no response, Dearon's smile fades to a frown.

'Do you think the role of an Elderman's mate is merely one of being his shadow?' he asks, but does not wait for me to reply. 'The instinct of the Wild Folk is to obey their leader, just as it is the instinct of the Elderman to lead. But blind obedience will only lead to destruction. The Elderman will tolerate no challenge from the members of the conclave, except the person he has chosen to share his life with. As much as the Elderman tells us how and where to hunt, chooses how we interact with the outside world and keep our blood-lines strong, so does his mate counsel us on whether to follow tradition or seek a change. While the Elderman leads by instinct much of the time, his mate will follow her mind and heart.'

'Yeah, I know that,' I say, trying to keep the defensive edge from my voice. 'Though it seems my father has done just fine after Mum died.'

'I'm not sure you can say the conclave is thriving when the Elderman's only daughter chooses exile.'

My fingers tighten around the steering wheel. 'It's temporary, you know that. I'm bound by the same promises as you.'

'Still, some of the joy died from the conclave with your mother.'

'Shame I'm not like her.'

'I think you resemble her more and more with each passing year.'

A tremor runs through me, though I cannot say whether it is pleasure or trepidation. The intensity of

Dearon's eyes becomes too much, and I fix my focus on the road.

'Was she happy?' I ask the car in front of us.

'She loved you a great deal. I believe there was a certain affection between her and your father, though I never observed them with that particular question in mind. But I do think the conclave flourished under their leadership, even if not everyone agreed with her plans for the future.'

'What plans?'

'Your mother was concerned about the conclave losing some of the old songs and stories. Each generation has its favourites, while others fade from memory. She wanted to begin a project committing our oral traditions to paper or electronic records.'

Dearon's words trigger a memory of a half-heard argument between my parents. My father was adamant that bringing more technology into the conclave would damage our future more than the forgetting of ancient lore.

'I guess she never got her way.'

'No, though I do think it's a good idea. But I'd like to take it a step further than she did and find a way to preserve the songs of every conclave in Britain. As much as we are the same people, we all have our own tales. It worries me that not all the stories are shared whenever the conclaves meet.'

'You're going to encounter a lot of resistance from the Elders.'

'So?' Dearon shrugs. 'I'm not afraid of a little conflict. My bigger problem is knowing what sort of technology to employ. To have any chance of persuading the Elders, I have to be able to provide them with a practical solution.'

'I can probably help you with that. The learning curve

this past year has been pretty steep, but I'm getting the hang of modern technology. The tricky part is storing the information in a way that will allow access to all the conclaves.'

'Thank you.'

'Have you ever met your birth parents?' I ask after a while.

'No.'

It is not a question I intended to ask, but something I have often wondered. Dearon's blood relatives are all detailed on the hide containing his family tree. I cannot recall a time when it was not common knowledge that Dearon had been adopted by our conclave to bring in fresh blood and stronger magic. He hit the jackpot when my father chose him as the next Elderman. With the hindsight of maturity, I find myself curious about whether he wishes his life had taken a different route.

I hesitate, but my curiosity wins out. 'Why?'

'My father died when I was very young, or so the stories say. My mother... disappeared.'

'How?'

'She left me in the cot one morning and walked away from the conclave. The trackers found no trace of her, though there was a delay before the search began. After that, my birth father approached the Elderman about giving me away. I can only assume he didn't want to raise a child on his own. He died shortly after I came to live with you.'

Why have we never spoken of this before? Even as the question flashes through my mind, I know the answer: since I found out the Elderman's plans for me and Dearon, I haven't wanted to know.

'I'm sorry.'

'What for? My real parents were loving and kind. That's what matters the most.'

'If you'd been given the choice, what—?'

The ringing of my phone interrupts my question. A glance shows Jamie's name on the screen. I fumble for the earpiece and nearly drop it.

'Hi, Jamie.'

'Sorry about not answering,' Jamie says. People are shouting in the background. 'I didn't want to ignore you, but today is not a great time to discuss those photos I sent you.'

A spike of adrenaline floods my system. 'What's wrong?'

'A child has gone missing in Hertfordshire. Normally that's outside my remit, but the boy is a Dog Shaman, so the powers-that-be sent me here to lend a hand.'

'Did he run away, or was he taken?'

'At the moment, we're not sure. But the family dog was killed, which makes me think it was the latter.'

'Killed how?'

'His neck was broken.'

'Can we help?'

'We're waiting for the dogs at the moment, but another tracker can't hurt. I'll send you the address.'

I hesitate and glance over to Dearon. 'Actually, I have someone from the conclave with me. We were hoping to look into the death of the woman in the photos together. Do you mind if I bring him? He's a better tracker than I am.'

Dearon covers his surprise by brushing hair off his face.

Jamie swears. 'I'm not thrilled about the prospect of strangers trampling all over my crime scene. However, if he can help us find this boy, then fine. But he's your responsibility. Don't let him do anything stupid.'

39

'I won't. Thanks, Jamie. We'll be there as soon as we can.'

'You'd better hurry. We'll start with the dogs when they arrive.'

I want to ask him if he will get us out of speeding tickets, but he sounds in no mood for jokes. Instead, I say goodbye and end the call. When the text comes through, I ask Dearon to read the address. With detailed instructions, I explain how to load the navigation app on my phone and enter the details. Luck is on our side in that our destination in St Albans is along the way. Next, I find Karrion's number and dial.

'Hey, Yan,' he says. The heavy metal in the background grows softer. 'Did you escape the conclave with your sanity intact?'

'Something like that,' I reply, and avoid looking at Dearon. Although I am using the earpiece, I have no doubt he can hear every word of the conversation.

'Do we go back to work tomorrow?'

'No, today. A Dog Shaman boy has gone missing in St Albans, and I offered our help in trying to find him.'

'Right.' Karrion switches off the music. 'Where do you want to meet me and at what time?'

'Can I pick you up from St Albans station in an hour?'

'Of course. Do we know what happened to the boy?'

'Not sure yet, though Jamie suspects foul play. They're going to bring in canine units.'

'If that's the case, you'd be better off taking Funja rather than me. Bird Shamans aren't known for our tracking abilities.'

'But you do have perspective no one else has. We're in this together or not at all.'

In the silence that follows, I wonder if he too recalls

how I sent him out of harm's way before facing Baneacre alone. We both paid a price for my choice.

'Yeah, thanks, Yan. I'll see you soon.'

'You didn't tell him I'm with you,' Dearon says when I end the call.

'No. This way he won't have an hour to prepare his third degree. Besides, I'll have plenty of time to bring him up to speed when we pick him up at the station.'

Dearon nods. 'I trust you know what you are doing.'

If only that were true.

5

IN SEARCH OF A CHILD

Karrion is standing outside the station when I pull up on a cobbled lane between a taxi rank and the bus bays. He steps towards the car, a broad grin on his face, and he is reaching for the passenger side door when he spots Dearon. It takes no more than a couple of seconds for him to recover from the surprise and he moves sideways to see Sinta behind Dearon. I imagine the roll of his eyes when he walks around the car and slides in behind me.

'Hey, Yan,' he says, and clicks on the seatbelt.

'Karrion, meet Dearon. Dearon, this is my apprentice, Karrion.' I keep one eye on Dearon as I turn on to the road.

'I recognised your scent,' Dearon says, giving Karrion barely a glance.

'Right. Nice to meet you too.' Karrion leans forward and grips the sides of my seat. 'So, what's the story?'

I tell him what little I know while we drive out of St Albans and to the village of London Colney. The main road takes us past a small green and over a shallow river. My navigator sends me right to Willowside, where the Dog Shaman's family lives. The far end of the close shows identical red-brick family homes, most of which have their front gardens decked ready for Christmas. I look at the plastic reindeer and snowmen and try to imagine living in a house like this. The image jars, and I concentrate on finding somewhere to park.

Although I spot the house, the area is choked by police cars. We park further away. A policewoman lets two German shepherds out of a van.

'Is Detective Inspector Manning inside?' I ask as we approach the front door. The woman nods.

Dearon looks at the front garden and the paved roads in both directions. 'If the boy was taken through the front, I'll be of no use here.'

'Me neither. Let's see what else the police have discovered.'

A police officer opens the door. I present to him my New Scotland Yard consultant badge and ask for Jamie. While we wait, I look around. A corridor straight in front of us opens to a lounge and stairs lead upwards. Strung along the wooden bannister is faded birthday bunting. Something about the muted colours leaves me feeling anything but festive. Along the corridor, the wall is decorated with photos of a couple with a dark-haired boy. A black Labrador retriever features in many of the photos, but several others depict different dogs.

Jamie strides in from the lounge, and his frown tells me the boy is still missing.

'Yannia.' He nods.

'Jamie, this is Dearon Wilder. He will become the next leader of our conclave once the current Elderman dies.'

'Nice to meet you,' Jamie says, but his smile falters before it reaches his eyes. 'Come on through.'

Dearon's nostrils flare as he identifies Jamie as a human, and his expression changes to disinterest. I suppress a surge of irritation. In Dearon's world, humans are an inconvenience to be tolerated and avoided as much as possible. That is why the conclave lands are surrounded by farms run by Shamans of all kinds; they act as a natural buffer between us and the humans. Although relations are not hostile, we prefer to ignore their existence as much as we can.

Living and working in Old London, I can afford no such narrow world view.

In the lounge, I ignore the gold and red Christmas decorations, and focus on the couple sitting side by side on the sofa. They are both in their late forties. The woman is sobbing and twisting a tissue in her bony hands. As I approach, I inhale: they are both Dog Shamans, though the man's magic is much weaker.

Through the sliding glass doors, I see a cluster of police in the back garden. At the far end, next to a shed, is a shape covered by a blue tarpaulin. Three steps take me to the glass doors. A six-foot fence separates the house from its neighbours.

Jamie introduces the couple as Connor and Ylva Eastman. He runs through our names, though from the glazed expressions of the Eastmans, I doubt any of them sink in.

'These are our best trackers on two feet,' Jamie says, and Ylva lifts her head.

'They are Wolf Shamans?'

'We're Wild Folk,' I say.

The widening of their eyes shows equal parts of alarm and hope. Behind me, Dearon's aura tightens as he shifts.

'Can you tell us what happened?' I ask.

'It was my husband's birthday,' Ylva says. 'We had arranged to have dinner in town and Cúan was supposed to have a sleepover with his friend Alexander in Alsop Close.' Tears spill from her eyes again. 'We thought that's

44

where he was. It wasn't until Connor spotted Shadow in the garden that we realised something was wrong.'

Connor wraps an arm around his wife's shoulders. 'Cúan was supposed to call us if he changed his mind. When he left Alexander's home yesterday evening, he told Alexander's mother, Martha, that he'd call to let us know. Martha had no idea something had happened until we rang her a couple of hours ago.'

'How long was he at his friend's house last night?' I ask.

'Only for an hour or two. Alexander had a new movie poster that frightened him. When Alexander wouldn't take it down, Cúan wanted to come home.' Ylva dabs her eyes with the soggy tissue. 'He is on the autistic spectrum and gets upset by unexpected things. We'd agreed with Alexander's parents that Cúan could come home if he wanted to. He's old enough to be left alone for a few hours. But when the house was quiet and the television wasn't on, we assumed he'd been away for the night.'

'What about Shadow?'

'We thought Cúan had taken Shadow with him. He often did when he spent time with Alexander. I was worried when I noticed Shadow's bowl still here, but I thought that Martha would have given Cúan an old ice cream tub or something for him.'

'Can you think of anywhere Cúan might have gone?'

'We've rung all his friends already, checked the local shops and the playgrounds.' Connor's voice wavers. 'He's gone.'

'How about anyone who might have wished him harm?'

'We lead a quiet, ordinary life here in London Colney,' Ylva says. 'Most of our neighbours don't even know we have magical blood. Cúan keeps telling people he can speak to Shadow and other dogs, but I believe most assume that is simply a child sharing a connection to his pet rather than a sign of magic.'

'Why would you keep your blood hidden?'

'Neither of us needs it in our work and, for us, it's not that big a deal. We are happy with the life we have and have no need for magic to augment it.'

While I am baffled by Ylva's attitude, all I can do is nod.

'How safe is this area?'

'It's fine,' Connor says. 'Cúan did most of the dog walking and he knows the other regulars. We always felt comfortable letting him walk Shadow alone. The only rule was that he did not go around the lakes by himself.'

'Did he ever mention feeling like someone was watching him? Or was there anyone who made him feel uncomfortable, especially when he was out with Shadow?'

Ylva and Connor exchange a glance. In their matching expressions, I see parents unable to conceive of someone taking their child. As much as I am used to asking these questions, they are unaccustomed to answering them.

'No,' Connor says. 'We hear everything the other dog walkers tell Cúan about their lives and their dogs. I don't recall Cúan mentioning anything specific recently, certainly nothing that gave me cause for concern.'

'Do you mind if we check out back?' I ask.

'Of course. Look anywhere you like.'

Jamie opens the sliding doors for us, and we step outside. Most of the grass in the back garden has been churned to mud and a few dog toys are strewn around. The police step aside as we approach the tarpaulin, and

46

I lift it. A black Labrador retriever looks pristine, but his head lolls back when I lift the body. Jamie was right about the cause of death.

'Do you know what he was like as a guard dog?' I ask Jamie.

'Apparently with Cúan in the house, he'd make a fuss of everything.'

'So it's likely the dog was killed to stop him barking.'

'Perhaps.' Dearon leans to look over the fence. 'Or perhaps Shadow was the lure.'

When I stand, I see that he is looking at the top of the fence, not over it. There is a smudge in the moss covering the panel.

'Do you think Shadow came out to investigate something and Cúan followed him?'

'It's possible.'

I turn to where the dog's body is. The spot is such that a black dog in the shadow of the shed would not be easily visible from the lounge. The more I look around the garden, the more I think Dearon is right.

'Has the dog been moved?' I ask Jamie.

'No. We just covered him up.'

'Karrion, can you give me a hand?' I push aside the tarpaulin again.

'Do you want me to pick him up?'

'Please.'

I study the ground beneath the dog, and Dearon crouches to do the same next to me. The grass sticks to the mud. I inhale, but detect no trace of blood. But where the dog's rump was against the ground, there is a faint impression of a footprint.

'See, there,' I say, and point to it. 'There's no tread detail.'

'And here,' he replies. On the edge of a patio slab are two clear impressions of the tips of boots. Again, there is no detail in the impressions, and I experience the first flash of unease.

'Can either of you smell any blood in the garden?' Karrion asks.

Dearon and I share a glance, and I shake my head.

'If that's the case, the boy was probably taken alive. I'm thinking that if the kidnapper entered the garden over the fence, he probably took the boy out through there.'

Karrion points to a back gate. It is in the corner of the garden, behind a stack of plant pots.

'Why not through the house?' Dearon asks.

Karrion tugs the row of hoops in his left ear. 'Assuming the boy was taken after dark, there would be far fewer prying eyes if our culprit left the way he came. All he'd have to worry about were people looking out of their upstairs windows. If the boy didn't go willingly, it would be madness taking him out of the front door. Even if the kidnapper had a car, it would still be a huge risk.'

'Karrion is right,' I say. 'And look here, there's grass stuck to the bottom of the gate. It was opened recently.'

'If that's the case, we need to be out there.' Dearon stands. 'Let's go.'

'No, we can't. If that's the route the kidnapper took, we could be destroying evidence. Hang on.' Calling upon the wilderness I sense beyond the fence, I leap as high as I can. 'There's a field out there and a footpath runs through it. We can find another way.'

Jamie has returned inside. We file into the lounge, and I draw him to the hallway.

'Where did the canine unit go?'

'They were following a scent from the front door. Why?'

'We're going to check out the back, if we can find a way to the field.'

'Did you find something?' Jamie asks, lowering his voice.

'So far, we only have assumptions and suppositions. As soon as I know something concrete, I'll let you know.'

'Thanks. I'm waiting for a Family Liaison Officer to take over here. I'm more suited to solving murders than comforting parents whose child is missing.'

I want to offer reassurance, but no words seem appropriate. We are not friends, and the distance between us seems greater than ever. So all I do is nod and lead the others out.

In Willowside, I use my phone to guide us to a footpath leading to the woods. Karrion and Dearon hurry behind me, the slap of Karrion's boots on the pavement the only sound accompanying us. Without noticing, I have shifted my weight to the balls of my feet to ensure my passing is silent. Dearon, wearing the soft-soled leather boots of the conclave, walks with all the grace of a predator.

The footpath takes us to the end of a small cul-de-sac. Toys are strewn across tiny front lawns and clumsy chalk drawings decorate pavements. Two canine handlers approach with their dogs.

'We followed a trail from the front door, but it led to the friend's house,' the woman we saw earlier says. 'Now we're checking the back of the property.'

'That's where we're headed too. We think they left the garden through the back gate.'

'Let us see if we can pick up a trail first.'

'Of course. The dogs are better trackers than we are.'

Dearon looks like he wants to argue, but I silence him with a look. We follow the dogs further along the footpath, until we emerge into the field. Beyond a walled playground, the pavement gives way to grass paths.

'Did anyone make a note of which house belongs to the Eastmans?' Karrion asks.

His aura is spread wide around him, and for the first time, I notice how weak it feels. He has had a month to recover from almost dying, but the progress has been slow. Too slow. I watch him now, trusting my feet to maintain balance on the uneven surface. He has lost weight. Although he has never been heavy, his face has grown thinner. It makes him look older, but also worn out. I want to ask him what has changed, but now is not the time. He is private enough not to want to tell me in front of Dearon and the police. It will have to wait.

'That house.' Dearon points to the far corner of the meadow.

'Are you sure?'

Dearon does not bother to reply to Karrion, and Karrion's magic ripples with his anger. While Dearon must sense it as clearly as I do, he strides ahead as if we are not there. I share Karrion's irritation, but neither of us says anything.

After a diagonal walk across the field, we have to push through brambles and nettles to reach a narrow stream. The trampled vegetation by the back gate is clear to see. The canine units give their dogs scent from a bright green shirt, and the dogs circle the ground. We leap over the stream.

'I could see into the house,' Dearon says.

'Where from?' I ask.

'As we were walking across the field. The Shamans were sitting in the lounge with a police officer.'

'Anyone who's tall enough or finds higher ground could watch the house,' Karrion says.

I nod. 'And I'm willing to bet that while people keep the blinds closed at the front of the house, they're not so concerned about the windows at the back.'

'Which means that when the lights are on, it would be easy to see that the boy was home alone.' Karrion pauses. 'Assuming he got as far as his home before he was taken.'

'And if Shadow was Cúan's dog, what would be the first thing he would have done when he got home?'

Karrion smiles, showing he understands. 'Let the dog out.'

'You don't know that for sure,' Dearon says.

'I'm pretty certain about this,' I say. 'When Shamans take animal companions, the needs of that animal will be as important to them as their own, if not more. Cúan will have learned to look after Shadow from the day he joined the family. And if Cúan is on the autistic spectrum, routines will be very important. So if he's learned he has to let Shadow out as soon as he comes home, he will do it, without fail.'

'Thereby giving the kidnapper the perfect lure to entice Cúan out,' Karrion finishes the thought for me.

'Here,' Dearon says.

He is crouching by the fence, pointing at the ground. Imprinted into the clay soil is a series of footprints. There is a groove of mud where the back gate has opened outward, and next to it is a partial print of a small trainer. The rest of the impressions lack any definition.

'The kidnapper is trying to disguise his tracks.' Karrion bends down to photograph the prints and the back gate.

'Perhaps.' I twist to look where we walked along the stream. 'Look at where Dearon stepped.'

On the bare ground, Dearon's footprint is clearly visible, but it shows no detail, just like the imprints next to Shadow's body and out here. It confirms what we already suspected.

'He's one of us,' Dearon begins just as the canine handlers hail us. The dogs are working at the ends of their long leads.

'We have a scent,' the female handler says.

6

THE TRAIL

The dogs take us across the meadow at a fast run. A pub called the Green Dragon comes into view, but the dogs veer left immediately after crossing a stream.

'Can you ask the birds to see if they can spot the boy?' I ask Karrion as we jog side by side along the muddy path.

'There are no birds around,' he says, his jaw set.

Casting my senses out, I find he is right. There are no songbirds in the bushes, no mallards or gulls over the stream, and no buzzards wheeling in the sky. As much as I want to say it is impossible, I turn my attention to Karrion instead. His magic is projecting outward, and I catch a fleeting impression of hostility from him.

Is he repelling the birds?

When he senses my stare, he turns his head away, teeth worrying his lip piercing. I say nothing.

We round a bend in the path. The stream flows into an oblong lake. At regular intervals, there are sections of the bank that have been cleared of the undergrowth and trees. They must be fishing spots, though I cannot see any fishermen.

The dogs rush to the edge of the water. They circle the area, tails wagging, but it is clear they have lost the trail. The handlers take the dogs back about twenty yards along the path. The dogs pick up the scent again, but it ends in the same place.

'This looks to be the end of the road,' one of the handlers says.

I approach the water's edge. A boot print leads into the water, as does a smaller one next to it.

'Look,' Dearon says.

A bright orange trainer is floating about fifteen yards from the shore. We scan the still surface of the lake for any sign of Cúan or his kidnapper, but see nothing else out of the ordinary.

'The boy was thought to be wearing orange trainers,' the second canine handler says.

'Pull the dogs back.'

The police look at each other, and then at me. I shrug, and they draw the dogs away from the water's edge. Dearon steps forward and rolls his shoulders. His body twists and contorts as long hair covers his clothes and he drops to all fours. It takes no more than thirty seconds for him to have shifted into a bear. The dogs howl and bark, straining against their harnesses with raised hackles and bared teeth. Dearon ignores them. With a huff directed towards me, he wades into the water and swims towards the shoe.

'Can you do that?' Karrion asks, his voice low.

His question prompts a memory of the challenge I fought in the Unseen Lands and the series of transformations that triggered a nigh-uncontrollable bloodlust. I thought I would be stuck forever as an abomination, somewhere between a bear, a lynx, and a boar, unable to find my way back to my normal form. Bradán saved me, as he did so many times during our journey to the Unseen Lands.

Realising I have been staring at my feet, I push aside the fear of losing control.

'No,' I lie. 'Not here.'

While I have been distracted, Dearon has reached the shoe. Instead of picking it up, he dives.

'What's he doing?' Karrion asks.

'He's looking for a body.'

Dearon dives four times, each time staying below the surface long enough that I grow restless and worried. After the fourth time, he retrieves the shoe from where it has floated and returns to the shore. I reach to take the shoe from his mouth and he glares at me, but lets go. As soon as he does, his form shimmers and contorts again as he turns back into a human.

'I couldn't find a body.'

Behind us, one of the canine handlers calls for a team of divers on her radio. The shoe I am holding looks pristine, if soaking wet. There are no tears, no sign of blood, and the laces are intact. I frown.

'The laces are undone.'

'So what?' Karrion asks.

'If Cúan had waded into the water, or if he had been thrown in and he lost the shoe while trying to swim ashore, I'd expect to see the laces still in a knot, even a loose one. Open laces suggest someone took the shoe off.'

'Maybe he knew they would weigh him down and he took them off himself.'

I cock my head, looking at Karrion over my shoulder. 'If that's the case, why can't we see more of his clothes floating out there? And if you were in a rush to remove your shoes in the water, why wouldn't you open the laces enough to kick the shoes off and no further?'

'Point taken. But if you've kidnapped a child, why would you lead him into the water?'

'To throw off trackers.'

'That can't be a good sign,' Karrion says.

'No, it can't.'

Borrowing the sight of a fox, I look across the lake. Faint tendrils of mist curl and uncurl over the water. Nothing else moves, and there are no birds anywhere. The air smells of damp soil and dried leaves. On the opposite side of the lake, narrow paths lead down to the water's edge and more fishing spots.

I let go of the magic and turn to where the path continues right. It rises up a few shallow steps and disappears behind trees. The next fishing spot is no more than a couple of yards from us and that is where I go. Karrion and Dearon follow me.

'Thought so.' I bend down to inspect the ground. 'He came out of the water again.'

'Cúan?' Karrion asks.

'No, the Wild Folk who took him.' I point to the footprint leading out of the water. 'See here. It's much deeper than the one that went in.'

'He's carrying the child,' Dearon says.

'That's my guess too. It's harder to follow Cúan's trail if he's not walking.'

Karrion leans down to touch the ground. 'I'm surprised there's no water. He must have been soaking if he didn't do what Dearon just did.'

'Cúan went missing sometime last night. It's been twenty or so hours. Any water will have evaporated hours ago.'

Calling to the canine handlers, I point to the Wild Folk footprint. 'Can the dogs pick up his trail from that?'

'We'll try.'

They set the dogs to work again while we hang back. When the dogs take off down the path, we follow at a fast run. The narrow track loops around the lake and on to a ledge between the shore and the back fences of houses.

'I was thinking,' Karrion says from behind me. 'In all the TV shows that feature kidnappings, the first twenty-four hours are always crucial. After that, the chances of finding the victim alive diminish rapidly.'

'Not what I wanted to hear.'

But at the back of my mind remains a nagging question: why would one of the Wild Folk kidnap a Dog Shaman child?

When the houses end, the path descends closer to the water. Soon we come to a crossroads in the path and the dogs turn away from the lake. A brief climb brings us to another smaller lake. A willow fallen into the water reaches towards a small island covered in shrubbery and tall saplings. It's no more than three or four yards from the shore, but as inaccessible as if it were in the middle of the lake.

The dogs rush down a set of steps to the water's edge, but before I have a chance to follow, Dearon stops me. His chin is lifted and his nostrils flare. Trusting his sharper senses, I follow suit. At first, all I smell is the mud and the water and the dogs and the sweating humans, but then I catch something else: something that triggers a primal hunger within me.

Dearon looks at me, wildness in his eyes. 'I smell fresh meat.'

7

THE ISLAND

The dogs lose the scent again. This time, there is no shoe floating in the lake. The path continues straight on, climbing high above the water, and a shallow wooden bank keeps the soil from crumbling into the lake.

'They're trying the same trick again,' one of the canine handlers says. 'We can pick up their trail from one of the other fishing spots.'

'That way.' The other points to our left. 'The bank is more accessible there.'

'We're going to check the island,' I say.

The police draw the dogs back. My phone rings.

'Where are you?' Jamie asks.

'The dogs led us to a series of lakes nearby. We found a shoe floating in one of them, which we think belongs to Cúan, but it was thrown there to distract us. The trail continued, but the dogs have lost it again. Dearon and I are about to check out a small island while the dogs try to find the scent.'

'Do we still need the divers?'

'For the moment, I'd say yes. We'll know more soon. Or so I hope.'

'Fine. Can you give me directions to where you are?'

'I'll leave Karrion to do it.'

After I have handed Karrion my phone, I empty my pockets into his free hand. Dearon steps off the bank, otter's fur covering his body a moment before his foot touches the water. I follow him, the hint of meat smell still tantalising my human nose.

Wetness spreads up my legs. I am standing knee-deep in the dark water and I stare down, wondering why my feet are not freezing. Then the cold hits me, and I hurry to insulate myself with fur.

The island is close enough that our upper bodies do not get wet before we reach the tip of the willow tree. Up close, the bit of land is barely large enough to be called an island and the steep banks look uninviting. A little further along, there is a gap in the undergrowth and I point towards it. Dearon nods and lowers himself back into the lake. The branches of the fallen willow scrape against my stomach and tangle around my legs, but I kick myself free.

How much harder must this have been for the other Wild Folk if he was carrying Cúan?

Turning around, I grope along the tree trunk and find a series of broken branches. I felt none break just now. Either Dearon did this or the other Wild Folk. Who else would be mad enough to swim in the lake in mid-December?

'This is the right spot,' Dearon says, and I cross the remaining few feet to where he is standing in shallow water.

Above us on the bank are deep tracks where someone slipped in the mud and pulled one of the saplings partly out of the ground. Dearon moves to do the same, but I stop him.

'I should go first. If we find something on this island, we need to make sure we preserve the evidence.'

Dearon shrugs, but shifts aside. Choosing a spot to the left of the footprints, I climb the steep incline until I reach level ground. From my vantage point, I see that the island is little more than a wooded ridge rising above the lake. Before I have a chance to enjoy the scenery, the smell of gore and meat hits me.

A narrow depression is nestled in the far side of the ridge. There, hidden under a layer of leaves, is the body. All I see is a splash of blood, shockingly bright against the ground, and a small pale hand clenching the end of a broken stick. My stomach growls.

Next to me, Dearon crouches on the ridge, nostrils flaring as he drinks in the scent of the body. In his eyes, I see my hunger reflected. It's at odds with the stab of pity I feel for the child, but my feelings cannot override the wild instinct to feed. There is meat before me, and the death of midwinter is almost upon us. I must feed now, while the carcass remains fresh, and thus ensure I will survive until life begins anew in the spring.

Beneath the urge to survive is another that sends a shudder through me. A faint voice at the back of my mind whispers that I must eat to ensure the pups in my belly will grow, that my clutch of eggs will be strong, that my fawn may be born healthy. I need not rely on my mate to provide me with food when there is plenty right here. But for the rest of the time, he will bring me what my offspring require.

I shake my head. This is madness. I am not pregnant, nor do I need Dearon to provide for me. While my instincts encourage me to feed on the carcass, the lessons of being a Wild Folk are so impressed upon me that my teeth clench.

What could cause a Wild Folk to break the ancient law?

With a warning glance at Dearon, I ease forward. My hunger becomes less important as I focus on the scene before us. Where the ground is devoid of leaves, there are deep grooves in the soil. The tracks look like those of a badger. I lift a clump of leaves where I estimate the head to be. Empty eyes stare at me. Another stab of pity lances through me. It is Cúan. From the way his head is lolling to the side, I know his neck is broken. Death would have been instant.

It is a small mercy, but one I am grateful for when I lift another section of the leaves and see that his torso has been torn open. He has been eaten. The smell of blood and intestines grows stronger, and my mouth waters. His skin is pale blue and mud is smeared on the edges of the torn flesh.

'Why would he do this?' I ask, and replace the leaves as they were.

Dearon nods. 'This goes beyond hunger.'

'He must have known it would be a matter of time before Cúan's disappearance was noticed. If all he wanted was a meal, why drag the body here and hide it under the leaves?'

'Leopards in Africa drag their kills up a tree to protect them from scavengers.'

As his words sink in, I look around me. No breeze stirs the wall of trees around the lake. A dog barks in the distance. I feel a thousand hidden eyes upon us, though our brown clothes keep us well disguised among the saplings. Nothing suggests we are being watched, and yet I cannot shake my unease.

'He's still here,' I whisper.

Dearon eases the hunting knife from his boot. 'The boy is hidden on this island because it is where he was most likely to remain undiscovered. The hunter intends to return to the kill.'

'Cúan was ten years old,' I say. 'He weighed perhaps six stone. Even ignoring the weight of his bones, there's plenty of meat on him. A hungry Wild Folk could consume, what? Three pounds of meat in one go. He'd get several meals out of the carcass before it decayed too much, especially this time of year when the cold preserves the body.'

'He will be resting after such a big meal, but sooner or later, he's going to return to check up on his kill.'

'We need to move the body.'

'I'll stay here,' Dearon says. 'There are several ways to reach this island. We can't have him sneaking in and out while we wait for the humans.'

'Fine.' I hesitate. 'Don't touch anything or go any closer to the body.'

'I won't.'

When I slide and scramble back down the slope, I spot Jamie standing next to Karrion. I feel his stare when I cover myself in fur again and swim to the shore. Karrion offers me his hand and helps me back to dry land. Jamie blinks and drops his gaze, but not before I see the longing etched on his face. My fur vanishes in a shimmer of magic.

'We found Cúan.'

'Right,' Jamie says, bringing his emotions under control. 'Is he—?'

'I'm sorry, Jamie. He's dead.'

Jamie swears. 'We should have got here sooner, got the dogs to it sooner.'

'It wouldn't have made any difference. He's been dead for hours. Most likely since last night.'

'Okay. Right.'

He makes a call to report the death.

A breeze brings the smell of meat to my nose. I turn partly away and fix my eyes on the trees on the opposite side of the lake. The bare branches are black against the grey sky. The longer I stare at them, the more I see patterns. I frown and rub my eyes. The patterns are still there. They remind me of something: the dance of snowflakes in the middle of the night, or frost blossoming across a window.

The patterns become clearer, and I grow aware of the power behind them. This is different from my new ability to see life and rot in everything: a consequence of embracing the wildness of the Unseen Lands. Over the past month, I have learned not to lose myself in the decay and not to stare at anything with my enhanced senses longer than necessary. Still, the image of Old London rotting and crumbling remains fresh in my mind, no matter how much I try to push it aside.

Without thinking, I reach out to the new power. Cold sears through me, worse than anything I have experienced before. I try to draw a breath, but my lungs are filled with snow. My pulse stutters as my heart turns into a block of ice. All through my body, the blood in my veins is replaced with winter rain. Snowflakes glue my eyelashes shut. Black spots swim across my vision, but my limbs are beyond my control. My body is no longer mine, but rather an ice sculpture for the Winter Queen's enjoyment.

She will take such good care of me.

'Yan!'

Karrion shaking me rattles my teeth. I blink, and he wipes something wet off my cheeks. Shivers wrack my body. They, together with my wet feet, the muscles aching from the long drive, and the pain that never goes away, coalesce into agony so strong, I want to lie down and never get up.

'Yan, what's wrong?'

I swallow, and warmth slides down my throat. Lifting a shaking hand, I see that my skin has a blue tint to it. Just like Cúan's. I push the thought aside and rub my face. Feeling returns with a rush of blood, and I grimace at the prickling pain. A little at a time, my body returns to me, and the pain eases.

When I try to speak, I have to clear my throat twice before the words form. 'What happened?'

'I've no idea. We were talking to you, but you didn't respond. Then you turned blue and started gasping for breath. I thought you were going to pass out.' Karrion looks around. 'Did someone cast a spell on you?'

Did they indeed? I trace the cold spot on my forehead and recall the exquisite agony of the Winter Queen's kiss. As much as being in the presence of the Fey rulers terrified me, I wanted to drown myself in her remote beauty. Even now, the thought of the Summer King's lips on her hallowed skin, when it should be my lips there, stokes a rage within me that is like a winter tempest.

'I think there's more to nature's mysteries than even I appreciate,' I say when I realise Karrion is still waiting for an answer, all the while making sure I keep my gaze away from the distant trees.

'What's that got to do with you looking like you were freezing to death?'

'That was my attempt to say that I don't know what happened without actually saying so.'

'But are you okay now?'

'Yes, I'm fine.' Something tugs at my memory. 'You said you were talking to me. What about?'

'Jamie asked where Dearon was.'

'He's guarding the body.'

I explain our theory that the killer is still nearby and likely to return to the kill. Jamie's expression darkens.

'But why?' he asks.

My eyes stray to the island. It takes a whisper of magic for my sight to sharpen enough to see Dearon's still shape among the trees. He can hear the conversation, if he chooses to listen. Either way, I have to be honest.

'Because the body was partially eaten. The killer is one of the Wild Folk.'

Karrion makes a noise of disgust at the back of his throat. Jamie opens and closes his mouth a few times, deep furrows appearing on his forehead. I observe with detached interest as fear, disgust, and anger, all flit across his face.

'And you're sure?' he asks, the words slow.

'As sure as we can be. The same goes for the other case. The body wasn't eaten by wild animals, but one of us.'

'I suppose a Wild Folk killer is preferable to the theory going around the Metropolitan Police. Even with evidence of so many different animals at the crime scene, they were muttering about werewolves being involved.'

I snort. 'You know as well as I do that werewolves don't exist.'

'I do. They don't. By their logic, if magic and ghosts are real, why not werewolves too?'

'Ghosts are just spirits, an echo of the people they once were. That's all. And there's an element of truth in the were-wolf legends, even if the creatures themselves aren't real.'

'Then what is real?' Jamie asks.

'We are.' I flash him my canines. 'The strongest among my kind are as close to werewolves as you're going to get. What are we, but monsters bestowed with the fangs and claws of nature? The wildest and fiercest of all beasts.'

'You don't really think that, do you?'

'No, but there are people who do. Where else would the legends have come from? As much as I dislike profiling, if someone cries werewolf, I'd be looking at the Wild Folk first.'

'And this?' Jamie gestures at the island. 'Are you capable of this?'

I hesitate a moment, debating whether he can handle the truth. Then I nod. 'Yes.'

'Christ, Yannia.' He takes a step back.

'The clue is in the name, Jamie. We are wilder than humans have been for thousands of years.'

'But would you really eat another person?'

'No.' He looks like he is about to argue, so I continue, 'You asked whether I was capable of it, and I am. But the circumstances would have to be extraordinary for me to break one of the fundamental laws that govern our existence. Besides, there are far more pleasant ways to fill my belly.'

When Jamie looks sickened, I advance on him, determined to drive home my point. 'You want to know what I feel when I look at a body? My instincts tell me that the meat is good for consumption, that there's plenty of it, and they urge me to gorge on the carcass. Who knows when I'll next find an unclaimed kill? I can taste the blood in my mouth, the edge of rot even you can smell. And you know why? Because I've eaten fresh kill, lapped up blood that is still warm, torn open a deer's flank to reach the flesh below.'

Jamie recoils, but I keep following him. 'I may look human, but I'm not. Nor is anyone else who carries the Wild Folk blood.'

8

THE VIGIL

'What would cause a Wild Folk to start eating people?' Karrion asks.

I force my eyes away from the island and tilt my head back. 'Usually an extreme environmental trigger, like famine. It happened during the Black Death, when some of my kind went mad with the fever and attacked the plague carts. They gorged on the dead and spread infected body parts across the villages, until Mages struck them down with fire and lightning. They continued to rage as they burned.'

'How do you know?' Jamie asks.

'Because others among my kind witnessed it and I have dreamed their dreams.'

'What do you mean?'

'I mean that the dreams of past generations of the Wild Folk are mine, just as those that come after me will one day dream my dreams. We can access the experiences of those that came before, learn from them, know how they lived and how they died. Their wisdom lives on so long as we still live in the wild places, where the magic is strong and untamed.'

'Do you get a choice as to what sort of memories you get to see, or are your dreams always controlled by your ancestors?' Jamie tugs at his right sleeve. 'That's such a weird question to ask.'

'At the conclave, we often have collective dreams, mostly chosen by the Elderman. In Old London, I rarely experience them, and most of the time, I have normal dreams.'

It is not true, but I have no desire to share with Jamie the premonitions about Dearon coming to find me or the time I tapped into residual Samhain magic and visited Dearon in his dream.

Jamie's phone rings. From his side of the conversation, I gather reinforcements have arrived. They had better hurry for the light is fading fast. There are no street lamps here, and the police will not have the heightened senses of the Wild Folk.

Looking towards the island, I cannot see Dearon through the gathering gloom. Although he could have slipped away unnoticed from the far side of the ridge, I trust he continues guarding Cúan's body. I picture him crouched on the ridge, the scents of the body pungent in his nose. A weaker Wild Folk would have moved as far away from the carcass as possible, but I believe Dearon will have stayed exactly where I left him. If there is one Wild Folk who can control his instincts, it is Dearon.

When did I grow to think so highly of him?

Perhaps the respect and belief in his abilities have always been there, and I have chosen to bury them under anger and disappointment. Had I not been promised to Dearon the day I was born, and my bargain with the Eldermen led me to reaffirm those old promises, I might still admire Dearon like I did when we were growing up.

'Are you sure you're okay, Yan?' Karrion asks.

Jamie is still on the phone, explaining the logistics of

removing the body from the primary crime scene. The frost that crept through me earlier has gone, though I remain shaken by its power.

'I'm fine, though a hot shower and some food wouldn't go amiss.' Perhaps it is my imagination, but I sound less convinced than I feel.

'Do you think the Winter Queen is messing with you?'

'I'm not sure she messes with mortals as such, certainly not here in the Dying Lands. From my brief visit, I got the impression that the Fey have become infrequent visitors. What Baneacre did in trying to establish himself as a ruler in Old London is unheard of in the Fey mythology.' My hand strays to my forehead again. 'As for what the Winter Queen wants with me and when she will call in the debt I owe her, that must remain a mystery.'

'I worry about you, Yan.'

'Thanks. Right back at you.'

We hug, and a wave of nausea washes over me. I stumble back and catch a glimpse of a necklace under his leather jacket.

'What's that?' I ask, pointing to his neck.

'Sorry, I forgot all about it.' He opens his coat to reveal a necklace of silvery discs stamped with skulls of different birds. While the intricate details tempt me, I keep my distance.

'You bought a cold iron necklace?'

'After what happened with Baneacre and Pheonix, it seemed like a good idea. Tinker Thaylor made it for me.'

'It is a good idea.' I shudder as I tug his coat closed. 'Just keep it away from me.'

'I thought you would have got used to cold iron while Lady B was treating your hands.'

'You'd think so, but if anything, my dislike for it has grown stronger.'

'Is it because of the Winter Queen?'

'Perhaps. But my trip to the Unseen Lands changed my magic and amplified it. That's reason enough for me to hate cold iron.'

Jamie ends his call and strides to the steps. 'I'm going to have to guide people here from the pub. Will you keep an eye on things while I'm gone?'

'Of course.'

'What's the plan for us, boss?' Karrion asks once Jamie has left.

The lake reflects the remaining light in the sky. The feeling of being watched has not left me, and I shiver as the damp chill of winter worms its way through my clothes. To keep my wet toes from freezing, I pace along the bank.

'I want to find that Wild Folk. Between you, me, and Dearon, we are far more likely to find him than the police are.' I scowl at the sky. 'But we can't do it tonight. We'd be plundering blind through an unknown landscape and he would hear us long before we got anywhere near him. So, first thing tomorrow morning.'

'Sounds good. I'm guessing Dearon will spend the night at yours, so I'll meet you there whenever you want.'

'It will be an early start as we have a lot of ground to cover. Besides, by tomorrow morning, Jamie may have more information for us.'

I face the island, my senses strained to catch anything out of the ordinary. Once again, I picture Dearon. Should I have guarded Cúan? My time in Old London has eroded the indifference towards others that comes naturally to the Wild Folk. Dearon is guarding the meat source of another Wild Folk, but I would have held vigil over the body of a dead child. Does he look at Cúan's remains and wonder what sort of a man he would have grown to be? Can he mourn the life lost and the grief of Cúan's parents?

But why would he, when they are mere strangers? Living in the wild requires survival skills, not sentimentality. Even the Shamans who act as a buffer between us and the rest of the world are regarded as allies, not kin. It has always been the Wild Folk way to isolate ourselves from the world. We have lived thus since the foreigners in shining armour marched through our land and built their wall across it. While the villages turned to the civilisation of the conquerors, we hid deep in the woods and moors; our wildness only surpassed by the Fey who were frequent visitors in those days.

The sound of approaching voices draws me from memories of my ancestors. Jamie leads a team of people to us. They are all carrying heavy bags. The first thing they do is set up floodlights, not only on the spot where we have been standing, but also at the nearby fishing bays. Soon, the whole island is bathed in a harsh glare. Nevertheless, Dearon remains hidden.

'Do you want me to call Dearon back?' I ask Jamie.

'Please. I doubt there's any risk of the killer returning now.'

I step up to the edge of the water and call Dearon. A brown shape soon slithers down the slope and slides into the lake. Unease causes me to shiver, but when I unfurl my aura, I recognise the power brushing against mine.

The closest police step back when Dearon glides to the bank and draws himself out of the water in a fluid motion. As he shakes himself, the fur disappears off his

71

body. Even so, he looks out of place in clothes sewn of hides and fur. At least he has had the presence of mind to hide the hunting knife.

We move to the top of the steps to give the police more space. The divers don drysuits and masks before wading into the water. They take more floodlights and set them up on the island. Safety lines between the divers and the people on dry land glisten in the artificial glare. Two of the divers return, and they take with them an inflatable raft.

'We're going to be here for a while,' Jamie says. 'I'm not sure there's anything more you can do. Thanks for all your help, though.'

'If it's all right with you, we'd like to come back tomorrow morning.' I bite my lip, unsure of myself in Jamie's company. 'We may be able to track the Wild Folk.'

'That's valuable help, so long as you leave the apprehending of suspects to the police or the Paladins.'

'Of course. I have no desire to step on official toes.'

'Good. Let's catch up tomorrow morning then.'

We say our goodbyes. A string of lights along the path guides us to where a gap in the trees opens to a road. With a final glance behind us, we leave the crime scene.

9

THE GREEN DRAGON

It takes us a matter of minutes to follow the road to the pub I spotted earlier, the Green Dragon. With my senses still connected to the wilderness, I smell food cooking and my stomach growls. Karrion laughs.

'Is that a suggestion that we should have an early dinner?'

'It's not the worst idea in the world.' I tilt my head towards Dearon. 'Are you hungry?'

'I could eat.'

'In that case, why don't you two get us a table and I'll give Sinta a quick walk. I'll bring the car around.'

Karrion is already agreeing when Dearon shakes his head. 'No, I'll come with you.'

'It's not far.'

'I don't think you should go alone.'

I take a deep breath, fighting to keep my temper in check. 'What about Karrion? He'll be all alone.'

'In a building full of humans.'

'Who never pose any threat to our kind... And for the record, I was going to walk back to the car along the road and not through the fields.'

'I'd feel better if you didn't go alone.'

'You don't think I can take care of myself? How do you

imagine I've managed in Old London for over a year without your protection?'

Dearon says nothing, crossing his arms, and my anger ignites.

'Fine, do whatever you want.'

Without looking back, I march towards the footbridge. Although I try not to listen, I can hear the whisper of Dearon's steps behind me. Karrion calls out after us.

'So, I'm going to get us that table.'

I hurry along a path to the main road, trying to widen the distance to Dearon. By the time I have rounded the corner past another pub, my calves are aching. I have little choice but to slow down. Dearon is wise enough to keep his distance. He follows a metre or two behind me, but makes no attempt to say anything further.

Sinta is asleep on the back seat, the chew I gave her untouched. I gather her in my arms and set her on the ground. She takes two steps and squats. I praise her while I top up her water bowl and retrieve a handful of dog food from my bag. Once she has eaten, I take her for a short walk around the streets. Although puzzled by Dearon following us, Sinta soon forgets him and focuses on sniffing the Christmas decorations and the few remaining flowers. Letting the puppy take me on a meandering path eases some of the tension I have been carrying. The mundane tasks of dog ownership draw my thoughts away from the body in the woods and the boy's torn flesh.

When Sinta begins to tire, we return to the car. I wipe her paws with an old towel and settle her on the back seat. She pulls the chew closer, while Dearon and I take our places and I start the car. Soon we stop outside the pub, and I give Sinta a final pat. As we approach the front door, I spot Karrion in a window seat.

He has chosen us a corner table near the door, away from the other people. Tantalising aromas of food tickle my senses, as does the rich warmth of wood smoke. I look around, but see no fireplace.

'I'll be right back,' I say.

As I walk to the bar, the sight of a large fireplace greets me. Small flames dance behind a grate, as alluring to me as an autumn candle to a moth. Ignoring the humans around me, I kneel by the hearth and reach for a twig and a curl of birch bark lying next to a log basket. My fingers bind them together with almost no conscious thought. I light the offering, words poised on my lips.

'Hearth Spirit, bless this hearth and ward this building. We thank you for the light and heat you provide.'

The offering burns with a flare of flames, and the scent of smoke intensifies. I sense a presence in the fire, and I smile. Wherever I go, he is always listening.

'I thought it would be good for you to venture outside of Old London again since you enjoyed yourself in Sussex.'

A chuckle I get in response is little more than a crackle of sap and heat envelops me. It eases the ache from my muscles and joints, as surely as if Wishearth embraced me. A flush creeps across my cheeks as I recall how he held me through the night after I had been poisoned, but I push the thought aside.

'Are you offering to buy me a drink in the country-side?' he whispers.

'Shouldn't it be the gentleman buying the lady a drink?'

I can just make out his dark eyes among the flames, and they are wreathed in a cascade of sparks when he laughs.

'Whoever claimed I was a gentleman? And you're no lady.'

'I'm so glad we had this conversation, but I need to go. Funja is not magically conjuring food in front of me and my foot is cramping.'

'You don't seem to need much of an excuse to abandon your friends. Is non-magical food all it takes?'

The banter could go on for a while. I stand and smile at the fireplace over my shoulder.

'Goodbye, Wishearth.'

'See you later?'

I hesitate and cover it with a nod. 'Of course.'

Warmth leaps from the fireplace and wraps around my hand. An echo of it lingers as I return to the other room, my steps lighter than before, despite my nagging conscience.

I find Karrion and Dearon sitting on opposite sides of the table. Karrion is scrutinising the menu as if his life depended on him memorising it, while Dearon stares out of the window. Both look relieved when I return, though Dearon hides it better.

'I ordered drinks at the bar,' Karrion says as I take a seat by an untouched cola glass. He has got himself a pint of pale ale, and water for Dearon. 'I hope you don't mind the beer.'

'Not at all. You're not driving and one pint isn't going to make you drunk.'

'Great. Here.' He passes me the menu. 'I already know what I'm having.'

By the time the waiter comes to take our order, I have made up my mind and ask for a steak and kidney pie. Karrion orders fish and chips, while Dearon opts for the gammon steak.

'Without the fried egg,' I say as soon as he has finished speaking.

'Why?' he asks.

'You're having dinner with a Bird Shaman.'

Dearon holds my gaze briefly before nodding to the waiter.

'Thanks,' Karrion says, his eyes fixed on his pint.

An awkward silence threatens to settle at the table, and with a sip of my drink, I tell Dearon my plan to return the following morning to search for the Wild Folk. He nods.

'I heard you talking as I was guarding the body.'

'While you were walking Sinta, I had a look at this area on my map,' Karrion says. 'The bad news is, we're right on the edge of the village and there's an awful lot of green to cover.'

'Show me.'

Karrion sets his phone on the table. Dearon looks at it without touching, while I locate us on the map and zoom in and out to study the area.

'We could do with a tablet for this sort of work,' I say as I lose my place for the third time.

'Shall I put it on the office supplies wishlist?'

I offer Karrion a crooked grin. 'We have a wishlist?'

'Yeah. It's important to dream about different coloured highlighter pens and paper clips.'

'Good to know.'

Turning my attention back to the map, I study it until I have a better idea of the area. Dearon leans closer so he can also see the screen, and our elbows touch. The casual contact draws more and more of my attention away from the map and to his warmth. When he shifts and our upper arms are flush, I let my eyes flicker to him. Dearon's expression betrays nothing. He is scrutinising the screen with a frown that creases the area between his eyebrows.

A flush has crept up my neck, and I reach for my glass. The cold liquid slides down my throat. When I set the glass down, I find Karrion observing me, a knowing half-smile on his lips. I roll my eyes at him and give him back the phone.

'Although there's a lot of green on this map, we can discount some of it. I doubt the Wild Folk is hiding in the Willows Activity Farm, though there are woods beyond it. A lot of this area is probably too open and too close to houses for his liking. If he's resting between feeds, he's not going to want dog walkers and fishermen disturbing him.'

'He'll also want to stay close to his kill,' Dearon says.

'As close as possible, at least. He may rely on the inaccessible location to keep it hidden. If he had a campsite selected before he killed Cúan, he's likely to return there.'

'Are we sure he doesn't live in London Colney?' Karrion asks. 'Maybe he has a flat here.'

Our food arrives, and we spend a few moments shifting around glasses, plates, and sauces. Normally Karrion and I would swap parts of our dinner, but this time, he steals nothing from my plate.

'Why would a Wild Folk be living here, among humans?' Dearon asks as he cuts into his gammon steak.

'I don't know. But if Yan can live in Old London, why can't one of your kind choose to live side by side with humans?'

'It's one thing for me to have chosen Old London as my home, quite another to survive out here. There's better access to nature, but as wary as we are of other magic users, we are ten times more suspicious of humans.'

'Maybe he has human relatives or he's married. To a human. Didn't you tell me a while back that it does happen?'

'I haven't heard rumours of a half-breed living in exile,' Dearon says. 'Have you?'

'No, though I'm out of the loop. While Karrion's theory is unlikely, it's not impossible. There's one thing that could confirm or disprove it.'

'What's that?' Karrion asks.

I tell him about Jamie's phone call yesterday and the photos he sent me. My laptop is in the car, but I describe the scene and the tracks as well as I can, keeping my voice low so the other diners cannot hear me.

'If the woman was attacked and eaten somewhere near St Albans, it's likely the Wild Folk has a permanent place here,' Dearon says. 'But if the death happened elsewhere in the country, we'll know he's on the move.'

'Could it be a coincidence?' Karrion asks.

'Two Wild Folk turning to cannibalism at the same time, when there has been no other recorded case of man-eating in our lifetime?'

'Make that in the lifetime of our parents too,' Dearon says. 'No, it must be the same person.'

Karrion draws a fork through his mushy peas. 'Earlier you said the most common reason for a Wild Folk to turn to cannibalism was an external factor. What do you think caused this one to start eating people?'

Dearon and I exchange a glance. Karrion has voiced the question that has been niggling at the back of my mind since we discovered Cúan's body.

'I'm not sure. There has been no catastrophic event that could have triggered this kind of behaviour. And since the Wild Folk who turn to man-eating are so few and far between, we can't even speak to one in the hopes of understanding the situation better.'

My frustration is mirrored on their faces, and I force a smile. 'We need to get that case file from Jamie for the other death. Perhaps then we'll know more.'

'Or we could just catch the guy tomorrow,' Karrion says, and sets down his cutlery.

Pushing away my plate, I try to keep the scepticism from my voice. 'Sure, how hard can that be? It's only one Wild Folk in the Hertfordshire countryside.'

10

RETURN TO OLD LONDON

We pay for the meal and leave. I pause outside the pub, turning to stare in the direction of Cúan's home. Do his parents know already, or are they still waiting, caught in a limbo where their son is simultaneously on his way home unharmed, and gone forever?

'There's nothing more we can do here tonight,' Karrion says, nudging my shoulder with his.

I wake up Sinta and give her a quick toilet break on the green. We have a long drive ahead of us, and I am eager to return to Old London.

We hit traffic on the M25, and our progress slows. None of us speaks; with the events of the day swirling around my mind, I cannot think where to begin with small talk. After a while, Karrion starts talking about his family's plans for Christmas and what his siblings have on their Santa wishlist. Although Dearon contributes nothing, the tilt of his head shows he is listening.

'Do they still believe in Santa?' I ask.

'More or less. Wren and Robin do, but I think Jay pretends to. I keep telling them Santa is really a snowy owl in disguise.'

'I guess that makes sense. It would explain how he gets up and down chimneys.'

'Exactly. Wren keeps calling me silly. She's inherited That Look from Mum.'

'What look?'

'You know the one mums have that tells you without a feather of a doubt that you're being an idiot. I'd hoped it would take Wren a little longer to perfect it. Living with one bossy woman is enough for me.'

'You could always move out.'

The suggestion is not serious. Karrion's half-siblings are much younger than he is, and their mother depends on his help to look after them. I have never heard him complain that he would like to live his own life or have more independence. He once told me his family are not cuckoos, and it sums him up perfectly.

'It makes more sense, financially speaking, to just have one place for the nest. Besides, we're going to have to move at some point when the boys will want their own rooms.'

'True. It's going to get crowded with the five of you in that flat over the next few years.'

'At least with Mum's recent promotion and my gainful employment, we can afford to do so when the time comes. Which reminds me, do you remember how Mum was pushing me to open a savings account now I have a steady salary?'

'And you were going to spend your money on piercings and hair dye?' I grin when he pokes my shoulder. 'Yes, I do.'

'I thought of something useful to do with the money that doesn't involve maintaining my dashing goth look.'

'Are you going to invest it in a new kind of pigeon repellent?'

'Funny.' Karrion huffs, but my teasing does not dampen his good mood. 'I'm going to get a driving licence.'

'Really? That's a great idea.'

'I know we don't often need a car in Old London, but I figured it wouldn't hurt to have a second driver in the family, especially since Mum hasn't driven in at least ten years. Besides, if you put me on your insurance, then you don't always have to be the one to drive.'

'Yes, but will I trust you with my car? I only had it repaired a month and a half ago.' I laugh to soften the words.

'Mum is alternating between thinking it's a good idea and a waste of money. I think she's coming round, though. Which reminds me, do you have any plans for Christmas?'

I glance at Dearon, but his attention is fixed on the tail lights in front of us. 'Not really. Why?'

'Mum and I wondered whether you'd like to spend Christmas Day with us. It will be pretty noisy and hectic, but neither of us likes the idea of you being alone.' In the rear-view mirror, he leans sideways. 'Other than Sinta, of course. You should bring her along. The brood is going to love playing with a puppy.'

Although I have been aware of Christmas for as long as I can remember, it is not a holiday that has ever been celebrated at the conclave. The Wild Folk celebrations hark back to older times. We observe the equinox – the vernal and the autumnal – as well as midsummer, Beltane, Imbolc, Lughnasadh, and Samhain. The one I loved the most as a child was the midwinter feast: a day of storytelling and tables laden with food. On one occasion, when I was ten or eleven, some of the Elders even sneaked out of the conclave lands to buy large tins of chocolates. The midwinter feast marks the darkest day of the year and the unbroken spirit of the Wild Folk. We tell stories that remind us about survival, perseverance, and ingenuity, while reaffirming the bonds of blood and friendship. Only together will we survive the winter and thrive for another year.

Realising that Karrion is waiting for my response, I meet his eye in the mirror. 'That sounds wonderful, thank you. Sinta and I would be delighted to come. You'll need to help me pick books for the brood and something for your mum. And let me know what food I can bring.'

'I'm not sure Mum will let you bring food, and if you ask me, I'd rather you didn't try to cook anything. Food poisoning is not the Christmas present I was looking for.'

'Harsh.' I pause for effect. 'But fair.'

'As for presents, you could help me figure out how to keep Old London's pigeons away from me.'

'You should not begrudge the love of your spirit animal,' Dearon says.

Karrion rakes a hand through his black hair and taps his lip piercing. 'In case you haven't noticed, crows and ravens are my spirit animals, not pigeons.'

'Impossible to say, when you keep driving away all birds in your vicinity.'

I shoot a warning glance at Dearon, who raises an eyebrow.

'Feel free to drop it,' Karrion says.

'If it's the truth, then I don't see the harm in—'

A shake of my head silences Dearon. Karrion slumps back in the seat with a creak of his leather jacket. We speak no more.

Once we reach Old London, I allow my aura to quest outward. It catches hints of other spell casters all around me, as indistinct as the background music at a restaurant.

Little by little, I become aware of the spell graffiti along a construction site, the whispers of old rites that have seeped into the buildings, and the thrum of power that runs through our part of the city. Something about Old London calls to the magic in my blood, and I know others feel it too. We gather here to find a community and safety in numbers in a world where humans outnumber us a thousand to one. Our magic has shaped it, just as the city has shaped us. No matter how abhorrent it is for a Wild Folk to live away from nature, I have found a life, a community, and a purpose in Old London unlike any I had at the conclave. That makes the old promises all the more difficult to keep, and soon I must choose a future for myself, one way or the other.

The evening traffic makes our progress slow, but eventually we drop Karrion off at Bride Lane, where his family lives. He promises to meet us at mine the following morning at seven, and we say our goodbyes. Once he shuts the car door and walks away with a wave, silence returns to the car.

'There's enough food at my place for breakfast, but we'll probably have to go shopping tomorrow,' I say as I turn the car around.

'Fine.'

Frustrated by Dearon's lack of willingness to lessen the awkward tension between us, I lapse back into silence until I park outside my home. By habit, I glance at the windows of the flat above mine, but they are dark. If Dearon finds it strange, he says nothing. I hurry to unpack the car, not wishing to linger in the dark street. Already my magic is faltering, hemmed in from all sides by technology, people, and pollution. But without a Leech feeding off my power, the gradual depletion is easier to bear.

A drop of rain lands on my forehead, then another, as I pick up Sinta and lead the way to my front door. My office feels damp, but I ignore it and walk upstairs. The first thing I do is open the window and let Sinta out. While she reacquaints herself with the garden, I unpack my bag and take Lady Bergamon's empty bottles downstairs. When I return to the lounge, Dearon is lifting Sinta back inside. I feed her and bite back a yawn. Although it is not yet late, fatigue weighs me down and I want nothing more than sleep.

'Shall I get the fire going?' Dearon asks, crouching by the hearth stones.

The chill of winter has crept into the room while the window was open, and my legs ache. But the thought of invoking a prayer to Wishearth and having him visit my fireplace with Dearon here triggers a twist of nausea in my stomach.

'I prefer a cooler temperature when I sleep.'

Dearon's eyes go to the remnants of a fire within the hearth, but he says nothing.

I find a towel in the wardrobe and hand it to Dearon.

'Do you want to use the bathroom first, while I find a pillow?' I ask. 'I know it's not that late, but we have an early start tomorrow.'

He nods and heads downstairs. I remain rooted to the spot, ears tracking his footsteps until the bathroom door closes. Forcing my aching muscles to move, I turn back to the wardrobe. The pillow Karrion has used when he has spent the night is on the top shelf, and rising on tiptoes, I reach for it. Dearon may be able to smell Karrion even after I have changed the pillowcase, but there is little I can do about that. I owe Dearon no explanation regarding Karrion.

When Dearon returns, I brush past him, keeping my eyes fixed to the floor. I am not certain why nerves twist in my stomach, but my cheeks flush as I descend the stairs. Last time Dearon spent the night in my home, I was so tired and sore that feeling nervous was beyond me. It seems as though this time, I am more than making up for it.

Having brushed my teeth, I linger in the bathroom while I undo my braid. My hair falls in a curtain of low waves around my shoulders, and I run a brush through the strands. When I start contemplating the state of my eyebrows, I know I am stalling and, with some reluctance, leave the bathroom.

Dearon is standing next to the mattress, and it occurs to me for the first time how out of place he looks in my home. As much as the décor is simple, it still screams of city living. It is no different from setting a bear down in Trafalgar Square and expecting it to blend in. From the subtle movement of his head, I can tell Dearon is tracking the sound of cars and people on the street outside. The silence is never complete at the conclave, but the background noise is natural rather than man-made. It took me months to grow used to Old London's hum, so I understand how disconcerted Dearon must feel.

He must sense my stare, for he turns to face me and the discomfort slips from his expression. It is replaced with something darker that defies definition. Or, perhaps I am not brave enough to give it a name.

Not trusting my voice in the heavy silence of the flat, I walk up to him. Dearon watches me, his eyes alone moving. When we are inches apart, I tilt my chin up. My hand trembles as I run my fingers across the smoothness of his cheek and onto the dark stubble along his jawline.

He remains stock-still while I trace the outer edge of his ear, the curve of his bottom lip, and the length of a faded scar on his temple.

I rise to bring our faces level, hands resting on his shoulders for balance. His settle on my hips. He leans forward to kiss me, and I wait until the last moment before ducking just out of his reach. He tries again, and again I avoid him. He growls, and my laughter is a mere exhale against his lips. I remain there, taking the time to enjoy his body flush against mine and his breath caressing my lips.

When I finally relent and kiss him, I keep the touch feather-light. He takes my lead and turns his head to kiss the corners of my mouth. His left hand slides through my hair to cup the back of my neck. I deepen the kiss, but keep the pace languid. When he sucks my lower lip into his mouth and grazes it with his teeth, I become aware of my heart pounding and a flush creeping across my body.

We kiss until I am trembling. Dearon is the first to step back, and he watches me with hooded eyes. Keeping his attention fixed on my face, he pushes down his trousers and shrugs off his shirt. I move to do the same, but he shakes his head. He peels off each piece of clothing I am wearing with agonising slowness, covering the bared skin with light licks and touches that have me clenching my fists to remain still.

When he is finished, he takes my hand and guides me to lie down on the bed. He remains crouched near my knees, and I experience a flash of uncertainty. All of me is bared before him, and I cannot help wondering what he thinks when he looks at my body. But as his gaze travels over me, it does not linger on the long red scar on my left arm, or on my hips – a little too wide for my liking

– or on my bony knees. When his scrutiny becomes too much to bear, I reach out to him.

Dearon seats himself next to me on the bed and resumes his exploration of my body. Hovering a hand just above my skin, close enough for me to feel its heat but not close enough to touch, he traces my limbs, across my torso and over my belly. When I try to arch into his hand, he pulls it back, a teasing grin curling on his lips. By the time he is finished, I am aching for him and I yank his head down. For a few moments, we both lose control, and an edge of wildness creeps into the heated kisses.

Dearon follows the line of my neck with nips that turn into bites when he reaches my shoulder. I groan and leave a mark of my own on his collarbone. All too soon, Dearon pulls back from his frenzy and resumes his teasing. He explores my body with his fingers and lips until ragged pleads slip out in time with my breathing. Then, and only then, does he relent, and I welcome him into me.

Moonlight casts a pale stripe across the lounge, but it does not reach as far as the bed. I borrow the sight of a cat sleeping in the flat next to mine to see Dearon better. He is biting his lower lip as he moves above me, and his jawline is dark with a dusting of new beard growth. His eyes are fixed on mine, and the intensity of his expression threatens to sweep me away. I tremble, the chill of the room penetrating the heat of our passion, and to ground myself, I focus on the tripping of my heart, the weight of him on me, the smells of his sweat and his magic, and the blooms of pain erupting from my legs. The physical sensations drown me in Dearon, and I am lost, closing my eyes at the last moment to hide how he overwhelms me.

His release follows mine, and he drops his head to rest on my shoulder. Warm gusts of breath caress my skin as my muscles relax. When he eases off me, I roll on to my side and groan. Moving my legs sends a wave of agony and nausea through me, and I clench my jaw to keep the bile from rising to my mouth. Dearon props himself up on to his elbow and tucks a lock of hair behind my ear.

'What can I do?'

He does not ask if I am okay, or apologise for the pain he caused. It was my choice, and he accepts that. We have never had the conversation, and yet, his actions are a tacit acknowledgement that he understands. Gratitude wells within me, providing a brief respite from the pain.

My voice is hoarse as I direct him to the kitchen and to the drawer where I keep my medication. He returns with a glass of water, two pills, and an apple. When I try to push myself up, my muscles shake too much and he has to help me remain upright. I gulp the pills and the water down too fast, and droplets cling to my lips. Dearon wipes them away, allowing his thumb to linger against my mouth, and I dart my tongue out to drag over the rough skin of his finger pad. There is smouldering heat in his gaze, and I look away while I eat the apple.

Once I have finished eating, he takes the glass and the apple core back to the kitchen, and I recline against the pillows. The pain still pulses through me in time with my heartbeat, and I am glad when Dearon returns. He stretches out next to me, his lips finding a bite mark he left on my shoulder. First his lips and then his tongue run over it, easing the hint of a dull ache. He moves on to kissing a bruise on my upper arm, his long hair stroking the sensitive skin in the crook of my elbow and causing me to shiver. Next, his lips find the Fey scar on my side.

The sensation tickles, and I squirm, only to have a hand on my sternum holding me still.

By the time the pain medication is taking effect, Dearon is nudging me to roll over. He works tension out of my shoulders and leaves a trail of kisses along my spine. Despite the chill of the room, my skin is flushed and I am panting. When I feel him hard against my shin, I shift my legs. He accepts the unspoken invitation, and his weight and warmth come to rest over me. I arch into him, and he chuckles, nipping my shoulder without breaking the skin. Drifting between asleep and awake, I am anchored by his presence to a world of desire. He parts my legs further, and pleasure overrides the flare of pain.

SUNDAY

11

THE MORNING AFTER

When I wake up, Dearon is propped up on his elbow, watching me. The subtle change in his aura indicates that he has borrowed the senses of wilderness to see in the dark. He reaches to brush his fingers along my cheek, and he frowns.

'Are you cold?'

My side of the blanket is bunched between us. I shrug. Without a fire, the room ought to be chilly, but I cannot feel the cold.

He shifts closer and touches the silvery line of a scar which is only a month old, but which was healed by Fey magic.

'Tell me about this.'

'You already heard the story. I told it at the conclave.'

'Yes, but I want to know the truth beyond the story.'

Although he is right next to me, the darkness has an insulating effect, protecting me both from Dearon and the Winter Queen's icy touch. Yet I hesitate. Will he think me foolhardy for bargaining with the Fey? Will he be jealous of the Winter Queen and the effect she has on me?

'What time is it?' I ask, buying time to think.

Dearon leans back and looks towards the window. Clouds have rolled in during the night, and I can hear a steady drum of rain. I would like to spend a whole day lounging in bed, but the thought of doing so with Dearon banishes the desire. One night of lovemaking has done nothing to change the reality of our situation.

'It's early. At least, early enough for a story.'

'Fine.'

I roll onto my back and stare at the ceiling, which is obscured by the darkness. It's easier than trying to track Dearon's expressions. I speak of my agreement with Bradán, our journey to the Unseen Lands, and the Fey Courts. My voice trembles as I recount the challenge, the battle, and the bargain I made, and it breaks when I relive our narrow escape from the Fey hounds.

All the while, Dearon listens without interrupting. When I finish, he drapes the blanket over me.

'It was quite an adventure you had,' he says, and his voice betrays neither disappointment nor admiration.

'I didn't think it through.' My admission surprises me. 'All that mattered was helping Lady Bergamon.'

Part of me expects him to tell me to be more careful in the future, but he does not. Instead, he shifts so he too is lying on his back.

'The bonds of blood, love, and friendship, give us courage and audacity, sometimes more than is wise. Your friend is lucky you were there to help her.'

I open my mouth to thank him, to explain, though explain what, I am not certain, and no words come. Dearon rises in a fluid motion. Sinta stands to greet him, and he picks her up. Opening the window, he sets her outside, seemingly unaware of his nakedness. A wet draught caresses my cheek and I shiver, despite not feeling the cold. Time to get up.

'Do you want to shower first?' I ask.

Like Dearon, I see no reason to cover myself. After last night, doing so seems unnecessary. A dozen different pains bloom when I stand, and I hang on to the mantelpiece while I wait for the initial pain and dizziness to subside.

'You go ahead. I'll keep an eye on Sinta.'

I choose a change of clothes from the wardrobe and head downstairs. The ache in my feet intensifies as I step on to the tiled bathroom floor. I put my clothes on the edge of the sink. Something is nagging at my consciousness, something I should remember, but it eludes me while I switch on the shower. Is it something to do with the case? I step under the spray and angle my face up. The pain flaring in my elbows and hips alerts me to the fact that the water is freezing, and I stumble out of the shower. How did I not notice it before?

It's the middle of winter. Why am I not cold like I should be? Is it the city changing me, or is this the Winter Queen's influence?

I have no answers, only questions, and I turn the heat up. Stepping under the spray again triggers an immediate feeling of suffocation from the excess heat, but I ignore the sensation, and shower in record time. I hurry to towel myself off and leave my fleece unzipped. When I leave the bathroom, the doorbell rings, followed by a rattle of keys as Karrion lets himself in.

'Good, you're awake,' he says. 'More importantly, you're dressed.'

'What?'

'I figured you and Dearon had a lot of catch-up sex to have.'

Perhaps it is an after-effect of the shower, but I feel all too hot and tug at the collar of my shirt. Karrion grins.

'Shut up,' I say, and head upstairs.

'I was thinking,' says Karrion, 'that it would be good to go through everything you have on the other crime scene before we return to St Albans. That way we can be on the lookout for any similarities.' We enter the lounge. 'Oh great, you're naked.'

Karrion turns to stare at the fireplace, thereby missing the frown Dearon directs at him. I bite my lip to keep from laughing. Dearon is standing by the window, Sinta's water bowl in one hand and an orange pteranodon toy in the other. Even after the night we spent together, he still looks out of place in my flat, no matter how much he is a picture of domesticity.

'Sinta just had breakfast, so I let her back out.'

'Thanks. The shower's all yours.'

Dearon nods and picks up his clothes before leaving the room. I remain frozen to the spot until the shower starts running, much like I did last night. Sensing Karrion's eyes on me, I bend down to straighten the blankets and switch on my phone.

'You know, that explains a lot.'

'What does?'

'Now I've met Dearon, I can understand why you and Wishearth... I mean, Dearon and Wishearth share a certain resemblance.'

'No, they don't.'

'Aside from the difference in height and build, yeah, they do. There's something similar in their eyes and their demeanour.'

Crossing my arms, I turn my attention to the window. Sinta is approaching a pigeon, her tail wagging. The pigeon glances inside and flies off.

'I knew of Wishearth long before I met him. His appearance and demeanour are beyond my control.'

'That's not what I'm saying. I just think that his resemblance to Dearon could explain why you're so fond of Wishearth.'

My friendship with Wishearth has always been complicated, not least because I never know when he is serious and when his gestures are a light-hearted joke. He is loyal to those who follow the old ways and who honour him with regular offerings. Things changed during my recent trip to Sussex for a friend's wedding. The investigation there and Wishearth's role in it gave me a chance to spend more time with him, away from the Open Hearth and my fireplace. He saved my life. The memory of his anguish at almost being too late still haunts my lonely nights, as does the feel of his arms around me as he held me.

Guilt fills me when I turn to the cold fireplace. The offering I made at the Green Dragon feels lukewarm compared to inviting him into my home and hearth.

'Whatever the reason, if you mention your theory to Dearon or Wishearth, I'll make sure you get tarred and feathered in pigeon down.'

'Threat duly noted.' Karrion puts the kettle on. 'So, about the other case?'

'Right. I don't have a copy of the case file, only the photos of the body.'

'That's a start.'

By the time Dearon returns upstairs, still running a towel through his wet hair, Karrion and I are sitting on our usual seats with the laptop and a plate of toast between us on the table. Coffee has helped dispel some of the fatigue from a night that involved far too little sleep. My aching joints demand painkillers, but I dare not take any when we have to head out soon. It would be useful if Karrion already had his licence.

'There's a mug of tea waiting for you in the kitchen,' I say.

Dearon's nostrils flare. 'You're drinking coffee.'

'It's a habit I picked up after moving to the city. When I'm working long hours, coffee gets my brain going better than tea.'

'Which do you prefer?'

I hesitate, feeling like we are no longer discussing hot beverages. 'Both have their time and place. Neither is worse simply because they are different.'

Dearon continues to the kitchen, leaving me wondering what he thought of my reply. I keep half an eye on him bringing his mug to the lounge and hanging up his towel, while Karrion finishes going through the photos and reaches for another slice of toast.

'Was it those animal tracks that made you think a Wild Folk was behind the woman's death?' he asks, and takes a long sip from his mug.

'Yes. And this.' I point to the boot print.

Karrion zooms in until the impression in the dirt dissolves into blurry pixels. 'It has no tread, like the tracks we saw yesterday.'

'We sew our boots from the hides we prepare,' Dearon says. 'Soft soles mean we can walk through the landscape silently.'

'It also makes it impossible to say for certain that the same Wild Folk left both footprints.'

I nod, toying with my mug. 'They look to be about the same size, though it's hard to say for sure from a photo.'

'The prints we saw yesterday didn't look huge,' Karrion says.

Dearon takes a slice of toast off the plate. 'He may be young, perhaps even a teenager.'

'But why would someone who's little more than a child start killing and eating people?'

Looking down at Karrion, Dearon shifts closer to the table. Karrion does not appear to notice the sign of dominance, and I resist the urge to put myself between the men.

'A teenager would make perfect sense,' Dearon says. 'If someone neglected their lessons and didn't learn the dangers of losing control, their wild instincts could override the human understanding of our laws.'

'You keep talking about control and instincts.' Karrion's gaze flickers to me. 'But how does it actually work?'

'Every time we borrow an aspect of nature, be it the sight of an owl or the nose of a fox, it is a transformation. As you saw yesterday, we can effect a partial change, like the fur covering my body, or the strongest among us can shape-shift like Dearon did. The challenging part about the process is learning not just how to transform feet into paws, but how to reverse the change. The more subtle the transformation, the more control it requires, until we learn to tap into the natural power around us to enhance our senses without resorting to a specific animal. We do it instinctively in a natural setting, and returning to the conclave reminds me every time how blind I am in the city.'

'Control is only part of the whole,' Dearon says.

'I'm getting to that.'

I reach to brush my fingers along the inside of his wrist. The skin there feels heated, or perhaps my fingers are cold. I cannot tell, and the confusion causes me to lose the thread of my thought.

'Control,' Karrion prompts me.

'Right. The other part is all about instincts. When we borrow an aspect of the natural world, we gain all of it. By tapping into an owl's night vision, we also get the instant reaction to a mouse creeping through a wheat field; the instinct to pounce and kill.'

'Which can be pretty inconvenient in polite company,' Karrion says.

'Especially if we catch the mouse,' I say with a crooked smile.

From the way his face lights up, I know Karrion wants to ask more, but I carry on with my explanation.

'Much of what we learn is controlling those wild instincts, especially when we tap into animals with high prey drive.'

Karrion plays with his lip piercing. 'Having a bunch of Wild Folk kids chase joggers because they're embracing their inner wolf would be bad PR for the conclave.'

'Exactly. So a lot of the early lessons focus on not letting the animal instincts override the laws that govern our existence.'

'Such as thou shalt not eat thy fellow human beings for breakfast?'

'Among other things. An adult Wild Folk with years of training and experience would only lose control under extraordinary circumstances, whereas it could happen easier with a teenager who is still coming to terms with his powers.'

'But if a teenager is missing from one of the conclaves, wouldn't you have heard about it?' Karrion asks.

'Not necessarily,' Dearon says over his shoulder as he takes his mug to the kitchen. 'Most conclaves prefer to deal with internal problems with little fuss.' Is it my imagination or is Dearon directing his words at me? 'It's only if a resolution cannot be found that the problem is opened to the collective wisdom of the Eldermen. The boy may be an issue his conclave is trying to tackle at the moment.'

'Not if he's here in the south.' I shake my head. 'There are no Wild Folk lands within two hundred miles.'

'Maybe he ran away,' Karrion says. Dearon frowns at him. Karrion continues, 'It's been known to happen. He could be lost and confused. In need of help.'

Instead of responding, I turn to the photo on the laptop screen. The victim's hand is visible among the seedlings; pale and bloodless against the greenery. Something about Karrion's words bothers me.

'A confused runaway wouldn't have gone to the trouble of misdirecting the dogs and hiding the body somewhere inaccessible. A boy overcome by the wild instincts would have killed Cúan in the back garden. In fact, a boy overcome by wild instincts would probably have eaten Shadow and left Cúan alone. What we witnessed yesterday indicates premeditation: a hunter who knows how to kill.'

'Yannia is right. He is a predator, whatever age he may be.'

'If that's the case, rather than reach out to the other conclaves to help find a missing kid, perhaps we should get in touch with them about trying to figure out who this hunter is.'

'We?' Dearon looks up from strapping his hunting knife to his calf.

Karrion crosses his arms. 'We're going to have to talk to them sooner or later.'

Before Dearon gets a chance to respond, I close the laptop lid and stand up. 'I think what Karrion means is that we're working on this case together and need to pool our resources. While I see what I can do about getting us the case file for the other death, perhaps you should get in contact with the other conclaves. Unless rumours of a teenager unable to control his wilder side have already reached you?'

The stiffness of Dearon's shoulders eases. 'No, I have heard no such thing.'

'That's what I thought. Can you reach out to the other Eldermen without physically visiting the conclaves?'

'Not easily, but I can ask someone at our conclave to carry messages for me.'

'What a shame you didn't bring a flock of carrier pigeons with you,' Karrion says, aiming his grin at me.

'Could you round some up for him?' I say, laughing when Karrion splutters his outrage.

'A Wild Folk is more reliable than a messenger bird and can carry longer messages,' Dearon says.

'Or you could set up a private WhatsApp group for the Eldermen. Hasn't Yan told you that modern technology has its uses?' When Dearon stares at him, Karrion raises his hands. 'I'm kidding. Is fun banned as well?'

'Okay, it's time to go now, if we are to maximise the amount of daylight we have available,' I say, lifting Sinta back inside before Dearon and Karrion end up at each other's throats. She dives at Karrion's shoelaces while I pack her bowl and a bag of food. 'Funja promised to have Sinta for the day, so we need to stop at the Open Hearth on our way.'

'Boris gets to play babysitter, eh?' Karrion grins and prises his shoelace from Sinta's mouth.

'According to Funja, it will do him good.'

Funja's Irish wolfhound companion, Boris, spends

much of his time snoozing in front of the huge fireplace at the Open Hearth. This is not the first time they have looked after Sinta for me, and I know Boris adores her. The feeling is mutual.

Karrion shrugs on his long leather coat and takes the bag from me. 'All right, let's go hunt a Wild Folk.'

12

THE LONG SEARCH

We park at the Green Dragon. I lean against the side of the car, stretching my stiff muscles. The rain has stopped, though the sky is still grey. A woman with two terriers walks across the green.

'How do you want to do this?' Karrion asks.

By the bridge, a sord of mallards takes flight. They are black silhouettes against the sky as they speed away from us. Karrion stuffs his hands in his pockets.

'Let's start with the lakes. That's the most likely hiding place for our Wild Folk.'

Dearon nods, his hair black against the whitewashed pub. It has dried during the drive and the ends are curling naturally around his shoulders. I have always envied his thick wavy hair, though, as a teenager, I would have been mortified if he'd ever found out. Now, I recall running my fingers through it as we lay catching our breath in the early hours of the morning, and it seems like the next best thing.

Together we follow the narrow road around the bend, dodging potholes filled with water. The route seems shorter than it did yesterday afternoon and we soon duck through the gap in the fence. Now that I'm focused on more than the path we are taking, I notice a field of some kind on the opposite side of the lake.

The ridge we are following is too narrow to afford a proper hiding place, but once the path dips down and the houses end, the woods grow denser. Karrion's hand brushes against withering nettles, and he swears. When we reach the first fork, he turns to me. Blue and white police tape sways in the breeze.

'Which way, boss?'

'I'd like to see what's beyond the crime scene.'

A uniformed officer approaches, an exasperated twist of his lips indicating that we are not the first people to stop by the tape this morning. His demeanour changes as soon as I show him my consultant's badge and explain why we are here. He lets us past the tape, and we climb the short incline to the next lake.

It is only now that I appreciate how close the nearest building is. A chicken wire fence separates it from the ivy-clad trees. In one of the ground floor flats, a woman is doing up her hair in front of a mirror. I mention the proximity of the building to the others.

'Should we speak to the residents in case someone saw something?' Karrion asks.

'The boy was taken after dark,' Dearon says. 'No one will have seen anything unless they have night vision.'

'Dearon's right. Plus any external lights on the building will have made the darkness even more impenetrable.'

On the island, Scene of Crime Officers are still working, with two rubber dinghies bearing supplies attached to the branches near the waterline. Two divers are in the water, and several more are holding on to safety lines or resting on the fishing spots near us. Jamie is nowhere to be seen, nor do I sense the presence of a Mage. Perhaps they have already been, or perhaps the case is clear-cut enough not to warrant the time of a magic consultant.

It takes us over an hour to work through the woods beyond the crime scene. By the time we reach the far end of the lake, we are all tired and covered in scratches. Karrion's knuckles are bleeding. While there were a few spots ideal for a Wild Folk to camp, we found nothing to suggest he had done so. The houses that surround the area are too close.

On the other side of the lake, a gravel path runs between the water and a field fenced with barbed wire. My chin lifts to sample the breeze. Among exhaust fumes and wet earth are the scents of fleece and fresh manure.

'There are sheep in that field,' I say.

'Does that mean there's no point in searching it?' Karrion asks. 'Are livestock afraid of Wild Folk?'

'No more than they'd fear a Bird Shaman. This is no B-list horror story.'

'There's a lot of ground to cover, though most of it is open. Where would he hide in that field?'

'It's not just that,' I say. 'What I want to know is why would the Wild Folk attack a child if there are sheep nearby? They are much easier prey and the kill can be hidden with minimal effort.'

Karrion cranes his neck to look across the field. 'Maybe he killed a sheep and the farmer took the rest away?'

'Either way, I want to search for signs of a recent kill.'

'There are trees ahead,' Dearon says. 'I'll follow the outside of the field and meet you somewhere near the middle.'

He leaves without waiting for a reply, and Karrion frowns. I roll my eyes.

A nearby kissing gate grants us access to the field. The ground is level, then rises in a gentle slope.

'Which way?' Karrion asks.

'If Dearon is going to the opposite end, let's follow the fence on this side and see what's over that ridge.'

A path snakes in the direction we are taking, and we follow it side by side. A steady drone of cars somewhere ahead grows louder. It is otherwise quiet. I find the lack of birdsong unsettling. Karrion walks beside me, shoulders hunched and his teeth worrying his lip piercing. His ragged power extends far beyond the limits of my senses.

We climb the low ridge, shoes sliding in the mud, and find that the field extends further than I expected. In the distance, it ends at the M25 and a small flock of sheep grazes against the backdrop of the always-busy motorway.

'So, apparently it's bigger on the inside,' Karrion says with a low chuckle.

'Shut up.'

I nudge him off balance with my shoulder, but my grin slips away as I survey the field. The ground dips and rises all around us, promising hidden spots and mischances.

'Karrion,' I say, keeping my voice gentle, 'we're going to need birds.'

He stiffens, and colour bleeds from his knuckles. 'There are no birds here.'

I slide my fingers over the back of his wrist, and he takes my hand.

'What Baneacre did wasn't your fault.'

'I know that,' he says, eyes fixed on the landscape. 'You've told me enough times.'

'Yet you don't believe me.'

'It's not that. I know he killed those birds.' Karrion's hand clenches around mine and then relaxes, his thumb running over the inside of my wrist. 'But I never want to feel another bird tortured like that.'

'And that's why...?' I tilt my head back to look at the empty skies.

'If I keep them away, they can't die because of me. Even if it was Baneacre who killed them.'

'Karrion, you're a Bird Shaman. You can't live without birds.'

'I can try.'

Frustration born out of fear rises in me, but I tamp it down. Getting angry at his flawed logic will not help either of us.

'I need your help, Karrion. If we had a flock of birds, we could cover this field in no time.'

He frowns. His eyes flicker down, then to me.

'There is no one here but us,' I say. 'No one to hurt the birds.'

Letting go of my hand, he rubs his face. His whole body is stiff, and he stretches his neck until it crunches. I wince at the sound. When he turns to me, my heart clenches at his look of indecision.

'I'm not going to fail you again,' I say, giving voice for the first time to a guilt that has slumbered at the back of my mind.

If I hadn't sent him out of harm's way, he wouldn't have nearly died trying to bring back the dead birds.

'It wasn't...' and his voice is lost in a sound that could be a laugh or a groan. 'Yan, we could spend all day arguing about which of us should take the blame.'

'That's what we're good at.'

He squeezes my shoulder and takes a few steps away. The press of his aura against mine changes. At first, nothing happens, but then the sky begins to darken. The birds wheel above us, all natural enmity between the species set aside to answer the call of a Bird Shaman.

Within the growing flock are crows and ravens, red kites and ospreys, buzzards and magpies, sparrow hawks and rooks, hobbies and jays.

Karrion stands in the eye of the storm of feathers, his head tilted up. His nose seems to transform into a beak, his hair into the gleaming plumage of a raven. A flock of pigeons lands at his feet, but he ignores them. He is connected to each of the birds, and the feather-width threads restore his aura. The more he uses his magic, the more powerful he becomes.

With a whisper of a command, he scatters the flock across the field. The birds of prey ride the thermals until they are distant specks in the sky, while the crows, ravens, magpies, rooks, and jays, swoop low over the ground. A few sparrows join them, more interested in chirping challenges than seeking carrion. The pigeons remain where they are, staring at Karrion with adoration until he dismisses them with another burst of magic.

'That way,' he says.

Near the fence, red kites and buzzards are forming a funnel. One of the birds swoops low and rises again, something grasped within its talons. It flies to us, diving to release the prize: a dried skin of a grey squirrel. Karrion kicks it off the path, and we continue towards the next concentration of birds.

When we reach the thick brambles separating the field from the road beyond, Karrion steps into the middle of a murder of crows. Their beaks are stained red. My pulse picks up speed, until I spot a flash of orange among the black feathers. Karrion ushers them aside long enough to reveal a fox carcass. The broken leg and bloodied face suggest it was hit by a car and crawled away from the road to die. We leave the birds to their feast.

Twice more the birds direct us to a carcass and twice more it turns out to be nothing but small ground game. If a sheep was killed on the field, no trace of it remains among the grass and dried stalks of thistle. The sheep move out of our way, but none appears injured or more fearful than I would expect.

'I don't think there's much more to be gained from this field,' I say, not bothering to conceal my disappointment.

'Dearon is over there.'

Karrion looks across the field, and his eyes hold the thousand yard stare of a sparrow hawk. A peregrine has joined the others late, and I borrow its sight. Dearon stands on the crest of a hill, a hand rising to shield his face. When I wave, he starts towards us.

'We should go.'

With the stealth of an owl gliding through the air, Karrion releases the birds. He raises his hand, and they swoop down. The touches are little more than the graze of a tail feather or a wing tip against his fingers, but he stands straighter and holds his head higher. I envy the birds for the healing they offer.

We meet Dearon next to a pair of gate posts in the middle of the field. All signs of the fence are gone, but a public footpath arrow still guides people towards the hedge ahead. Karrion moves to step between the gate posts. Dearon stops him.

'Don't.'

'Why? There's nothing here.'

'No gate leads to nowhere and all paths must take you somewhere.'

Karrion turns to me. 'That doesn't make sense.'

'It does.' I draw him away. 'The old stories speak of Fey

traps. You may think the gate leads nowhere, but you might end up in the Unseen Lands, bound to an eternity of servitude.'

'Oh.' Karrion gives the rotting posts a wide berth. 'I didn't know.'

'City living risks your life,' says Dearon. 'Don't they teach you anything there about the dangers of our world?'

Crossing his arms, Karrion glares at Dearon. 'They teach us plenty. Do you know how to touch-type or use spreadsheets? Do you know how the tax system works, or the powers and responsibilities of the Circle of Shamans and the High Council of Mages? Do you know how to make contactless payments? These are all things relevant to living in the city and surviving there.'

Dearon considers this for a long moment, and then nods. 'You are correct. I had not appreciated the differences in our experiences.'

Karrion raises his eyebrows and looks from Dearon to me and back. I shrug, but he is not ready to let the point drop.

'Besides, if I don't know something, how can I know to miss it?' says Karrion.

'True,' says Dearon.

'Did you find anything?' I ask Dearon.

'Only thickets and rabbit holes. There are further fields, though from the tracks, dog walkers are frequent visitors.'

'There are no signs here that someone has killed a sheep recently. Or else they've been careful about covering all traces of their crime.'

'He must have satisfied his hunger elsewhere.'

Cúan's mangled body flashes across my mind. A familiar frustration sends my pulse tripping. This case makes no sense. Why eat people when there is livestock available? What are we missing?

We walk back the way Dearon came. Across a narrow track is a small meadow with footpaths cut through the brambles and saplings. In the distance, the pale light of the overcast day touches the front of the Green Dragon.

'Which way do you want to go next?' Karrion asks as we walk towards the car.

'Hang on.'

A flash of blue in a narrow spinney of oak, cherry, and horse chestnut, draws my attention to the right, and I veer off the path. The others follow. In the widest part of the spinney, a blue tarpaulin is stretched between trees. Beneath it is a damp layer of cardboard. The ground in front of the shelter is clear of leaves and packed solid from regular footfall. A carrier bag hangs from a branch, rustling in the breeze. I take it down. Inside is a brown banana skin, a tuna sandwich wrap beginning to smell, and scraps of other litter.

'Someone was staying here until recently.'

'So?' Karrion peers into the bag and scrunches his nose. 'It's probably just a temporary shelter.'

'I disagree. Look around you. The area is clean, and the rubbish bag suggests someone was keen to keep it that way. And check this out.' I point to the back of the tarpaulin. 'See how there's a layer of leaves on the bottom of the tarp? Someone weighed it down with rocks and it's been that way for several months at least.'

'Yannia is right.' Dearon has walked further into the spinney. 'Whoever has been living here has even gone to the trouble of digging pits for his waste.'

'How do you know?' Karrion asks.

'I can smell it.'

Karrion grimaces. 'Nice.'

'It is a fact of life.' Dearon returns to us. 'But as much as this camp is different from the conclave, the basics are the same. This was someone's home.'

'How do you know they're not intending to return?' Karrion asks.

'There are no belongings here,' I say. 'If a homeless person was to go to the shops, in an area like this with less footfall, they would be unlikely to take everything they own with them.'

'But there are any number of reasons why a homeless person would decamp,' Karrion says. 'Maybe they've gone to a shelter?'

'It's possible, though the timing is coincidental. Keep an eye out for a homeless person while we search the rest of the area.'

'Which way are we going next?' asks Karrion.

'For the sake of time,' I say, 'we ought to split up. Karrion, I want you to follow the river to that activity farm. Speak to a member of staff and ask if they've lost any animals to dog attacks or something similar. Provided there's a way past the farm, I also want you to see what the area is like.'

'I'm guessing it'll be footpaths.'

'Me too. Dearon and I are going to search over there,' I point up the slope, 'and take a quick walk to the far side of the motorway.'

'Okay,' Karrion says. 'Where do you want to meet?'

'Call me when you're finished and we'll figure something out.'

'Sure.' He checks his phone and slides it into his back pocket.

'Karrion?' I call after him. He turns. 'Don't search

beyond the farm, just see what's there and come back. Confronting a Wild Folk on your own would be dangerous.'

'I won't be alone.'

Right on cue, a red kite lands on Karrion's outstretched arm. As much as I want to tease him about unnecessary melodrama, my joy at seeing him interacting with a bird silences my tongue for a few seconds.

'Even with a flock of pigeons, you'd be in grave danger.'

'Don't worry, Yan. I'll be careful.'

Karrion looks like he wants to hug me, but his eyes flicker to Dearon and back. He nods, and leaves, the bird still clinging to his arm. I wonder if he has realised that the talons are digging into his leather jacket.

13

HUMAN FEAR

When I turn, I find Dearon watching me. His expression is softer than before; puzzled rather than dominant. What has caused the change? Before I have a chance to voice the question, he speaks.

'Shall we?'

We follow the path up the shallow slope and through a gap in the hedge, where it opens to a landscape of brambles and briars. Twice we flush a pheasant into flight, and both times, Dearon's hand reaches for a bow that is not there.

There is no sign of the Wild Folk among the brown shrubs and coils of thorns. Dearon points towards a steep set of steps leading up to the footbridge over the motorway, but my attention is drawn away from it. The breeze carries a tang of an unwashed body, barely distinguishable over the stink of the exhaust fumes and rubber. Dearon follows me without a word. He tries to edge past me, but my pointed look halts him. I lead the way.

A man wrapped in a dark blue sleeping bag is huddled on a pile of cardboard. At first glance, he appears to be dozing, but a horn blares and his head jerks up. I stop, motioning for Dearon to stay back, and the man fixes a suspicious glare on us.

'What do you want?'

'We were on our way to the shops, and I wondered if you needed anything.'

'A sandwich would be nice.' The furrows across his forehead become less pronounced. 'Thank you.'

'No problem. We'll be right back.'

I lead Dearon to the edge of Sainsbury's car park. Even after we are out of earshot, I keep my voice low.

'Can you watch him? But keep your distance.'

'Sure, but why?'

'Even without the bow and arrows, you look pretty intimidating. Someone whose situation is already vulnerable doesn't need to be made to feel unsafe.'

Dearon stares at me, confusion written in the purse of his lips. 'You think I'm intimidating?'

'Yeah. You wear your power like a dark cloak, and even to those who can't detect your magic, it gives you an air of otherness. Whether you're angry or merely channelling the Elderman's abilities, people don't need to see your frown to know you're dangerous.'

When his expression doesn't change, I reconsider his words. Did I answer the wrong question?

'I'm not afraid of you.' When he reaches to brush hair from his face, I know I got it right the second time. 'Let's face it, I'm going to find it hard to fear someone who was once trampled by a goat. But I respect your power, just as I've been brought up to respect your position as the next Elderman.'

'You could have stopped after saying you weren't scared of me.'

'And what? Miss the opportunity to remind you about the goat?'

'It was a very large goat.'

'Dearon, I was there. It was a pygmy.'

'It seemed huge when it was charging towards me.'

'Such a shame you didn't notice the puddle.'

'You didn't seem too unhappy about it at the time.'

We manage to keep a straight face for a few seconds before laughter gets the better of us. Wiping my eyes, I lean against his side and try not to notice how his eyelashes are brushing his cheek when he blinks, or the hint of heat on his neck. Dearon's eyes are drawn to my lips, and laugher gives way to something darker. I swallow and turn to look towards the entrance to Sainsbury's.

'I'll see you soon.'

When I move to walk away, fingers caress the back of my hand. I glance over my shoulder, but Dearon is already walking in the opposite direction.

I collect a basket on my way in. The sandwiches are next to a kiosk and I select two: a tuna and sweetcorn and a BLT. A stand advertising yoga accessories is next to Christmas chocolates, and after a moment of deliberation, I tuck a rolled yoga mat under my arm. From the clothes aisles, I pick up socks, gloves, and a fleece, erring on the side of caution with sizes. A rucksack follows. As I wander past the food aisles, I add a bag of apples and another of bananas to the basket, then select canned goods that can be eaten cold. For Dearon and me, I get rolls, roasted chicken breasts, and flapjacks, and choose a tray of sushi for Karrion. I pick up a bag of toilet rolls and hesitate next to the hand sanitisers, opting for wet wipes instead. A toothbrush, toothpaste, antiseptic cream, and plasters, complete my purchases.

As I pack the supplies into the rucksack, I cannot help thinking how inadequate the gesture seems. No one should be spending December sleeping next to a motorway. No one should be cold and alone, not at Christmas or any other time of the year. My upbringing taught me that no people outside the Wild Folk conclaves matter, but my time in Old London has eroded old behaviours and prejudices. Now I understand that every life, be it a human or one of us, is precious.

When I approach the footpath, Dearon appears from between parked cars. I lift my chin to confirm the homeless man has not moved.

'Didn't he only ask for a sandwich?' Dearon eyes everything I am carrying, and I pass him our lunch supplies. While I waited to pay, I texted Karrion to say I'd bought him lunch. Dearon and I will have to eat our chicken before Karrion joins us.

'Yes. That doesn't mean he didn't need other things.'

'How do you know?'

'If you were in his position, would you ask a stranger for help?'

Dearon offers no response, and I weave between parked cars to the opening in the hedge. The look of suspicion returns to the homeless man's face when he spots me.

'I bought you a few supplies,' I say, setting the rucksack and toilet rolls next to him. 'And I thought a yoga mat would be warmer to sleep on than cardboard.'

His brow furrows as he takes the blue mat from me. 'Why did you buy all this?'

'Because I need your help, and it seems only fair I return the favour.'

He stares at me for a long time. Dearon shifts behind me, but I ignore him. The homeless man nods.

'What do you need?'

'Information.' I hold out my hand and introduce myself.

'Terry.' The handshake is fleeting.

'Is that your shelter in the copse?' I ask, nodding in the direction of the fields.

'Yes.'

'Why did you leave?'

Terry pulls the rucksack closer and opens it. I packed the sandwiches and a carton of orange juice on the top. Beneath them is the packet of wet wipes. He scrubs his hands, even reaching to clean under his nails. Once finished, he folds the used wet wipe and hides it in his pocket. With deliberate slowness, he opens one of the sandwiches. Hints of tuna, mayonnaise, and sweet corn reach my nose, and my stomach growls. Terry takes a bite.

'Did something happen to make you leave?'

Washing down his mouthful with a swig of orange juice, Terry flickers his eyes to me and away.

'It was nothing, really. Just the wind and my mind playing tricks on me.'

'Will you tell us what happened? Please?'

When Terry speaks, he directs his words at the sandwich. 'I woke up in the middle of the night, certain someone was watching me. At first, I thought it was just a bad dream, but then I heard growling. I grabbed my sleeping bag and the backpack next to me, and I ran. With every step, I expected to be attacked, but I got to the bridge and the pub in one piece. I spent the rest of the night walking around Sainsbury's car park, too afraid to sleep. When I went back the next morning, someone had looked through my camp. I gathered the rest of my belongings and haven't been back since.'

'How do you know someone had been in your camp?'

'A few items weren't quite where I'd left them. I know where I keep my things.'

'Was anything missing?'

'Nothing.'

'Did you see any tracks?' Dearon asks.

Terry laughs. 'I grew up in London.'

'When did all this happen?' I ask before Dearon presses the point.

'Three nights ago.'

The day before Cúan went missing. Is it significant? I am not certain.

'What about since then? Have you seen or heard anything out of the ordinary?'

Terry sets down the sandwich and replaces the top on the orange juice. He shakes the carton.

'I stepped out to that field yesterday afternoon shortly before it started getting dark, to relieve myself. You see, I haven't slept during the night since that awful growl woke me. Best stay in the light and be alert, you know. I can then rest during the day here, close to people, but far enough away that I won't be disturbed. In any case, as I was coming back, I thought I saw someone walking across the footbridge. But when they got to the top of the steps, they weren't a person anymore.'

'What do you mean?'

'I thought they were walking a dog at first and they'd bent down to tie a shoelace or something, but nothing else came off that bridge.'

'What did the creature look like?' Dearon asks.

'Like a big dog, but not quite. It could have been black or brown, I couldn't say for sure in the fading light. Although it walked on four legs, there was something awkward about the gait.'

'Did you notice anything else?'

'No. It glanced in my direction, and I got the hell out

of there. Spent the rest of the night begging for change outside Sainsbury's, and then huddled in the middle of the car park in a trolley shelter. I didn't come back here until a couple of hours after the sun had risen.'

'What about the person on the bridge?' I ask. 'What can you tell us about him?'

'Not a lot. He was little more than a silhouette against the motorway. Though he was moving fast.'

'Fast how?'

'He wasn't running, but like he was walking with a purpose.'

I turn to Dearon, who shakes his head.

'Thanks for your time and for answering our questions, Terry,' I say.

'This bloke I saw, is he dangerous?'

I see no reason to lie. 'Very. You'd do well to stay in well-lit areas for the time being, or go elsewhere.'

'I like this spot, or my campsite at any rate. People are generous by the shops. I'll stay put and just keep an eye out. Thanks for the supplies.'

'Any time. Be safe.'

As we leave, I glance back. With a hungry Wild Folk roaming the area, Terry may not survive the night.

14

THE LAIR

We leave the way we came and walk far enough from the motorway that I can call Karrion. He is on his way back from the farm, and we agree to meet by the bridge. While we wait, Dearon and I eat our lunch, standing amidst the dried grass and low blackberry bushes. Dearon licks chicken grease from his fingers and opens the packet of flapjacks.

'Our first instinct is to shift forms to hunt,' he says. 'Do you think that's what he was doing when Terry saw him yesterday?'

'Either that, or he was returning to his kill. It doesn't make sense to go after new prey when there's plenty of meat left on the carcass.'

'Which means it's likely he was watching us last night,' Dearon finishes the thought for me.

'I expect so. It wouldn't have been hard to sneak through the woods and hide somewhere along the lake-shore.'

'We should have been able to detect him.'

'He knows how to stay downwind just as well as we do. The smell of the body was so strong we might have missed him even if the wind had turned.'

Dearon nods and takes the water bottle I offer him.

'But why didn't he kill Terry when he had the chance? Why go after a child instead?'

'The camp is visible from all sides. Killing Terry would have been easy, but hiding his body less so. While Cúan's body has less meat on it, the Wild Folk could carry him and consume most of it before the meat spoiled. Moving Terry would have been much harder, especially if our assumption is correct and we're after a teenager. What's more interesting is that the Wild Folk scared Terry without killing him.'

'How so?'

'He could have snapped Terry's neck in his sleep, no doubt about that,' I say. 'So why wake him up by growling instead?'

'Perhaps he wanted Terry on the move?'

'But why? It wasn't to chase and kill him.'

Dearon turns his back on the bridge and stares over the open landscape we have just searched. His eyes narrow, and I wonder what he sees.

'Could he have simply been in the way?' he asks.

'What do you mean?'

'Terry's camp was more or less opposite the Dog Shamans' home. Scaring him away could have been the Wild Folk's way of eliminating competition and ensuring he could stalk his prey in peace.'

A part of me wants to tell him off for not referring to the Eastmans by name, but it would be futile. Who am I to force him to think as I do?

'You could be right,' I say. 'If that was the reason, killing Terry would have drawn attention to the area, whereas very few people are going to take notice of a homeless man moving on.'

'Even so, I keep coming back to how strange it is that

he killed the jogger and ate her on the same spot, but he went to great lengths to hide the Dog Shaman's body.'

'There's something we're missing.'

'Like what?' Dearon asks.

'I don't know. But when we figure it out, this will all make sense.'

'You seem optimistic.'

'Hazards of the job,' I say, and wave at Karrion walking up the hill.

'Hey, Yan.' Karrion takes the tray of sushi and the chopsticks. 'How did it go?'

Karrion eats as we cross the motorway and head along a gravel path. I explain what we have discovered. He listens in silence until we come to a set of traffic lights.

'You did better than I did. The staff at the farm looked at me funny until I whipped out my Met consultant's badge. They took me to a shepherd who confirmed all their animals were alive and well. He started quizzing me about dangerous dogs, and I beat a hasty retreat. Beyond the farm, there's a path following the river, with paddocks and small woods along the way. From the map, it looks like there's some sort of manor house up there, more woods and a gravel quarry. But I didn't go far enough to see them for myself, though I do think someone could probably find a secluded spot to hide.'

We cross the road.

'I wonder if he was aware of the farm?' I say. 'It would be much easier to take a sheep or a goat than to target a person. So why did he go after Cúan?'

Karrion throws the empty sushi tray in a bin. 'As soon as we find him, you can ask the question.'

A sign to our left indicates that we are entering Arsenal Football Club's training grounds. I hesitate, wondering if we should turn back until I spot a public footpath sign ahead.

The path cuts a line between football fields and is bordered by hedges. Leaves crunch underneath our feet. Eventually, we come to a crossroads. In front of us, a gap in the trees opens to another field.

'Which way should we go?' Dearon asks.

I turn to look back. Have we come too far? Normally, this distance would be nothing to a Wild Folk, but expecting one to travel past football fields and over major roads to return to their kill is a big ask. Nothing about the situation feels right. I am reluctant to give up now, so I load the map on my phone. Were we to walk far enough, we would reach the village of Shenley. But if we continue straight on, we will encounter woods as well as fields, which offer more options.

'This way,' I say, and step through the gap.

Beyond the football training ground is a landscape of ploughed fields. We continue on to a deep depression. At the bottom is a series of sheds built from corrugated iron sheets. Outside one, two men are readying a small aeroplane for flight. A strip of grass acts as a runway. While Dearon and I carry on, Karrion jogs down the hill to speak to the men and returns a few minutes later, shaking his head.

The woods are narrower than I expected, and we soon emerge back into the light. Horses are grazing in the field ahead of us.

'Look,' Karrion says.

He has turned to where the land slopes down towards an overgrown track. Half-hidden behind saplings and tall piles of rubbish is a small cottage. The roof has holes in it, and the windows are empty spaces. I see no outward signs of anything awry, but something about the abandoned cottage gives me a deep sense of disquiet.

'What do you think?' Karrion asks when I have been quiet for too long.

'It's a possibility.' I glance at Dearon. 'We've been so focused on his animal instincts that we've forgotten about his human side.'

Dearon nods. 'Even Wild Folk like a roof over their heads.'

'We should have a look,' I say. 'But we have to be quiet.'

The swish of grass against our shoes sounds too loud to my ears as we walk down the hill. The building may be a red herring, but the thought does nothing to alleviate my unease. A shotgun going off in the distance causes me to jump, and Karrion steadies me with a hand on my elbow. His eyebrow is raised, and I nod. He lets go.

Once we reach the track, it's easier to keep quiet. Dearon glides forward with a purpose, his toes touching the ground first. Next to him, I feel loud and uncoordinated, though Karrion makes more noise than I do. When Karrion steps on a twig, Dearon casts a warning glance in his direction, but says nothing.

As the track curves towards the cottage, I spot a brown skip filled with rusting appliances, pieces of plastic, and broken ceramic tiles. A tree is growing in front of the cottage, and during the summer months, it would obscure most of the gaping doorway and sagging porch. Now the bare branches scrape the air and scratch against the edge of the roof.

Dearon draws my attention to the back of the building, where the grass indicates that someone has been in and out of the cottage several times. A thrill of excitement runs through me, and I see my thoughts reflected in the shine of Dearon's eyes. We are finally getting somewhere. He makes a show of sniffing the air. Calling upon the nose of a fox asleep under the skip, I wait for a gust of wind to blow past the house; then I inhale.

The smell of meat is unmistakable, and it carries an edge of rot. Has he killed again? There is also an under-current of an unwashed body and damp. Something about the scent teases the edge of my thoughts: a mirage of insight just out of my reach. Perhaps Dearon already knows what I am still grasping to understand, but I dare not ask the question out loud.

When he moves to approach the porch, I stop Dearon by grabbing the back of his sleeve. He frowns at me, motioning towards the house. I shake my head, and he glares at me. When it becomes clear I have no intention of letting go, he turns around and we retrace our steps until we are further from the cottage.

'What are you doing?' I ask, keeping my voice low.

'Taking a closer look.'

'Can't you smell him?'

'I smell something, but that doesn't mean he's there. Besides, even if he is, so what? The two of us can easily overpower him.'

'There are three of us here,' Karrion says.

'If we think we've found his hiding place, we need to call Jamie and the Paladins. Let them come and do the apprehending. We can watch the house from a distance and make sure he doesn't slip away.'

'This is a Wild Folk matter. There's no need to get humans involved.'

'If he's attacking and eating people, he's dangerous. There's no shame in asking for help, Dearon.'

His shoulders stiffen as he stares down at me. 'What aid could a human possibly give to the future Elderman of a Wild Folk conclave?'

'Could we maybe not have this conversation here?' I hiss. 'When you chose to accompany me, you accepted that this was my case and that you'd be playing by my rules. Don't renege on that promise now.'

'Have you paused to consider what you're asking? How could you leave the fate of one of our own in the hands of humans and Paladins?'

Dearon turns away before I have a chance to reply and strides towards the cottage. I curse, balling my hands to fists, and follow him. Karrion trails behind me. When he kicks a stone that hits a branch by the track, I whirl around to tell him off. I stop myself. It is Dearon I am angry with, not Karrion, who mouths an apology and slows down.

At least Dearon has the good sense to be careful. His feet morph into a lynx's paws, allowing him to move with the stealth of a hunter. I follow his lead and slow down my breathing. If we can convince the Wild Folk to surrender himself to us, all the better. Afterwards, I can explain to Dearon that in the Southern Lands, killers must face the judgement of the Heralds rather than the Eldermen.

The smell of meat grows stronger as we creep towards the cottage, though it remains faint. It is unlikely there is a body in the building. I sharpen my hearing, but the house is a void within a landscape of sound and life. The doorway looms dark and forbidding, and I call upon the sight of an owl to penetrate the gloom. Ahead of me, Dearon stops and indicates that I should go around to the next window. He spares no glance at Karrion.

A change in the air pressure pricks up the hairs at the back of my neck. It's the only warning I get before a dark shape explodes out of the porch window and flies at Dearon. He has just enough time to raise his arm to shield his throat, and blood sprays when the creature's teeth clamp down on his forearm. A low growl rises from the misshapen snout as the attacker shakes its head. Dearon's free hand shimmers and contracts into claws. The creature howls when the claws rake down its neck and across its shoulder.

My muscles unfreeze. I call upon the teeth of a bear, my jaw elongating to accommodate them. I leap forward, but my foot lands on a hidden roof tile. A searing pain lances through my knee and hip as the joints sublux and slip back, and I stumble, breathless and stunned. The snarl of the creature forces me to rise, but black spots swim across my vision when I try to shift weight on to my right leg.

The creature's back is slick with blood where Dearon's claws have wounded it, but the matted black fur has prevented worse damage. It releases Dearon's arm to leap at his throat again. He blocks it a second time, and the force of the attack sends him stumbling. The creature drops back, but before Dearon has the chance to shift forms, it rushes at him again, this time aiming lower. Dearon goes flying back. The crack of his head hitting the ground vibrates through me. The pain in my leg forgotten, I charge to defend him.

A brick whistles past me and hits the creature on its shoulder. It shrieks and whirls around on top of Dearon, claws slicing through his leather vest. A second brick misses it by an inch. Karrion is standing next to a pile of building debris, holding two roof tiles.

'Get away from him!' he screeches, his features darkening into the countenance of an eagle.

With the creature's attention fixed on Karrion, I dive at it and knock it off Dearon. Its claws catch my arm, and my snapping jaws find a mouthful of fur. The creature shakes me off, only to take another hit from Karrion's missiles. With a half-howl, half-shriek, it turns and rushes around the corner of the building. Over the roar of blood in my ears, I listen to it moving through the undergrowth until the sound fades away.

Fear speeds the transformation of my face as it returns to normal. Dearon is lying on the ground, bleeding from a dozen wounds on his arm and chest. I drop on to my knees next to him and gently lift his head. My fingers feel around his hair and come back wet.

I become aware of Karrion repeating my name and look up. He is standing a few feet away, hands filled with pieces of brick and wide eyes scanning the area around us.

'What?' I manage around the lump in my throat.

'Call for help.'

The pain from the cuts on my arm registers as I find my phone and dial a number. My hands shake so much it takes me three attempts to get the number right. It seems like an eternity before the call connects.

'Brotherhood of Justice, what's your emergency?'

I search for the words, but my mind is blank. That was not the number I intended to dial. Blood slides down my palm and drips off my middle finger.

'Hello?'

'Sorry,' I rush to say, my brain finally in gear. 'I need an ambulance, but I dialled the wrong number. We're not in Old London.'

'Give me your location, and we will dispatch an ambulance from the nearest hospital.'

I stumble over the words as I explain where we are.

There are no roads nearby, and I agree that we will meet the ambulance by the airstrip. It will not be easy to carry Dearon there, but we have no choice.

'Wait,' I say as the operator is about to end the call. 'Can you alert the police too? We think this is where a killer has been hiding.'

'The police are on their way and I will pass them all the information you've given me.'

'Thank you.' I end the call.

Next to me, Karrion is beginning to relax his defensive stance. He shrugs off his long coat and the black jumper underneath. Once he has taken off his T-shirt, he tears the fabric into strips and we wrap them around Dearon's arm in a makeshift bandage. Karrion's nipple rings flash in the pale afternoon light as he dresses himself.

The cuts on Dearon's chest and abdomen are mostly shallow, but there is one that looks deep. As much as I hate to increase the bleeding, we have to move him to the airstrip. I shrug off my thermal shirt, heedless of the chill of the winter air, and pack it as well as I can between the wound and Dearon's leather vest.

With my mind clearer, details about the attack are coming into focus. I crouch down and find the clump of fur I tore off the creature. Bringing it to my nose, I inhale deeply. Beneath the smells of blood and wildness, there is an undercurrent of pheromones that sends my pulse tripping once more. I must have made a noise, for Karrion's hand comes to rest on my shoulder.

Standing up, I allow the fur to float down to the ground as I meet his gaze.

'The Wild Folk we're after is a woman.'

15

A CALL FOR HELP

'Are you sure?' Karrion asks.

'Positive. I can smell it.'

Before Karrion has a chance to reply, Dearon groans behind us. We both hurry to him as his eyes flutter open and stare past us. I help him to sit up. Dearon twists to the side and vomits. When his retching brings up nothing but bile, he relaxes against me. From my coat pocket, I take the bottle of water, and he drinks the last two mouthfuls.

'We need to get you out of here,' I say, and stuff the bottle back in the pocket.

Karrion skirts around the vomit to take Dearon's arm and together we raise him to his feet. Dearon groans. A pigeon lands on the edge of the skip, and Karrion's magic reaches out to it. The pigeon coos and flies off.

Where Dearon's arm is draped across my neck and shoulder, wetness chafes against my skin. The smell of blood fills my nostrils. It reminds me of the way I buried my tusks into Tem's stomach and tore through his intestines. The memory leads me to a startling realisation: I have spent most of my life wishing I was as powerful as Dearon, but I have power he will never attain. He may be the future Elderman, but I am prepared to kill to protect those I love.

With our support, Dearon is able to stagger on, though our progress is slow. I keep glancing at him, taking in the unfocused eyes and the face tight with pain. Are we making things worse by moving him? What if he has internal bleeding? Could his neck have been damaged by the fall?

'Yan, it's going to be okay.'

Karrion's words ground me, and I slow down my breathing until it no longer comes in panicked gasps. Dearon trips over a rock and more of his weight shifts on to me. It reawakens the agony in my leg. I cast my aura out, seeking power from the nature all around to remain upright and moving. The weft of life here is frayed, tainted by pollution and human habitation. It cannot sustain me for long, but I hope it will supplement my inner reserves until we reach our destination.

The pigeon returns, cooing softly as it circles us. Karrion looks up, and the unfurling of his magic brushes along my aura. He nods.

'There's a shortcut ahead. A gap in the hedge that will save us a lot of walking.'

'Great,' I say, gritting my teeth. 'Lead the way.'

We change direction and our progress slows in the tangled undergrowth. The pigeon stays with us, but Karrion ignores it. I search the hedge and spot a gap just wide enough for one person to squeeze through. Manoeuvring Dearon through a thorny hedge is not going to be easy, but what choice do we have?

'Yannia.' Dearon coughs. 'It was a woman.'

'I know. Let me worry about that and you focus on walking. We need to get you to a hospital.'

'No human medicine.'

The spike of anger lends me strength. 'I'm going to do

135

whatever it takes to make sure you get back to the conclave in one piece, including taking you to a human hospital if needs be. Now shut up; you've caused enough trouble for one day.'

Dearon turns his head so his breath ghosts over my ear. 'I'm sorry,' he whispers before he goes limp in our grip.

'Shit,' I mutter, trying to keep my balance under the added weight. Dearon's hand is slick with blood, and I struggle to maintain my grip on it.

'He's still breathing,' Karrion says, voice tight from exertion.

'Good. I'm not sure either of us knows first aid.'

'In our line of work, it wouldn't be a bad skill to have, especially given how accident-prone you are.'

'Put a comment about it in the suggestion box,' I say, gasping when I step in a hole and my ankle twists.

By the time we have part-carried, part-dragged Dearon through the gap in the hedge, I am shaking from pain and exhaustion. My connection to nature's power is fraying, and I almost sob with relief when I see that we are no more than thirty yards from the airstrip. The sight of our destination gives us both the push we need. With every step, Karrion seems to bear a little more of the burden. I glance at him past Dearon's lolling head. Karrion's biceps are visible against his leather jacket, and they look larger than I recall. Has he started working out? I push the thought aside as irrelevant.

As we are easing Dearon to the ground, an ambulance appears in the distance, followed by a police car. Karrion waves at them while I sink next to Dearon, pain rearing to overwhelm all else.

Soon paramedics are there, opening their bags and asking what happened. I try to explain, but the words are jumbled. Eventually, Karrion steps in, while I watch the paramedics fit an oxygen mask over Dearon's face and hook him up to a heart monitor. Amidst my clouded thoughts, one stands out.

'He needs to go to a hospital in Old London.'

One of the paramedics looks up, her gloved hands red with Dearon's blood. 'Why?'

'We're not human. He's one of the Wild Folk.'

While their faces register surprise and alarm, neither stops the first aid they are administering. 'We need to stabilise his condition before it's safe to transport him any great distance. He's going to Watford in the first instance, and the Paladins of Old London can then organise the transfer with our doctors.'

'But—'

Karrion silences me with a hand on my shoulder. 'They're right, Yan. He needs help now.'

I turn back to Dearon. Under the perpetual tan that comes from living outdoors, his skin has a sallow tinge to it. There is blood in the corner of his mouth and streaked in his long hair.

'Okay.'

The paramedics move Dearon on to a gurney and lift him into the back of the ambulance. Even the jolt of the gurney locking into place does not wake him up. Karrion helps me to stand, and I lean on his side to keep my balance.

'Is all of that blood his?' the paramedic asks, pointing at my arm.

My jumper has stuck to the wound, stemming the bleeding. The cut aches, but it is no worse than any of the other pains hammering my body.

'Most of it. Don't worry about it.'

137

'Do you want to go with him?' Karrion asks, his hand finding mine.

'I...' Glancing from the ambulance to the police car and back, I silence the tripping of my heart. 'No. We have a killer to catch.'

After I explain that Dearon has no phone and is staying with me, I give the paramedics my contact details. They promise that someone at the hospital will let me know when Dearon is ready to be transferred to Old London and which hospital will continue treating him.

We watch in silence as the paramedics shut the ambulance doors and drive away. Karrion and I explain the situation and our position with the Met to the police officers who have stayed back while the paramedics worked.

After the police call for a SOCO team and a canine unit, we retrace our steps and lead them to the abandoned house. Rather than go in and risk contaminating the scent trail, we peer through the windows. Mounds of leaves and debris give the inside an uneven look. The rooms are small and empty, any signs of human occupation having long since been cleared out. There is a pile of rags in the corner, and next to it, a lump of meat on top of a plastic bag. Were it not December, there would be flies swarming all over it.

'It's odd, I can't see luggage or anything,' Karrion says.

'What do you mean?'

'We know she's not from around here, not least because she's Wild Folk. If she's travelled from the Northern Lands, I'd expect her to have at least a backpack or some camping gear. There's nothing here.'

The more I think about it, the more Karrion's words make sense. Only a few among us would be strong

138

enough to remain in another form for any length of time, let alone undertake a strenuous journey across human lands. If she is not one of the Eldermen, which is clear from her gender alone, she ought to have taken advantage of human transportation. Why then is she hiding in an abandoned cottage?

'Perhaps her gear got lost or stolen?' I suggest, but I do not sound convinced even to my ear. Once again, I am struck by the feeling that I am missing something important.

'It's possible, though I pity the person who tried to mug her.'

Another police unit arrives, and the officers cordon off the cottage with blue and white tape. Upon seeing the paleness of my face, the police agree that we can hand in our statements to Jamie. There is little more we can do at the crime scene.

'Shouldn't we try to track the Wild Folk?' Karrion asks as we begin the long walk back to my car.

'I'm not that good a tracker. The only way to do it would be shifting forms and I don't have enough power for that here. Carrying Dearon depleted a lot of my magic. Besides, she's one of us. She knows as much about tracking as I do, which means she's equally capable of hiding her trail.'

'I guess. It just feels wrong, leaving like this.'

Stuffing my hands in my pockets, I chew my lower lip. 'It does. But you saw her. We're no match for her, not when we're exhausted and wounded.'

'Are you sure she's Wild Folk? Because she looked more like a werewolf to me.'

'They don't exist,' I say, my tone weary. 'And yes, she's one of us.'

'But her form? What was up with that?'

'I don't know. If she's powerful enough to assume animal form, it should have been recognisable. What she was doing looked like it was a halfway point between herself and a wolf.'

'Didn't you say that when you were in the Unseen Lands, you were a bear, a lynx, and a boar at the same time?'

The memory of the battle under the watchful eyes of the Winter Queen and her dark hounds sends a shudder through me. I close my eyes. The rage of the bear was mine, as was the bloodlust of the boar. My transformation was so complete, I came close to forgetting how to revert to my own form.

'That's different. I shifted into a bear and then borrowed aspects of a boar and a lynx. But most of me was recognisable as a bear. At least, I assume so. There were fortunately no mirrors at the Courts.'

'So what could cause this?'

'I don't know!' I instantly regret my sharpness. 'No songs or stories of old mention this. Perhaps the Elderman might remember something, but he's at death's door. And Dearon is unconscious. We're on our own.'

'Good job we do our best work together.' Karrion smiles at me. 'Though I don't think we're as alone as you think. Jamie can help us.'

My first instinct is to question what aid Jamie could offer, but Karrion is right. He may be able to tell us something about Cúan's death that we missed last night, plus we still know next to nothing about the dead jogger. I reach for my phone and dial his number.

Jamie takes his time. When he finally answers, I hear voices in the background. 'Manning.'

I switch him to speaker phone and stumble over the words as I explain what happened and what we discovered. Jamie swears, the voices fade, and a door closes.

'Didn't you say the Wild Folk was a man?'

'We assumed she was.' In hindsight, I struggle to recall why. 'But her gender changes nothing. She's still eating people and is extremely dangerous.'

'Okay. I'll call someone at New Scotland Yard and ask them to forward you the whole file on that murdered jogger. As for what you discovered today, let the local police deal with it. The powers-that-be reassigned me to investigate a politically volatile case in Old London, so there's little help I can offer for now.'

'What's happened in Old London?'

Jamie hesitates and sighs. 'It looks like one of the Council members strangled his girlfriend.'

'Which Council member?' I think back to the list of Mages I have vetted so far and the few that are still outstanding.

'Gerreint Lloid.'

The phone slips through my numb fingers and lands on the grass. Karrion catches me just as my knees buckle. He eases me on to the ground, and I clutch handfuls of grass to try to stop the world from spinning. A distant part of me listens as Karrion tells Jamie we will call him back. The noise in my ears increases to a roar, and I lean my head between my knees.

'What's wrong, Yan?'

In my haste to deliver the Elderman's tonic and find Cúan, I never told Karrion about the Council meeting and Gerreint's true nature. My throat is tight and it takes three attempts to get the words out, but at least the world has stopped spinning.

'Gerreint Lloid is a Leech.'

'What? How do you know?'

'I went to the latest Council meeting to try to tick the last few names off my list of Mages. He was one of them. There's no question about what he is.'

'Did he spot you?' Karrion asks, alarm written across his face. He was not there to help me fight off Jans, and the knowledge still bothers him.

'I don't think so. He was in a rush and just ran past me.'

'Did you tell Jamie?'

'No.' When I was hurrying away from Lloid, it never occurred to me to call Jamie. 'But I told Mr Whyte.'

'So Lord Ellensthorne knows. That has to be good, right? He's as keen to clean the Council of Leeches as we are before the general public discover what Leeches can do.'

When I offer no response, Karrion crouches in front of me. He tugs at the row of piercings on his left ear as he searches my face.

'What's wrong, Yan?'

'I never paused to consider the consequences of my actions.' Slamming my fist against the ground sends a spike of pain up my injured arm. 'How could I have been so stupid?'

'Sorry, I don't follow.'

'All this time, we've been vetting the High Council of Mages and the Circle of Shamans, but neither of us stopped to consider what would happen if we actually found a Leech. What the hell was I thinking? That Lord Ellensthorne would simply pat them on the back, congratulate them on a fine con, and send them on their merry way? Any Leech impersonating a Mage or a Shaman in high places has the knowledge to bring down the entire political structure of Old London. There's no way Lord Ellensthorne would let them walk away unharmed.'

'But surely there's a difference between having someone quietly assassinated, as reprehensible as that is, and framing them for murdering a third party?'

'I guess.' Neither of us looks convinced. 'But the timing is suspicious.'

'True.'

Pushing myself off the ground, I accept Karrion's help in standing. The world spins and settles. A dozen aches and pains wash over me, tempting me to leave the investigation to others. I didn't sleep much last night, and the fatigue is catching up with me. But this cannot wait.

'We need to visit that crime scene and see what's going on for ourselves. The police won't know what they are looking for.'

'I'm all for it, but what about the Wild Folk woman and Dearon?'

Guilt overtakes the pain, and I hesitate. Too many things are demanding my attention, none of them less important than the others. Something of the lessons I've learned in the past couple of months returns to me.

'Dearon is at the hospital and there's not a lot we can do for him. Once they've stabilised him, he'll be going to Old London anyway, and we can catch up with him there. As for the Wild Folk,' I turn a circle in the middle of the football field, 'she could be anywhere. We're not bloodhounds. To find her, we need to figure out who she is and why she has started eating people. We can't do that out here.'

'Okay, Yan. You're the boss.'

We hurry along the gravel path towards the motorway as quickly as my sore leg allows. When I glance at

Karrion, he seems troubled. I let my fingers graze his knuckles, and he looks my way. Although I do not voice the question, he understands it just the same.

'While we're on the subject of consequences, what happens if we prove that Lord Ellensthorne framed Gerreint for the death of his girlfriend? Or at least ordered someone else to do it? He's a powerful man, and our investigation into Braeman's murder showed just how ruthless he can be.'

Once again, Karrion surprises me. Should I not have been the one to voice that concern? Perhaps his city upbringing has given him an insight into political intrigue that I do not possess.

'Lord Ellensthorne has too much to lose for him to be personally involved in anything like that. Then again, we know Mr Whyte is aware of the situation, since he's paying us to find the Leeches. How far is Lord Ellensthorne willing to go to protect his allies? I don't know, Karrion; maybe I should look into this alone.'

'Whoa, stop right there, Yan. Remember what you promised after you ditched me and took on a Fey Lord by yourself? We're a team and we're going to do this together.'

'But think of your family.'

'I am. Did it ever occur to you that I might consider you as part of my family?'

Pleasure washes through me, but it cannot quell the rising tide of fear.

'Lord Ellensthorne is bound to know about your mum and siblings. I can take care of myself. They can't.'

'You've met Mum, right? Be that as it may, we can't let Lord Ellensthorne decide whether people live or die. He's a politician, not a dictator, and as much as we may have a Shadow Mage running the city, these aren't the Dark Ages.'

'I understand, but I hate the thought of putting your family at risk.'

'They're already at risk because Lord Ellensthorne is playing God and because we know stuff about him that we shouldn't. And our employment is proof that he's hiding facts from the Council and the Circle that could endanger us all.'

'We have very little proof,' I remind him.

'Since when has the press cared about proof? All they need is speculation.'

'There'd be a witch hunt and we'd all suffer.'

'I'm not saying we should pigeon him out to the media, but perhaps it wouldn't hurt to remind him discreetly that we have the means to do so. A package left with someone we trust and instructions on what to do with the information if something were to happen to us could go a long way in ensuring our safety.'

'Who were you thinking of? Fria?'

'Don't be daft.' Karrion pulls a face. 'We can't trust this with a Cat Shaman. It has to be someone good at keeping secrets.'

The answer is obvious. 'Lady Bergamon.'

'Yes. Lady B would be perfect.'

'I'll mention it to her when I next visit. She's expecting me. And by the way, have you considered a career in politics?'

'That would mean too many dealings with arrogant Mages. We get enough of that in our line of work, thanks very much.'

'Their loss is my gain,' I say, and Karrion nudges me with his shoulder.

145

After we have crossed the motorway, I steer Karrion towards Sainsbury's and explain that I want to deal with my arm before we return to Old London. We pick up first-aid supplies and find a quiet corner of the car park. Peeling back my sleeve causes the wound to start bleeding again. I douse it with plenty of disinfectant and Karrion applies butterfly bandages to seal it. He wraps bandages across my forearm to complete the process, and I shrug my coat back on.

'Car next?' he asks, and drops the rubbish in the nearest bin.

'Would you mind getting us coffees and snacks while I go back to the car? There's a cafe upstairs, I think. I'll need to take meds if I'm to get through the rest of the day.'

'Of course.'

'I'll see you back here in a few minutes.'

As I head towards the car along the main road, I call Jamie again. This time, he is quicker to pick up.

'Yannia, what was that all about?'

'Sorry, I wasn't feeling well and the news took me by surprise. Listen, could Karrion and I come to take a look at that crime scene?'

'What's a dead Mage got to do with a Wild Folk kidnapping and eating children?'

'Nothing, as far as I know.'

'Then why do you want to get involved in this murder investigation?'

'I'll tell you everything I know, but I'd prefer to do it in person rather than over the phone.'

'Fine, if you think you can bring something to the investigation that we don't already have.'

Approaching my car, I dig out the keys and disengage the lock. 'I'm counting on it.'

16

A LIFE OF LIES

The caffeine and the painkillers kick in when we cross the invisible border between New and Old London. My arm still aches, but it's easier to ignore now my mind is already turning over the puzzle of the Gerreint Lloid case and its timing mere days after I exposed him as a Leech. The address Jamie texted me takes us near Liverpool Street station, and I have to drive around for a few minutes in search of a parking spot.

'This doesn't seem like the typical area for a Council member,' I say as I reverse into a space vacated by a delivery van. 'But Jamie specifically said the body was discovered at Lloid's residence.'

Karrion, who has been staring at his phone for the past twenty minutes, looks up. 'That's part of Lloid's political play. He's from humble origins rather than one of the old bloodlines, and that's made him very popular with the general Mage population of Old London. Even after he accepted the seat on the Council, he said he was going to stay where he was living, refused the accommodation allowance offered to all the Council and Circle members, and continued to be seen as the advocate for the common Mages.'

'I bet that made him popular with the likes of Lord Ellensthorne.'

We step out of the car, and I stretch my stiff muscles. I eat the last bite of my brownie and drink the remains of my cold coffee.

'It shouldn't come as any surprise that it was Gideor Braeman who appointed him to the Council as part of keeping up with the modern times. And hey, it says here that Lloid was keen to improve the relationship between our kind and the humans. How much do you want to bet it was through greater control over our magic?'

'Sounds like he was a carbon copy of Braeman,' I say, leading the way across the street. 'It's a surprise really that Lord Ellensthorne hasn't already fired anyone who shared Braeman's opinions.'

'I don't think he could. Braeman had the support of many influential Mages on the Council, including the likes of Jonathain Marsh. While there's no doubt that Lord Ellensthorne wields considerable power within the Council, I don't think his support is as solid as he'd like to make everyone believe.'

'Still, I wonder if we should be looking beyond family trees to the policies and opinions of the Mages we've yet to check.' I call the lift down. 'That could give us further red flags to watch out for.'

'Maybe.' Karrion indicates I should go through the doors first. 'But if I were a Leech hiding in plain sight, I'd want to keep a low profile, especially after Braeman's death. I'd be gradually shifting my stance to be more in keeping with the current Speaker. Or it could be that the other Leeches were only mirroring Braeman's policies because he was protecting them. Now he's dead, they're free to pursue their own agenda.'

I rub my temples. 'Have I mentioned recently how much I hate politics?'

'Duly noted.'

The lift doors open to a drab green corridor. Faded purple doors have numbers on them, but the Paladin standing guard steers us in the right direction. Next to him, a folding table contains the protective-clothing supplies. I check that blood has not seeped through the bandage around my arm. We don the crime scene suits, and while I draw up the hood and pull on two sets of gloves, I try to imagine Dearon's face if he had to jump through all these hoops. Perhaps it's just as well he's not with us.

Although Lloid's door looks no different from the others along the corridor, it's thicker than I would expect. The lock has been forced. As humble as the setting may be, when we duck under the crime scene tape, we step into a whole different world. The interior is decorated in the lifeless fashion of black chrome furniture and white walls. A subtle pressure against my aura indicates that the flat is warded, though I have no way of telling the purpose of the wards.

Jamie stands in the hallway with Mery, the forthright Mage consultant we have encountered before. Under her hood, Mery's fringe shifts to the side, revealing her luminous green eye as she turns to us. Her blue eye seems dull in comparison.

'Well, if it isn't the PI dream team. My day was already looking pretty delightful, what with all the paperwork I've got to fill in, but now it's complete.'

'You wouldn't have so many reports to write if you prepared them as you went along,' Jamie says.

'We can't all be star pupils like you, boss.'

Ignoring the jibe, Jamie leads us to the main bedroom. The covers on a king size bed have been tossed to one side, revealing crimson satin sheets. There is a large mirror affixed to the ceiling over the bed. The doors of a wardrobe are open, displaying a wide array of bindings, leather masks, whips, and other items, the function of which I care not to consider. Next to me, Karrion whistles.

'What was Lloid in to?'

'We can safely say he liked pain.' Jamie opens his notebook. 'The victim's name is Leina Parez. She was the long-term girlfriend of Lloid, though they didn't live together. Based on the fact that we found a leather whip wrapped around her neck, the cause of death was strangulation.'

'Who called the Paladins?' I ask.

'A neighbour heard screams and became concerned. The first Paladins on the scene had to break the door and force the wards down. Given that Lloid has a seat on the Council, the flat is heavily warded.'

'I'd like to see a list of those wards.' How many of them will be identical to those we found in Braeman's study?

'Sure, I'll ask Mery to send you a copy of her report.' Jamie raises his voice. 'If she ever writes one.'

'I heard that,' comes a response from the corridor.

'Have you got Lloid in Paladin custody?' Karrion asks.

'No, we can't find him. He attended a Council meeting on Friday morning, and that's the last sighting. But given that it's the weekend, he hasn't missed work yet. I have people looking into his phone records and finances to see if they might tell us where he's hiding.'

'When did the victim die?'

'Early this morning.'

This makes no sense. If Mr Whyte and Lord Ellensthorne acted immediately after I called them, who killed Leina? And if Lloid was not apprehended straight away,

why did he kill his girlfriend? Could her death be uncon-
nected to his true nature? Is that too much of a
coincidence?

Jamie calls over a Scene of Crime Officer and asks to
see her camera. He flicks through the crime scene photos.

'This is how we found her.'

I take the camera from him, and Karrion leans over
my shoulder to peer at the screen. Leina is on the floor
next to the bed, hands bound behind her with a pair of
thick leather cuffs. She is naked, her body covered in
bruises, and the ends of the black whip rest on the floor
next to her neck. The sight of the terror on her face
causes a familiar fear to spike through my mind. But I
fought off my attacker.

'It looks like she was beaten,' Karrion says, his voice
tight. I am glad we got here after the body was taken away.

'The abuse looks to have been systematic. We'll have
to wait for the pathologist report to know more about
how recent the bruises are and what could have caused
them. There are plenty of faded scars on her as well.'

'I'm not surprised, given the cupboard of horrors over
there,' says Karrion.

'What can you tell us about the victim?' I ask Jamie.

'Not a great deal as yet. She worked as an associate at
a law firm and had a flat-share near Blackfriars station.
Interviewing her flatmates is on my list of things to do.'

'Do you mind if we look around?'

'Please do. You know the drill: don't remove anything
from its context and get the SOCO team to document
your findings.'

The bedroom has an en suite shower room, and I
glance inside. Everything looks clean and a pungent tang
of bleach rises from the shower. There is a pink tooth-

brush in a holder next to the sink. A hairbrush with long black hairs clinging to it is on the counter next to a hair dryer. Two sets of towels hang from chrome hooks. Stepping further into the room, I pull down my facemask and inhale. No blood anywhere, at least so far as I can tell with bleach hanging in the air like fine mist. It is not what I expected.

Back in the bedroom, I walk to the cupboard. While the contents puzzle me at first, I soon notice a curious detail: while there are whips and paddles among the other items, I see no knives or anything intended to draw blood. The cupboard smells of leather, metal, and dust.

'I can't smell blood,' I say, and replace the mask over my face.

'What do you mean?' Jamie looks up from his notebook.

'These items may have been used to cause pain, but not to maim.'

'That doesn't mean things couldn't have escalated. This could have been a power play gone wrong.'

'It's possible.'

'Check this out,' Karrion calls from near the bed.

He is crouching next to the bedside table, and when I join him, he points to a small heart copper token partially hidden between the wall and the table. A Crime Scene Officer photographs the token and slips it into a clear evidence bag.

'Why would Lloid have a warding token lying around when there are permanent wards on the flat?' I ask.

'Depends on what the ward does,' Karrion says. 'Mery can find out, right?'

Jamie nods. 'The token could have been there for weeks or months.'

'I don't think so. The reason it caught my attention was that the flat is immaculate. There's no dust on the token, so it must have either fallen down recently or been used for a ward in the past week or so.'

'We'll check it for prints at the lab.'

A second wardrobe in the room contains more mundane clothes and linen. The green silk cloaks of the Council hang side by side with suits. There are gaps on the shelves. Going back to the bathroom, I find no sign of a razor, deodorant, or cologne. It looks like Lloid packed an overnight bag before he disappeared.

Or is that what someone wants me to believe?

Uncertain what to think, I point this out to the others. Karrion has been looking through the bedside table and now glances over his shoulder.

'I have three empty watch boxes and two Western Union envelopes. Lloid changed a thousand pounds to dollars and another grand to euros three months ago. The envelopes are empty.'

'He could have simply forgotten about them,' Jamie says.

'True, but consider the flat. Does this look like the home of a man who casually leaves empty envelopes lying around? Nothing here is out of place.'

'You've got a point.'

I turn away, the mask hiding my smile. It pleases me to see how much Karrion has grown in confidence. Two months ago, he would never have argued with Jamie like this. The apprenticeship is going from strength to strength, all thanks to Karrion's hard work.

'It looks like he's left the city and possibly the country too,' I say. 'Karrion, have you seen a passport anywhere?'

'No.'

'If he kept spare currency in the bedside cabinet, it's likely his passport was there too.'

The other bedside table contains two sets of silver earrings, coconut-scented hand cream, and three dog-eared paperbacks. Under the bed is a large storage box with a yoga mat and women's workout clothes.

'Leina appears to have spent a lot of time here, but she hadn't quite moved in.'

'So what caused Lloid to kill her?' Jamie asks.

I can think of a reason, but keep the thought to myself as I leave the master bedroom to explore the rest of the flat. Mery is standing in the doorway, both eyes glowing and her aura questing outward while she makes notes on a clipboard.

Tossed on to the leather sofa at an angle is a black handbag. A set of keys is balanced on the top. I open the handbag to find everything I would expect, including a phone. The lock screen shows a photo of Leina and Gerreint standing on the Millennium Bridge at dusk with the lights of Old London behind them. They look happy as they stand cheek to cheek and grin at the camera. A host of notification icons lines the bottom of the screen.

Jamie walks in, and I show him the phone.

'It's locked, but there could be something interesting on it.'

'The tech guys should be able to unlock it,' he says, and asks a SOCO to bag the phone.

I look around the lounge and the open-plan kitchen. There are no signs of a struggle anywhere. It's as though Leina let herself in, set her handbag on the sofa, and surrendered to her assailant. I wait until Jamie has left the room, then I inhale. At first, I detect nothing beyond the people in the flat, but then a tremor tugs at my instincts. Turning around slowly, I take some time to find the brown spot where the coffee table leg rests on the pale green rug. I call Jamie back in.

'There's a drop of blood on the rug.'

'We'll test it, though it could be from a stubbed toe.'

'It's possible, though the stain is fresh enough for me to smell it. If luck is on our side, Leina struggled and wounded the person who attacked her.'

'But there could be any number of reasons why Lloid's blood is on the rug.'

Casting a sideways glance at Jamie, I stand. The crime scene suit rustles around me.

'You assume the blood is Lloid's and that he killed Leina.'

'It looks like the most logical explanation.' Jamie holds his hand up to silence my objections. 'But I know not to jump to conclusions. I'll ask one of the Crime Scene Officers to collect it.'

Something about the flat is bothering me, some detail I have missed. I look around again, chasing the thought, and my eyes land on the stilettos.

'Where are her clothes?'

'What?' asks Jamie.

'Leina's clothes. Her shoes are there. Presumably she set them down next to the shoe rack because it was full, suggesting that Lloid was here when she arrived. Her handbag is on the sofa. She was naked when she was murdered. So where are her clothes?'

'Good question. Hang on.' Jamie leaves and returns after a few minutes. 'None of the Crime Scene Officers have bagged any clothes.'

'Given the handbag and shoes, it's safe to say she wasn't dressed in anything as casual as workout clothes.

Maybe she came straight from work. If the clothes are not here, it's likely the killer took them.'

'I'll get some officers to check all the bins nearby in case the killer dumped them somewhere. There could be trace evidence on them.'

'That's what I thought,' I say.

The smaller bedroom is an office. A MacBook Air lies on a glass table, the lid down. The windowsill is lined with tiny pots containing succulents. A black bookcase is full of books about politics, city planning, and economics, and the lowest shelf contains a series of ring binders. The only artwork in the room is a painting of a girl and a crow hanging above the table. It feels like an odd choice for a Leech.

I choose a ring binder at random and open it to find old bank statements. All the transactions are annotated, and ticks confirm that the amounts add up. Lloid has been meticulous in his record keeping.

My first instinct is to put the ring binder back, but I hesitate. The most recent bank statement on the file is dated three years ago. I sit cross-legged on the floor and set the ring binder down next to me. From the shelf, I find another that is up to date and I go through Lloid's bank statements. By the time Karrion comes to find me, my legs have gone numb and my pelvis aches, but I have been too engrossed in the task to notice.

'There you are. I was beginning to wonder if you'd sneaked out without me.'

'What?' I look up. 'Why would I do that?'

'I don't know, but we've been searching through the rest of the flat for the past hour and I haven't heard a peep from you. What have you been up to, besides making a mess?'

156

The ring binders are spread out around me, all open at different places. My notebook is on my lap, and I have been scrawling page after page of notes. Now I push aside one of the files and straighten my legs with a groan.

'Turns out Lloid kept meticulous records of his finances. I've been going through his bank statements to see what I might learn about his life.'

'Any luck?'

'Yes. We can safely say that Lloid isn't a wealthy man, but he never lives beyond his means. This flat is affordable, though he took a loan to redecorate, and the interest is fairly high. His Council salary covers most of his expenses, but he'd be struggling if it wasn't for an added bonus every month.'

'What's that?'

'He receives a standing order for five thousand pounds from Igneous Wealth Management.'

'Five grand? Wow. How come?' Karrion asks.

'I'm not sure, but I think it has something to do with this.' I hold out several sheets of paper stapled together.

Karrion takes the papers from me and flicks through them. Although his eyebrows rise at the sight of the sums, he hands them back with a shrug.

'What's the Cuckoo Trust?'

'Some sort of private settlement, only most of the information is missing from those accounts. What I do find interesting is that there are three unnamed beneficiaries who each receive sixty thousand a year from the trust.'

'And you think that's what the standing order is?'

'Yes. I have three years' worth of trust accounts on this file and bank statements showing the same.'

'Why would someone be paying Lloid every month?'

157

Glancing at the open door, I lower my voice. 'I can think of a few reasons.'

'You think it's got something to do with his true nature?'

I turn to the page showing a summary of the trust. Much of the description means little to me. A date shows the trust was set up twenty-five years ago and it is run by a corporation in the Channel Islands, which has discretion over who should benefit. There are no named beneficiaries, only references to a letter of wishes from the settlor, which has been updated at times. The settlor is referred to only by their initials.

'Look at this. The settlor is one GRB. Do you happen to recall what Braeman's middle name was?'

'I haven't a clue,' Karrion says, and fumbles past the layers of the crime scene suit to find his phone. He types for a few moments. 'Richart.'

'Yes.'

'So you think Braeman set up a trust to support others like him?'

With another glance towards the door, I replace the trust accounts in their proper place among the others.

'We can speculate about that later.'

'Fine. Did you find anything else of interest among Lloid's papers?'

'A regular direct debit to something called Sensual Pain. The amounts have varied over the years, but at the moment, he's paying them five hundred a month.'

'Is it just me or does that sound dodgy?'

'I looked up their website, but you need to be a member to see any of it. All I found was an address.'

'That's better than nothing. Is it in Old London?'

'Yes, near One Magic Change.'

'Good, then it will be easy for us to check it out.'

Closing the file, I return all the ring binders to their rightful places. Karrion is looking through the desk drawers and soon calls me over. Hidden beneath cheque books and warranty documents for the MacBook is a small velvet box. As I open it, the tiniest suggestion of power caresses the inside of my wrist. I shiver. Nestled within the cushioning is a solitaire diamond engagement ring. A series of small gems encircles the band.

'That must have cost a decent chunk of money,' Karrion says.

'It could explain the cheque for ten grand that had no explanation next to it. I wonder if Leina knew?'

'But if he was going to propose, why kill her?'

'You assume the killer was Lloid?'

'Are you suggesting otherwise?'

'I don't know,' I say, and close the box with a snap.

A glint of metal beneath the papers catches my eye. I reach for it, and my fingers close around a key. It has no tag or any identifying features. From the size and shape, it could open anything from a padlock to a small door. Unable to see any direct connection to the case we are investigating, I put the key back where I found it.

The bottom drawer contains a series of boxes filled with mana gems. The power causes the hairs on my arms to stand up, pricking against my clothes. On top of the boxes are two leather armguards with flat gems fitted into tight slots along the inner seam.

'What are those?' Karrion asks.

'I'm guessing they're a way for a Leech to cast Mage spells in public without needing to drain someone's power first.'

'He must have gone through a lot of gems. Though I must say, this looks like a clever system.'

'Mana gems can be recharged, but you'd still need a Mage to do it. It would be helpful to visit Thaylor to ask about the costs and how many gems would be required to cast typical Mage spells.'

'Good idea.'

Jamie enters the office, and we give him a brief account of everything we have discovered, with none of our speculation. That will have to wait until later.

'I'm about to head off,' he says. 'There doesn't seem much point in my standing around watching the SOCO team do their job. But I'm interested in what you told me about the regular money coming into Lloid's account. What is he getting paid for?'

Karrion and I exchange a glance, but neither of us says anything.

'I gather you have an idea,' Jamie says.

'We do, though I can't say anything more than that here.'

Jamie's expression darkens. The old distrust settles between us. I lay my hand on his arm, and he seems startled.

'Wait. I promised I would tell you everything and I will. But the information I have is extremely sensitive and the fewer people hear it, the better. If we're finished here, we can find somewhere to speak in private. Perhaps early dinner at my place?'

'Fine.' Jamie's stony expression relaxes. 'From what you said earlier, I expect you can make sense of this case.'

'I'll paint you a clearer picture, but it may not be what you are expecting.'

160

17

ALLEGIANCES

We leave the crime scene suits in a bin provided outside Lloid's flat and head out. Next to the car, I check my phone again, but there have been no missed calls in the ten minutes since I last looked. No doubt A&E has queues and the staff are doing everything they can for Dearon. Why then do I feel so guilty about not having gone in the ambulance with him?

Karrion orders Thai food, and we pick it up on our way home. Jamie is already waiting by the steps that lead down to my front door. I let us in and hurry through the dark office. The air in the lounge smells damp, and I open the window, only to realise that the dusk is no drier. Instead, I build a fire in the hearth.

When it comes to making the dedication to Wishearth, I hesitate, glancing over my shoulder at Jamie. He and Karrion are occupied emptying the takeaway bags. I rush through the words and let the burning offering fall on to the logs. A coil of smoke caresses my cheek.

I set three glasses of water on the table, while Karrion brings us plates and steals half of my prawn curry. Once we all have our food, he perches on the edge of my mattress, and Jamie and I take the armchairs. We eat in silence for a few minutes, before Jamie sets down his fork.

'You've drawn out the suspense as long as you can, I think.'

Dipping a prawn cracker in the sauce on my plate, I glance at Jamie and away. 'You must understand that I tell you this in the strictest of confidence. It is only the fact that a crime has been committed that forces me to break the discretion I extend to all my clients.'

All traces of amusement slip from Jamie's face. 'Go on.'

'Gerreint Lloid is a Leech.'

'What?'

Jamie's shock triggers a sense of déjà vu. The memory of finding out the truth about Braeman is still fresh in my mind. Why shouldn't it be, when my first big case took place only a couple of months ago? Yet I feel as though it has been years since I sat on the sofa in Braeman's study as the foundations of Old London's society crumbled around me.

'Lord Ellensthorne hired me to vet the High Council and the Circle in case there are more Leeches following in Braeman's footsteps. As the present Speaker so tactfully phrased it, I'm the only one in Old London capable of sniffing out the truth.'

Karrion stabs a prawn with more force than necessary. He is still angry with Lord Ellensthorne for using me as his personal bloodhound.

'You're certain about Lloid?' Jamie asks.

'Yes. He ran past me two days ago in his haste to get to the Council meeting. His scent was quite clear.'

'Was he the only one there?'

'Yes.'

'Shit.' Jamie sets his plate down and rubs his face. 'Did he catch you?'

'No.'

162

'Are you sure?'

Jamie was not there when the Paladins carried Jans from my flat, but he came the following morning and sat in on my statement about the attack. Is that what he recalls, or are his thoughts firmly at today's crime scene?

'Yes.'

'If he wasn't suspicious of you, perhaps the girlfriend caught on to his secret and he had to silence her. Then, upon realising what he'd done, Lloid fled before anyone knew she was missing.'

'Perhaps.'

'But you don't think so.'

'I'm not sure what to think.' Staring into the fire, I seek the courage that would allow me to speak freely. 'I screwed up, Jamie.'

'How so?'

'I should have paused to consider the consequences of my actions and I didn't. Lord Ellensthorne's assignment was good for Old London and, I'm ashamed to say, great for the finances of my PI business. They both clouded my judgement, so I never thought about what would happen if I actually uncovered another Leech.'

'What are you saying?'

'That on Friday, within minutes of having discovered Lloid's secret, I told Lord Ellensthorne, or rather his agent. Two days later, Lloid has disappeared and his girlfriend is dead.'

Jamie rises and paces across the room. He pauses to rest his hand against the bricks of the fireplace as he stares at the blaze before turning back to us.

'That's a serious accusation you just intimated, Yannia.'

'I know.' I set aside my plate, my hunger forgotten.

'That's why I waited until now rather than revealing all this at the crime scene.'

'A wise choice.'

Karrion has been listening to the conversation, all the while shovelling food into his mouth, seemingly with no regard for the flavours. He crumbles prawn crackers on to the remaining sauce.

'So how are we going to nail Lord Ellensthorne?' he asks.

I shake my head. 'We can't.'

'What? Why?'

'We have no proof.'

'I get that, but we'll find the evidence.'

When I say nothing, Karrion rises. 'We are going to investigate him, aren't we?'

Fixing my gaze on my plate, I drag my fork around the remaining food. The hand Karrion lays on my shoulder is gentle, but his eyes are narrowed.

'Seriously, Yan?'

'I'm not giving up,' I hurry to say. 'But it's not as simple as all that. If we go after Lord Ellensthorne with anything less than cold ironclad evidence, he's going to bury us, and Jamie too. If we tip our hand, he's going to destroy all the evidence. If we give him reason to suspect anything is amiss, we endanger anyone we hold dear. Worst of all, we don't know what happened to Lloid. What if he's innocent of Leina's murder? If Lord Ellensthorne knows we're hot on Lloid's trail, Lloid may not survive long. What's more incriminating than the man himself? He may be a Leech, but that doesn't mean he deserves to die.'

'Yannia is right,' Jamie says. 'Lord Ellensthorne has the power to end careers.'

Karrion crosses his arms. 'I didn't realise that was your priority.'

Jamie's harsh laugh seems too loud in my small lounge. 'Do you still believe the world is black and white, even after everything you've seen with Yannia? Do I want a guilty man to go free? Of course not. Am I prepared to sacrifice my career? Not sure. But one thing I can say for certain is that others at New Scotland Yard will gladly throw the three of us under the bus to save their careers.'

'So what are we going to do?' Karrion asks.

Brushing hair from my face, I search for answers among the dancing flames. 'We're going to have to beat Lord Ellensthorne at his own game.'

More relaxed now, Karrion helps himself to the rest of my curry. 'Can we do that?'

'It's not going to be easy, but we'll have to try.' I turn to Jamie. 'As much as our priority is to track down the man-eating Wild Folk, I'd like us to remain involved in the Lloid case.'

'Of course,' Jamie says. 'It's a good job we have this consultancy arrangement in place and Lord Ellensthorne has known about it since Samhain. Changing our working arrangements now would no doubt rouse his suspicions.'

'I agree. It would also be best if the truth about Lloid remained between the three of us.'

Jamie's chuckle is softer than before. 'You've just asked me to chuck the entire rule book out of the window. If my superiors find out about this, my career *is* over, as surely as if Lord Ellensthorne willed it so.'

I cannot decide whether he expects me to apologise and I offer him an uncertain smile. 'Do you have a better idea?'

'No. Holding back information about the case just doesn't feel right. My world was a lot more by-the-book before you came along.'

'Nuance can never be a bad thing.'

'Depends on whether it pays the bills or not.' Jamie drinks the rest of his water. 'How do you want to play this?'

'We're waiting for the file on the eaten jogger and that will be our priority. Tomorrow, I'd like to speak to Leina's flatmates with you to find out whether it's likely she knew Lloid was a Leech. Perhaps that will yield an alternative suspect for her murder. Those trust accounts I found in Lloid's study are an interesting lead, but one Karrion and I are going to struggle to follow up. I doubt a company like Igneous Wealth Management will divulge the names of the beneficiaries. But the trustees may speak to a Detective Inspector.'

'Do you think the payments have something to do with Leina's murder?'

'Probably not, but they may enable us to identify two more Leeches. There are three beneficiaries, remember, and each of them receives the same amount. Lloid is one of them, and it stands to reason that the two others are likely to be in similar positions of power. If we find out who they are, we can then come up with a plan as to what we should do about them.'

'What do you mean?' Karrion asks, and steps into the kitchen long enough to put the kettle on.

'If I uncover another Leech within the Council, do I dare tell Lord Ellensthorne? But if we have advance notice of someone likely to be a Leech, we can watch them, learn their habits, and continue to surveil them, even after I've informed Mr Whyte. That way, if Lord

Ellensthorne is getting rid of the Leeches permanently, we can gather the evidence we need to put a stop to it.'

'You make it all sound simple.'

'It won't be. Lord Ellensthorne is more cunning than any of us appreciate, and he's had several decades to perfect his power plays. Nothing about this is going to be easy, especially as one false move will tip our hand.'

'How do you think Leina fits into this?' Jamie asks.

'I'm not sure,' I reply. 'Perhaps she was with Lloid when they came to capture him. Perhaps she was alone in his flat when they broke in. Perhaps there's a whole other side to this story that we haven't seen yet.'

Karrion leans against the kitchen door frame. 'Who's they?'

'No idea. But I don't see that Lord Ellensthorne would ever personally take part in the removal of a dangerous Leech.'

'So the first step is identifying his henchmen. Mr Whyte must be one of them. I knew straight away there was something dodgy about him.'

'Are you sure you didn't just dislike his arrogance?'

'What's the difference?' Karrion shrugs.

'Just because someone is unpleasant and has a privileged view of the world, and our society, doesn't make them evil, I'm afraid. Also, I don't think anyone in the past century has had henchmen.'

'Henchmen, assistants, loyal followers, it's all the same to me,' Karrion says, and ducks back into the kitchen.

Jamie has been tapping his lower lip with his index finger, his expression growing grave. 'If the trust accounts enable us to trace the other two Leeches, what are we going to do with them?'

I open my mouth to reply, but no words come out. We are still sitting in silence when Karrion enters carrying three cups of tea. The warmth seeps into my fingers as I cradle the mug in both my hands, but it does little to ease the turmoil of swirling thoughts.

'I don't know.'

'We must decide now.' Jamie takes a sip from his mug. 'You said you didn't pause to consider the consequences of your actions before. It's time to do so. What will we do about any other Leeches we find?'

'Lock them up,' Karrion says, leaning against the mantelpiece.

Jamie's eyebrows arch. 'Indefinitely?'

'It's true that impersonating a Mage or a Shaman to gain a personal or a political advantage must be illegal,' I say, each word measured, 'but I doubt it's a crime punishable with a life sentence. That said, any Leech has the power to destabilise our entire society. We were all sworn to silence about Braeman, but what's to stop a Leech from contacting the press about this? To protect the magical community, any Leech in league with Braeman would have to disappear for good.'

'Can you see an alternative?' asks Karrion.

'No.' I stand, stretching my legs as a new certainty takes shape in my mind. 'But I'm a PI, as are you. Jamie is a police officer. We are neither the judge nor the jury. It's not up to us to change the course of other people's lives. Let those who mete out justice do so.'

'Are you suggesting we tell my superiors at the Met after all?'

'I'm saying that when the time comes, we tell the Paladin General. We already know how far he is willing to go to protect Old London, but that he is not without compassion. I trust him to make the right choice. Besides, with him we only need to disclose one facet of the story and not the whole picture.'

'Can we trust him?' Karrion asks.

'More than I'd ever trust Lord Ellensthorne. After what happened with Marsh, we know that the Paladin General will put the safety of the citizens of Old London before everything else.'

'Even if it means executing Leeches?' asks Jamie, his voice soft.

Setting down my mug, I cross the lounge to kneel in front of the fire. The logs have reduced to glowing coals, so I add more wood, even though the room is warm enough. When I begin inspecting the blackened bricks, it is clear I am stalling.

'I don't know, Jamie,' I say as I rise. 'All I know is that I have no right to determine whether someone lives or dies, but neither does Lord Ellensthorne.'

'We'll figure it out when we get there.' Karrion rests his hand on my shoulder. 'The important thing is that we're aware of the consequences of our actions now.'

'Next we have to get a few steps ahead of the Shadow Mages.' I offer the others a wry smile. 'No big deal.'

Jamie finishes his tea. 'I don't know, the three of us make a formidable opponent.'

'We also have allies,' I say, thinking about Lady Bergamon and Wishearth. The image of Fria slinks through my mind and disappears into the shadows. 'Though we need to be careful about who we trust.'

'But there will no longer be secrets between you, me, and Karrion. Agreed?'

I meet Jamie's eyes, and nod. 'Agreed.'

18

DISTANT DEATH

Once Jamie has left, I clear away the remains of dinner. Karrion and I complete our witness statements for the events of this morning and email them to Jamie. I glance at my watch.

'I ought to stop by the Open Hearth to pick up Sinta. Funja and Boris have no doubt had enough of puppysitting for one day.'

'Shall I come with you?'

'Sure.'

My phone pings as we ascend the stairs to the street. I read the first line of the email and slip the phone into the back pocket of my jeans.

'The crime scene file has arrived.'

'Great,' Karrion says. 'We can go through it when we get back. It's still early.'

'You'd better let your mum know you've had dinner here.'

Karrion writes a text message while we walk, and I admire his easy mastery of technology. If I had grown up in the city, perhaps I would be as comfortable with smartphones and computers as he is.

We are halfway to the pub when a drop of water lands on my cheek. I look up to see a dark cloud obscuring what little of the night sky is visible in the city. Another, larger, raindrop splashes against my forehead.

'I don't suppose you brought your skull umbrella?' I ask as the rain begins in earnest.

'Nope.'

Tugging on my coat sleeve, Karrion quickens his steps. I do my best to keep up, all the while ignoring the flares of pain in my knees and ankles which grow to a steady throb. By the time we round the corner, we are lost in a roar of rain and we run the rest of the way. The lights of the pub are a welcome beacon. Karrion pushes open the door, and we duck inside.

We both pause by the door, shaking water from our coats. Karrion's hair is plastered to his forehead and the row of hoops on his left ear glistens with droplets of moisture, but he is grinning. The laughter that escapes his lips is infectious, and I lean against the door while I catch my breath. Beside us, the fairy lights around a Christmas tree blink in random patterns.

'What would you like to drink?' I ask at last.

'You got dinner, so let me buy drinks. Brandy?'

I nod, and while he joins the crowd by the bar, I circle around it towards the fireplace and the table that sits in the darkest corner of the room. Wishearth is there, as I knew he would be, with his back against the wall, the collar of his coat turned up, and a pint of Guinness in front of him. A small fire burns in the fireplace, and Boris reclines on a raised dog bed in front of it, head up and eyes closed as he enjoys the warmth. I wave to Wishearth and murmur a greeting to Boris, who wags his tail.

Sinta is curled up next to Boris, fast asleep. Her day at the pub must have exhausted her, for she does not stir when I crouch to pet Boris, who lifts his head and rests it against my neck.

171

'Are you seeking to recreate our night of adventure in Lady Bergamon's garden?' Wishearth asks, leaning forward in his chair. His words are low enough that I barely catch them.

My thoughts flash back to the trek through the sodden garden and to his warmth against my back as I drifted off to sleep. I recall the anguish in his voice when he told me he couldn't bear the thought of almost being too late to save me in Sussex two weeks ago. No trace of those shared moments is on his face now. There are many questions that leap to my mind, but I voice none of them. Each of them would reveal more about the inner workings of my mind than I care to show him.

'As much fun as that was, not really,' I say instead. 'We just got caught out.'

He does not question my choice of pronoun, but his eyes stray past me to the bar. Karrion approaches with two brandies. I take the offered glass, and the alcohol lifts some of the numbness within me. A look passes between Karrion and Wishearth; too quick for me to guess at its meaning. Wishearth takes a sip from his pint.

'It feels almost criminal to wake her up,' Karrion says, gazing down at Sinta.

Wishearth rises from his seat, and flames flare behind the spark guard. 'You know the adage about letting sleeping dogs lie, but are you aware that the same applies to Wild Folk?'

'What?' asks Karrion, sneaking a look at me.

'Oh yes. When they are between sleep and wakefulness, the Wild Folk are at their most volatile. They're not quite human and will likely turn savage unless you appease them with coffee and bacon rolls.'

Karrion grins. 'I guess that explains something about

Yan. And it gives us a new weapon against the Wild Folk we're hunting.'

'To catch one of the Wild Folk, you must first consider what makes them wild.'

'But they're wild by default.'

'Is that so?'

I have been following the conversation without interrupting. Sparks glow in Wishearth's eyes, whereas Karrion seems to alternate between irritation and awe. I hold back a laugh. Wishearth's cryptic clues are less frustrating when they are aimed at someone else.

'It's in the blood,' I say to the pocket of silence in an otherwise bustling pub. 'The wildness is in the blood.'

'What happens when the blood is no longer enough?'

'The blood is all there is,' Karrion says, looking from me to Wishearth and back. 'Isn't it?'

Wishearth leans against the side of the fireplace, satisfaction evident in his relaxed posture. 'I think that's enough mystery for one evening.'

Before I have a chance to reply, Funja enters from the kitchen. He smiles when he spots us, his eyes all but disappearing behind the creases on his face.

'You have come to take our guest home, *da*?'

'Yes. Thanks again for having her.'

'It was our pleasure.' Funja pats my arm. 'She is quick and headstrong, like her mistress.'

'I've noticed,' I say with a laugh.

Funja picks up Sinta and places her gently in my arms. She sighs and buries her nose in the crook of my elbow, but does not stir. Careful to maintain my hold on her, I drain the rest of the brandy, cough, and hand the empty glass to Karrion.

Having said his goodbyes, Funja heads towards the bar

and stops to speak to a couple of regulars. I turn to Wishearth, but he speaks first.

'I'll let Lady Bergamon know that you'll stop by to-morrow.'

'Thanks,' I say when nothing else comes to mind. Next to me, Karrion frowns.

Outside, the rain has stopped, but the air is thick with moisture. All the scents arrest both my and Sinta's atten-tion, until Karrion nudges me with his shoulder.

'Did we make plans to go see Lady B?'

'No. The thought crossed my mind, but I hadn't decided when.'

'Do you think she'll be able to help with the case?' Karrion asks. 'Cases.'

'Maybe. I was going to ask her to tend to Dearon's wounds when he's released from the hospital.'

'Right. Of course.'

'Though it's possible Lady Bergamon could be useful,' I say after a while. 'She has a knack for finding people.'

'Do you think she could use her magic to find the Wild Folk?'

'We don't know her name. Gerreint Lloid was who I had in mind.'

'Good idea. We can ask Lady B tomorrow, seeing as it appears we're going to visit her.'

We pause while Sinta squats under a tree. A drop of moisture lands on my ear from the branches above.

'How did Wishearth know you were planning to visit Lady B if you'd only just thought of it? Is he telepathic?'

'Goodness, I hope not.' My cheeks heat, and I hurry Sinta along.

Karrion lengthens his strides to keep up with us and he casts a curious glance my way. 'Are you blushing?'

'No.'

'You are. Does that mean you're thinking about Wishearth in ways you don't want him to know about?'

'Of course not.'

Karrion's laughter is pure delight in the secret he has discovered. I shove away the memories of Wishearth's arms around me, the heat of his breath on my skin, and his eyes on my lips. He is not mortal, nor does he act like one. My life is complicated enough without entangling myself in his smoky presence. Yet whenever we are alone together, I am little more than a moth drawn to his flame.

'You'd be a lot more convincing if you weren't resembling a lobster.'

'Give it a rest, Karrion.'

My tone is stern enough that he brings his mirth under control. We walk in silence until my phone rings. The number is unfamiliar, and when I answer, a nurse introduces herself.

'Are you Dearon Wilder's next of kin?'

I hesitate. His parents are dead. The Elderman is at death's door and the rest of the conclave is difficult to reach. However conflicted I feel about the unexpected title, practicality wins.

'That's correct. How is he?'

'Mr Wilder was transferred to Old London a couple of hours ago and one of our doctors has reviewed his notes. The cuts required stitches and we want to keep him under observation in case he has a concussion. But he's been very distressed since he arrived. I can see here that the hospital staff in Watford had to sedate him in order to clean and dress his wounds.'

'He's a Wild Folk. We don't really do modern medicine.'

'We meant no disrespect. But if left untreated, his injuries could become serious.'

'I understand. No offence taken. Can I pick him up tomorrow morning?'

'That depends on what the doctors say. Someone will ring you when we are ready to discharge him.'

I thank the nurse and end the call. It has done away with my embarrassment, reminding me of all the work ahead of us. Tracking down the Wild Folk will be more difficult without Dearon's help.

'Are you okay?' asks Karrion.

'Fine.' I force a smile. 'I was just thinking we're going to be busy with two cases to solve.'

Karrion shrugs. 'We can do it.'

The corner of my mouth lifts. 'I'm beginning to believe in your endless optimism.'

'As you should.'

Back home, I feed Sinta and lift her through the window while the kettle boils. Karrion makes himself a coffee, while I drop a lemon and ginger teabag in my mug and leave it to steep. We carry our drinks to the lounge, and I call up the crime scene file on my laptop. Setting the computer down at an angle that allows us both to see the screen, we read.

Although the death was undoubtedly suspicious, the file is smaller than I expected. The victim is Holly Smith, a thirty-five-year-old maths teacher. Her body was discovered on the outskirts of a village called Souldrop in Bedfordshire.

According to the pathologist's report, the cause of death was laceration of the throat and subsequent exsanguination. Shortly after Holly had been killed, an animal or animals unknown had eaten parts of the body.

A biologist had been called in to determine what kind of animal was behind the attack and to make sense of the tracks around the body, but their report was not included in the file. If they had been slow to submit their findings, that could explain why Jamie had sent the photos to me. The pathologist also discovered signs that the flesh from Holly's thighs had been removed with a blade.

'Does this confirm what you already suspected?' Karrion asks when we have both finished reading.

'I don't think there's any question that a Wild Folk killed and ate her.'

'But she was left where she was killed,' Karrion says. 'According to the file anyway. Why?'

'She may have been too heavy to move. There may have been no suitable cover nearby. Perhaps the Wild Folk was interrupted before she could move her.'

'But isn't it risky to start eating a body out in the open like that?'

'It is,' I say. 'Very risky.'

'Then why do it?'

'Without seeing the lie of the land and the tracks beyond the immediate vicinity of the body, it's impossible to speculate.' I check the file. 'It's been two weeks since Holly was killed. All the tracks will be long gone.'

Karrion leans back, passing his empty coffee mug from hand to hand. 'She was killed two weeks ago. Cúan two days ago. That's quite a long time between kills.'

'It's also quite a distance between kills.' Something in his thoughtful expression makes me smile. 'Are you thinking what I'm thinking?'

'That there may have been others in between?'

'Sounds like you were.' His aura swells with his pride,

177

and my smile widens. 'Though I was thinking on a bigger scale than you.'

'How so?'

'Bedfordshire, even rural Bedfordshire, isn't Wild Folk country. Unless she has the aid of a Mage and a teleportation circle, the Wild Folk must have got there somehow. She may have a car, though it's more likely she travelled on foot. If she's turned to killing humans, I doubt Holly was her first victim. It's a long way from the wild Northern Lands to Bedfordshire.'

Karrion sets down his mug and stretches his back. His right arm narrowly misses my lamp.

'How can we find out?'

'We'll need Jamie's help. Though he's not going to be pleased if I ask him to contact every constabulary between Old London and the Scottish border.'

'There can't be that many murders taking place across the country,' Karrion says. 'Right?'

'Think bigger, Karrion. If we ask for just murders, we're missing out on vital information. No predator is successful all the time. We need information about animal attacks, people being stalked, and attacks that failed.'

'Why animal attacks?'

'You saw what she looked like when she leapt out of the abandoned house. On a dark country road, could you tell the difference between her and a big dog?'

'Point.' Karrion glances past me at the dark window. 'I definitely wouldn't want to come across her alone at night.'

'I wouldn't either.' My thoughts flash to my battle with Tem in the Unseen Lands. I hope I will never come that close to losing control again.

'I can see what you mean about Jamie not being pleased. Compiling all that information is going to take ages.'

'If he does the initial requests, we can do the rest,' I say.

'But what about the time it takes us to make sense of it all? Shouldn't we be focusing on figuring out where she is now?'

'The problem is, she could be anywhere. We'll have time to work on that while we wait for the constabularies to get back to us. But in order to understand where she is going, we'll need to know more about who she is and what set her on this path. If we can trace her movements, we'll have a better idea of which conclave is hers.'

'That makes sense, I guess. Are we going to have a road trip up north to visit the conclave?'

Dearon's words about tamed wolves becoming dogs flash from my memory, though the sting they carry has lessened. 'No. As he's the representative of our Elderman, we'd best leave that to Dearon.'

'In that case, let's hope he will have recovered by the time we've found all the answers.'

'It's not Dearon I'm worried about as much as the other Wild Folk.'

'You think she's going after someone else?'

I rise and take our mugs to the kitchen. Karrion follows and looks through my cupboards until he finds a packet of chocolate Hobnobs.

'Sooner or later, she's bound to,' I say. 'I just wish I knew why she's started killing people.'

'Could she simply be an opportunist?' asks Karrion as he offers me a biscuit.

'What do you mean?'

179

'Animals are the main source of food for Wild Folk, but it must be far easier to hunt at the conclave, where there are lots of people to help. If for whatever reason a Wild Folk was travelling alone, humans start looking like easy prey, or so it seems.'

Shaking my head, I lick the chocolate from my fingers. 'That's not reason enough to break our gravest laws, especially when there is plenty of livestock out in the fields. There has to be another reason. She may have chosen Holly at random, but the kill was deliberate, and don't forget that she made an effort to conceal Cúan's body.'

'She cut off the meat from Holly's thighs, but didn't do so with Cúan. Why do you think that is?'

'If I had to guess, she ate her fill from Holly and took as much as she could easily carry with her. Given that with Cúan, she was still in the area two days later, she must have intended to eat all of him. And there was a chunk of meat at the abandoned cottage. She probably took it as a snack. It would have been unwise to visit the carcass during the day.'

'But why did she want to stick around this time?'

Instead of responding, I scroll through the crime scene file again. 'Did you see any mention here about whether Holly had magical blood?'

'No. I figured that meant she was human.'

'It seems like a logical conclusion. I wonder...' I stare at the flames in the fireplace as I try to fit the puzzle pieces into a coherent picture.

'Yan?'

'Sorry,' I say, realising that I have been silent for a while. 'Could the fact that Cúan was a Shaman make a difference?'

'Are you suggesting that she's a Leech instead of one of you guys?'

'No. She's definitely not a Leech. All I wondered was whether it made any difference to her if the victim was human, or one of us.'

'Do you think it would?'

'I don't see how. But we're clearly missing something.'

'Nothing better than two baffling mysteries to solve instead of one,' Karrion says with a wry grin, which is replaced by a yawn.

'It's late. You should go home.'

'No objections from me. I'll meet you here at eight?'

'Sounds good.'

After Karrion has gone, I email my request to Jamie and let Sinta out. The cut on my arm has bled through the bandages. I clean the wound properly and dress it. The tightness across my palm draws my attention away, and I spread my fingers wide, watching as the silvery scar tissue becomes taut. Even if I recover the full function-ality of my hands, I am forever marked by the Fey. As if summoned by the thought, a shiver of frost runs down my spine. I hurry out of the bathroom.

An ache in my legs and my wounded arm leads me to select two extra tablets, and I eat a banana. The pillows smell like Dearon when I lie down, and the loneliness that had been a frequent visitor until I adopted Sinta surges over me. As I lie still, my attention is drawn to the pain, which has increased into a crushing throb threatening to shatter my bones. Sinta clambers over the blankets towards me, and I welcome her warmth against my neck. Even a hint of a smoky presence in the fire-place cannot dispel the bleakness that settles in my heart.

As I lie with my back to the fire, my thoughts turn to the Wild Folk we are pursuing. Where is she now? Has she settled down for the night in another abandoned building or in a thicket of brambles, the chill of the winter biting at her skin and slowly petrifying her muscles? Does she share the bleakness I feel, so far apart from my homelands and the company of my kind? Or is she concealed in the shadows, lying in wait for her next victim?

MONDAY

19

LEINA PAREZ

My phone wakes me up, and I grope for it while untangling my legs from the blankets. Sinta whimpers, her back end wagging as she licks my chin. I pick her up with one hand and head for the window. My bare foot lands in something cold and wet. I swear as I answer the phone.

'I haven't had that effect on a woman since my ex-wife left me,' Jamie says, and laughs.

'Sorry. The joys of puppy ownership include a wet foot.'

'There are worse things to step on.'

I agree with Jamie as I open the window and set Sinta outside. She trots away from me, tail curling over her back, and I turn to switch on the light. The puddle is closer to the laid-out newspaper than Sinta has managed before.

'Did you ring about my email?' I ask as I wipe the floor and my foot, grateful that she only had one accident. My arm twinges, but the pain has lessened during the night.

'Yes. That's quite a task you set me.'

'Sorry,' I say again. 'We'd struggle to find out the information without you.'

'I understand; besides, it's a police case anyway. That you've thought to ask the questions you did is already progress. I've set the ball rolling, but it's going to take a while for me to hear back from the various constabularies.'

'That's fine. I'd say there's no hurry, but there's no telling what the Wild Folk is going to do next.'

'While we wait, I'm heading to speak to Leina Parez's flatmates this morning. Do you and Karrion still want to join me?'

'Absolutely. Where do you want to meet?'

'Why don't I pick you up in an hour? I'll bring breakfast for all three of us.'

'Sounds good. Remember, no eggs.'

'Right, thanks. I keep forgetting about the Bird Shaman thing.'

Jamie says goodbye, and I text Karrion to let him know about the change of plans. By then, Sinta is ready to come back inside, eager for her breakfast. I close the window and hurry to get dressed, more out of habit than the cold. The ache in my legs has not eased during the night like I hoped it would, but it has transformed into a ragged pain that makes my joints feel raw. Biting back my frustration, I wash more pain medication down with a glass of milk and eat a banana.

Karrion arrives five minutes before Jamie, and I am still brewing a pot of coffee when the doorbell rings again. While Karrion hurries downstairs, I set out mugs, milk, and sugar. Jamie enters with a bag. Bacon and sausage smells waft from it. Sinta greets Jamie with far more enthusiasm than last night, but to her evident disgust, he ignores her.

While we eat, Jamie's phone keeps pinging. After the third time, he sets down his breakfast roll, wipes his fingers on a napkin, and checks his phone. He grimaces.

'By lunchtime, I suspect the whole police force of England will be after my hide.'

'Sorry we've made you unpopular,' I say.

'Just make good use of the information these poor buggers are having to dig out for you.'

'We'll do our best.'

Once our plates are empty and I've refilled our mugs, Jamie draws a small tablet from his briefcase.

'The Met is inching towards the twenty-first century,' he says with a sardonic twist of his lips.

'How will you cope without parchment and quills?' Karrion asks, eyes twinkling with laughter.

'It's you I'm more worried about.' I wink at Karrion. 'If New Scotland Yard is phasing out carrier pigeons, you're going to be even more popular.'

Karrion scowls, but he cannot help a small chuckle.

'We got a preliminary report from the pathologist who examined Leina Parez,' Jamie says, tapping on his tablet. 'We put a rush on the post-mortem, given the sensitive political connections of the case.'

'Anything interesting there?' I ask.

'Plenty. She died yesterday morning. It came as no great surprise that the cause of death was strangulation. She was also beaten on more than one occasion over the past few days. The ligature marks around her wrists and ankles indicate that she spent long periods of time restrained in the same position. She was severely dehydrated and the pathologist estimates that she had not eaten since Friday, approximately lunchtime. The odd thing is that as much as everything points to a bondage game gone horribly wrong, there was no sign of sexual assault.'

As Jamie lists Leina's injuries, the words coalesce into sensations and experiences in my mind. Hunger gnaws at my belly, thirst parches my throat, and my body becomes a mass of pain beneath blows that fall across it.

Her pain is my pain, not because I have experienced similar abuse, but because I can imagine it. Perhaps within the subconscious memories of past Wild Folk generations, an ancestor recalls what such treatment felt like.

My imagination leads to a startling conclusion. The mug in my hand trembles.

'She knew she was going to die.' Pity overtakes the horror of Leina's injuries.

'How do you figure that?' Karrion asks.

'If they didn't give her food or water, she must have realised they weren't keeping her as a hostage. She wasn't raped. If her captors didn't see to her basic welfare, they must not have cared whether she lived or died.'

Karrion nods. 'Then it must have been only a matter of time before they were done with her.'

'She spent her final days with that knowledge as company.' I bow my head and massage the bridge of my nose. 'She struggled against her bonds, perhaps earned several beatings for her troubles. In the end, all she could do was wait to die.'

'That's not cool.' Karrion rises and takes his mug to the kitchen, but not before I catch a glimpse of the anger and disgust on his face.

'It's a terrible way to die,' I say. 'All the more reason for us to catch the killer.'

Jamie puts away the tablet. 'I doubt any of us needed extra motivation.'

'What puzzles me,' I say as Karrion returns to the lounge, still looking glum, 'is why Leina wasn't killed until yesterday morning.'

'Maybe Lloid had a use for her,' Jamie replies.

'Or maybe she was used as a bait to lure Lloid to his flat.' Karrion slumps on the end of my mattress.

'But if Lloid was lured to the flat, why didn't we find his body there?' I ask. 'The trap doesn't seem to have been effective.'

'We have no concrete proof that anyone other than Lloid was involved.' Jamie raises his hand to silence our objections. 'Though we're still processing evidence.'

'*If* it was Lloid who killed Leina,' I say, 'why would he have waited two days before strangling her? It would have been wiser to kill her on Friday and then flee the country to get a head start on his escape.'

Jamie drains his mug. 'That's true. Perhaps speaking to Leina's flatmates will shed some light on the mystery.'

We tidy away the breakfast things, and Karrion does the washing-up while I get ready and lift Sinta out to the garden. Looking around for anything she might chew, I set up the spark guard in front of the cold remnants from last night's fire and drop yesterday's socks in the laundry basket. A cupboard in the kitchen is filled with cow hooves, fish skins, and other chews, and I hide a selection around the lounge while Sinta busies herself by growling at the blackcurrant bush next to my woodshed. She rushes to the window when I call her, but her ears droop when I set her on her bed and we head for the door. We hear a yowl of outrage behind us, which is cut short by what I can only assume is the scent of a hidden treat.

Jamie drives. He navigates the morning traffic past Farringdon station and towards the river. Leina Parez had a flat-share in one of the narrow old houses a few hundred yards from the luxury buildings along the northern bank of the Thames. The entrance hall looks clean, but worn, and it's immediately clear that this area is a notch down from the opulent homes we have visited in our past investigations. A poster on the inside of the front door advertises a self-help course to improve incantations and enhance evocations. Jamie slows his steps, looking at the fine print with interest. Karrion rolls his eyes behind Jamie's back. After a warning shake of my head, we both pretend not to notice Jamie taking a photo of the poster.

The lift takes so long to arrive that we give up and take the stairs to the fourth floor. Rap music blares through one of the doors we pass, replaced by the theme tune for the Old London news broadcast. By the time we reach the correct door, my ankle is aching, but I push the discomfort aside. Jamie knocks.

The person opening the door, dressed in a grey pinstripe suit, has closely cropped black hair and thick-rimmed glasses. My eyes flicker up and down.

'Yes?' The voice is surprisingly soft.

Jamie introduces us all, and we show our consultants' badges. 'We're here to talk about Leina Parez.'

'I'm Jhoel Hannegan.' His eyes stray to Jamie's badge. 'Though I haven't received official confirmation of the name change. The rental agreement is under Janene Hannegan.'

With a nod, Jamie makes a note of this, and Jhoel invites us in. As I walk past him, I inhale. Beneath subtle cologne, the velvety scent of a Shadow Mage is unmistakable. At least he appears to lack the arrogant sneer that I have come to associate with Shadow Mages thanks to my dealings with Lord Ellensthorne and Mr Whyte.

The front door leads straight to an open-plan living room and kitchen. A battered old sofa is tucked into the far corner of the room, and assorted armchairs and bean bags take up the rest of the space. The room has an air of bohemian comfort. I relax.

'Please take a seat,' Jhoel says, pointing towards the sofa and checking his watch.

We sit, side by side.

'What's this about?' he asks, looking at the three of us with open curiosity. 'Is Leina in trouble?'

Jamie and I exchange a look, both caught off guard. It makes sense that Jhoel has not heard the news, and yet the thought of having to be the ones to explain what has happened fills me with trepidation.

'I'm sorry to have to tell you that Leina was murdered yesterday morning,' Jamie says, his left hand clutching the handle of his briefcase.

Jhoel's eyes widen. 'Murdered? Leina? That's not possible. Who would want to hurt her?'

'That's what we're trying to find out. We were hoping that you and her other flatmates could offer us an insight into her life.'

'Anything you need,' Jhoel says, words slow as he turns to stare out of the window.

Silence fills the room. I shift, uncomfortable witnessing Jhoel's grief. Karrion glances at me, uncertainty written across his face, while Jhoel's features are blank. Only his hands clenching and unclenching on his lap reveal something of his inner turmoil. His eyes glisten, but no tears fall.

At length, Jhoel clears his throat and rubs his eyes. He rises from the enormous green armchair and plucks a tissue from a box on a circular dining room table. After blowing his nose, he discards the crumpled tissue in a bin.

'I think I'm okay now. It doesn't feel real.'

191

'It may take a while for the news to sink in. Do you have someone you can talk to?' Jamie asks.

'Yeah, my girlfriend. Though she's also going be devastated.' Jhoel shakes himself like a dog might. 'How can I help?'

'How long have you lived here?' asks Jamie.

'Five years, give or take a few months.'

'And Leina?'

'She moved in about six months after me. The two of us, plus Ande who's on holiday at the moment, have been here the longest.'

'Did you and Leina know each other before she moved in?' I ask.

'Yes. We were both trainee solicitors at the same firm. That's where we met and became friends. We both wanted a place reasonably close to the office, but couldn't afford anything decent on our own, so we decided to look for a bigger place that could fit four or five people and we'd share the costs. That's how we found this flat. Leina was on a fixed contract elsewhere, so there was a delay before she moved in.'

'Where did Leina work last?' Jamie asks.

'At Hayes, Alcock and Bryan in New London. Her speciality is family law.'

My eyebrows rise at this. 'Isn't it odd that she was working in New London? She was a Mage, wasn't she? Is it a human law firm?'

'Yes, an East Mage. And yes, it was unusual. Leina was headhunted. She wasn't sure whether she'd be a good fit, given that almost everyone else there was human, but the pay was good and the work challenging. Her plan was to stay there for a few years then find a job in Old London that would fast-track her to an appointment as a partner.'

'Did she have any problems at work?' Jamie asks.

'Nothing major.'

'But something happened?' I prompt.

'Leina told me about a partner who was being difficult. He's one of those crusty old men who think that women should only make tea and type letters. She said he was always undermining her work.'

'Was there an indication of violence from the male partner?'

'No. Leina was more concerned about being passed over for a promotion. She isn't,' Jhoel pauses and looks out of the window, '*wasn't* the type of person to be cowed by a threat of violence.'

'How so?' Karrion asks.

'For one, Leina was an accomplished capoeirista. For another, she was a dominatrix.'

Karrion makes a strangled sound and begins to cough. I elbow him in the ribs. A hint of amusement lifts the sadness on Jhoel's face.

'Was she a professional dominatrix?' I ask, conscious of how strange the question is.

'She used to supplement her income by working at a club, but she gave that up a few years ago, when she qualified as a solicitor. Recently, it's been just a hobby. Gerreint is a submissive. They were a match made in heaven.' Jhoel pauses. 'Well, a match made in a bondage club anyway.'

'Is that how they met?'

'Yes.'

'Do you know the name of the club?'

'Leina never said and I never asked. She was always very private about that side of her life. I got the impression that just telling me she was a dom was a big deal. Ande also knew, I think, but I'm pretty sure none of the others did.'

'If she was that private, I'm guessing she didn't talk about her clients,' Jamie says.

'Never.'

'Do you know whether her work as a dominatrix led to physical injuries or a threat of violence?'

'The whole point of being a dom was that she was always in control. Her shifts at the club seemed a form of release for her, in a non-sexual way, and she came home looking relaxed. Much like each time she took part in a *roda*.'

'*Roda*?' Karrion frowns.

'It's what they call sparring in capoeira circles. The groups in Old London use spells as well as the physical moves.'

'And what's capoeira again?' Karrion asks, tugging at the row of piercings on his left ear. 'The name sounds vaguely familiar.'

'It's an Afro-Brazilian form of martial arts that combines self-defence moves with music and dancing. Leina's parents emigrated from Brazil before she was born and practising capoeira was her way of connecting with her roots.'

'Was she a member of a particular group?' I ask.

'Yes, there's one not far from here. It's on Birchin Lane.'

'What was Leina's relationship with Gerreint Lloid like?' asks Jamie.

'They were in love. Truth be told, I'm surprised Leina still kept her room here. I've been expecting them to find a place together for the past six months.'

'Are you aware of any tension between them?'

'None,' Jhoel says, shaking his head for emphasis. 'They were great together. Leina had a string of short, toxic relationships before she met Gerreint, but with him, her restlessness seemed to melt away. I've never seen her happier than when she was with him.'

'And these previous boyfriends, could any of them have wanted to harm Leina?' I ask.

Jhoel thinks for a moment, playing with the clasp of his watch. 'There was one guy, Curt Wegner, who became a bit stalkery after she broke up with him. I seem to remember that he knew about her dominatrix work and, in his opinion, that made her a glorified prostitute. In the end, she threatened to flay him with a cat-o'-nine-tails if he didn't leave her alone.'

'Do you know where he lives?' asks Jamie, scribbling in his notebook.

'No. Leina may have his number in her phone, though I doubt it.'

I too have made a note of the name. 'Can you think of anyone else who might have wanted to harm her?'

'No. She was a kind, bright young woman who wasn't in the habit of making enemies.'

'Do you know if she was planning to spend the weekend with Gerreint?'

'She was. On Friday morning, she took an overnight bag with her to work. She's been gradually transferring more of her clothes to Gerreint's place, but most of her work clothes were still here.'

This strikes me as curious, though I leave the thought unspoken. There was no overnight bag in Lloid's flat. Did the killer get rid of it when he disposed of Leina's clothes? Why then was her handbag left untouched? There are far too many points about the case that do not add up.

Jamie looks at us, an unspoken question in his eyes, and closes his notebook.

'Thank you for your time, Mr Hannegan,' he says.

Jhoel rises, straightening his suit jacket. We are following him to the door when a final question jumps to my mind.

'Did you ever notice Leina coming home low on power?'

As he turns to me, Jhoel frowns, a hand coming up to rub his jaw. Jamie has stopped next to an umbrella stand crammed full of silk parasols and giant fans.

'Low on power?' The floorboards creak when Jhoel shifts his weight. 'I can't say I make a habit of monitoring my friends' power levels. She was drained after a major *roda*, I suppose, but nothing else springs to mind.'

We thank him again, and leave. Outside, Jamie checks his phone, while I zip my coat against the winter chill. A breeze from the Thames ruffles Karrion's hair, bringing with it the scents of the river silt and the salt of the sea. As my chin lifts on its own accord, I long to drive out of the city so that I may run on my beach, free and wild. The time I spent at the conclave and St Albans has gone some way towards replenishing my power reserves, but carrying Dearon to the paramedics left me depleted and weaker than I should be.

'Do you think she was telling the truth?' asks Karrion into the silence between us.

'Who?' I turn to him, relinquishing my connection to the sea breeze.

'Jhoel, or Janene, whatever her name is.'

'Him, Karrion, not her,' I say.

Karrion begins to speak, but he stops himself.

'He's choosing to identify as a male. We should respect that.'

'Right.' Karrion's cheeks turn pink. 'Sorry.'

'There's no need to apologise. You didn't do it in front of Jhoel.'

'I need to return to the office,' Jamie says, putting his phone away. 'Where are you off to next?'

'To the capoeira group. I want to see whether their account of Leina matches Jhoel's.'

'So you don't trust him,' Karrion says. 'Do you think he lied?'

'Not necessarily, but that doesn't mean he told us everything either. I must admit, however, that I have a certain prejudice towards his account because he's a Shadow Mage.'

'How do you know?' Jamie asks, and shakes his head. 'Sorry, I forgot you do that as a matter of course.'

Karrion's expression darkens. 'Do you think he's in league with Lord Ellensthorne?'

'I doubt every Shadow Mage in Old London is on his payroll. There was nothing about Jhoel to suggest he comes from the old bloodlines.'

'Still, it won't hurt to be suspicious.' Karrion glares at the building behind us. 'Just in case.'

'We're already suspicious,' I say. 'At the moment, we have no proof that Jhoel's been anything but honest with us. We shouldn't fall into the trap of thinking every Shadow Mage is evil, just because Lord Ellensthorne is morally questionable. His source of power makes him no more evil than Light Mages' power makes them good. Just remember Reaoul Pearson.'

'Let me know if you find out anything that sheds further light on the case,' Jamie says. 'Do you need a lift?'

'I think we'll walk.' Next to me, Karrion nods. 'I'll call you later for an update.'

Jamie waves us goodbye and heads for his car. I remain rooted to the spot, craning my neck to look up at the flats. Jhoel painted a picture of a strong woman capable of taking care of herself. If Leina was a dominatrix, no one could have tricked her into shackles. It ought to have been her restraining the submissive. How then was an accomplished capoeirista overpowered, especially without the neighbours hearing anything? Who did it? What is the purpose behind her death and does it have anything to do with the Leech hiding in plain sight?

20

SPELL RODA

We follow Queen Victoria Street towards the Royal Exchange. Near the Bloomberg Arcade, wide wooden plant boxes are filled with hardy roses and tiny evergreen trees wreathed in fairy lights. The sight of the roses blooming despite the late season reminds me of my intention to visit Lady Bergamon. I mention this to Karrion, whose face lights up with eagerness. He is always willing to explore the mysteries of Lady Bergamon's garden, not realising that there are far more secrets to uncover than he appreciates.

The Royal Exchange, with its war memorial and porticoed front, houses the largest collection of magical texts and reference books in the country. A few people are hurrying up the steps as we cross the road in front of the building, dodging those ascending the stairs from Bank Tube station. With a subtle suggestion from Karrion, a flock of pigeons takes flight.

'It might be worth paying the Royal Exchange a visit,' I say as we turn to Cornhill and walk alongside the large building.

'Why? Are you planning on refreshing your knowledge of Mage rituals?'

'No, but aren't you at all curious about what the oldest

199

magical library in the country has to say on the subject of Leeches?'

'Maybe.' Karrion stuffs his hands in the pockets of his leather jacket. 'How about you dive into dusty books while I follow a suspect at a discreet distance and duck into a speakeasy for a word with a dodgy informant?'

'You still haven't given up on the glamorous view of our job, have you?'

'I live in hope.'

'Feel free. Just don't hold your breath while you wait for a damsel in distress.'

'With my luck, she'd turn out to be Fria.'

I laugh. Fria, a Cat Shaman thief, has become a valued contact over the past couple of months. While Karrion appreciates her looks, the natural enmity between Bird and Cat Shamans puts him automatically on his guard. He has complained more than once that someone as beautiful as Fria should not have been born a Cat Shaman.

We turn to Birchin Lane, and I keep an eye out for any sign of a gym or a dojo. The tall buildings surrounding us cast the narrow street into shadows. A man in a suit hurries past, leaving the scents of cologne, horsehair, and fresh hay lingering in his wake.

A door across the street catches my eye. Tacked to the red surface is a poster showing a man dressed in white, executing a kick while spinning on his hands.

'I think that's it,' I say as I cross the road.

Through the door, I hear singing and clapping. I hesitate, wondering whether I should knock when the door opens. Two teenagers carrying rucksacks step out, chattering in Portuguese, beads of sweat still clinging to their foreheads. We step aside to let them pass, and I catch the door before it closes.

We come to a narrow hall, with stairs leading up to our right and a door of frosted glass in front of us. The voices I heard before seem to come from the far side, and I test the handle to find it unlocked.

The room beyond is larger than I expected. In the far left corner, temporary walls separate an area for changing rooms. Next to them is a tall stack of blue mats. The scuffed wooden floor is bare, the walls are painted white, and fluorescent tubes hanging from the ceiling light the room. There are twenty people milling around, dressed in white trousers and T-shirts. Near the back wall, three men are holding instruments that look like a cross between a small drum and a bow. Next to them, two teenagers are setting up tall drums, while a third holds a pair of bells and a rattling oblong metal shape.

'Can I help you?'

A man approaches us, dressed like everyone else. His features are narrow and pointed, and he is pulling his long violet and silver hair into a ponytail. Up close, his eyes resemble liquid mercury, and when he smiles, he reveals a row of pointed teeth.

I need not use magic to identify him as Feykin. The blood of the Fair Folk runs strong in his veins, that much is clear from the press of his aura against mine. I envision him astride a towering war horse, a horn of bone and silver in his hand, leaning forward in his eagerness for the hunt. In my vision, I run silently beside him, my dark paws eating up the ground while bloodlust urges me on.

Stumbling back, I collide with Karrion. He holds out his hand to steady me, concern written across his face.

'Are you okay, Yan?'

'Fine, I just felt faint for a moment.' I force a smile at the Feykin, fixing my gaze on his sharp nose rather than the unsettling eyes. 'Sorry.'

'Would you like to sit down?' he asks, pointing to a row of plastic chairs along the wall. 'The *roda* is about to start.'

'Do you mind if we watch?'

'Not at all. Come find me if you have any questions.'

The Feykin returns to the others, while we move to the nearest chairs. They shift as we sit down, and pain flares in my collarbones. I brace my elbows on my thighs.

'Are you sure you're okay?' Karrion asks.

'I'm fine. He's a powerful Feykin, and our auras meeting triggered a memory of sorts about the Coin-Sìth. Actually, it was more like a vision.'

'The hounds can't harm you here, can they?'

'I don't think so, but that doesn't make the memories any more pleasant.'

He has no chance to reply before the capoeiristas form a circle, standing shoulder to shoulder. The musicians begin to play, and everyone in the circle claps their hands in time with the music. Power crackles through the air, causing the hairs at the back of my neck to stand.

One of the musicians sings, the words indistinguishable over the clapping. With each word, the threads of magic in the air join and unravel, forming a weave over the *roda* that connects each capoeirista. Beside me, Karrion watches with interest, but I am left with the impression that he does not sense the power like I do. Perhaps if it was a circle of birds instead of people, things would be different.

A young woman steps forward and bows to a tall, rangy boy of perhaps sixteen. He joins her at the centre of the *roda*, pleasure evident on his smooth face. They move as one, together, yet in opposition. Red light flares above them. The woman moves for a low kick, and her bare feet glow green as they swing through the air without making contact with her opponent. A smell of limes drifts across the room, but it is overtaken by the scent of dry autumn leaves. The North Mage attacks in turn, his kick higher, yet it makes no contact.

It takes me several minutes to realise that as much as the *roda* appears to be a form of ritualistic combat, the object is not to harm the opponent. Rather the focus seems to be the harmony of the movements and the way the capoeiristas combine dance with magic. Power crackles overhead, and when the Feykin takes his place at the centre of the *roda*, cherry blossoms and birch leaves float over the musicians, not touching them. The scent is a mixture of blood, ashes, and summer nights. He must be descended from the vassals of the Summer King, who have a rightful place beside their lord and master when the Fey ride and hunt and kill.

The memory of the Summer King's casual cruelty is distracting, and it's only when Karrion nudges me that I realise the *roda* is finished. With a final bow, the Feykin and his opponent withdraw from the circle. Everyone applauds, and Karrion and I join in.

'What do you want to do now, boss?'

'We'll take the Roman approach, I think.'

Karrion frowns, then grins. 'Divide and conquer, right?'

'Well remembered.'

'What can I say? I taught you well.'

I stand. 'Keep telling yourself that.'

We split up to mingle. With every person I speak to, I ask the same questions: did they know Leina well, what was she like, and did she have any known enemies? As I move around the room, I am aware of the diminished auras of the combatants and the movements of the Feykin. Wherever he goes, I make sure I'm as far away from him as I can be without being obvious.

My strategy works until I get speaking to one of the instructors, who offers me a leaflet about their beginner courses. I fold the leaflet and tuck it into my pocket just as I sense the trickle of summer rain against my aura.

'Are you thinking of joining us, Wild Woman?'

The Feykin's hair is down once more. Under the harsh lighting of the room, the shades of it resemble heavy clouds heralding a storm. Although his tone is polite, there is an undercurrent in his voice I cannot place. Finally, his words register and I open my mouth to ask how he knows what I am.

'I can sense the source of your power just as you can sense mine,' he says, answering the unspoken question. 'My kind whispers tales of the Wild Woman who battled one of the lords of old, wielding a weapon of wood and metal, modern and ancient, forbidden and feared. The shock of your actions crossed the threshold between the worlds. My kind takes pride in their long memories.'

Casting my senses inwards, I reach for my reserve of power. Even as I do so, I know that in the middle of the city, where nature has little hold left, I will be no match for a Feykin of such lineage should he choose to attack me.

Giving all of myself to nature here will offer no help.

'There was a great deal at stake that night,' I say, trying to mask the defensiveness of my words.

'I cast no judgement upon you or your actions, Wild Woman.' His eyes gleam, and I am left with the impression that there is much he leaves unsaid. 'Should you wish to learn the art of capoeira, you are welcome here.'

'Thanks.' I back away, narrowly missing a collision with one of the musicians. 'I may join your next beginner course.'

Although all my instincts warn against it, I turn my back to the Feykin and scan the crowd for Karrion's plumage of black hair. No attack comes from behind, though I can still sense the mercury eyes boring into me. What the encounter means, I am not yet certain, and I am in two minds about attempting to figure it out. When I chose to oppose Baneacre, it never occurred to me that the Feykin in Old London would take note. Now I wonder how many more enemies I have made.

Declan Pheonix's serpentine eyes rise from the confines of my memory, and I shudder. I only returned to the site of the incomplete Fey Mound once, but found nothing except rubble and rubbish. The tricksy Fey was gone, but knowing he continues to reside in Old London leaves me uneasy. Pheonix supported Baneacre's claim over the city and cannot have been happy when his new king fell before ascending to the throne. Instinct tells me our paths will cross again, though I am less than certain that it will be a good thing.

'Are you done?'

Karrion appears at my side, still looking around with open curiosity. Across the room, a woman heading for the dressing rooms offers him a shy smile. He stands up a little straighter and runs a hand through his hair.

'Yes, I think so,' I say, and he forces his attention back to me, thereby missing the look of disappointment on the woman's face. 'Let's grab a coffee somewhere and compare notes.'

We leave in silence. My thoughts return to the *roda* and the power I sensed in the room. Everyone around the circle contributed to it, though most of the time the combatants' magic manifested as colour and scents. Only the Feykin created tangible shapes as he participated in the *roda*. Despite this, in the aftermath, everyone I spoke to was low on power.

A *roda* would be a treasure trove for a Leech, though I sensed none present.

As soon as we step out of the front door, Karrion turns to me, having to raise his voice over a motorcycle driving past. The sound of the engine echoes between the buildings.

'Did you find out anything interesting?'

'Not much. Everyone said that Leina was lovely and a gifted capoeirista. A young woman said that while Leina gave her all to every *roda*, she wasn't a particularly powerful Mage.'

'Could that be because Lloid was draining her power?'

'The thought occurred to me too, but the woman said Leina had always been weak, even before she began dating Lloid.'

'If she wasn't that strong, it would have been risky for a Leech to try to steal her power,' Karrion says.

'I agree. But if Lloid didn't get his East Mage abilities from Leina, where did they come from?'

'Shall we add that to the list of mysteries we need to solve?' Karrion flashes me a wry smile.

'What about you? Any interesting nuggets?'

'Much of it was what you just told me. But one guy did mention there was someone who used to come to watch Leina train. Originally they were friendly, but towards the end, Leina was threatening to call the Paladins if he didn't leave her alone.'

'Did our witness know the man's name?' I ask.

Karrion's smile widens, showing his pleasure at the question. 'He thought possibly it was Curt.'

'The stalkery ex-boyfriend? Let's hope Jamie can track him down.'

We reach the Royal Exchange, and my steps slow as I look up at the building. Karrion sighs.

'You still want to go do some research, don't you?'

'I do, but I'm not sure it's the best use of our time just now. It's almost lunchtime, and we haven't been to see Lady Bergamon yet.'

'If it's a choice between musty old books and Lady B's awesome garden, I vote for the latter.'

'Of course you do. Your attitude is strange, given that of the two of us, you're the one with a university degree.'

'Yes, in Fine Arts. I spent as much time with a paint-brush in my hand as I did writing essays.'

Still looking at the library, I weigh our options. When the stone facade offers no insight, I check my phone. No missed calls from the hospital.

'Let's visit Lady Bergamon first,' I say at last. 'We can always come back later.'

Since Jamie gave us a lift this morning, we catch a bus. I'm glad to sit down and rub my aching knees.

'Do you need meds?' Karrion asks.

'No, I think I'm okay for the time being.'

'What do you think Lady B's garden is going to be like? Do you reckon it has recovered from Baneacre's deluge?'

I consider the question while the bus shudders to a stop at a red light. 'Lady Bergamon seemed better last week when I saw her, though still weak. I expect her healing goes hand in hand with her domain's. Every time I've seen her recently for bandage changes, the garden has looked a little better.'

'How do your hands feel now?'

'They're okay.' I flex my fingers and watch as the silvery scar tissue bunches up and stretches tight. 'It's unlikely the scars will ever heal, given that they were caused by Fey power, but I should have the full use of my hands again.'

While modern medicine and Lady Bergamon healed my hands, the silver scar on the side of my abdomen is a reminder of not just my time in the Unseen Lands, but the favour I owe the Winter Queen.

'This is us,' Karrion says, and presses the stop button.

As we alight, my head turns to look down Ivy Street. At the far end, hidden by a curve in the road, lies a house with a gateway to a different version of Old London.

21

TEMPERANCE

Lady Bergamon answers the door almost immediately, smiling. Karrion turns from the row of pots containing seedlings to greet her.

'Wishearth said you'd stop by,' she says. 'Come in.'

'Sorry we're later than planned.'

'No matter. You lead busy lives and I am old enough that time is less pressing.'

She closes the door behind us, and I head towards the kitchen without needing to be told to. Both doors I pass are shut. Behind one is a lounge, where the dining room table was protected by a circle of power on the night of Samhain. Behind the other is a library with lead scrolls stamped with runes of a forgotten language. Does she know I explored her home, perhaps with more freedom than was warranted, while she lay unconscious upstairs? Nothing in her demeanour towards me since Samhain has indicated that I have caused offence.

'The kettle just boiled,' Lady Bergamon says. 'Why don't you step outside and I'll be right with you?'

As we cross the threshold, my vision blurs. For a moment, I am uncertain of my balance, but it is not the terrible vertigo of Baneacre leeching Lady Bergamon's magic out of her domain. Rather it is another sign that the garden is returning to normal.

In Old London's past, the sun peeks through clouds. It's a cold day, early winter or late autumn, but the temperature is warmer than in the city of today. The wild power greets me. A wreath of spruce branches hangs from the back door, decorated with holly berries.

Is it Christmas Lady Bergamon celebrates, or an older festival tied to the magic behind the changing seasons?

Three of the seats around the wooden table have sheepskins on them. She is well prepared for our visit. When Lady Bergamon appears with a tray of drinks, she is carrying a folded blanket under one arm. She hands it to me.

'I hope you don't mind taking tea out here, despite the chilly day. Recently, I have been reluctant to be away from the garden for any length of time.'

'It's not a problem,' I say, and once I have sat down, I drape the blanket over my legs more out of habit than because I feel the cold.

Lady Bergamon serves us tea. I no longer feel surprised or uncomfortable when she stirs a spoonful of honey into a cup of her pain-relieving infusion and places it in front of me. While she cuts slices of lemon drizzle cake for us, I turn to look along the stretch of lawn. In the distance, fruit trees all but obscure a vegetable patch and a greenhouse. Both are too small to give Lady Bergamon self-sufficiency, even with the disrupted order of seasons yielding more than one crop a year. There must be other cultivated areas in her domain, though I have never glimpsed them.

Beyond the greenhouse, the edge of the forest is barely visible. I call upon the sight of a hen harrier, but see nothing out of place along the tree line. Yet I cannot shake the feeling of being watched. Is Bradán out there, staring at us from the gloom of the forest, or is my unease a mere throwback to Baneacre's menace in the sodden domain?

My thoughts are interrupted when Lady Bergamon says my name, and I turn back to the table. She has set a plate next to my cup. I smile my thanks as I force my attention away from the memories of terror, darkness, and relentless rain.

'Sorry. Thank you for the tea and cake.'

'You're always welcome in my home, Yannia.' Lady Bergamon sips her tea. 'How can I help you?'

I hesitate, suddenly uncertain. 'We... I wanted to ask a favour, possibly two. But I'm conscious that you're forever helping me out. I can pay you, of course.'

'Yannia.' She silences my stumbling words by laying a hand on mine. The thumb brushing against the side of my wrist is at once rough, smooth, and soft. 'You saved my garden and my life. Any aid within my power is yours to have.'

'Thanks.' I smile, and she withdraws her hand. Taking a bite of cake, I wonder where to begin. 'Dearon was hurt.'

A look of surprise and alarm passes across her face. She remains silent while I recount our hunt for the Wild Folk and the brief skirmish outside the abandoned house.

'Dearon will resist human medicine,' I say. 'That's our way. But his injuries were too serious to leave unattended.'

'Whereas my healing comes from plants and nature.'

'I was wondering, if it isn't too much trouble, whether you would examine his wounds once he's released from the hospital.'

'Of course. Whatever healing I can impart I'll gladly give.'

A tension I was unaware of is eased. I relax in my seat, appreciating for the first time the tart sweetness of the cake and the warmth spreading through me. Some of the guilt I feel over Dearon's injuries slips away, replaced by the knowledge that I am doing something tangible to help.

'The second favour?' asks Lady Bergamon.

'Remember the Leech I told you about on Friday?'

Lady Bergamon nods.

'It looks like he killed his girlfriend, then disappeared.'

'Looks like?' She arches one thin eyebrow.

'We're not sure whether he's behind the murder or not. But the fact remains that he's disappeared and we need to find him. If he killed Leina, he needs to answer for his crimes. If he's been framed, he's probably in grave danger.' I set my fork down, and the clatter of metal against porcelain is louder than I intended. 'You found Brother Valeron when he didn't want to be found, and I wondered whether you could do so again with the Leech.'

Clouds obscure the sun just as Lady Bergamon's expression darkens. The winter air seems forbidding. Next to me, Karrion shivers.

'Using plants and blood to locate the missing takes a great deal of power,' Lady Bergamon says, her words directed at the lawn rather than us. 'The cost is more than I have to spare. Baneacre's blight on the garden runs deeper than it looks. Healing this land will take years. I don't know how long it will be before I can wield my magic as freely as I once could. But for now, I'm afraid I cannot help you.'

'We understand,' I say. 'I don't want you to think I'm making a habit of asking you instead of doing my job.'

'I know that. Under different circumstances, I'd be glad to help.'

We speak no more as Lady Bergamon tops up our cups and cuts everyone another slice of cake. The warmth has spread to my limbs, easing the ache that resides there permanently, but the pain has not gone. The pain never goes away. This is my reality now, and I have come to accept it.

The clouds drift away. Lady Bergamon closes her eyes and angles her face towards the sun. Without intending to, I allow my aura to expand outwards, acknowledging Karrion's presence but skirting around him. Lady Bergamon feels different, as though her magic is less well defined. Hundreds of tiny threads connect her to the plants, and they in turn form part of something bigger. It's as though she is the centre of a delicate, intricate lace weave.

As soon as the thought registers, I know I am mistaken. Lady Bergamon's connection to her garden is more multidimensional. It's not just the plants forming threads in her patterns of magic, but also the air, the soil, the very bedrock deep beneath our feet. The waterways, though no doubt controlled to an extent by Bradán, are hers, while the wind rustles the nearby branches in a melody only she discerns.

Before I get a chance to pull back my questing aura, the awareness of the patterns of Lady Bergamon's power intensifies. The weave brushes against my skin. I look down, expecting to see threads spreading across my hand, but there is nothing there. The tastes of clean air, fresh green shoots, and dry leaves cause me to swallow. A hum fills my ears, as if unseen fingers pluck the cords of the power like harp strings. Red stains appear on the weave. They do not mar its beauty, but rather strengthen it. I see, for the first time, how blood and the stars and the moon all play their part in the greatest act of magic Old London has ever experienced.

Lady Bergamon's power goes beyond plants, beyond the growth and decay of the natural world. The name for her kind is on the tip of my tongue, and I'm opening my mouth to speak it when something wet lands on my cheek. My awareness returns to me in a flash, so forcefully I jerk back, and Lady Bergamon stands.

'Winter showers,' she says. 'They always come at an inopportune moment. Karrion, will you please bring the sheepskins inside?'

She busies herself by clearing the table, but I catch the sideways glance she throws my way. How many of my thoughts did she guess? Why is she so resistant to the truth?

In a flash of trepidation, it occurs to me that Lady Bergamon may not trust me. We are bound by the bonds of friendship and survival, but that does not mean I am entitled to her secrets. I have shared my past and my cases freely with her, but now that I think about it, she has not reciprocated. While there are many things I suspect, what I know for certain about Lady Bergamon would not fill a sheet of paper. I recall the intimacy of Wishearth leaning over Lady Bergamon's prone body, whispering to her, and wonder how long it will be before I share such a connection with her. Will a mortal lifetime be enough?

Guilt from overstepping boundaries mingles with disappointment as I follow Karrion and Lady Bergamon inside, carrying the blanket. The kitchen is cramped with the three of us there, and I fold the blanket in the smallest possible space so as not to poke the others. Lady Bergamon's smile is warm as she takes the bundle from me and sets it on one of the chairs.

'Send word with Wishearth when you and Dearon are ready for my visit.' Despite the warmth of her tone, it is time for us to go.

I thank her again, and we are almost at the door when she calls after us. Lady Bergamon hands Karrion a small red flower with five petals and tall anthers. I recognise it as an azalea.

'Not patience this time?' Karrion asks as he examines the flower.

'You have changed, therefore my advice to you must also change.'

Karrion stammers a thank you, and we leave. The seedlings in the front garden are a far cry from the usual display of colour and growth, but there is enough power in the plants to offer Lady Bergamon protection from the prying eyes of her neighbours.

'Are you okay?' Karrion asks as we weave past the larger pots, through the wrought iron gate, and to the pavement.

'Fine. Why?'

'After Lady B said she couldn't help us find the Leech, you adopted that faraway look that suggests you're trying to stare the secrets out of the universe. Lady B was watching you, and it looked like she grew a little paler right before the rain started. In fact, I got the impression the shower was intended to distract you.'

'It wouldn't surprise me. She's entitled to her secrets.'

'Speaking of secrets, what's up with this?' Karrion asks, twirling the flower between his fingers.

'Hang on.'

I open the browser on my phone. A quick search later, I scroll through the results.

'There are several meanings for azalea. My guess is that she didn't mean it as a Chinese symbol for womanhood.'

'Let's hope not, otherwise I need to have an awkward conversation with her.'

'The meaning that makes the most sense is temperance.'

'Temperance?' Karrion frowns at the flower.

Something flashes across his face, and if I had to guess, I would say it was guilt. Glancing back, I wonder at Lady Bergamon and what she sees when she studies us. What advice is she offering Karrion that makes no sense to me, but holds meaning for him? What does she see that I cannot?

22

FORTNEM AND MASSON

'The Royal Exchange next?'

Karrion's question draws me away from my thoughts just as my phone beeps. I missed a call while we were visiting Lady Bergamon, and the voicemail has arrived. Dialling the number, I listen to the automated greeting until it changes to the voice of a young woman. I save the message.

'Someone from the hospital has left a voicemail. Dearon's discharge has been delayed until this evening. I can pick him up at six.'

Karrion checks his phone. 'That gives us plenty of time for sleuthing. Though I want a proper lunch. Lady B's cake was great, but I need more than that for my brain to work properly.'

'Let's stop for lunch then. Never let your mother claim that I don't feed my apprentice at regular intervals.'

'That's the spirit.'

We find a cafe a few minutes' walk from Ivy Street. As we enter, I look around for magic-detecting charms, but none are visible. Perhaps the owner feels no need to know whether the customers are human or not.

The cafe is nearly empty, and we choose a table in the far corner, away from the other customers. A smiling waitress comes to take our order, and Karrion gives her a lazy grin. I nudge him under the table with my foot.

'Focus.'

'I was,' he says, but he curbs his enthusiasm when the waitress returns with our drinks.

I take two pills with a mouthful of my cola. Although the effects of Lady Bergamon's tea still linger, the ache in my legs is beginning to push to the front of my mind. When the food arrives, Karrion tucks into his fish finger sandwich with gusto, while I rake a fork through my salad. My thoughts are jumbled, too many ideas and emotions vying for my attention. All the while, an undefined sense of urgency is causing my leg to jiggle in a restless pattern.

'Eat up,' Karrion says. 'Otherwise the meds will make you feel sick.'

I spear a forkful of rocket and tuna, then another. The tartness of the dressing and the salty fish chase away a hint of nausea. While I retrieve my notebook from my pocket, I continue eating with little focus on the taste.

'You didn't answer my question earlier,' Karrion says.

'What question?'

'Are we going to the Royal Exchange next?'

'Oh, that.' I open the notebook and let my pen hover over a blank page. 'Yes. I keep thinking that if we know more about Leeches, we might have a better idea of how Lloid thinks and acts.'

'Surely not all Leeches are the same.'

'No, but they must share some common goals and desires, like Wild Folk or Bird Shamans do.'

'Yeah, steal power and remain undetected by the rest of us.' Karrion stabs his fork into the pile of salad on his plate and sends a cherry tomato flying through the air.

It lands near the door. No one but us appears to have noticed the small missile.

'Every person has the capacity for evil. But not every Shadow Mage is evil, nor is every Wild Folk a man-eater. There must be exceptions to every rule. Being born with the ability to drain power from others doesn't automatically mean every Leech is capable of murder.'

Karrion pushes his plate away. 'I'm surprised that you of all people would say that.'

'Why? Because a Leech attacked me?' I run a hand over my face, trying to find the right words. 'I'm still angry at what happened, and the fear that I could be attacked again will probably never fully disappear. But that doesn't mean I think every Leech must be evil, just like I don't think every man is evil. As much as I'm still healing, I don't want the trauma to define me. It's better to forgive and move on than to allow the anger to consume me.'

'That's...' Karrion watches me, his brow furrowed. 'That's a pretty cool way of looking at it.'

'It's easier said than done.' I laugh at his look of surprise. 'What? Did you think I turned into a saint overnight? It's a goal, and one day I'll get there. For now, I'm working on remembering that the world would be a better place if everyone was a little quicker to forgive.'

'Fine, fine, let's go to the sodding library.'

This time, we laugh together. Affection lights Karrion's expression as he takes my hand and squeezes it. Then his attention is drawn to the counter, and he sobers.

'Shit, now the waitress thinks we're together and she's pissed off.'

'That's what you get for thinking you're Don Juan.'

'The Mage known for his infidelity? Nah, I'd rather be

Casanova born again. He must have been related to birds of paradise to get all the chicks.' He raises his hand when I start to speak. 'No, I don't want to hear any more suggestions about hen houses.'

'You don't know that I was going to say that.'

'I do know, so shut up.'

Taking the notebook from me, Karrion turns the blank page towards himself. After sketching a quick caricature of a pigeon running away from a raven, he looks up.

'Right then, we'd better come up with some sort of a plan.'

'That was my plan,' I say.

'So a plan about a plan. That sounds like a plan.'

Resisting the urge to roll my eyes, I recover my notebook and pen. 'In addition to the library, we also have that lead from Lloid's bank statements to follow.'

'The place that was something to do with pain?'

'Sensual Pain.'

'It sounds like a fetish club.'

'You never know, maybe it's a support group for pigeon haters.'

'I live in hope,' Karrion says. 'Library first, then the club. That should keep us entertained for a bit.'

'I'd also like to speak to Tinker Thaylor about the mana gems we found in Lloid's office.'

Karrion grins. 'I'm never going to say no to a trip to One Magic Change. While we're there, remind me to pick up a few spell crackers for the brood.'

'Aderyn is going to love you.'

'I wasn't going to set them off inside. Contrary to the common belief, I'm neither stupid nor suicidal.'

I pay and we leave. The painkillers kick in as we reach the bus stop, and I sway. Karrion steadies me with a hand on my elbow. I preempt his concerned question with a reassuring smile.

Instead of going straight to the library, we take a detour to let Sinta out and feed her. My conscience twinges at having to leave her again, but I also feel guilty about asking Funja and Boris to look after her every day. I will have to investigate other dog-sitting options tonight.

Given that we are likely to continue our investigation until it is time to pick up Dearon, I opt to take my car as we return to the heart of Old London. After finding a parking spot, we cross the road and climb the marble steps of the Royal Exchange. Karrion pushes open the heavy door and we step inside. A small antechamber contains a cloakroom and signs to the loos. Another set of double doors leads to the library.

Light floods the tall atrium from windows set high above us. A dark reception desk sits opposite the entrance, and on both sides of a screen decorated to resemble a Turner painting, a reading area is visible. Glass walls separate the bookcases lining the perimeter across three floors. A few people are browsing the shelves, but I am surprised by the silence. Even the traffic noises from outside do not seem to penetrate the hushed quietude of this place of knowledge.

Behind the desk sits a small man with salt and pepper hair shading his large hazel eyes. His stubby fingers hover over the keyboard, as if our arrival has interrupted his typing mid-sentence. Dressed in a pristine suit jacket, white shirt, and a burgundy tie, he looks like he belongs in a bank rather than a library. Perched just behind his left shoulder is a large raven. As we approach, Karrion caws a greeting. The raven inclines its beak a fraction.

'Can I help you?' The man's soft, refined voice is just

221

loud enough to reach us. Pinned to his suit lapel is a tag that says "Fortnem". The scents of moss, frost and autumn leaves identify him as a North Mage.

'We're looking for a book about Leeches,' I say.

'Do you have a library card?'

'No.'

'About half of our books can be lent out, but the rarest texts and many of the powerful Mage ritual scrolls must remain here. If it's only general information about Leeches you are after, you can check the book out.'

While I deal with the formalities of applying for a library card, Karrion sidles closer to the raven. It clicks its beak in warning.

'I wouldn't go too near Masson if I were you,' Fortnem says. 'He doesn't like strangers touching him.'

'That's okay, I'm a Bird Shaman,' Karrion replies.

Fortnem does not look up from entering my details on the computer. 'Perhaps that might help you with an ordinary raven, but not with Masson.'

'What?' Karrion leans closer to Masson despite the warning glare from the bird. 'What is he then?'

'A servant nature spirit who has chosen to manifest in such a form.'

The idea of a Mage using a nature spirit as his servant feels wrong, but Fortnem speaks as if it's perfectly normal. I have heard rumours of Mages binding spirits to do their bidding, but as I have never encountered it, I assumed it was one of the many urban myths giving Old London an air of mystery. Has anyone ever tried to bend Wishearth to their will and did they walk away from the attempt unscathed?

'I didn't know spirits could choose their form,' Karrion says, bringing my attention back to the conversation.

'Certainly,' says Fortnem. 'They must manifest in a physical shape to interact with our world. Masson has been serving my family since the beginning of the eighteenth century.'

Karrion turns to me, a grin forming on his face. 'So Wishearth chooses to look middle-aged and a bit rough around the edges?'

'Wishearth?' Fortnem looks up with interest.

'Not important,' I hurry to say, uneasy. Instinct tells me to keep my friendship with a powerful Hearth Spirit a secret.

As if sensing my discomfort, Karrion returns to my side. 'Masson is looking pretty good for a three-hundred-year-old raven. Not a grey feather in sight.'

Fortnem's brow knits in irritation. 'I told you, he's not a raven. Spirits don't age like mortals do, but rather remain the same through the ages.'

'Is it easy to get a spirit to serve you?'

'Usually it takes a complex ritual to bind a spirit and a great deal of skill to bend them to a Mage's will. Only the oldest and most powerful families manage it.'

'Wouldn't it be easier to befriend a spirit instead?' Karrion asks.

Fortnem's irritation turns into confusion. 'Befriend a spirit? Why would any spirit choose the companionship of mortals?'

'I don't know.' Karrion stuffs his hands in the pockets of his leather jacket. 'Maybe they're bored or don't like drinking alone?'

'Spirits don't get bored,' Fortnem says angrily. 'And they certainly don't drink.'

Karrion looks like he wants to argue, but I silence him with a nudge of my knee.

223

'Fair enough,' he says, taking the hint.

'Here.' Fortnem passes me a library card. 'You're all set. The general lore about magical races is on the second floor. I'll show you.'

'Won't someone need to man the information desk?' Karrion asks, sounding a little too eager to avoid Fortnem's company.

'I am still here.'

It takes me a moment to realise that the hollow formal words come from Masson. His eyes are cold as they regard us. Something in his demeanour causes me to admire Fortnem's courage for spending all day with his back to Masson. The creature looks like he would enjoy pecking someone's eyes out.

'Great,' I say, stepping back.

Fortnem rises and shuffles around the desk. His gait is unsteady, and when I look down, I see that his left leg does not seem to bend at the knee. Although he walks slowly, his balance is good enough that he does not require a cane.

He leads us through a side door and up two flights of steps. A wall plan in the stairwell indicates that the rarest and most dangerous books are housed in a restricted area in the basement. I wonder if the library also supplies kits for setting up one's own demon-summoning circle, and I stifle a laugh.

On the second floor, we pass a narrow shelf containing books about humans and the deficiency that is their lack of magic. My amusement fades. I hope Jamie never sees these books.

At last we come to a section about past and present magical races. A few of the subsections catch my eye: Druids; Plant Shamans; Wyrmkin. Feykin have their place on the shelves, but the Fey are not there. They must have a category to themselves elsewhere. A brief glance along the shelves shows that Mages and Shamans have the greatest volume of texts. I crouch near the end. Two dusty volumes are crammed into a corner, the leather covers so faded I struggle to make out the titles. The first is called *The Winged Walkers; a Christian Myth or the First Race?* and the second *Beast Kin of Old*.

'I'll leave you to it,' Fortnem says. 'You can check the books out downstairs.'

As I stand up, my eyes drift to the reading room below. Masson rises from his perch. The expanse of his wings is more than twice that of an ordinary raven, and near the tips, the feathers pale to translucence. He circles the room once, causing alarmed looks from the people seated at their desks, and returns to his post.

'He creeps me out,' Karrion mutters, glancing over his shoulder.

'The man or the spirit?'

'Both.'

'You're not wrong.'

There are three books on Leeches. I pick one of them up at random and flick through it. There is far too much text for me to learn anything new while here. The best I can do is take all three books with me.

'I expected there to be more than this,' I say once my arm is laden with the books.

'Who'd want to write academic texts on creatures that are little more than monsters from legends, when they could be out there doing magic instead?'

'Some people must prefer books to spells.'

'Yes, but how boring is that?'

On our way back down, we pass a section on the history

225

of Old London. A title catches my eye, the silver words contrasting against a black cover: *Paths of the Forgotten*. The wording puzzles me, but I have more than enough mysteries to solve without delving into the riches of this library. There will be time for that later, or so I hope.

Fortnem checks the books out and tells me to bring them back in two weeks. Karrion rummages around his pockets and hands me a crummy shopping bag. I thank Fortnem, and as we leave I feel the penetrating stare of Masson at my back.

23

SENSUAL PAIN

It takes us nearly half an hour to find the address for Sensual Pain. We search every darkened doorway and back alley for an entrance flanked by burly bouncers and lit only by a purple light. Eventually, Karrion spots the number on a discreet silver plaque. A glass door leads to an airy reception area decorated in white. There are no seasonal garlands here; plants provide the only contrast of colour against the stark decor. Even the receptionist, with her platinum blonde hair and white trouser suit, looks bleached and faded, but the smile she offers us is warm.

'How may I serve you?'

Her turn of phrase throws me, and I hesitate.

'Do you prefer to suffer or to inflict suffering?' she asks, her gaze flicking from me to Karrion and back.

Regaining my composure, I clear my throat and show her my New Scotland Yard ID card. 'Could we speak to the owner of this place, please?'

'Of course.' She types on a tablet set into a recess within the desk. 'Please take a seat. Someone will be with you in just a moment.'

We have a choice between plastic chairs or a deep leather sofa. The mere sight of the former triggers an ache in my collarbones. As soon as I sit on the sofa, I regret my choice. The seat is wide and the cushions soft, causing me to sink backwards.

A middle-aged man in a grey suit walks in, a tall umbrella dangling from his arm. He greets the receptionist with a smile and swipes a white keycard through a reader set into the wall next to an internal door. The angle of the sofa is such that I cannot see beyond his disappearing back.

Another couple of minutes pass before the same door opens and a woman in a midnight-blue kimono steps into the reception area. Her high cheekbones and narrow eyes give her a vulpine air, and her chestnut hair is pinned up in a chignon. Although her features have been fashioned to look like those of a geisha, my first thought is that she is not Asian. With the heavy make-up, it is impossible to estimate her age. Her small feet are covered with white split-toe socks, and she stands on wooden platform sandals.

'Ms Wilde?' she says in a voice that resembles the sound of wind rustling the undergrowth. 'This way.'

I understand the reason for the sofa in the reception area when I struggle to rise, resorting to clutching the armrest with both of my hands. There is nothing graceful about the movement, and straight away, I feel at a disadvantage. Up close, I catch the subtle scents of rice fields, cherry blossoms, and blood. Although the combination is unfamiliar, there is no question as to what type of magical blood she possesses. She is Feykin. A master manipulator.

We follow her through the door, down a short corridor to a gilded lift. The only sounds are the swishing of silk and the tap of her shoes. Up close, I notice that the kimono is tied with a wide *obi* decorated with a lake scene of herons fishing.

When I moved to Old London, I had a brief relationship with a Japanese Monkey Shaman. She told me about the history of Japan and the geisha culture. More of the information must have stuck than I realised, for now I pick out all the details of the outfit. The make-up, the hairstyle, the style of the kimono, and the way the *obi* is tied all indicate that she is a fully fledged geisha rather than a *maiko* apprentice. But why the elaborate costume in the middle of Old London?

Inside the lift, the woman swipes a key card that appears from the folds of her long sleeves. Without her pressing a button, the lift begins to move, and it takes us to the top floor. There, the doors open directly to a large room. Lacquered cabinets and silkscreens painted with scenes of mountains, cherry blossoms, and shrines seem out of place in the middle of Old London. From somewhere within the room comes soft shamisen music. A low square coffee table sits to one side, surrounded by cushions.

A couple of feet in front of the lift doors, our host slips off her shoes. Without prompting, we follow her example. She walks to the side of the coffee table affording a view of the lift, and she sits, motioning for us to do the same. I choose the seat opposite her, while Karrion sits to my right. On the table is a wooden tray containing a small brown teapot and three cups. Tiny foxes decorate the tea set.

The woman still does not speak as she pours green tea into the cups. Her movement draws my attention to her hands, and I marvel how she can keep the long sleeves of the kimono dry as they sweep the table. The action may be mundane, but she is no less graceful than if she was dancing across a moonlit glade.

While the Feykin we met earlier filled me with dread, this woman has a different effect. All at once, she is a mother soothing me to dreamless sleep, a lover of great skill, the coolness of spring water on a hot day, and the tranquillity of a starry sky. Her power is no less, and indeed the subtleness of it makes her more dangerous because few would spot the trap before it closed upon them.

Heedless of my stare, she hands two of the cups to us. As they have no handles, I cradle mine in my palm as I take a sip. The tea is hot and strong, sending a thrum of energy through me. Karrion sniffs his cup suspiciously before drinking from it. He winces, indicating that the hot liquid burned his tongue.

'What's your name?' I ask when I run out of patience.

She smiles as if she has just scored a victory. There are silver flecks in her amber eyes.

'You may call me Mad-Aim.'

'Do you own this place?'

Topping up our cups, she takes her time. 'After a fashion.'

'And what is Sensual Pain?'

'A safe haven for those prepared to embrace their deepest urges. We cast no judgement upon our guests.'

'So it's a fetish club?' Karrion asks, impatience colouring his voice.

Mad-Aim arches an eyebrow. 'You say it like it's a bad thing.'

'Isn't it?'

'Here there are no sins, only desires as yet unfulfilled,' she says, eyes fixed on my lips. I cannot force myself to look away. 'Who am I to refuse those in need?'

Karrion runs a hand through his hair and tugs the

230

piercings on his ear. When he says nothing, Mad-Aim smiles.

'I assure you that what we do here is perfectly legal,' she says. 'The Paladins inspect the premises regularly. But we are discreet. I will not be giving up my client list, even to aid a Paladin investigation.'

'No need.' I shift to a more comfortable position on the cushions, my knees protesting, and she looks surprised for the first time. 'What we're after is information about one of your clients, whose identity we already know.'

'This client being?'

'Gerreint Lloid.'

Her expression betrays nothing. 'What is your interest in Mr Lloid?'

'His girlfriend was murdered in his flat and he has gone missing. We're trying to piece together his private life to gain insight into what may have happened and where he could have gone.'

'I see. What makes you think he was a member of this club?'

'His bank statements showed he was paying a regular monthly amount to you.'

'What is it that you would know?'

'That monthly standing order. What did it pay for?'

'The services of this place.' Mad-Aim sweeps her hand across the table, narrowly avoiding dipping the sleeve of her kimono in Karrion's teacup. 'What else?'

'What did the services entail?'

'Control or freedom. Suffering or pleasure. Control, freedom, pain and pleasure. They are all entwined, all roots of the same stem.'

'Was he a frequent visitor?' asks Karrion.

231

'Once a week. Sometimes more.'

'What did he do here?'

'That,' Mad-Aim says, 'is between him and his companion.'

I cast a warning glance at Karrion to get him to tamp down the irritation. 'It's important,' I say.

'Of course it is. Why else would you ask?'

'Please,' I say.

Mad-Aim's eyes flash with pleasure. I have just lost a point in the game we are playing, though I am uncertain of the rules or the desired outcome. A throb flares behind my left eye, and I long for the simplicity of the conclave life. What ever possessed me to think I could handle the politics and machinations of Old London, let alone thrive in the city? I am a wild animal, nothing more.

'Very well,' she says, to my surprise.

She slips her hand off the table, her attention briefly diverted down. Then she refills our cups once again. When I glance at the table, a fourth cup sits empty next to the teapot.

It takes no more than five minutes – five silent minutes – for the lift doors to open. My back is to them, and I twist around to see a figure executing a low bow. My eyebrows jump.

The woman is dressed in a fluffy pink robe and white bunny slippers. Her long blonde hair is tied up in pigtails, and she is carrying a lollipop in her hand. The red of it has stained her lips. She approaches, bows again, and seats herself at the table with a creak of leather that is at odds with her outfit. The scents of an East Mage drift across the table when she takes the offered cup of tea.

Mad-Aim introduces us to her. 'Crysthal, they would like to know about your sessions with Gerreint Lloid.'

Crysthal looks at Mad-Aim in astonishment and a silent exchange passes between them. Eventually, Crysthal nods.

'What would you like to know?' she asks in a broad East End accent.

'What was the nature of your sessions with Mr Lloid?' I ask.

'Submission.'

'His or yours?'

Crysthal's lips twitch as she exchanges a look with Mad-Aim. 'His, of course.'

'So he came here for what, exactly?' Karrion asks. 'Pretending to be someone's side table?'

'He came here to lose control. Nothing more, nothing less.'

'Was sex involved?'

'This is not a brothel.' Crysthal's eyes flash with anger that is also reflected on Mad-Aim's face.

'I'm sorry,' Karrion says. 'I didn't mean to offend you.'

There is a pause; a heavy silence which fills the room and steals away the oxygen. Finally, Crysthal nods.

'Was there anything unusual about Mr Lloid's sessions?' I ask.

Another pause follows while Crysthal tips back her teacup, then swirls the lollipop between her lips. 'He seemed desperate for punishment. While he never challenged my control over him, he begged me to treat him the way he deserved. Also, his visits were unusually vigorous.'

'In what way?'

'I was tired after the sessions. Drained, even.'

Karrion and I exchange a glance.

'Do you mean physically?' I ask. 'Or low on power?'

233

'Can you tell the difference?' Crysthal releases the lollipop with an audible smack.

'Yes.'

'Well, I can't. I was tired. There's no more to it than that.'

'What about Mr Lloid?' asks Karrion. 'Did the sessions have the same effect on him?'

'I haven't the foggiest. By the time I was done with him, he was a quivering mess on the floor.'

Hiding my expression behind the teacup, I try to imagine what Crysthal must have done for such an end result. My mind comes up blank.

'Do you know why he wanted to submit?'

'Why does anyone want to lose control?' It is Mad-Aim who answers the question, and I shift my focus to her. 'Only those brave enough to take the leap can appreciate the absolute freedom of relinquishing all power to someone else. Once you have done that, all of yourself is laid bare and you can truly understand who you are.'

'Do you use magic in any of your sessions?' I ask Crysthal.

'Rarely.'

'How about with Mr Lloid?'

'Not that I recall.'

'What about him?' Karrion asks. 'Did he ever cast spells in your presence?'

'I don't know what you think goes on here,' Crysthal says, 'but it's not a magical show-and-tell.'

Neither of us can think of anything else to ask, and I thank them. Mad-Aim rises in a move so fluid, it's as if her limbs are forest streams and skeins of spider silk. She extends her hand, and when her cool palm touches mine, I glimpse a flash of a crimson fox slinking through

234

shadows. I frown. The fox has more than one tail.

Heedless of my confusion, Crysthal rises with another creak of unseen leather. She bows to Mad-Aim. After only a brief hesitation, Karrion and I follow her example. Mad-Aim remains where she is while Crysthal leads us to the lift. The last things I see before the doors slide closed are Mad-Aim turning away and the curiously vulpine expression on her porcelain face.

'As entertaining as our chat was, feel free to be strangers,' Crysthal says as she presses a button for a floor beneath us.

'Why?' Karrion asks, irritated again.

'For one thing, I doubt either of you could afford to become a member. For another, just the fact that you had to ask proves that you don't belong here.'

She leaves before either of us has a chance to reply. The last we see of her are the bunny slippers and the series of bruises that travel up her calves and disappear beneath her robe.

'What did you—?' Karrion begins, but I shake my head. Although I cannot see a camera in the lift, I have no intention of comparing first impressions while inside the club.

Karrion seems to guess the direction of my thoughts, for he glances towards the ceiling and stuffs his hands in his pockets. I check my phone; our audience with Mad-Aim took less time than I expected.

A man enters the lift, dressed in a glittering blue robe adorned with silver stars. The hem brushes against the floor, revealing the tips of leather boots curling upwards. In his hand, the man carries a heavy wooden staff tipped with a glowing purple crystal, and a pointed hat matches the robes. His expression is sour as he glares at us.

'You'd think that if someone had a wizard fetish, they'd at least get a Mage to handle it,' he grumbles as the lift comes to a halt at another floor and he walks out again. He leaves the scents of grass and wool hanging in his wake.

Karrion waits just long enough for the lift doors to have closed before bursting out laughing. 'That poor man.'

'I'd say he's a wolf in sheep's clothing, but it's more that he's a Sheep Shaman in... actually, I don't know what that was.'

'Awesome is what it was. I hope he gets paid well for that level of humiliation.'

'You never know, he may get off on it,' I say.

'Judging by the look on his face, I don't think so.'

We leave the club in a lighter mood than we entered it, but as we walk through the doors, I cannot help glancing back. It is a structure of contradictions, of secrets and practices I cannot fathom. We are still in the dark about many things concerning Gerreint Lloid, and yet I feel as though I know him better than before. Whether that will help us find him remains to be seen.

24

MAGIC ON OFFER

'Is it time for us to head to the hospital?'

I check my phone again, although it has been no more than a minute or two since I last looked at the time on the screen.

'Not quite. We have time to visit One Magic Change first, given that the hospital is practically next door.'

My conscience twinges at the environmental impact of taking so many short car journeys, but today, convenience wins. We park as close to the hospital as we can and enter One Magic Change through a corridor of glass and steel, which is now flanked by two enormous Christmas trees. At the heart of the shopping centre, next to the stairs leading up, two Mages are passing flaming swords between them. After an unseen signal, they enact a short fight. Each time the blades strike together, coloured lights and rose-scented petals rain down on the enchanted audience. Children clap and cheer, while a group of tourists takes selfies in front of the Mages. Karrion rolls his eyes, but he says nothing as we climb the stairs and the atrium disappears from sight.

The smells of solder and ozone tickle my nose as Karrion pushes open the door to Tinker Thaylor's shop. Next to the door, bells chime once with the clear notes of a nightingale, then with the shiver of aspen leaves.

Upon hearing the chimes, Tinker Thaylor peeks through the enchanted bead curtain hiding the workshop from view, and smiles.

'Yannia, Karrion. This is an unexpected pleasure.'

The shop has changed since I was last there. Many of the smaller display cases are gone, replaced by a large machine that takes up most of the floor space. It looks like a giant version of an old-fashioned cash register, and the front bristles with levers and antennae. I cannot even begin to guess its function.

'Can you spare us a moment? I'd like to ask you a couple of questions about Mage magic and mana gems.'

'Of course. Hang on a moment.'

Thaylor disappears behind the curtain and returns moments later carrying three wooden stools. She sets them next to the shop counter and indicates that we should sit.

'Is it common for Mages to use mana gems?'

'Depends on the Mage,' Thaylor says, leaning against the side of the counter. 'Most keep a store of gems in case of an emergency. There are certain spells that require too much power for the majority of Mages to cast them without the help of artefacts. And there are some among us whose innate power reserves are so feeble, they are largely dependent on the gems.'

'Can any Mage create them, or does it require specialist skill?'

'All of us learn it as part of our education, but not everyone is prepared to put in the time and the power to create them. For some, most gems are beyond their means.'

'How so?' Karrion asks.

Thaylor adjusts the goggles that enlarge her already

enormous eyes. 'The vessel holds great importance. In theory, any solid object can receive raw power, but in most cases, it seeps out almost immediately. Only precious and semi-precious stones can hold magic indefinitely.'

'Hence they're called "mana gems",' I say.

'Exactly. The purer the stone, the better it stores power. But not every Mage can afford to buy diamonds and rubies just to squirrel away some extra magic.'

'Making it a hobby of the aristocrats,' Karrion finishes the thought.

'Yes, although, ironically, they are the ones least likely to bother creating gems themselves. It's easier to buy them from the likes of me and the other Mage shopkeepers at One Magic Change.'

'Are the different Mage powers separate?' I ask. 'Or can any Mage use them regardless of the creator's type?'

'Mage magic is Mage magic. It doesn't matter whether the gems were created by a Light or a South Mage.'

Karrion shifts, trying to get comfortable on the low stool. 'Can other spell casters use mana gems?'

Thaylor dips her hand into the large pocket in her pitted and stained leather apron and rummages around. When she withdraws her hand, a small amethyst rests on her calloused palm.

'Call a bird,' she says, and passes the stone to Karrion.

He stares at the gem, brow furrowing in concentration, but I sense no change in his aura. After a while, he exhales through pursed lips and looks up.

'As far as I can tell, it's just a stone.' He turns to me. 'You try.'

I take the offered mana gem. It is an irregular oval, with smooth edges and a polished surface. Where it rested against Karrion's palm, it feels warm. I unfurl my senses, searching for something beyond the physical presence of the stone. At first, it is no more significant than the stool I am sitting on. But as I open my awareness to the power running through everything around me, I find a spark at the centre of the gem. As far as I can tell, it's like an island surrounded by the sea: visible, but out of my reach. Yet there is something there, some connection to the web of power I almost see. If I can find the right thread, the right way to view the web, perhaps I can draw the magic out of the gem and set it free.

'Yan?'

Karrion's voice breaks my meditation, and I look up, becoming aware of my hunched shoulders and my face inches from my cupped hand.

'Sorry. Did you say something?'

'You've been staring at the stone for a couple of minutes, and I was starting to worry.'

'I'm fine,' I say, and pass the gem back to Thaylor. 'But I can't access the power.'

Thaylor puts the mana gem back in her pocket, but there is a searching gleam in her eyes as she regards me. 'As you can see, only a Mage can use them.'

'What about Leeches?'

'What about them?' Thaylor asks.

'Can Leeches use mana gems?'

'I don't see why they would. Besides, as far as I know, Leeches are all but extinct. I'm sure they have better things to worry about.'

'But if a Leech was able to access the power within the gems, how would the kind of spells they were able to cast be determined?'

Thaylor runs her fingers over a healing scab on the

back of her left hand as she thinks. With the leather apron and tunic, her grey hair and the goggles, she is like a cartoon insect that has come to life.

'I suppose they would take the power as it was put into the gem,' she says at last.

'A mana gem created by a North Mage would give them the power of a North Mage?'

Thaylor nods. It's as I expected. Lloid must have been careful in choosing the supplier of his gems to maintain the illusion that he was an East Mage.

'But all of this is academic,' Thaylor says. 'Leeches can't use mana gems.'

When neither Karrion nor I offer any reply, her shrewd eyes bore into mine.

'There's something you're not telling me.'

'Aren't PIs supposed to be mysterious and secretive?' I force a smile.

'Perhaps. But I'm beginning to wonder if you don't know of a Leech who has been using gems.'

'Didn't you just tell me it's impossible?'

'I did, but most Mages would tell you that it's impossible to identify a spell caster from the traces they leave behind, and yet I've created a machine that can do just that. Because I think something is impossible doesn't mean I can't change my mind.'

'You're a wise woman, Thaylor,' I say.

'It's not the confirmation I was hoping for, but I suppose it's the best I can squeeze out of you. Is there anything I can do to help?'

'When you sell mana gems, can you tell with each of them the type of Mage who created the stones?'

'Yes. For the most part, I charge them myself. But I keep a list of those who do it for me.'

241

'Do you ever get specific requests?' Karrion asks.

'As in, gems created by a Shadow Mage?' When Karrion nods, Thaylor shakes her head. 'Not that I recall.'

'The gems can be reused, can't they?' I ask, thinking about the spell detection machine Thaylor sold me. It's powered by mana gems.

'Correct.'

'Can a Mage use more than one stone at a time?' I am fairly certain I know the answer, having watched Lord Ellensthorne feed power into the ward separating him from Baneacre, but it pays to be thorough.

'Yes. It takes practice to draw magic from several external sources at once, but it's easy enough. After a while, it becomes second nature to us. For the most powerful spells, multiple mana gems are a necessity.'

'Thank you.' I stand, stretching my tired legs. The wound on my arm is aching. Karrion rises next to me, followed by Thaylor.

'You're welcome,' Thaylor says, a wry smile creasing the corners of her eyes. 'Perhaps one day you'll even tell me what these questions were all about.'

'I'll do my best.'

'While you're here, do you want to take the commission you ordered? I have it waiting in the back.'

'Please.'

Thaylor picks up the stools and disappears through the curtain.

'What did you order?' Karrion asks in a whisper.

I grin. 'That would be telling.'

'Have I mentioned that you're no fun?'

'Frequently.'

Thaylor returns with a parcel wrapped in brown paper and tied with string. I accept it with care, knowing how delicate each element is. But I need not have worried. Layers of cardboard and bubble wrap keep one of Thaylor's fine creations safe. All I need to do is make sure I keep the package out of reach until Christmas. I pay, and we leave.

'Do you mind if we stop downstairs?' Karrion asks.

'Not at all.'

Karrion leads the way to one of the small shops on the ground floor, little more than a large cupboard draped in reds and golds. My eyes water from the brightness. A round woman behind the counter looks up from a cross-word when we enter, and she smiles.

'Hello, Karrion. How wonderful to see you. How's the brood?'

'Finding their wings, thanks for asking. And in Wren's case, finding her voice too.'

'A bit of a nightingale, is she?'

'More like a screech owl.'

The woman winces and laughs. Karrion draws me forward.

'This is Amenda. I've been coming to her shop since I was old enough to open the door. Amenda, this is my boss, Yannia.'

'Yours must be the famous spell crackers Karrion is so fond of talking about.' We shake hands, and out of habit, I identify her as a South Mage.

'The very same. Mine last longer than most.' Amenda glances at Karrion. 'I take it that's why you're here?'

'I figured the goslings deserved a treat.'

'The phoenix ones?'

'Always. What's the point of a spell cracker if it can't fly?'

'The pegasi can fly,' Amenda says.

'A horse with wings? Where's the fun in that?'

I look around the shop while Amenda packs the crackers in a paper bag. There are a few spellbooks and scrolls for sale, but most of the items are intended for tourists. A collection of wands promises colourful smoke for up to fifteen minutes, while top hats have a magical compartment that allows the user to store a rabbit or a dove. There are balloons that shape themselves into animals, flashing confetti, napkins that make unwanted food vanish, and straws that change the flavour of the drink.

After I've spent a few moments marvelling at the sort of things people are prepared to spend money on, my attention is drawn to a series of small paintings on the wall. They all depict Old London landmarks, but the scenes are overlain by threads that connect everything – people, cars, buildings and trees – in an intricate web.

'What are these?' I ask when Karrion has paid.

Amenda joins me. 'They're depictions of how Mages view the world. A friend of mine painted them.'

I have never asked how a Mage sees the world, so now I am surprised to find that they perceive magic in a similar fashion to Wild Folk. We, too, sense the weave that connects all living things. In the wild country, the threads are thicker and stronger. Here in Old London, I barely sense them and I get no relief from what little natural power remains in the city.

Now I recall how I used wild magic to cast a circle, which has always been something reserved for Mages alone, and I wonder how much more overlap there is between Mages and my kind.

25

THE RELUCTANT PATIENT

We walk from One Magic Change to the hospital. Ten yards from the entrance, a lamp post twisted out of shape is covered in bouquets. Some of the blossoms change colour while I watch, but the jaggedness of the transformation suggests that the enchantment placed upon the flowers is fading. Just like the roses and tulips themselves, the cheap illusions cannot last forever.

Dearon is sitting on his hospital bed when we reach the ward. My steps falter. He looks out of place in the middle of a building filled with technology and human medicine. Instead of his usual vest, he is wearing a hospital gown over his leather trousers. The vest must have been ruined in the attack and the subsequent first aid.

He barely looks up when we approach. His eyes are dull and his head hangs low. Most of his right arm is covered in bandages, and I fancy I can just see the outline of more around his torso. At the back of his head there is a large plaster. An image of my fingers covered in his blood causes me to blink rapidly.

A nurse arrives with Dearon's discharge papers. Given that he is yet to acknowledge any of us, she gives me instructions on how to keep his wounds clean. After all the injuries I have sustained recently, I am well versed in ensuring stitches stay dry and don't burst. I voice none of this. When she tells me to make an appointment with Dearon's local surgery for regular check-ups, I have to bite my cheek to keep quiet. The only one Dearon will trust to oversee his recovery is the Wild Folk healer at the conclave. I hope he will accept Lady Bergamon's help, and I'll do my best to make sure he does.

When I lay a hand on Dearon's bare arm, he stirs and slowly raises his head. He blinks twice before his eyes focus on my face, and a frown forms between his eyebrows.

'Yannia?' he whispers in a voice that is hoarse from lack of use.

'Time to go home,' I say, lacing my fingers with his and tugging him off the bed. He obeys, and I have to grab him with both arms when he overbalances.

'Home?' The word is slurred with confusion and hope.

'My home here in Old London.'

Dearon says nothing as we lead him out of the hospital and to my car. He slumps in the seat, and I lean across him to fasten his seatbelt. After I do so, I twist around to look at Karrion.

'Could you do me a favour and buy Dearon a couple of T-shirts and a fleece? He didn't bring much with him, and I think he'd be more comfortable wearing something other than animal skins while he rests.'

'No problem,' Karrion says, and leans forward between the seats, casting an assessing look over Dearon.

'Thanks.' I give him my credit card.

'I'll see you later at your place?'

'Sure.'

Patting my shoulder, Karrion leaves. As I join the evening traffic, Karrion jogs across the road behind the car. Dearon's head lolls, and he is soon snoring.

Luck is on my side and I find a parking spot right

outside my front door. A white van is parked nearby, and its open back doors reveal a collection of furniture. The sound of a door opening draws my attention to the building. I watch as a middle-aged couple walks down the steps from the flat that used to belong to Jans, both smiling as they speak in low voices. When I step out of the car, they stop and look at me with interest.

'Are you moving in?' I ask, hiding my rising tension by forcing a smile.

'Yes. Are you a neighbour?' the woman asks.

'I live in the flat below you,' I say, and nod towards the stairs for good measure.

'Nice to meet you. This is Drake and I'm Lyn.'

I introduce myself, and we shake hands. As we do so, I borrow Sinta's nose. The smells of warm scales, dry skin, and serpents overpower all else. They are both Snake Shamans. Some of the tension leaves my body.

After a minute or two of small talk, I take my leave and walk around the car to help Dearon out. He follows me without a word, and his obedience unnerves me more than any number of insults could. This is not the normal Dearon – *my* Dearon – and the thought threatens to force me to examine feelings I am not yet ready to confront. I choose to focus all my energies on making sure we survive the steps down without falling, and I do the same inside.

Sinta greets us with enthusiasm. I leave Dearon leaning against the wall while I lift Sinta outside and tidy up the accident she has had in our absence. While she barks at a pigeon and leaps at the low branches of the blackcurrant bush, I lead Dearon to the bed and draw back the covers. He offers no help when I peel off the hospital gown and unlace his trousers. Although I have seen him naked several times, I avert my eyes as I undress him and guide him to lie on the side of the mattress nearest to the fireplace. He shivers, and while I cannot feel the cold, I draw the blankets over him and build a fire.

'Hearth Spirit, the protector of the home and the guardian of the weary, see us through another winter night safe and sound.' I let go of the offering. 'And could you let Lady Bergamon know that we would welcome a visit from her?'

The flare of flames is muted, but the heat caresses my cheek briefly. I close my eyes. It would be easy to pretend I was alone in my home, communing with Wishearth like I always do, or that it was just Dearon and me here. Both of them in the same space is an equation that does not balance. I am in the middle, drawn first one way and then another, never quite at peace.

Whimpering from the garden draws me from my introspection. I lift Sinta in and close the window. Tucked at the back of my freezer is a container of chicken soup, and I set it in the microwave to defrost while I look through Dearon's medication. I doubt I can persuade him to continue taking antibiotics once the sedatives wear off, but perhaps I can crush the pills and hide them in mugs of tea, at least for a day or two.

When the soup is warm, but not hot, I carry a bowl to the mattress. Dearon seems stuck somewhere between asleep and awake, and I struggle to rouse him. When nothing else works, I pull him up long enough to sit behind him so his head rests on my shoulder. The position reminds me of Wishearth holding me on the same spot, but I banish the memory by coaxing Dearon to take small spoonfuls of soup. Some of the liquid dribbles down his neck, and I dab it away with a tea towel. Once the bowl is empty, I lay him back down and get more soup.

I sit on the hearth stones, the fire all but scorching one side of my body, and alternate between watching Dearon and the flames. He looks peaceful; the lines on his forehead smoothe out, giving him the appearance of a man a decade younger. It has never occurred to me to wonder whether he is burdened by his role as the future Elderman, but I recall a time when the only lines on his face were caused by laughter.

We are no longer the children who would escape to the woods and hide from the chores the Elders gave us, choosing instead to fill the days by watching the squirrels leaping through the branches, the hen harriers wheeling and diving, the caterpillars eating through nettle leaves, and the steady progression of cirrus clouds across the sky. Life was simple back then because there was no future beyond an endless line of days filled with adventure and the simple pleasure of being together.

Now those carefree children are gone, replaced by two adults who never seem to know how to speak to one another. We choose silence instead, or venomous barbs, or sex, but none of them achieves anything beyond keeping us locked in a holding pattern. Yet as I look at him now, my heart yearns for the boy he once was and for the honesty of childhood. We have lost too much, left behind too many good things that once defined who we were.

What are we now, together and separate, other than pieces that no longer fit, forming a picture neither of us recognises?

The front door opens below me, and I track Karrion's ascending steps. Sinta growls, but I silence her by picking her up and setting her on my crossed legs. She huffs a protest and lies down. Karrion steps in, a greeting on his lips, but upon seeing Dearon's still form, he raises his hand instead. I take the bag he offers. He has bought Dearon three T-shirts, a green fleece, a pack of white sport socks, and a pair of tracksuit bottoms.

'Thanks,' I whisper.

'Shall we get back to work?' he asks, keeping his voice low.

In response, I yawn. He chuckles, and the sound settles a restless, uncertain part of my being. Sinta reaches to lick the side of my wrist.

'No. Go home,' I say. 'We can pick up the investigation tomorrow morning.'

'Okay.' He approaches and squeezes my shoulder.

I wait for the soft sound of the closing door before I ease Sinta off my lap and put away Dearon's new clothes. After washing the dishes, I am debating whether to check my emails when the doorbell rings. Sinta howls, then looks at me. I shake my head, scoop her up, and hurry to open the door.

Lady Bergamon stands in the gloom of the winter evening, this time dressed in a grey fur-trimmed cloak. She is carrying the basket without which she never seems to leave her house. I step aside and take her cloak.

'I appreciate you coming so quickly.'

'Of course. I knew to expect Wishearth's call.'

Upstairs, she kneels next to Dearon without a word and folds the blankets across his hips so his torso is exposed. Dark bruises spread from under the bandages, which look at odds with his tanned skin. Lady Bergamon strokes her fingers down a bruise, and Dearon shifts in his sleep.

'Tell me about his wounds,' she says.

'His arm took the worst damage and has a series of deep cuts from the Wild Folk's claws. The wounds on his chest are shallower. He also hit his head when he fell.'

At Lady Bergamon's instructions, I hold Dearon's head up so she can examine the wound there. When she nods, I rest his head down gently.

'The hospital has done well in first aid,' she says, 'but the difficulty will be keeping him still long enough for the wounds to heal. His arm is a particular concern of mine as significant scarring there can impede hunting. Your kind are not like wolves, where the strongest leads, but he will need his full abilities to command the respect of the conclave.' Lady Bergamon's eyes flicker to me. 'Or your respect.'

I frown at the implication. 'I wouldn't think less of him if he didn't make a full recovery.'

'Yet you fear that is how he feels towards you.'

'I've never told you that.'

'You didn't have to, my dear. It's quite clear in the way you choose to live your life. What you fear most is pity, especially from those you love. You accept help, albeit grudgingly at times, but will not tolerate people feeling sorry for you, certainly not someone like Dearon. What you cannot see is that when he accepts all of you, that includes the illness and the pain. They are part of what defines you. Having to live in pain has placed great restrictions on your life, but it has also fuelled your determination, your stubbornness to find a place in a hostile environment. Many, those ungalvanised by the fires of pain, would have given up long ago.'

My field of vision wavers, and I sit next to the mattress, hugging my knees close to hide the tremor in my hands. Soft fingers stroke the hair away from my face.

'Do you know what concerns me?' Lady Bergamon asks, and I shake my head. 'That you are so used to fighting and pushing through the pain and adversity,

251

you'll lose sight of how to stop fighting. Forcing yourself to continue will not give you peace. Only accepting your achievements as enough will.'

Her words remind me of Obeajulu's prophecy. *You have the courage to find your path, but in order to find peace, you must look beyond courage.* How can Lady Bergamon, who knows nothing about the impromptu fortune-telling session, mirror Obeajulu so closely? Or is it only me who seems to be stumbling blindly through the days and weeks in Old London?

'I guess I'll need to work on that.'

My words are a deflection, and when Lady Bergamon twists her lips, I know she realises it too. But she does not press the point. A rush of gratitude envelops me. She has more wisdom than I can ever appreciate, but it's her generosity that touches me the most. Yet, it would be foolish to promise I will do as she says when I do not fully understand what that entails. With every aspect of my life being a struggle, how can I stop fighting without giving up?

'I prepared a salve for you to put on the wounds when you change Dearon's bandages,' Lady Bergamon says, reaching into her basket, and I force my focus back on her. 'This second jar contains an unguent that's good for easing the soreness of bruises. Finally, I've brought a pain-relieving tea for him. Make sure you keep it separate from your usual mixture. This one contains extra ingredients that will make him drowsy and hopefully speed up his recovery. The more he rests, the cleaner his wounds will heal.'

'Thank you.' I take the jars. 'Is your tea safe to mix with antibiotics?'

'Yes, though I'd add extra honey to mask the taste.'

'That was my plan.'

'Good. If his condition worsens, call me immediately.'

'Of course. Is there anything I can give you in return for your medicine?'

Lady Bergamon strokes my cheek with her smooth, rough, soft fingers. 'I owe you more than even a lifetime of healing can repay. While I appreciate the sentiment, stop asking.'

'Okay. Thank you.'

'You've said that often enough already.'

'Right. Sorry.'

Huffing her exasperation, Lady Bergamon stands. After pausing to pet Sinta, she heads for the door. I follow her down and drape the cloak over her shoulders. She turns to press a fleeting kiss on my cheek and leaves without a word. I watch her go until the breeze forces me to move for fear of Dearon getting cold. While the pain in my legs has grown worse, I am beyond feeling a chill.

The kettle boils while I feed Sinta. I brew a cup of pain-relieving tea from separate jars for both Dearon and me, adding crushed antibiotics and two extra spoonfuls of honey to his. By the time I have taken my evening medication and finished my mug, his tea has cooled enough that I can spoon it into his mouth.

When I return upstairs after brushing my teeth, his brow is furrowed and his hands clench the blankets. Perhaps the sedatives have worn off and he is feeling the pain of his many wounds. I stroke his hair, but it has no effect on his agitation. I recall a song my mother used to sing when I was ill or frightened. My voice is reedy, rusty from lack of practice, but I soon recall the tune and the words. I sing of the full moon watching over the weary travellers, of the fire keeping them warm through the hours of darkness, of the stars that contain the legends of the universe. The next song is about sunlit days, of hidden glades, and moss-clad trees, where the Fey revel and the Wild Folk commune with the spirits of nature. My third song recounts the paths of our lives, the choices we make, and how the threads of the trails always bring us together, always bring us home.

I sing until the lines of worry on Dearon's face fade into the smoothness of sleep, and I carry on singing until the terrible absence of my mother freezes the words in my throat. The tears that brim in my eyes never fall, but my whole being aches to be in my mother's arms, to ask her advice on so many things. I'm not sure where I would even begin.

But my mother is gone, and I have no choice but to hug Sinta until the turmoil of emotion stills into a pool of loneliness. Standing up on achy legs, I switch off the lights until only the flicker of flames remains. When I crawl under the blankets, Sinta clambers over the pillow to take her place, nestled against the crook of my neck.

She would be good for me, Wishearth once promised, and he was right.

I stare at Dearon, asleep on my bed, and try to imagine a future where he lives here with me, where we are partners. But it's a fantasy, nothing more. Is that even what I want, or is the idea of him being part of my Old London life a mere product of seeing him hurt and vulnerable?

The darkness of the room and the glowing embers of the dying fire offer no answers, only more questions. I force my eyes shut, knowing that I will need my rest. But even now, when nothing is certain and my thoughts are in constant turmoil, I cannot help reaching for Dearon's hand.

TUESDAY

26

WATCHED

I wake up long before dawn to a cold and dark flat. Dearon is pressed against my back and Sinta is sprawled next to the mattress, all four paws in the air. Despite the nagging pain in my hip, I lie still for a moment, simply listening to the two breaths stroking the silence of the room. This is how it feels, not waking up alone.

Soon the pain forces me up and I ease out from under the covers without waking Dearon. Sinta scampers to her feet, and I let her outside before getting dressed. Only ash remains in the fireplace. Moving as quietly as I can, I make space for a new fire and whisper a dedication to Wishearth. A bowl of natural yoghurt, mixed seeds, and chopped mango serves as my breakfast, and I leave the coffee until later.

Something about the early morning stillness permeates my being. I leave my laptop where it is, charging on top of the side table, and pull the first library book from my bag. The title is *The History of Leeches*, which seems like a good starting point for my research. The leather cover is shiny and the edges of the pages yellowed, but otherwise the book doesn't look like it has been read often. I move around so that the firelight illuminates the pages, and I begin to read.

"The origins of the Leech are shrouded in mystery. Some claim that it is the most recent of the magical races and that its beginnings hark back to Medieval Europe, where the first Leeches were followers of Vlad the Impaler. They drank the blood of the impaled victims, thereby giving rise to the vampire mythology, and found a way to absorb power from the blood. Others say that there were once such things as Leech Shamans, whose quest for blood and greater power led them to embrace the darkest of practices. What such practises may be, one can only speculate.

"Of all the rumours and supposed facts we know about the Leeches, the only certain thing is that they are the most elusive and perhaps the rarest of all the magical races, barring such extinct types as Plant Shamans and Wyrmkin. Even when one manages to track down a Leech, persuading them to share their origin stories and racial mythology is difficult, to say the least. On more than one occasion, the author was left with the impression that they do not know for certain themselves."

I skim the rest of the chapter and select passages from later parts of the book at random. The author appears to have spent a couple of hundred pages talking around the fact that he has no idea where Leeches come from and the ones he was able to track down either do not know themselves, or refused to tell him. Before I grow too frustrated, I set aside the book and pick up the second one, again flicking through the pages without reading them properly.

A section heading catches my eye, and I pause.

"A Leech is a creature driven by hunger. It is not hunger as most people understand it – the need for nourishment and the pleasure of food and drink – but rather an all-

consuming obsession that dominates every aspect of a Leech's life. One man described eating until he vomited without ever feeling the slightest relief from the ache gnawing at his insides. A Leech's hunger is stronger than any other impulse, stronger at times than even their survival instinct. That is why, when a Leech feeds, the risk of killing their victim is high. They are lost in a feeding frenzy and cannot control the desire to have just a bit more magic.

"Even when a Leech is able to rein in their impulses and take a little power from their victim, this can only be temporary. Feeding for them is like a growing addiction. Sooner or later, they will need more than is safe to take and they will resort to draining their victims dry. In that sense, they are like the vampires of popular culture. Ultimately, as beings of instinct and hunger, Leeches must, and will, kill."

Setting the book down, I stare at the grey light creeping across the sliver of sky visible through my window. The words in the book bother me. Not for their sensationalist tone, but because I feel as though there is subtext. I spend the next half hour skimming the chapters, but the feeling persists.

The book implies that while Leeches can walk and talk and dress like the rest of the population, they are little more than savages prepared to commit murder to satisfy their base urges. Everything in the book is at odds with what I know of Gideor Braeman and Gerreint Lloid. Even Jans kept up the pretence of civility to a great extent, until the combination of a Wild Folk and a North Mage became too much for him to resist.

Could it be that Leeches are masters of hiding in plain sight? Perhaps those interviewed for the books lied to protect the secrets of their kind. Or could it be that there are two distinct subtypes of Leeches: the wild predators driven by their hunger, and the masters of disguises and false identities so in control of themselves that they can store Mage power and learn to cast spells?

Is there a difference between the way the book described Leeches and how most people in Old London view Wild Folk? While we are not seen as outright killers, the consensus seems to be that all Wild Folk are uncultured savages. Perhaps all this book is good for is highlighting the difference between perception and reality.

My head aches, and I regret the earlier decision not to make myself a coffee. Before I have a chance to close the book and stand up, Dearon stirs. He raises his injured hand to rub his face and grimaces when the wounds catch. I press my fingers against his shoulder, and he blinks in an attempt to focus on my face.

'Take it easy. You've been asleep for a long time.'

'Where am I?' he asks, his voice hoarse.

'Back at my place. Still in Old London.'

'There were humans. And Paladins. They stuck needles in me.'

'You were in a hospital. Your wounds needed stitches and they were concerned about a concussion.'

'I'm fine,' he says, the stubbornness in his voice reminding me of the Dearon I am used to.

'Sure you are. A few herbs can definitely heal deep wounds and possible swelling in your brain.'

Dearon frowns. Fatigue tempers his irritation, but only a little. I regret my sarcasm. Why can I not be civil to him even for a moment? My experiences in Old London have proven that I am as capable of compassion as the next person, but it all seems forgotten whenever I am near Dearon.

'Are you hungry?' I ask, hoping he will accept the implied apology.

'Yes.'

'How is the pain?'

He shrugs as much as he is able to lying down. From his expression, I know his first instinct is to say that he is fine, but he pauses. Perhaps he is thinking along the same lines as I am: this brief cohabitation will be far more tolerable if we rein in the impulse to argue all the time.

'It's not so bad at the moment, though my arm aches.'

'Lady Bergamon dropped off a mix of pain-relieving tea she prepared for you. I'll make you a cup.' When he looks like he is going to argue, I hurry to add, 'It contains only natural ingredients. Her healing is all plants, not human medicine.'

'Fine.' Dearon nods. 'Thank you.'

I help him to stand and support him down the stairs. While he's in the bathroom, I fill the kettle and put bread in the toaster. I wish I had eggs to fry, but out of respect for Karrion, I make a point of not buying eggs in Old London. Dearon will have to settle for toast.

Breakfast is ready when he returns to the lounge. He insists on sitting up while he eats and settles cross-legged on the mattress. I bring him a plate and a mug, and he murmurs a thank you.

After a few bites, Dearon sets his plate down. 'The Wild Folk. She's a woman.'

'I know. I caught her scent when she attacked you.'

'Did you find her?'

'No. Karrion and I couldn't track her, not while we were carrying you to an ambulance. When we were done, she had too much of a head start.'

'We can't just let her go.'

'I'm aware of that,' I say. With a deep breath, I soften my tone. 'We're trying to figure out where she came from and who she is. That should give us a better idea of why she was eating a child in Hertfordshire. She wouldn't have ventured so far from our lands for a snack.'

'If you want to find out which conclave she belongs to, you're going to have to talk to the Elderman.'

'Actually, I was hoping you'd do that for me. It's more your area than mine.'

Dearon looks surprised by my admission, but says nothing. The press of his mouth softens, leaving me with a desire to kiss him. I resist the temptation and pass him a slice of toast from my plate.

'But to engage in Wild Folk diplomacy, you're going to have to recover from your injuries. So eat up and drink your tea.'

By the time we have finished our breakfast and Dearon has drunk a mug of antibiotic-laced tea, his eyelids are drooping. I add a log to the fire and wash the dishes. Dearon is asleep when I return to the lounge. I curl up on one of the armchairs with my laptop. Jamie has forwarded me several emails from different police forces in the country. Taking a sip from my second mug of coffee, I open the first email and read.

The dawn has paled to a ragged cloud front when Sinta's growl draws me away from the computer. She is standing by the lounge window, ears up and tail stiff. At first I think she is asking to go out, but there is something in her body language that conveys alarm and outrage. Opening the window, I lift her out. She shoots off across the small lawn, howling and heading for the bushes by the woodshed. While this is not the first time she has chased pigeons and cats – real or imagined – from the garden, I cannot shake the feeling that something is different.

When Sinta does not reappear within a minute, I find my garden shoes and follow her out. The growling leads me to the shadows behind the shed, where Sinta alternates between sniffing at the ground and leaping against the brick boundary. My appearance elicits little more than a cursory glance and a brief pause in her growling.

'What's wrong?' I ask. Part of me feels foolish to be asking questions of a dog, but in the past weeks, I have fallen into the habit of talking to Sinta. She is yet to respond, however, and this morning is no exception.

I crouch to inspect the ground. Beneath mouldering leaves and the debris of the seasons, a few impressions in the earth catch my eye. They are small and no deeper than half an inch. Sinta's scampering has shifted the leaves enough that had I not been looking for anything out of place, I would have missed them. But there is no mistaking the partial boot prints. They show only the front half of the foot, where someone landed next to the wall with every attempt at stealth, and another set facing the other way, when they leaped on to the wall to get away. My thoughts flash to Fria, who has spied on me in the past, but I am certain I would find no trace of her. She is a professional.

There is one further detail that convinces me of the identity of the intruder: none of the prints shows any sign of treads.

A Wild Folk was in my garden.

Given that I know of only two Wild Folk in the city – Dearon and me – my stealthy visitor would almost certainly have been the woman we were tracking in Hertfordshire.

The boundary wall is tall, but not beyond my reach. Calling upon the agility of a squirrel, I grasp the top of the bricks and pull myself up to an awkward perch. To my left runs the alley separating my row of terraced houses from the next. The alley cleaves the series of gardens in two. In front of me and to my right are the tiny back gardens of houses just like mine. Most of the fences are wood panels, but not all. From my vantage point on top of the wall, I can see a good distance, but there are plenty of hiding places in the gardens. The only movement I see is a cat sitting by a back door, licking its paw.

If the Wild Folk did visit my garden, she is gone now. But why was she here? And why, of all the places she could have gone, is she in Old London? To get here, she'd have had to travel through areas filled with humans. What would drive a Wild Folk to go against all of her instincts?

I lower myself down and stop, my hand against the cool bricks. The question is wrong. To attack people, she has already gone against the strongest of Wild Folk instincts. I try to imagine what could drive me not just to leave my conclave, but to resort to cannibalism. Nothing comes to mind. My thoughts keep turning back to a different question: why is she in Old London?

Sinta's growling has subsided since I gave the situation my full attention. I praise her quietly. Her guard instincts are better than mine, and once again, I recall Wishearth's promise that she would be good for me.

Another question keeps me rooted to the spot in the shadow of the shed. How did the Wild Folk know where to find me? There is no way she could have tracked me here from St Albans. Even a Wild Folk as powerful as Dearon would have struggled to keep up with a car. How then did she do it? Did she rely on the fact that I am the only Wild Folk living in Old London? But how could she have been certain I lived in the city? Something about the equation does not add up; there is something I am missing. If only I knew what that something was.

My phone vibrates in the back pocket of my jeans. I fumble for it, my fingers stiff from a cold I cannot feel, and I see Jamie's name on the screen. We exchange pleasantries before the purpose of the call becomes apparent: he is ringing for an update on the Lloid case.

While I coax Sinta away from the woodshed, I recount everything Karrion and I did yesterday. Determined to keep my promise of sharing everything with Jamie, I hold back nothing, including our speculation that Lloid visited Sensual Pain to steal power from an East Mage. Jamie asks a few questions to clarify details, but otherwise he listens to my account without interrupting.

'That all sounds interesting,' he says once I have finished. 'But I can't see how any of it is going to help us find Lloid.'

'I'm not sure it will. But what's quite clear to me is that there's more to the case than it seems. Everything I've heard about him and Leina makes me think that he didn't kill her.'

'You may be right.'

'Did the forensics come back with conflicting evidence?' I ask, catching his troubled tone.

'Not a lot. The bathroom was completely clean, though that's no surprise given how strong the smell of bleach was. All the fingerprints collected belonged to Lloid or Leina, except for the heart copper warding token Karrion found behind the bedside cabinet. That print came back as unknown.'

265

'It could belong to whoever created the token.'

'I agree,' Jamie says. 'Except that if Lloid or Leina set the ward, I would have expected to find their prints overlapping the unknown one. Also, we didn't find any other tokens anywhere in the flat. You need more than one to set up a ward, even I know that much. So where were the rest?'

A brief smile lifts the corner of my mouth. 'Now you're beginning to sound like me.'

'That's because I think you're on to something. There's more. Mery delivered her report and the flat contained all the permanent wards you'd expect, plus a few extras. Given everything you told me on Sunday, I checked the list of wards against those around Braeman's study. I'm sure it won't surprise you to hear that the two lists were identical.'

'It's what I expected. But that in itself doesn't prove a lot. I'd expect most aristocrats to have similar warding in place.'

'True. Mery said that the heart copper token was used most recently for a silence ward, which is odd given that the walls contained a permanent one. Whoever brought that token to Lloid's flat intended to make sure they had the right ward.'

Warding tokens are split into two different types: some that are nothing more than discs cast from a metal of power – heart copper, true silver, or cold iron – which anyone with knowledge of protection magic can use to raise a ward. I used to believe only Mages and Paladins had the power to do so, but Wishearth taught me otherwise. To cast the simplest of protections, a circle, all one needs are foci and magical blood. The second type caters for those not wishing to create their own wards. Packs of tokens pre-enchanted with a ward are available. They require a word of power to activate and tend to be single-use. Once the ward is broken or it lapses after a set time, the enchantment fades away, leaving only the tokens behind.

Including metals of power in the construction of walls and doors makes it possible to create permanent wards that can be raised and lowered without terminating the magic. Some work with a small object, others with a password. Even people with little or no power can control wards with a linked object.

'Assuming someone other than Lloid murdered Leina, they would have wanted to make sure no one could hear what was going on in the flat. Unless they had scouted the flat and its permanent wards beforehand, they wouldn't have known for sure that one of them was for silence. More than that, they couldn't rely on Leina divulging the correct password.'

'I suspect you're right. There were a couple of other points of note we've discovered.'

'Do tell.'

Papers rustle in the background. 'First of all, we did more digging into Lloid's finances. Turns out he was pretty much broke five years ago, right before the payments from the trust began. A month later, he became the assistant of one of the East Mage Council members. A year on, he was on the Council.'

'It sounds like the trust changed his life,' I say, no longer surprised.

'His finances aren't the only thing that's changed. It took some tracking, but he was living under a false name in Old London. His false identity was expertly created and must have cost him a pretty penny. In the end, we found out his real name by comparing his dental records from Old London with the wider database.'

'So who is he?'

'His real name is Geraint Davies and he was born and raised in a small village outside of Cardiff. We contacted his parents, but they haven't heard from him in over ten years. They had no idea he'd changed his name or that he was living in Old London.'

'Do you believe them?'

'Yes, I think they were telling the truth. But there's something else interesting there. His parents swore they're human.'

The next question dies on my lips as I consider this revelation. Could two humans birth a Leech? Or is one of Lloid's parents lying about their nature? If his parents are lying about this, could they be lying about everything else? And if they are a family of Leeches, why would Lloid have cut all ties over a decade ago? It stands to reason that if he was trying to live in Old London while keeping his identity hidden, he would need all the help and advice he could get.

'It sounds like your reaction is pretty much the same as mine,' Jamie says. 'I don't get it either.'

'Assuming we believe them, it's unlikely Lloid would have gone there. Though it wouldn't hurt to check to be sure.'

'I've asked the local constabulary to do that. They reported no sighting of Lloid anywhere in the village. While it's not conclusive proof that he's not there, at least everyone will be on the lookout for him.'

'True. We can leave the question mark over his origins aside for the moment. What else did you find?'

'We contacted the Igneous Wealth Management people

in charge of those standing order payments. They couldn't tell us anything without a court order and it's looking unlikely we'll get one.'

'Why?'

'The payments have gone on for years, so it's going to be hard to prove that they are connected to the murder.'

'Damn. We needed that information to figure out who the other two Leeches are.'

'I'll keep trying, but without new evidence, that line of inquiry may have run its course. Another possibility is contacting the trustees of the Cuckoo Trust, though I'd expect a similar answer there. I'll give it a shot anyway.'

'Thanks, Jamie. Was there anything else you found out?'

'Let me see.' He goes through the papers again. 'The fingerprints on the whip that was used to strangle Leina were smudged, but all the ones we were able to identify belonged to her or Lloid.'

'Meaning either Lloid did it or the killer wore gloves.'

'Yes. Also, and this is rather strange, Leina called in sick on Sunday morning, saying she had food poisoning and wouldn't come to the office on Monday and a few days after.'

'Are you sure it was her?' I ask.

'The law firm gave us the recording from their automated absence line, and we compared it to an interview she gave about capoeira a few years ago. It was definitely her.'

'So whoever was holding her prisoner forced her to make that call. Why?'

'My best guess is so she wouldn't be missed for a few days longer. And perhaps to give the impression that all was normal on Sunday morning.'

'Is it just me or does it feel like there's an elaborate double bluff going on here?' I ask. 'Lloid disappeared on Friday, Leina called in sick on Sunday and died shortly afterwards. Who knows, that call may have been the last thing she did before she was killed. I just can't get my head around it all.'

'Yeah, it's weird,' Jamie says.

There is a pause in the conversation, which I use to tickle Sinta's side. She huffs and totters away. A glance back towards the shed reminds me of something else I wanted to ask Jamie.

'Have there been any further reports of people going missing that could be related to the Wild Folk we're trying to track down?'

'No, but I'd only get a call if the victim had magical blood. Don't forget that people go missing in the UK every day for all sorts of reasons.'

'What about in Old London?'

'Given the smaller population, that's a different story.' I hear the sound of fingers tapping a keyboard. 'No one has been reported missing in the past two days.'

'Good.'

'What makes you think she'll be heading to Old London?' Jamie asks. 'It seems unlikely for a Wild Folk, present company excepted.'

I hesitate, but choose the truth. 'Because I think she was in my back garden less than an hour ago.'

Jamie swears. 'How could she have found you?'

'That's what I'd love to know.'

'Is Karrion coming over?'

My temper flares at the implication, but I keep the angry retort to myself. This is not the first time Jamie has implied that I need Wishearth and Karrion to keep me safe.

'He was always going to. We have work to do on the two cases.'

A silence follows. Perhaps Jamie is taken aback by the sharpness of my tone. My head aches and I cannot bring myself to care.

'Right. Good. Keep in touch with any progress you make.'

It is only after we have ended the call that my conscience twinges. I was unfair, taking my frustrations and fears out on Jamie. If we are going to keep working together, I have to learn to be more professional.

I call Sinta to me and carry her in. Dearon is still asleep. Shivering, I look around my home. I have regained the sense of safety I lost when Jans broke in, but now the cold room has an inhospitable feel that even the bright flames cannot dispel.

As if sensing my thoughts, the fire and sparks rise and warp into a face. Wishearth's brow is furrowed and his black eyes are devoid of his usual mirth.

'Yannia, watch out. Something wild is stalking you.'

27

PATTERNS OF DEATH

Karrion knocks before he enters, no doubt worried about repeating the eyeful of naked Dearon from the other day. I am still staring at the fireplace. The flames have returned to normal, but Wishearth's warning haunts me. Did he watch the Wild Folk sneaking into my garden, or does he know something I don't? I wanted to ask him that, and much more, but he was gone before I could utter a single word.

'What's wrong?' Karrion asks when I offer no greeting.

Shaking myself from my reverie, I make more coffee. Karrion has brought his mother's homemade carrot rolls filled with ham and cheese. Aderyn still seems to think that I cannot feed myself without her aid. Given the emptiness of my fridge, she may be right. While we prepare breakfast, I tell Karrion in a low voice everything that has happened this morning. His expression grows darker the further my story progresses, until I mention Jamie's concern about Karrion coming to protect me. Then, Karrion rolls his eyes and his shoulders relax.

'Jamie's a moron,' he says.

'A little bit, though he means well. I was a bit rude in my response.'

'I hope he learned his lesson.'

'Assuming he knows what the lesson was.'

'Yeah, there's that.'

When my tale is finished, we sit in the armchairs in the lounge. I let Karrion digest all the information while he consumes two of the rolls. Dearon shifts on the bed, but does not wake up.

'Where do we start?' Karrion asks when he has finished eating.

'Even if the Wild Folk has travelled to Old London, we still need to figure out who she is and why she's killing people. Let's start by working through my emails and see if the collective police force of England has come up with the goods. I've already gone through a few of them, but we have a lot of reading ahead of us.'

'Should we head downstairs? We may need to print stuff and we'll disturb Dearon if we're comparing notes here.'

'Good idea.' I pick up the laptop and my coffee, while Karrion leads the way. Once the door is closed, I voice what I did not dare say in front of Dearon. 'Though he may already be disturbed.'

Karrion snorts, splashing some of his coffee on his hand. He curses, and while I switch on the heater in the office, he wipes the coffee off the stairs.

My inbox has thirty unread emails from different constabularies. Some we can discard with only a glance. A bull that escaped from an activity farm is not what we are looking for. Others are trickier, and those we print out. Karrion organises the cases into stacks, based on the county of the constabulary. Once my printer stops churning out paper, we read.

It takes us a couple of hours to go through all the cases and put our notes in a coherent order. We swap stacks part of the way through and take a break for me to let Sinta out and check on Dearon. By the time we are finished, the office is hot and musty, and I long for the cool chill of the garden. Unzipping my fleece, I feel a flash of irritation burst through me. I should be out in the wilderness, hunting my traitorous kind the only way a Wild Folk knows: with my nose and all the instincts of a predator.

'Are you okay?' Karrion's fingers brush the back of my hand.

'Fine. Why?'

'You looked cross for a moment. Like you were contemplating murder.'

'Sorry. I was just lost in my thoughts.'

'If that's your thinking face, I worry about what goes on in your mind.'

I grimace, and he laughs.

'Right, let's go through this.'

Aside from Cúan and Holly Smith, we find five other cases that could be connected to the Wild Folk woman. The first is a teenage boy, Josh Bridges, found dead in the woods outside Derby. His body was discovered near a popular off-road trail with his mountain bike nearby. Some of his injuries were consistent with a fall, but there was also evidence of wild animal activity. A bird watcher came across the body shortly after death. His arrival goes some way towards explaining why so little was eaten.

Karrion flags up an A&E report filed by a doctor on call in Bradford. A homeless man named Pete Williams was brought in with severe puncture wounds on his arm. He claims to have been sleeping in a doorway and was woken up when a huge dog was trying to bite his arm off. His screaming scared off the dog and summoned help. The doctor noted that the victim's blood-alcohol level was high and dismissed the story as drunken embellishment. However, the bite marks were undoubtedly canine, which is why the doctor felt it prudent to report the incident to the police in case there was a dangerous dog loose in the area.

'What about this?' Karrion asks, and offers me a sheet of paper. A body was found washed up in Calder Valley near Halifax. I scan through the details and shake my head.

'No, the victim drowned. Any animal activity on the body was minimal. It's not just the deaths that are important, but also the eating that follows.'

'I figured this sounded like a natural setting.'

'Plenty of people die in the woods and fields of this country without Wild Folk having anything to do with it. But if we stalk a human, they're not going to die by drowning.'

'Point taken. I think this one is a better match.'

Amy Fields was jogging late at night near Chesterfield when she became concerned that she was being followed. She made her way to a nearby pub and escaped without a scratch on her. The incident may have gone unrecorded, were it not that Amy is a police sergeant. When she retraced her steps the following morning, she found huge paw prints criss-crossing her tracks. The incident was recorded as a wild animal sighting, though it was the only one of its kind in the area.

Our final candidate is the oldest of the cases, and I only include it after hesitating. Gary Hickson, a fifty-year-old actuary, was found dead near Windermere in the Lake District. The coroner ruled the cause of death to be a heart attack and thereby natural causes, but animals had eaten large parts of him.

'What was an actuary doing deep in the Wild Folk territory?' Karrion asks.

'There are roads through our lands and humans have the right to use them. Over the years, we've had to concede parts of our wilderness as national parks, though we're the ones who manage them. But those areas are far from the hearts of the conclaves, to keep curious humans away from us.'

'Based on this, it looks like the Wild Folk is attacking people all over the place,' Karrion says.

'Maybe. But maybe not. Can you find a map of the country that we can print?'

It takes a few attempts, but we manage to print a map across several pieces of paper. I tape them together and arrange the cases we've picked out in date order. Starting with the oldest, I mark the locations on the map, moving further and further down. When I have finished, understanding dawns on Karrion's face.

'It's not random at all,' he says.

'No. Over the past couple of months, the Wild Folk has been travelling down the country, and she's been stalking and killing people along the way.'

Karrion traces his finger along the route I have marked on the map. He stops next to St Albans and looks at me.

'All this time, she's been heading towards Old London.'

That is the conclusion I, too, have reached. Is it because of me, or is the Wild Folk simply drawn here by the same mysterious pull that entices all magic users to gather in the heart of a human metropolis?

'We pretty much knew that already, given Sinta's reaction this morning and Wishearth's warning. But her journey tells us something far more important than her destination.'

'How so?' Karrion asks, turning to scrutinise the map.

'These cases establish behaviour. If we look at them in chronological order, we'll see that this all began in the Lake District two months ago. Gary died and a scavenger fed on his body. Three weeks later, the Wild Folk had made her way to the outskirts of Bradford, where she attacked the homeless man, Pete. He wasn't an easy target, but slowed by alcohol, cold, and living rough, he posed less of a risk than most people. Three days later, Amy Fields was stalked just outside Chesterfield.'

'Do you think the Wild Folk felt she was an easier target than a man?'

'That's not really what I was thinking. In less than a month, the Wild Folk went from scavenging to hunting a healthy human. That she didn't make a kill is no surprise, given that all big predators are successful only some of the time. The larger the game, the greater the likelihood of failure, but the pay-off is also better. I'm willing to bet she stalked plenty of others who escaped and either never noticed anything was amiss or didn't report it to the police.'

'What about successful kills? Are there likely to be more of those out there?'

I consider this for a moment. 'I doubt it. When someone goes missing, people notice. You'd have to be very lucky to target a victim who has no one in their life. Also, the Midlands is pretty built up. Outside of the Wild Folk lands, there isn't much wilderness and hiding a body wouldn't be easy, especially if you bear in mind that our Wild Folk made little attempt to hide her kills until Cúan.'

'Why do you think she did that?'

I trace my finger along the dots on the map, from the Lake District down to Old London. 'With Cúan, her behaviour changed. I wish I knew why.'

'He's the first child she's killed,' says Karrion. 'Josh Bridges may have been only sixteen, but at six foot, he could have been mistaken for an adult. Cúan definitely couldn't have been.'

Something about that does not seem right. I return to the cases we separated from the rest and read through them again. The nagging sensation at the back of my mind resolves into a clear thought.

'Everyone aside from Cúan is human.'

'A coincidence?' Karrion asks.

'I doubt it. Until Cúan, she was an opportunistic hunter, eating Josh and Holly where she killed them. But she took Cúan alive, covered her tracks well, and went to a great deal of trouble to hide the body. It's as though Cúan was more valuable somehow. Why?'

'Maybe he tasted better?'

The question could be considered flippant, were it not for Karrion's teeth worrying his lip piercing. He may be closer to the truth than I have been, and yet I cannot put my finger on it. I should know, but I understand my kin no more than I understand humans.

'It could be a coincidence that her behaviour changed the first time she killed someone with magical blood,' I say, but cannot conceal the hesitation in my voice. 'After all, how likely would you be to encounter one of us anywhere other than Old London? Humans outnumber us a thousand to one, maybe more. Perhaps the answer eludes us because nothing she has done makes sense. A Wild Folk living in a conclave should never resort to eating a dead human, let alone hunt a live one.'

'Could that be where our logic fails us?' Karrion asks. 'Maybe she's not from a conclave.'

'No.' I shake my head. 'Remember how she shape-shifted at the abandoned cottage? While her use of the wild power was unusual, she's received training to be able to do that. Regardless of why she's now in Old London, she's originally from a conclave.'

'Then how do we find her?'

'By understanding her better.' I stand and switch off the radiator. 'It's time Dearon did his part.'

28

REACHING OUT

Dearon is slow to wake up when I call his name, and he stares at us, uncomprehending, until I help him to sit up. I have prepared him a mug of pain-relieving tea from my jar to avoid the added sedatives, with the taste of anti-biotics again hidden by honey, and he drinks it without a question. While I see to his injuries, he keeps his eyes fixed on the hearth stones and his torso partly twisted away from Karrion, who is sitting in his usual armchair. An awkward silence fills the room, broken only by my murmured instructions.

When Dearon has finished his tea, he sets the empty cup next to the mattress and uses his good hand to rub his face. His fingers against his stubble make a scratching sound, and I wonder if he would like to shave. There is several days' worth of growth along his jaw, but I did not think to ask Karrion to also buy a razor.

Dearon lets his hand drop and looks at me.

'You've been putting something in the tea you keep giving me. Am I going to fall asleep again?'

'It's for your own good.' I cross my arms. 'Besides, it's only natural ingredients to help with the pain and healing.'

The statement stretches the truth as far as the anti-biotics are concerned, but Dearon need not know that.

'You didn't answer my question.'

'No, you're not going to fall asleep straight away, unless you're tired. We need your help.'

Dearon glances at Karrion, but says nothing. Instead, he pulls himself to sit cross-legged on the bed and winces when the stitches pull.

I spread our makeshift map on the blankets. Keeping the explanation as brief as I can, I recount what we have discovered while Dearon was in the hospital or asleep. As much as I am tempted to leave out the part about the Wild Folk being in Old London, Dearon deserves to know everything. The further I get, the graver his expression becomes.

'Where's my knife?' he asks when I have finished.

The hospital gave me what few personal effects he had on him when he was admitted, and I now retrieve his knife. He tests the reach of his injured arm, a frown firmly in place.

'Where's your knife?' he asks, setting his down next to the pillows.

'In the wardrobe.'

'Fetch it.'

My first instinct is to argue about the order, but it feels counter-intuitive. I retrieve the knife and, when Dearon holds out his hand, pass it to him. He pulls it from the leather scabbard, checks the blade from every angle, and tests the edge with his thumb. Seemingly satisfied, he hands it back to me.

'Keep it with you at all times,' he says.

'It's a risk, carrying a knife like this in the city. If the Paladins stop me, I'll be in trouble.'

'So don't let them stop you.'

Doing my best to curb the growing irritation, I roll my eyes and leave the knife next to my car keys. On the map, I point to the Lake District.

'We think this is where she's from. Now we need to find out who she is.'

'More than one conclave has a territory border near Windermere. I will need to speak to several Eldermen to see if anyone is missing a conclave member. But she may not be from any of them.'

'What makes you say that?' Karrion asks, finally joining the conversation.

'If she'd turned into a man-eater, why would she do so on her doorstep?' Dearon says.

'But won't someone have noticed a stranger tramping through your lands?'

'I've no doubt about it, but we are far more tolerant of our own kind within the conclave borders than we are of Shamans or humans.'

Karrion aims his next words at me. 'Should we have looked for more cases further north? Maybe we need to ask Jamie to forward us everything from Scotland as well?'

'I'm not sure that fits with the patterns of behaviour,' I reply. 'Let's go with our first conclusion and revise it if it leads nowhere. Jamie's not going to thank us if we cause unnecessary work for the constabularies.'

Pulling my phone from my back pocket, I show Dearon how to unlock it. 'Find out what you can from the Eldermen of the Lake District conclaves. Someone up there must know something, even if it's just rumours.'

It takes three clumsy attempts before Dearon has opened the phone app. He dials a number from memory, listens for a while, then leaves a short message identifying himself and requests that the Shaman asks the Elderman to call him back as soon as possible. I am surprised to find that he remembers my number by heart, no doubt because of the tentative communication we have established in the

282

past month. Heat rises to my cheeks, and I take Dearon's empty mug to the kitchen to hide the reaction.

Dearon leaves several more messages, all identical, and then offers the phone back to me.

'It will likely take some time before anyone responds, even if the Shamans listen to the messages straight away.'

'Keep the phone, just in case. Just swipe right when a call comes in. I'll make a quick trip to the shops to get us something for lunch.'

'I'll come with you,' Karrion says, and jumps up, catching the side of his head on my lamp in the process. He winces and heads for the door.

I gather together a hemp shopping bag, my wallet, and keys, before following him. Dearon clears his throat. When I turn back, he is pointing at the knife. I sigh, having no energy for another argument, and shove the knife in the bottom of the bag.

'Were you two always like this?' Karrion asks when we have ascended the steps to the street.

'Like what?'

'Constantly arguing about everything.'

My first reaction is to disclaim the statement, but neither of us would believe it. 'No. Once upon a time, we were as close as you and I are; closer, because we grew up together. We bickered a lot, but it was just teasing and joking and a bit of fun. I didn't know about my father's plans for us or that Dearon knew, while Dearon thought I knew. So in hindsight, I guess there was always a subtext we were missing.'

Jogging between cars to cross the road, I glance back towards my flat. Upstairs, new curtains have appeared in some of the windows. I force my attention to the pavement.

'When I found out, I was so angry I thought the force of it would cause me to implode. It's as if my insides were rearranged and that anger never went away, not completely. Every time I speak to Dearon, a spark of it returns and turns me into someone I don't quite recognise.'

Karrion gives my hand a quick squeeze. 'I'm sorry.'

'It's not your fault. It's no one's fault, except my father's for keeping it a secret for so long.' I hesitate before voicing a thought I have never spoken out loud. 'My mother's too, I suppose. She knew and that made her complicit. Even when she was dying, she didn't tell me.'

'Maybe she didn't want to spoil what little time she had left with you.'

'Whatever, it was the wrong choice.' I have to swallow around the traitorous words. 'I've never thought of her in this light. It's been easier to cast my father and Dearon as the bad guys, while mourning her.'

'You're allowed to only remember the good stuff,' Karrion says.

'Am I? You've talked about your father and the circumstances of his death, telling it the way it was, both the good and the bad. Shouldn't I do the same?'

'Only if you're ready.'

'How do you manage it so well?'

Karrion brushes locks of hair off his forehead. 'I like talking about Dad. It keeps the memories clear and it's like a part of him shares my life when I remember him. Besides, I want the brood to know the sort of man he was, even though he's not their father. Better to have him as a role model than the swallow who abandoned Mum and migrated south.'

'As far as good role models go, I'm pretty sure you're all the youngsters need.'

I laugh when he blushes, and we walk the rest of the way to the shops in comfortable silence.

Dearon is on the phone when we return and offers us no greeting. Karrion pulls a face, but follows me into the kitchen without a word. While the salmon we bought roasts in the oven, I make a root vegetable mash and a salad. The shop we went to bakes its own bread, and we found a sourdough loaf that was still warm. Karrion cuts thick slices and slathers them in butter. It helps to dull the edge of hunger. I grin when melted butter runs down my chin.

By the time lunch is ready, Dearon has finished the call. Since I only have two armchairs and no proper table, we fill our plates in the kitchen and Karrion perches on a stool. For a few minutes, we eat in silence, but eventually, my curiosity gets the better of me.

'Did you find out anything yet?'

'Only rumours of unrest within one of the conclaves I contacted, but nothing that will help us.'

'So how come you were on the phone for at least an hour?' Karrion asks, a laden fork halfway between the plate and his mouth.

'A phone call between the Elders of two conclaves is the exception rather than the rule. There were plenty of formalities to observe before I could ask for information. It has been some time since the Eldermen last convened, and we also had other matters to discuss.'

'Let's hope the other conclaves have something more definitive for us,' I say before Karrion replies to Dearon.

Dearon receives three more phone calls while Karrion and I clear the kitchen, do the washing-up, and walk Sinta. When we return and Dearon is still not done, we retreat to the office to review the emails from the constabularies to make sure we have not missed anything. I am tempted to ring Jamie to find out whether he has made progress on the Lloid case, but I resist the urge. If he has something to share with us, Jamie will call.

The light coming through the high windows of the office is fading when the need for caffeine tempts us upstairs. Dearon is standing by the window, staring out and cradling his chest with his free hand. Without acknowledging us in any way, he says a respectful goodbye and ends the call. Turning, he offers me the phone.

'Her name is Cathwulf Bleake and she is a half-breed.'

29

OUTCAST

We sit in the lounge, cradling mugs of coffee or, in Dearon's case, tea. A fire is blazing in the hearth, and I sense a hint of a smoky presence among the flames. Perhaps Wishearth is as keen to find out the latest developments in our case as we are.

'For many years, no one at the conclave knew of Cathwulf's existence. Her mother is human and she was raised in a village not far from the conclave's Lake District lands. The Shamans were the first to relay stories of a girl with an unusual fascination for the wilderness. After the Elderman ordered an investigation, it came to light that the girl carried Wild Folk blood, though she had not yet come to her powers. It was only then that one of the conclave members confessed to having had a brief affair with a human many years previously.'

'Didn't you tell me a while back that such affairs are strongly discouraged?' Karrion asks me.

'I did and they are,' I say. 'But sometimes love has little regard for species.'

'You assume it was love,' Dearon says, disapproval clear in the narrowing of his eyes.

'Love, attraction, lust, call it whatever you want. Few are immune.'

The dark aura around Dearon expands, filling the room

with the smell of ozone. Karrion shivers, while I pull myself straighter in my chair and respond to Dearon's challenge by tilting my chin.

'Sorry, I distracted you from the tale,' Karrion says.

Dearon holds my gaze for a few seconds more before the press of his magic against me eases. The flames in the hearth flare and then settle down.

'When the girl – Cath, as she insisted on – was twelve, the Elderman visited her mother and struck a bargain that saw the girl move to the conclave. A family took her in on the understanding that she cut all ties with the human world. After some initial resistance from the girl, she threw herself into her studies. But she was hampered by her lack of experience and knowledge about our way of life that Wild Folk children grow up with. She made mistakes with herbs and mushrooms, could not read the stars, and everyone at the conclave could hear her coming from hundreds of feet away.'

'It can't have been easy for someone raised by humans to learn to live Wild Folk life,' Karrion says.

Dearon inclines his head a fraction, but this time, he refuses to be drawn away from his narrative. 'When she came into her powers, several years later than is customary for most Wild Folk, it became clear that her blood was weak. The human half of her was too strong.'

'Wait.' I set my mug down. 'Her blood was weak? Don't you remember how she was when she attacked us? That sort of shape-shifting requires a tremendous amount of power. I doubt I could have achieved that before my visit to the Unseen Lands. There was nothing weak about the Wild Folk we encountered.'

Raising his hand, Dearon silences further objections from me. 'There are inconsistencies in the story, but I do believe Cathwulf is the woman who attacked us.'

'Sorry. Carry on.'

'The conclave did their best to train her in the use of her power, but she struggled. In particular, hunting became a stumbling block for her. While she eventually mastered catching game birds and coneys, the group hunts led by the hunt master defeated her, time and time again. With weak blood, she was unable to use the strength of nature to increase her stamina. Having been raised a human, she lacked the instincts to follow the Elderman without question. Without an innate understanding of the landscape, the seasons, and the turn of the weather, she became easily lost. Without appreciating the slow dance of the stars across the skies, she lacked the patience of acceptance, and didn't understand how change would be as gradual as the seasons.'

'I'm not surprised.' Karrion sets his mug down with more force than necessary. 'It's like raising a bird in a tiny cage for years and one day expecting it to fly. You can't turn a human into a Wild Folk.'

Dearon shrugs. 'I cast no judgement over the actions of the conclave, merely relay their tale.'

'But what caused her to leave the conclave and become a man-eater?' I ask.

'On that point, the Elderman was less clear. According to him, this autumn during one of the big hunts, Cathwulf fell behind and became lost. The hunters expected her to eventually find her way back to the conclave, but she never returned. That was the last anyone saw of her.'

'And no one went looking for her?' Karrion asks.

'Eventually, they did, but by then, a couple of weeks had passed. They found no trace of her.'

'What about the Elderman's sentries?' I ask.

Each conclave has sentries posted along the borders to monitor anyone entering the Wild Folk lands. They are lesser spirits of trees, water, and soil, and respond to the Elderman alone. My father always refused to satisfy my curiosity about the sentries, and for a time, Dearon and I made it our mission to patrol the borders to try to spot one. We never did. Now that Father is dying, the sentries should report to Dearon. Perhaps he will finally answer my questions on the subject. As his mate, I may even gain some understanding regarding the sentries. That is, if I choose to take my place at his side.

'They said that a shadow had passed and continued beyond the conclave lands. Even when pressed, they would divulge no further detail.'

'And that was it?' Karrion asks. 'Didn't anyone care that one of their own had gone missing?'

Dearon stares at Karrion and me for a long while before answering. 'They did care, otherwise they would not have gone looking for her. A missing half-breed wouldn't have been a great loss to the cohesion of the conclave. That said, the Elderman expressed concern that Cathwulf was the second Wild Folk who had abandoned our way of life in recent years.'

This time, it is my aura that expands with my flaring anger. Bitter words fly to my lips, intent upon inflicting the greatest possible pain on Dearon, but the scent of woodsmoke coiling from the fireplace halts me. Heat caresses the backs of my hands, easing the tension from my body. I let go of the magic I had gathered to me.

'You can hardly compare me to Cathwulf. I've neither abandoned the Wild Folk ways, nor broken our sacred laws.'

'Yet you live in the city,' Dearon says, keeping his words even.

'Temporarily, as you and my father are so keen to remind me.' Breathing out the last vestiges of my anger, I ask, 'Does the Elderman blame me for Cathwulf's disappearance?'

'Not directly. He is more concerned that you've set a dangerous precedent, which may threaten our way of life in the future. Old London, or any of the big cities in the country, offer many a lure to the younger generation.'

'If the youngsters prefer the cities to the Wild Folk way, perhaps it is the conclaves that need to change.'

Dearon rubs his face, shoulders stiff, but offers no response. It seems he has silently agreed to disagree with me on the subject.

'I don't suppose you thought to ask the Elderman about the dead human found within the conclave lands?' I ask.

'I did. He said exactly what I expected him to say: the Wild Folk lands are a haven for wildlife, so it was no surprise that scavengers had fed on the body. But none of his people had any part to play in the condition of the body or the death itself.'

Like Dearon, I too anticipated such a response. To Wild Folk, it would be inconceivable to entertain the idea that one of our kind has violated the taboo of eating human flesh. Only irrefutable evidence, like finding a Wild Folk engaged in the act of killing, would alter such certainty.

'So we now know who she is,' Karrion says into the silence that settles over us. 'Does that help us find her?'

'If she heard rumours about my living in the city, that could explain why she was in my back garden this morn-

291

ing. But what Dearon has just told us still doesn't explain why she ate human flesh.'

'Are you sure it wasn't just wild animals helping themselves to the body, like the Elderman said?' Karrion asks.

'Pretty sure. Scavenging a corpse is a more logical tipping point than gnawing on a homeless man's arm miles from the conclave. But why did it come to that? Even if she became lost in the conclave lands, she had the skills to hunt smaller prey while she found her way back to the heart of the conclave. There's a trigger, a catalyst we are still missing.'

'We will have to ask her when we capture her,' Dearon says.

'That may be easier said than done. First, we need to figure out where she's likely to be hiding.'

'It's got to be a natural place, I reckon,' Karrion says, unlocking his phone and calling up a map of the city. 'I doubt she will have checked into a hotel. The trouble is, Old London doesn't boast a great variety of parks. There are a few walled gardens and small green spaces, but nothing that could properly hide a murderous Wild Folk. She'd need at least a haunted house or a dank cave as her lair.'

'Both are in short supply in this city.'

'Yeah, I know. Could she be lurking in the Thames?'

I exchange a glance with Dearon and see my thoughts reflected in his eyes. 'Without knowing the extent of her shape-shifting abilities, I can't say for sure, but I doubt it. As much as we are at home in every kind of wilderness, full submersion in a polluted river isn't going to be easy, or a long-term solution.'

'Could we ask Lady Bergamon to get in touch with the

plants in Old London in case they've noticed something unusual?' Karrion asks.

Before I have a chance to reply, my phone rings and I reach for it. 'It's Jamie.'

When I answer, Jamie wastes no time in getting to the point.

'A little girl in Old London has gone missing.'

30

THE TRACKS OF A PREDATOR

Once I have finished the call and relayed the news to the others, Karrion takes our mugs to the kitchen, then throws on his leather jacket with a flourish. Dearon stands and grips the table for support.

'You should rest,' I say. 'You've spent far too long on your feet this afternoon.'

'I should come with you.'

'Not a chance. You're not going to be of any help if you keel over as soon as you get out of the car. Are you going to lie down, or do I have to drug you again?'

His brow furrowing into a glare, Dearon settles back on the bed. Some of the lines around his mouth ease, suggesting that staying upright cost him dearly in pain and exhaustion. I add a couple of logs to the fire and whisper a quick request for Wishearth to keep an eye on him. Sinta has been asleep next to the fireplace, but I wake her up long enough to take her out. She squats with clear disapproval and, once back inside, curls up next to Dearon on the bed.

'Where are we going?' Karrion asks as we are hurrying out.

'Not far from the Museum of London. It's close enough that we might as well walk.'

'Do you feel up to it?'

'So long as I don't have to run.'

Sharpness in the air suggests a frost will arrive overnight. The Winter Queen is watching over the city, or so it seems as I breathe the cold air deep into my lungs and revel in the burn of it. While I long to lie at her feet in front of her oaken throne, this is the next best thing. Better to stay out here, where I can breathe freely, than to slowly roast alive in my flat. That Hearth Spirit would rather see me burn to a cinder than be free.

What am I thinking?

The surprise at my own thoughts is so strong, I stumble and collide with Karrion's side. He reaches a hand to steady me, concern written across his face.

'Are you okay, Yan?'

I rub the spot on my forehead, but doing so sends searing cold through my limbs, triggering a pain so intense, I gasp. Karrion pulls me to a stop, and I drop my hand.

'Why don't we take the car? We haven't gone far and it's better for your pain.'

'I'm fine. This damned Fey mark is wreaking havoc on my thoughts.'

'How so?' he asks, but instead of answering, I carry on walking, scared that voicing my thoughts will only make the pain worse.

The address Jamie gave me takes us to one of the long grey blocks of flats in Barbican. The ground floor units have tiny back gardens, whereas the upper floors have to make do with balconies built from the same dreary grey as the rest of the building. Karrion stops by the front door and cranes his neck up.

'This does not look like a place for a Wild Folk.'

I agree with him, but say nothing. All the nearby buildings appear to have been made using the same mould, and there is hardly any greenery in sight. We are far from the affluence of Lord Ellensthorne's residence.

The communal hallway smells of stale grease and dusty concrete, but it has been swept clean. Jamie is waiting for us by the stairs, studying a leaflet advertising magic wands to boost spell casting.

'Do magic wands work?' he asks when we approach him.

'Not even a little bit,' I reply. Perhaps I should have tempered my tone, but now does not seem like the time to indulge his obsession with magic.

'I see.' He turns to a corridor next to the stairs. 'Follow me. The crime scene unit has already been and they've released the scene.'

'Wait. We've got news.'

Keeping my voice down, I recount what Dearon learned from the Elderman about Cathwulf. Jamie makes a note of the exact location of the conclave where she was raised.

'This is great progress,' he says. 'I'll ask the local police to track down her mother in case she's had recent contact with... Cathwulf, and to find out about any other family members.'

'Usually in such circumstances, the child is encouraged to cut all ties with the human family, but we may get lucky. Cathwulf hasn't exactly been acting like a typical Wild Folk.'

'The more we learn about her, the better our chances of guessing her current behaviour.'

I want to argue that it's not as simple as that, since she had to give up the life she knew as a child to become a member of the conclave, but it would accomplish nothing. So I nod instead, and Jamie leads the way towards the crime scene.

We have not gone further than around the corner when we spot a Paladin standing guard by a door. She steps aside when we pass, and we enter a dimly lit hallway. To our right, there is a narrow alcove for coats, with a stack of empty cardboard boxes underneath. An arched doorway to our left leads to a kitchen barely large enough to fit the appliances, the sink, and a narrow counter. We pass two closed doors before the hallway ends in a lounge that has a media unit, a sofa, and a dining room set, but little else. All the furniture feels too large for the space and nothing matches the off-colour beige walls. Two metal bowls sit on the floor next to the sofa, and the flat contains the unmistakable smell of cat urine.

A middle-aged couple is sitting on the sofa. As soon as we approach them, the scents of hay and horse hair reach my nose: they are Horse Shamans. They both share the same pale complexion and eyes rimmed with red that follow in the aftermath of a tragedy, and I experience a stab of pity for them.

Crouching next to the sofa, I introduce Karrion and myself. The woman offers me a weak handshake, while the man maintains his hold on her shoulders, as if she is likely to disappear if he lets go.

'I know you've already been through this with the police and the Paladins, but would you mind telling us what happened? The more information we have at this stage, the better.'

'Our daughter Thina is missing,' the man, Phillep Marshell, says, his voice cracking.

'How old is she?'

'She turned eleven last month,' Roselind Marshell says.

'When was the last time you saw her?'

They exchange a glance, and Roselind bites on her lower lip hard enough to draw blood. 'This morning. We couldn't afford after-school clubs anymore, so Thina either stayed with friends or played on her Xbox until I came home. But today she had an INSET day and I couldn't take the whole day off, so she was home alone in the morning.'

'Are you sure she didn't visit a friend?' Karrion asks. 'Or go to the shops, or for a walk?'

'Her coat and shoes are in the hallway,' Phillep says. 'Also, we only moved in last week, so Thina doesn't know her way around the streets yet. She promised not to venture out without one of us, and she's not one to break her promises.'

Changing direction, I ask, 'You have a cat?'

'Yes.' Phillep frowns. 'Why?'

'Where is it?'

'He's here somewhere.'

Roselind stands and leaves the room. Her murmured voice carries from one of the bedrooms. She returns a few minutes later carrying a huge Maine coon in her arms. He is charcoal grey, with a paler mask around his face, long tufts on his ears, and deep orange eyes. The haughty stare embodies the arrogance of cats, and my immediate thought is that he is related to Fria.

Karrion responds to the presence of the cat with the ruffle of unseen feathers, but it extends no further. A single animal is less of a threat to him than a Cat Shaman.

'Is he okay?' I ask.

'Fine. Were you expecting otherwise?'

Glancing at Jamie, I debate how to answer Roselind's question and how much to reveal. Jamie gives me a subtle nod.

'Another child went missing last week in what may be a related case,' I say. 'In that instance, the family pet was killed.'

'What makes you think the cases are connected?' Phillep asks.

'Only that in both cases, the victims were children and Shamans,' Jamie replies for me. 'Once we have processed all the evidence, we will have a better idea of whether there is a link or whether the timing of the cases is coincidental.'

'What... what happened to the other child?' Roselind asks.

The lines around Jamie's eyes deepen. He did not want them to ask this question.

'We were able to recover his remains.'

Phillep gasps and reaches for his wife's hand. She lets go of the cat who falls gracefully, hisses his disapproval, and saunters away, tail high.

'He was murdered?' Roselind whispers, knuckles white as she clutches Phillep's hand.

'That is our preliminary conclusion, though the case is far from finished,' Jamie says.

'Do you think Thina is dead?'

Jamie meets Phillep's stare head on. 'It's too early to say.'

'But we'll do everything we can to find your daughter,' Karrion says.

Both Jamie and I give him a silent warning, but the tension in the room seems to have got the better of him.

Karrion paces to the patio doors and back, hands wrapped around his torso. His biceps strain the leather jacket.

'Can you think of anyone who might have wanted to harm Thina?' I ask.

'Who would hurt a little girl?' Phillep asks, shaking his head.

'Does the work you do pose any risk to you or your family?'

'My wife is a teacher and I... I'm unemployed. My days are spent at the jobcentre trying to find work.'

The tightness around his jaw does not invite further questions on the subject, and I leave it alone.

'Is the cat Thina's pet?'

Roselind frowns, but nods. 'She wanted a pony, but we couldn't even afford riding lessons. A cat was the next best thing, and she even named him Black Beauty after her favourite book. They adore each other. Whenever Thina is home, he follows her around like her shadow.'

'Interesting.'

'What are you thinking, Yan?' Karrion asks.

'We once used birds to crack a case. I'll give Fria a call to see if she'd be willing to speak to Black Beauty. Perhaps he saw something that could help us.'

Karrion's expression falls. 'You're going to call Fria? But she's so... annoying.'

'That doesn't mean she won't be helpful.'

'There's something I'd like to show you outside,' Jamie says. 'Follow me.'

Jamie pushes aside a heavy curtain and slides the patio door open. The back garden contains a narrow faded deck and a few square feet of muddy grass. The neighbouring gardens are separated by brick walls, while the back is wood panelling.

'The kidnapper gained entrance through this door. The lock was forced, and she left these behind.'

Next to a bare flowerbed are four large paw prints. Karrion and I both crouch to inspect them.

'How come they're not of even depth?' he asks.

'Think about an animal jumping over something. The front feet land first, bearing most of the weight. Hence the difference.'

Bending further, I borrow the nose of Black Beauty. All I smell is mud and a hint of plaster. The SOCO team must have taken casts of the prints. Something about the scene bothers me, and I lay my hand on the mud between the deepest impressions. A vague unease settles over me as I stare down.

'A feather for your thoughts.'

'These prints are huge.'

'The beast we fought on Sunday wasn't exactly small,' Karrion replies.

I shake my head. 'If Cathwulf transformed into an animal to scale the wall, assuming she could take on a proper form instead of the hybrid we saw her as, she would have chosen something with great agility. A lynx would be my first choice. But these prints are far too big for a lynx.'

'Don't you scale to size?'

'Not to this extent. To become a lynx capable of leaving such big prints, a Wild Folk would be a giant. Even in her misshapen form, she was about my height.'

'We also found some stray hairs in the paw prints,' Jamie says, and scrolls through the photos on his phone. 'Here.'

I take the phone from him and zoom in on the picture. Three hairs lie within one of the indentations, two orange and one white. I rub my forehead, trying to make sense of the information.

'They are not lynx hairs.'

Karrion leans over my shoulder. 'They look more like tiger or leopard hairs.'

'Which is impossible,' I say.

'How come? They're still animals.'

'It would be no different from you being able to speak with bats simply because they fly.'

'But bats are a different species to birds,' Karrion says.

'The point still stands. We borrow shape from the nature around us, not from the wild of distant lands.'

'Maybe Cathwulf visited a zoo on her way to Old London?'

'That's not wilderness; it's captivity for the amusement of people.'

'But there are hardly any lynxes left in the UK, so how come you said that would be okay if a tiger isn't? Wouldn't you be just as likely to go to the zoo to see a lynx?'

'Perhaps, but lynxes have been part of the ecosystem of this country for thousands of years and without human interference, they'd still be thriving. They form a part of the same wilderness that Wild Folk belong to. Thus their form is available to the strongest among us. It doesn't matter that there are only a few lynxes left in the wild when my ancestors have hunted as them for countless generations.'

Karrion shrugs. 'Then I'm all out of ideas.'

'Me too, for now.' I return the phone to Jamie. 'There's something else in this garden that feels strange to me.'

'What's that?' asks Jamie.

'It's tiny. To jump over the fence, Cathwulf must have

known where to land. Otherwise, why risk crashing into a patio chair or a planter and alerting Thina to her presence? Yet the wood panels are flimsy and climbing would damage them. Jamie, did the Crime Scene Officers notice any damage to the other side of the fence?'

Jamie consults his notes. 'Not that I'm aware of.'

'Jumping clear over the fence is possible, but not easy. A Wild Folk could certainly manage it in the shape of a lynx, though it would take a lot of power. But only a fool would make the jump blindly.'

'Didn't we also decide that Cathwulf had probably been watching Cúan before she took him?' Karrion asks. 'It was easy to see into the back of the house after dark.'

'You're right.'

Karrion stands on his tiptoes, hand on my shoulder for balance, and cranes his neck to look over the fence.

'There aren't any trees nearby for some woodlandly surveillance work.'

'Those offer a range of options,' I say, pointing across the road at the blocks of flats that are almost identical to the one we are next to.

'How would a Wild Folk gain access to a flat or the roof of a block of flats in Old London?' Jamie asks.

'I'm not sure they would,' I say. I don't know how to express the unease at the back of my mind.

Jamie puts his notebook away. 'What are you suggesting?'

'I don't know. Something about this doesn't feel right, and yet the timing is too much of a coincidence.'

An insidious cloud of menace seems to hang over the garden. Try as I might, I cannot ignore the feeling that I'm missing something vital. But the most important matter now is finding Thina while she is still alive.

'Hey, how did Cathwulf take Thina away?' Karrion asks, interrupting my thoughts.

'We assume through the front door,' Jamie says. 'The SOCO team lifted a number of prints.'

'But how is a Wild Folk who appears to be travelling on foot going to spirit away an eleven-year-old girl without anyone noticing?'

Jamie glances at me. 'Are we sure she doesn't have a car?'

My first instinct is to say yes, but I hesitate. 'No, we're not sure. It's not the Wild Folk way, but you need not look further than me to find an exception. Who's to say she isn't also an exception?'

Even as I pose the question, I think back to the misshapen creature that exploded out of the abandoned cottage, and the smell of dirt and sweat. If Cathwulf had her own transport and money, why would she have slept in a derelict building instead of the car? And why would it have taken her so long to reach Old London? My instinct tells me she is travelling on foot and thus has no means of transporting a kidnap victim discreetly.

'Maybe there's a simpler explanation,' Karrion says.

'Such as?' Jamie asks.

'Could she have lured Thina away with a promise of sweets or whatever else kids are into? Spell crackers, maybe?'

'It's not a bad supposition. As much as parents tell their children not to speak to strangers, the right sort of lure could override the warning. But why Thina?'

Jamie puts away his notebook. 'Maybe Cathwulf came across her somewhere in Old London; near a school, perhaps?'

Tilting my head back to stare at the few stars visible

in the city, I try to find a way to articulate what feels so wrong about the situation. 'If she's merely a cannibal, there are easier places to hunt people than Old London, or any other part of London. She must be here for a different reason. Whatever the reason, why go after a child?'

'Easier to carry and hide?' Karrion suggests.

'Yes, but a missing child is going to be noticed and acted upon far sooner than an adult. If she wanted an easy victim, she should have kept attacking homeless people during the hours of darkness or someone returning home from a club, drunk. Why Thina?' Before Karrion has a chance to say anything further, I stop him. 'I'm not suggesting we debate the topic now, but it's something to bear in mind. The more we understand Cathwulf, the more we can anticipate her next move. It's more important to figure out where she could have taken Thina.'

Glancing back towards the Marshells, visible through the glass doors, Jamie lowers his voice. 'We know what she's likely to do to Thina. Where would you go, Yannia?'

'I'd drive out of the city and find secluded woods, where I could kill Thina and hide the body from people and other predators,' I reply, keeping my tone dispassionate. Next to me, Jamie takes a step back. 'If there was a stream or a lake nearby, I might consider submerging the body in a watertight container to slow the decomposition, though the temperatures are cool enough to stop the meat from spoiling too quickly anyway. But assuming Cathwulf doesn't have the option of using a car, my first guess would be an empty building nearby, possibly even a building site which is not currently active.'

'The Paladins are already going through the area

searching for suitable hiding places and I've asked the police in New London to do the same.'

'Good. The second-best option would be a natural setting. I doubt she'd jump in the Thames, with or without Thina, but a boat moored along Old London's river border could be a possibility. My guess is, she'd gravitate towards a park.'

'Yes, but which one?'

'None of the green spaces in Old London are large enough to hide a child, let alone a grown woman.'

'Great.' Jamie rubs his chin. 'There are plenty to choose from in New London. We'll have to call in more police patrols to help comb through all of them.'

'Won't that run the risk of Cathwulf bolting or rushing to kill Thina to hide the evidence?' Karrion asks.

I glance at the phone to check the time. 'Possibly, though she may already be dead. It's far easier to hide a dead or unconscious body than a struggling child. That said, we do have one advantage on our side: although it's dark, there are still plenty of people moving about the city. Cathwulf isn't going to risk moving Thina, dead or alive, with steady footfall in the parks. So we have a window of opportunity while she's going to have to stay hiding.'

'What if we don't find her in that time?' Karrion asks.

'Then she's going to slip away with her kill and we'll have no chance of finding her until she takes another child.'

We look at each other in the small decked garden, the enormity of the task weighing heavily on us.

31

A NEEDLE IN A HAYSTACK

'Can you drop us off at my place?' I ask Jamie when he offers us a lift. 'We'll cover more ground if we have two cars. Also, I want to ask Dearon if he has any thoughts about tracking Cathwulf to a specific location.'

'Really?' Karrion asks. 'You're going to ask Dearon's advice?'

My first instinct is to protest that my doing so is not as strange as Karrion makes it sound, but that would not be true. Of all the people in my life, Dearon should be the last one I'd go to for help. Yet during his time in Old London with me, he has shown a grudging respect for my abilities as a PI. The least I can do is extend him the same courtesy.

'Why not? I'm not so foolish as to jeopardise the life of a little girl because I'm too proud to ask for help.'

'Fair enough.'

When we reach my street, Jamie parks behind my car. The dark and barred windows of my office look uninviting in an otherwise lit street. As I unclip my seatbelt, I turn to Jamie.

'Do you want to come in?'

'Is Dearon back from the hospital?'

'Yes.'

'In that case, I'll wait down here. Your lounge would be pretty crowded with the four of us.'

'Good choice, mate,' Karrion mutters as he exits the car.

Sinta remains silent when I let us in, and I wonder if Dearon has taken her for a walk. Bracing myself to tell him off for not resting yet again, I open the door to the lounge and find Dearon propped up on pillows on the bed with Sinta asleep next to him. I stop in my tracks, and Karrion collides with my back and mutters an apology.

Upon seeing us, Dearon struggles to stand, and he grimaces. I hurry forward and offer him my arm, which he takes.

'She came back,' he says through gritted teeth.

'Who did?' I ask, briefly thinking about Fria.

'Cathwulf.'

'She was here?' Karrion and I ask at the same time.

'Sinta scared her off a second time before I had a chance to speak to her.'

'But that can't be right,' I say. 'Why would she come here if she's kidnapped a child?'

Karrion tugs at the hoops on his left ear. 'That means Thina is dead, doesn't it?'

'Even then, it makes no sense. Cathwulf is like any predator hunting big game: after a kill, she will gorge herself and remain close to the carcass, guarding it against other predators. That's why she hid Cúan's body on the island. For her, the risk is even greater as she's hunting people. If Cathwulf took Thina, she wouldn't have ventured away from her, whether she's dead or alive.'

'Yannia is right,' Dearon says, eliciting another incredulous look from Karrion. 'If Cathwulf has taken another child to eat, she would stay close to the body, especially after what happened with the Shaman boy.'

'His name was Cúan.' Karrion tilts his head in a challenge.

Dearon shrugs. 'Cúan. I apologise.'

'Let's back up a little,' I say before another miracle happens and Sinta develops the ability to fly. 'What makes you think Cathwulf came here again?'

'Sinta woke me up by growling at the window. When I let her out, she shot across the lawn, howling and barking. I sensed a whisper of power, but by the time I had climbed out, Cathwulf was gone. All she left behind were a few faint footprints and a clump of mud.'

'Where's the mud? Maybe we can use it to figure out which park she's hiding in.'

Dearon leads us into the kitchen. The mud is on the counter on top of a piece of kitchen roll. It is no bigger than my thumbnail and shows on one side a pattern of neat stitches.

'I think it fell off the bottom of her trousers,' Dearon says.

'This is great, but how are we ever going to find anything based on this alone?' Karrion asks. 'It's not like we have time to run extensive tests on the exact composition or anything. The longer this takes, the fewer people there will be out and about. If Thina is still alive, she won't stay that way for long. We need to be out there, instead of standing around, admiring a clump of mud.'

'You need to learn patience, Shaman,' Dearon says, and I duck to hide my smile at Karrion's indignation. While he tries to protest, Dearon continues without showing any sign of noticing Karrion's irritation. 'There is as much information here for us as there is in a bird's nest for you.'

'I don't know many raven nests with a map pointing to the location of a kidnapped child, but go on, amaze me.'

Instead of responding, Dearon offers the piece of paper to me. I examine the mud closely, spotting something white sticking out of the side. When I tug on it, I find it is a tiny green feather, soft as down. I show it to Karrion.

'It's from a parakeet,' he says straight away, as confident as if I had asked him to read the newspaper headlines. 'But that in itself isn't going to help us much. There are parakeets all over London, both Old and New.'

'No, but it's a start. Do parakeets also live outside the city?'

'Some, but they're not as common there as in the big parks in New London. Tourists feed them.'

'See, that does help,' I say, and offer Karrion an encouraging smile.

'Not a lot it doesn't.' Karrion paces to the windows and stares out, as if willing Cathwulf to appear from the shadows of the garden.

Dearon looks like he wants to tell Karrion to be patient again, but I silence him with a shake of my head. I use my nails to split the clump through the middle and bring the pieces up so I can smell them. Borrowing Sinta's nose, I close my eyes to make sense of the threads of nature. There is dark soil there, stagnant water, decomposing leaves, and something I cannot place, although the memory of a similar scent teases the edges of my mind. After chasing the elusive idea for a minute or two, I pass the piece of paper to Dearon.

'What do you think? Your nose is better than mine.'

His aura expands outward as he calls upon the power of nature. I feel it sliding along my awareness, smooth and familiar and intimate, before it separates into fingers that quest outward. He takes magic from the garden, from Sinta, from the spider in the corner of the ceiling, and even from Karrion. Only I remain untouched. Borrowing power from another Wild Folk uninvited would be akin to reading their private correspondence, going through their wallet, and sleeping in their bed.

The ease with which Dearon uses his magic even in Old London demonstrates clearly the difference between us. While I recall the lessons of my youth as well as any other Wild Folk, he lives them every day. It galls me to admit it, but Dearon was right when he accused me of having lost some of my wildness. By adapting to life in the city, I have become feral rather than truly wild, and the loss of a part of who I am pains me more than I care to admit. But Old London is another aspect of my identity, equally precious. No matter which future I choose for myself, I cannot remain unchanged.

Oblivious to my thoughts, Dearon considers the fragments of the mud and identifies many of the components I already detected. He hesitates, then nods to himself.

'There's something else present too. I believe it to be a form of algae.'

'Could she be near or in the Thames after all?' Karrion asks.

'No. This is from a body of water that flows slowly or not at all. A stream, or perhaps a lake.'

'There's some sort of water in most of the parks,' Karrion says, his frown deepening.

'What if we assume that she's somewhere north of Old London or level with it, given that she's travelled down from the Northern Lands?' I ask. 'Then the obvious choices would be Hyde Park and Regent's Park. The latter houses the zoo.'

Dearon shakes his head. 'That would discourage a Wild Folk, not draw one in. What creature of the wild wants to be in the vicinity of caged kin?'

'Fine, Hyde Park then,' Karrion says.

'It's a good place to start,' I say. 'But we also need to bear in mind that she could have been drawn to larger spaces south of here, like Richmond Park or Hampstead Heath. If that's the case, we're going to need a cohort of Paladins to conduct a proper search.'

Karrion paces to the door and stops. 'Okay, but let's at least start with Hyde Park and then see where we're at. Standing around discussing our options is wasting precious time.'

'One should not hunt deer until one has studied the tracks,' Dearon says.

'One can do whatever the hell one wants, but we need to find this Shaman girl alive, not dead. So let's get to it.'

'You're both right,' I say. 'As annoying as the delay has been, we've gleaned valuable new information. Time to act on it.'

Before I have a chance to suggest that Dearon lies down, he flicks on the kettle and takes a mug from the drying rack.

'I'll stay here,' he says. 'My wounds mean I would not be of much use either tracking Cathwulf or persuading her to surrender to the Paladins. Once she has been caught, I can act as the messenger for her conclave's Elderman in determining her fate. And if she returns a third time, perhaps I can convince her to give herself up without a fight.'

I almost point out to Dearon that once Cathwulf is caught, she is going to appear before a Herald and pay for her crimes in Old London, but it seems foolish to start an argument about that now. Let him assume the conclaves have authority in Old London until we have found Cathwulf. What happens thereafter will be a headache for another day.

'Good idea,' I say when the silence has gone on for too long. 'There's food in the fridge, make sure you eat something so the tea won't make you feel sick.'

We have almost reached the door when Dearon calls after us.

'Yannia, do you have your knife?'

'No,' I say, twisting to regard him over my shoulder. 'I'm going to hunt her the Wild Folk way.'

32

THE HUNTER

Once we are outside, I let Jamie know what we have discovered. He takes a map of both Londons from the glove compartment of his car and spreads it across the steering wheel.

'Even if you're right about Hyde Park, it's a lot of ground to cover. I'll see if we can get some canine units there.'

'Karrion and I can do a fair bit of searching between us. But I'm not so confident about our guess that I think we shouldn't search Regent's Park at all.'

'I can coordinate the search there. That way we'll cover more ground at the same time. I'll also see if I can direct a few mounted units of Paladins over to Richmond Park, at least. They'll be faster on horseback.'

'Good idea. I'll call you when we reach Hyde Park, and Karrion will keep you updated during our search.'

'Why not you?' Jamie asks.

'I'm going to need all the power I have for the search. It's easier to keep hold of it than to distract myself with phone calls.'

'That makes sense.' A familiar wish to witness my magic shines in Jamie's eyes. I ignore it.

'If at any point you think you've found Cathwulf,

314

don't approach her,' I say. 'She's more powerful than you can imagine, especially when cornered.'

'Understood. I'll call for reinforcements.'

'You'll need Paladins. Their swords and chains will draw the magic out of her. After that's gone, she's just a young woman who's been living rough for the past couple of months. But whatever you do, get those chains on her.'

Even as I give the advice, I shudder. There is nothing more unnatural than a Wild Folk cut off from the wilderness. A small part of me feels guilty that I am about to inflict the same fate on Cathwulf, but she cannot go on kidnapping and eating children. Every action has a cost and she must pay for hers.

Jamie nods in agreement and reaches for his phone. Karrion and I walk around the corner to my car. By the time we have slid in, Jamie's car is going past us. As I fasten my seatbelt, Karrion stares straight ahead.

'She's after you,' he says, voice tight.

'Yes.' I turn the car around and choose the fastest route out of Old London, cursing the evening traffic. The cars cast haloes of white, red, and flickering orange along the dark shop windows. More than once, I fancy I detect a glimpse of a different landscape in the reflections: one of snow, frozen rivers, and black bare branches reaching towards steel grey skies. Is it a warning or a premonition of what the future holds for me? 'She must have a reason. But if she knows who I am, she must know by now that I'm involved in the investigation and that I'll be hunting her.'

'Maybe she was planning to turn herself in?'

'She could have done so this morning, but as soon as Sinta started barking, she bolted.'

'Lost her nerve?'

I say nothing in response, trying to get the puzzle pieces to form a recognisable picture. All I have are jagged edges that grate against each other, refusing to do anything beyond baffling me. The Cathwulf seeking me out jars with the one who took Thina.

'Are you worried?' Karrion asks.

'Yes, but not about Cathwulf coming after me.'

'About Thina, then?'

'We've made more assumptions than I'm comfortable with. What if we're wrong and she dies because we've pursued the wrong path?'

'Doesn't the balance of probabilities indicate it was Cathwulf?'

'I never could get the hang of calculating those. But isn't it dangerous to put someone's life at risk on something as flimsy as probability?'

Karrion tugs on the blue-black tuft of plumage over his forehead. 'What choice do we have?'

'Not much,' I admit. 'I'm not even suggesting we change our course of action, but it doesn't stop me feeling there's an element to this that we aren't seeing.'

'But you heard what Thina's parents said. They have no enemies. Who other than Cathwulf would want to harm Thina?'

Who indeed? I have no suggestions and it's not until we stop outside Hyde Park that I find a way to voice the thought that has been bothering me since Jamie's phone call earlier.

'The trouble is, I'm struggling to see why Cathwulf would have chosen Thina out of all the children in Old London, even if she did so at random.'

I text Jamie to say we have arrived, and we enter the

park at Hyde Park Corner. Despite the chill in the evening air, there are plenty of people walking dogs, jogging, or simply cutting through the park. Their relaxed postures only increase my tension as we weave between them along one of the main paths, trying to get an impression of the area hidden by the shadows. We walk the park lengthways, skirting around the Serpentine until we are on the opposite side from where we began. Already frustration fuels my impatience, and I kick a stone off the path. Leaves rustle in the bushes where it lands.

'This is no good. We're never going to find her by walking the footpaths,' I say.

'I can use an owl's sight for a while, but your senses are going to be much sharper than mine.'

'Maybe you should wait somewhere central while I search the park?'

'No way,' Karrion says. 'Remember what you promised after Baneacre? We do this together or not at all.'

A familiar fear of Karrion being hurt rises to the surface, but he's right. We are stronger together. If he trusts me to look after myself, then the least I can do is trust him to do the same.

'You're right. Just stay close and try to walk as quietly as you can.'

As we step off the path in the direction of a thick clump of bushes, a woman walking a Great Dane smirks at us. I flush at the implication of her look, but carry on regardless. Her opinion is of no consequence.

Behind me, Karrion's aura expands with the softness of downy owl feathers, but once again, I am struck by the thought that his magic is weaker than it should be. Did Baneacre cause so much damage that even now, over a month later, Karrion has not recovered? I should have asked him whether he was okay, should have pushed the point even when he was avoiding the subject. What sort of a friend am I?

'If you run out of power, just say the word.'

'I'm fine,' Karrion says, but his voice is tight with exertion.

A small part of me is tempted to repeat the suggestion that he waits in one of the lit areas, but I know he is not going to agree. It is better to let him go on for as long as he can, and then figure out a solution.

When a branch slices across my cheek, I force myself to focus and call the power of the wild beasts that roam the darkness. The blacks fade to greys as the darkness hinders me no more. I rest my hand briefly on Karrion's arm and move forward, leading the way through the undergrowth.

Half an hour later, when Karrion's magic is sputtering, I accept that our second plan was no better than the first. We make too much noise travelling through the undergrowth, and our progress is too slow. Cathwulf can evade us easily, even if she is burdened with a body. There is only one way I can find her, but after my experience in the Unseen Lands, the thought fills me with fear so complete that I stop in my tracks.

'You okay?' Karrion asks after he narrowly avoids colliding with me.

'To hunt a predator, I need to become one,' I whisper, the smell of blood and intestines as strong in my nostrils as when I plunged my tusks into Tem's stomach.

'What are you going to do, start munching on my arm?' he asks with forced lightness.

'No, but I have to stop acting like a PI and start acting like one of the Wild Folk. I was born to hunt, to stalk prey,

318

and to pounce when they least expect it. That's how Cathwulf is behaving, and I need to do the same.'

'We agreed to do this together.'

I glance over my shoulder at Karrion. His pupils are wide and his irises a clear yellow colour. I wonder if anyone has ever told him how beautiful he is when he uses his magic.

'So we did, but we can't catch her like this.' When I see that he is about to argue, I continue, 'I'm not ditching you, but you may not be able to keep up with me.'

'Doesn't that amount to the same thing?'

'What do you suggest, Karrion?' I ask, more sharply than I had intended. 'That we let her kill Thina just so we can stumble around the bushes together? That we allow Cathwulf to escape so you don't feel left out? We need to find her.'

Karrion shoves his hands in his pockets, shoulders tense, and lets go of his power. The amber of his eyes fades to his usual colour. With that, some of the anger drains away.

'You're right. Go do your thing. What can I do in the meantime?'

'Call Jamie and tell him to ignore all calls of weird animals being spotted in Hyde Park. The last thing we need is animal control here or a trigger-happy police officer with a dart gun. The fewer humans we involve, the better.'

'Does that include Jamie?'

When I hesitate, Karrion laughs and his shoulders relax. 'That's mean,' he says.

'If he thinks I need you and Wishearth to keep me safe, I'm allowed to think that he's safer if he keeps away from magical conflicts.'

'Just don't tell him that,' says Karrion.

'Not a chance.'

'Okay.' Karrion opens his phone. 'I'll call Jamie. You go save the day.'

'Karrion? If you hear any howls or screams coming from somewhere in the park—'

'I know, I'll stay away.'

'No. Come running.'

His teeth flash as he grins. As low as he is on power, I still feel the effect my words have on his aura. After he has switched on his phone torch, he heads for the nearest footpath, leaving me alone in the darkness.

As soon as the sound of his footsteps fades away, my fears return tenfold. It is one thing to give myself to the power of the Wild in the Unseen Lands, quite another to attempt it in the middle of human London. Even at the conclave, a transformation would be almost impossible. Moreover, this time I have no Bradán to help me regain control of myself. What if I get stuck in a different form and remain a monster for the rest of my days?

Pain in my hands alerts me to the fact that my nails are digging into my palms and my breathing has grown shallow. Forcing my fists to unclench, I count seconds for my inhales until I feel calmer. A panic attack is not going to resolve anything. To ground myself, I gather twigs and dried leaves into a pile and pretend to strike a match. The barest hint of wood smoke seems to tickle my nostrils. I wind together strands of dried grass and make the pretend offering.

'Hearth Spirit, the guardian of the hearth and the home, watch over me tonight. Help me to find the power and to control my magic. Wishearth, please help me find Thina.'

Wishearth's dark eyes seem to materialise out of the semi-darkness. Sparks flare from them, and I swear I can feel the heat caressing my cheek. Something warm and not quite substantial takes my hand and turns me in a circle. At first, I am confused by his message, but then I see that the answer is right in front of me.

Beneath my feet, beneath even the human-made concrete paths of the park, dark soil awaits me. Moles and earthworms tunnel through it, insects burrow into it, and every speck is teeming with bacteria. Above me, the wind rustles the leaves on the trees as the final nutrients are drawn back into the fibres of the wood, ready for another spring. Shapes leap from branch to branch, squirrelling away the last of the autumn's nuts, while birds settle into their nests for a rest. Countless mice, grey from the city's soot, venture away from the shadows to feast on the crumbs left by tourists and residents alike.

There is life everywhere around me, and the power of it is mine for the taking.

I reach out, opening myself to every tiny thread of magic running through the park, and it suffuses me with a warmth only the Wild Folk know. The power of nature pulses, throbs, crawls in my veins and I allow it to define me. For what am I, if not wildness personified, nature at her greatest, the only one who understands the harmony of life and death?

The imagined scent of smoke fades away as the wildness of countless generations of Wild Folk connects me to shapes long remembered but never assumed. My limbs contort, fur covers my body, and my face elongates into a muzzle. I meet the ground with my front paws before I fall over and find my new centre of gravity with an ease that is all instinct. A shiver runs through my body, causing the hairs along my spine to rise then settle back into sleekness.

I have chosen a lynx as my form, for I am a solitary hunter. No pack will aid me, no murder will accompany me with a rustle of shadow feathers. It will be just the woods, my prey, and me, all connected by the threads that bind all living things together. My sole purpose will be finding the right path to follow.

Lifting my chin, I sample the night air. Even at the conclave lands, when I borrowed the senses of the animals around me, I never encountered such a tapestry of information. It tells the tales of the trees, of the birds that call the park their home, of the people who have passed today and in times gone by. All have left subtle impressions of their passing, invisible to the naked eye, but obvious to a careful observer.

A branch snapping has me whirling around, claws extended and my lips pulled back in a snarl. Karrion jerks backwards, alarm written across his face, and raises his hands in what could be a gesture of appeasement or defence.

'Jeez, Yan. I didn't realise you could transform that fully.'

My ears remain flattened back as I retract my claws and hide my fangs. Karrion relaxes.

'All I wanted to say is that I got hold of Jamie and he said he was going to head this way once he's finished in Regent's Park. So far, he hasn't found anything.'

With my tail up, I turn and saunter off. I have no patience for the trivialities of the two-legged. The hunt beckons me, the night air a far stronger lure than the words of the Bird Man, no matter how much a small part of me rails that he is important.

'Right,' Karrion calls out after me. 'I'm just going to follow at a distance and try not to get in your way.'

The bushes swallow my sleek form before he has finished speaking, but the thunder of his gait remains persistent in my wake. I flick my ears in irritation. A shrew scurries across a narrow path, and I twitch, eager to leap after it. My stomach growls with the hunger of a predator uncertain of the timing of her next meal. The shrew would be a tasty morsel, an appetiser before the other animals in the park, all tamed by people and slow to react to a predator like me. Frost tickles my nostrils, causing me to sneeze, clearing my thoughts. I have far bigger prey to hunt.

Time loses all meaning while I slink from shadow to shadow, all senses trained to detect even the slightest hint of another killer on my territory. For this island of wilderness belongs to me, just as the city around me is mine. It is not the unspoilt wilderness of the conclave, but I have made a home for myself here and I will defend it until my final breath.

I avoid the Serpentine and the wider paths. There are people there, and their tame wolflings are a temptation I prefer to avoid rather than to fight. Their meat will be slack from sedate life, tasteless from lack of wildness, and it is not the way I want to fill my belly. Better to hunt the real prey and—

The unmistakable aroma of rotting meat reaches my nose, and I stop so abruptly, my claws dig into the soft soil. Tilting my chin up, I find the scent again. There is no question about it: I have found my prey.

33

THE WILDEST OF THE WILD

I extend my paw, sampling the leaves on the ground. At the first rustle, I draw back and find a different path. Since I detected a trace of a decomposing body in the park, I have moved with deliberate care, doing everything I can to ensure I remain hidden. Twice I have had to chase the Bird Man back, hissing at his incessant noise. The second time he swore at me and promised to stand still until the screaming began.

To reach the source of the enticing smell, I have to cross the main path and get over a metal fence. The latter does not concern me, for it is barely a leap for a cat of my size, but there are still humans around. Their noise will alert my prey.

In my lynx form, I no longer feel any concern for the Horse Child, or for any other inhabitant of the city. My blood sings with the urge to stalk, chase, and kill, and I surrender to it without a fight. Why should people concern me? They are not my kind, nor do I owe them allegiance. My sole purpose is to track down the predator that has invaded my territory and is killing with greater efficiency than I have achieved. Ours will be a fight to the death, and already I can feel her warm blood sliding down my parched throat.

There is a gap in the humans walking past my hiding

place, and I take the opportunity to dash across the road in a flash of pale fur. A single languid leap sends me over the fence. I land in a bare patch of earth, silent, and with my senses alert for any sign that my approach was detected. A chill wind ruffles my fur, but the cold holds no sway over me. For the first time in more than a turn of the moon, I am free.

Beyond the trees, a small clearing is a break in the grey shadows. I need not my instincts' warning to know I must skirt around it, towards the smell of meat somewhere close by. My nose leads me to a clump of hazel bushes, where buried under dried leaves and plastic bags are ragged chunks of flesh. Saliva fills my mouth, and I swallow it back as I rein in the hunger that consumes all other thoughts. Through the haze of primal want, all I know is that the meat comes from a human.

But here in the darkness only my eyes can penetrate, who would know if I satisfied my hunger?

The hairs along my body prickle a warning. I hear nothing except my own shallow breathing, but I realise that alone is a sign of danger. All the sounds of the woods around me have ceased, indicating that my approach was not as subtle as I thought. With as much care as I can muster, I back out of the bushes and turn around. The clearing remains empty, but now I am certain someone is watching me. But where?

Bushes shudder as a figure explodes out of them. I leap across the clearing, out of the way, as the creature rolls and finds its balance. Arching my back, I hiss a warning and a challenge.

Cathwulf looks thinner than the last time I saw her. Once again, she is a hybrid of many animals, rather than having chosen a single form. Her muzzle is that of a bear, the rest of her head resembles a wolf. She remains bipedal, but her feet are deer's hooves. A tail of black feathers fans behind her. She snarls at me, the sound a primal reflection of inhuman rage, and the park echoes from its force.

I am still taking stock of her form when she charges. Her speed is that of a deer, but, with the agility of a lynx, I leap aside and slice shallow grooves through the fur covering her body. She bellows in pain and turns quicker than I expected. A glancing blow to my side sends me flying across the clearing. I cough, ignoring the pain as I leap to my paws.

She comes at me again. This time, I dodge in another direction and leap out of the way when she attempts to hit me a second time. Despite her apparent rage, she is a cunning opponent. I slash at her clawed hands, and beads of blood fly from her knuckles. The sharp edges of her hoof barely miss me as she stamps forward.

It soon becomes clear that while I am faster in my lynx form, she is stronger. Her blows wind me, while I struggle to get my claws to penetrate her matted fur. Her aura ebbs and flows around her, unlike anything I have encountered in the past. I have difficulty accepting her as one of my kind.

The sound of breaking branches behind me attracts my attention, but only for a moment as I dodge another blow coming my way. I slide between her feet, twist, and leap onto her back. My jaws close around her neck, and I rake with all four paws. For the first time, I feel the fur give away and my claws sink deeper into her flesh. She bellows, trying to shake me off, but my jaws are locked tight. I am not strong enough to incapacitate her with a bite through her spine, but I am not letting go without a fight.

When nothing else will dislodge me, Cathwulf throws herself backwards, intent upon crushing me under her weight. I let go at the last minute, twisting in the air with all the grace a lynx can muster, but she grabs my foreleg before I have a chance to dart away. The burst of her magic singes the edges of my aura, and she flings me away with the strength of a boar. I land on the far side of the clearing. A sharp edge of a rock slices my calf open. When I struggle up, a blinding pain behind my front paws indicates that one of my ribs is fractured, possibly broken. The agony is so great I slump back down.

Footsteps approach, or are they the drumming hooves of charging horses? My mind is dull with pain, but beneath it is an urge to stand and keep fighting. I must defend my territory and kill the intruder. Blood wells from a hidden cut in my mouth, but it is my own blood and thus does nothing to parch the terrible rage burning within me.

I finally blink my eyes into focus only to see Cathwulf almost upon me. Her lips are peeled back in a silent snarl, but before she leaps onto me, a large branch hitting her side sends her off balance. She crashes into the bushes with a yelp.

A few yards away, the Bird Man stands, breathing hard, another length of branch raised in a challenge. His eyes are wide, and the acrid smell of fear comes off him in waves. Yet he advances towards me, jaw set.

'Don't you dare touch Yan again.'

An overwhelming desire to protect the Bird Man pushes the cacophony of aches and pains to the back of my mind. I stand and shake myself, spraying more blood on the ground. My injured hind leg hurts, but it holds my weight. I can carry on fighting.

The threat has little effect on Cathwulf, who flies out of the shadows with the rage of a bear separated from her cubs. The Bird Man swings the branch at her head, but she catches it. Her claws gouge deep furrows into the wood before his grip loosens. She tosses the branch aside and snarls at him.

What little colour remained on his face drains away. He dodges the first blow, but the second catches him across the chest and he is thrown back. His boot lands on an exposed root and he has to flail his arms to remain standing. A trail of blood slides out of the tear in his coat.

It is the sight of the blood, more than his gasp of pain, that stokes the fading embers of my rage into a blaze. Calling upon the stealth of a stoat, I slink forward and sink my teeth into the back of Cathwulf's leg. She shrieks, but before she can do anything else, I bite through the tendon.

At last, sweet, thick blood fills my mouth and slides down my dry throat. The effect is immediate. Power surges through me like a tempest wave, pounding me mercilessly against the cliffs. The pain from my injuries fades away, and all I care about is getting more of the blood and its power. I must consume every last drop of it.

All of this flashes through my mind with the speed of a diving buzzard. Without thinking, I reach up with my claws. Cathwulf is turning, and my new-found strength means her fur no longer hinders me. I slice deep cuts into her thighs and over her knees. Blood slicks her fur as she screams and stumbles back. Her damaged legs cannot find balance, and she falls. She has barely hit the ground when I am leaping on to her chest. Claws strike my sides, but I am immune to the pain as thicker fur sprouts to ward me against the damage. Someone is calling my name, but it's coming from a great distance and cannot tear me away from the terrible hunger gnawing at my insides.

My teeth close around Cathwulf's throat. All it takes is a little pressure and she will die. I will lap her warm blood, feast on her flesh, and all the power will be mine. But even as I prepare to kill her, the memory of Baneacre's smoking body at my feet flashes across my mind. I stood over him, ready not just to defend my city, but to please my Queen, and I shot him in cold blood. If I do it again, what will that make me?

I almost bite down when something collides with the back of my head. The blow is not hard enough to knock me out, but there was enough force behind it to make me pay attention. Unclenching my jaws, I turn to find the Bird Man standing behind me, holding a thick branch.

'Time to stop, Yan. You caught her. She's not going anywhere.'

The fog of hunger and rage still clouds my thoughts, and I blink several times before I recognise the Bird Man as Karrion. Animal instincts give way to human logic, and I ease back.

Cathwulf's body contorts and shimmers as the fur, claws, and fangs recede. Before us lies a young woman, filthy and malnourished. Her clothes are dirty and torn, and, in several places, they are covered in fresh blood. Matted strings of greasy blonde hair form an unlikely halo around her. The aura that surrounds her is ragged and weak, as if the fight has consumed the last of her power. Tears cleave paths across her dirty cheeks. She rolls on to her side and sobs.

I stand over her, still in my lynx form, and see that she is no monster, but a mere human.

34

BLOOD AND POWER

'Yan, it's time to turn back.'

I look from Cathwulf to Karrion. He has lowered the branch, but the wary expression has not left his face. Now, for the first time, I notice the phone in his other hand.

It takes a concentrated effort to focus on my form. A wild instinct whispers that it would be better to run away from this place to the true wilderness, to hunt, kill, and feed in peace. That would be a life for a Wild Folk, far from the noise and stink of humans. I could find a mate, dig myself a den, and have a litter of kittens.

Dearon, asleep on my bed, floats past my thoughts, but I dismiss him with a low growl. He would not accept the life I seek any more than I accept the life he has chosen. It is easier to remain a lynx and only meet him during the brief mating season. What use have I for a mate?

'Yan?'

This time, recognising Karrion takes longer. The animal is taking over. What strange power I gleaned from Cathwulf's blood is fading, and with it comes crushing fatigue. Soon, I will be too tired to change back. I look down at my wide paws, perfect for moving silently through a winter landscape and for running down prey, and try to imagine my hands instead. The paws shimmer, and I almost lose the transformation when a wild hope surges through me. Gritting my teeth, I force myself to focus first on my hands, then on my arms, torso, legs, and finally my head. The process falters more than once, but eventually, I crouch next to Cathwulf in my human form.

'Call Jamie.'

As soon as the words slip past my lips, every injury Cathwulf inflicted on me wraps me in a blanket of pain. My ribs ache in several places, I bleed from various superficial cuts, but the leg is the worst. I shrug off my jacket and fleece, pulling off my T-shirt. Once I have dressed again, I tear the fabric into strips and use some of it as a makeshift bandage around my calf. Then I do the same with the cuts I left on Cathwulf. The wounds Dearon inflicted on Sunday have opened again and several look infected.

Karrion finishes his call. 'Jamie's on his way with the Paladins.'

He approaches Cathwulf cautiously, the branch held high, but she appears too weary to offer any further resistance as we turn her first one way, then another. The smell of her unwashed body is so strong I gag and have to turn away before I finish tying the last of the temporary bandages.

'Could you do me a favour?' I ask Karrion, glancing into the bushes behind us.

'Anything.'

'I found some... meat, over there, but didn't have time to investigate further. Can you check whether Thina is there? I may have missed her in my haste. Don't touch anything, though.'

Karrion swallows, then nods. He looks at the branch, hesitates, and hands it to me. I accept it without bothering to point out that I have far better defences against

Cathwulf than a piece of wood. Karrion disappears, and I track his movements by the flashes of his phone torch and the sound of breaking branches. When he returns, his expression is grim.

'She's not here. I saw the meat you mentioned, and it looks to me like it's from someone larger than a small child.'

Relief washes over me, replaced by confusion. I turn to Cathwulf.

'Where's Thina?'

'Who?' Her sobs have subsided while I tended to her wounds, but her voice sounds hoarse. A small part of me wonders when she last spoke to another person.

'The Horse Shaman girl you took.'

She shakes her head. 'I didn't take a girl.'

Karrion steps closer, fists clenched and his mouth pressed into a thin line. 'Don't you dare lie about that.'

'Why would I lie?'

Cathwulf's simple question throws Karrion. Frowning, he looks to me for direction.

'We know you killed a Dog Shaman boy in St Albans and hid his body on a small island,' I say. She nods. 'What happened after you attacked us outside the abandoned cottage?'

'I continued my journey.'

'And when you grew hungry?'

'I found food thrown out by restaurants and shops. Some of it had gone off, but most was edible if I was hungry enough.'

'What about meat?' I ask, casting a meaningful glance towards the bushes.

'There was a homeless woman, half-dead from drink and the cold. I ate my fill and took as much meat as I could carry. She tasted bad.'

The more she speaks, the more a spark of life returns to Cathwulf's eyes. Talking about meat seems to energise her, and her attention slips from me and towards her buried cache. I shift to block her view, and a flash of anger twists her features into those of a monster. A glance at my hands stained with her blood is enough to calm her, but a hint of steel remains in her expression.

'Tell me why,' I say.

'Why what?'

'Why did you start eating people?'

She shrugs. 'Why not?'

'To consume the flesh of mankind is forbidden.'

She lifts her chin. 'Do you always follow every rule?'

'Some laws are ancient and immutable for a reason. We're not cannibals, nor shall we ever be cannibals.'

'What if,' her voice drops as she leans closer, 'I told you that's exactly what we once were?'

'That's absurd,' I say, trying to lace my voice with conviction.

'Is it? Since I first tasted human flesh, the dreams have been coming frequently. Did you know that this whole island was once unspoilt wilderness and we were some of the earliest people who came here? There were battles, fights over territory, and it was foolish to let the meat go to waste. We ate what we killed and we grew immensely powerful.'

I try to imagine a world of monsters like Cathwulf, grotesque, strong, and hungry. The image jars, but not as much as it should. There are too many stories of Wild Folk going mad from disease or hunger to dismiss her claim outright. But just because there is some truth behind her words does not justify her actions.

'What happened in the distant past doesn't mean it should happen again.'

'Do you have any idea how much power we once had? Why settle for being a bumbling herbivore when we could claim our place as the top predator in the country and the world?'

'You can hardly call the Wild Folk herbivores.'

Cathwulf is growing more animated, and she uses her shaking arms to push herself into a sitting position. 'Then why ignore the greatest source of power and food for us? Why not realise your true potential and embrace your wildness?'

'Because I can bear in mind the consequences. Humans have already done a great job of wiping out wolves, tigers, lions, sharks. We would be hunted down like vermin and the killing would be indiscriminate. Your selfish quest for power endangers us all.'

'Or perhaps it encourages others among us to be true to themselves.'

'I doubt it. Why else would you have left the Wild Folk lands and travelled all the way to Old London?'

She flinches, but tilts her chin. 'I came to find you.'

'Why?'

'Because for over a year, I've heard stories about the Wild Folk who abandoned our ways and still manages to thrive in a city. That is more absurd than us eating people. You should be a mere shadow of your old self, but instead, you're far more powerful. Your chosen mate is the future Elderman of your conclave, not you. How, then, are you able to assume full transformation?'

'Trade secret,' I say. The last thing I want is to explain to her about my visit to the Unseen Lands.

'I wanted to know how you manage to retain the wild

power in the city; I wanted to learn from you. The power I gain from the meat doesn't last. There has to be a way to make it last.' Her voice trails off in the petulance of a teenager. I try to recall if I know her age.

'So your ability to effect transformation, even a partial one, came from eating people?' Karrion asks into the silence that follows.

'Yeah. I'm half-human. What chance would I have otherwise?'

'Right.' Understanding dawns on Karrion's face. 'You ate people to get power?'

Cathwulf nods. When neither Karrion nor I say anything, she chooses to elaborate.

'Dead meat allowed me to survive. Fresh meat allowed me to thrive. But magical blood evolved me into something greater than I could ever imagine. That's when the dreams from our past came and showed me that I was only doing what came naturally to us.'

'The power is in the blood,' I whisper, recalling Wishearth's words. At last, I understand.

Cathwulf nods again. 'You have tasted warm blood, felt its richness slide down your throat, enjoyed the thrill of taking down your prey. When you drink the blood, that kill is yours and yours alone.'

I have no reason to argue with her.

'But what if I told you that human blood tastes a hundred times better? That it makes you feel alive in a way no other prey can. And what if I told you that magical races have their own distinct taste? All those scents that allow us to identify magic in others are present in the blood. The Dog Shaman tasted like he smelled, and it was addictive. He gave me so much power I felt like a god. But it never lasts. I need to find a way to make it last.'

I think back to how close I came to tearing open Reaoul Pearson's throat. Would I have appreciated the taste of his blood? Would I have thought it any different to that of a deer or a hare? Would it have left me craving for more? Now that I have battled Cathwulf and felt the jolt of power that came from drinking, albeit inadvertently, her blood, I know the memory will haunt me.

'The key to power is the blood,' Cathwulf says. 'That's one of the first things we learn as Wild Folk. But what if I tell you that key can be taken? Not borrowed, but claimed. Can you imagine what we could be?'

'You're insane.'

'Perhaps,' she says, to my surprise. 'But that doesn't mean I'm not right.'

'There's one thing I still don't understand,' Karrion says. 'The whole time we've been looking for you, Yannia has been repeating that all the rules of the Wild Folk mean that eating people is forbidden, the worst taboo, punishable with death, and all that jazz. What made you take a bite from the dead body in the first place?'

'I already told you: I was hungry.'

Karrion looks to me for an explanation, but I only raise my eyebrows in confusion. 'Sorry, that doesn't explain anything at all.'

'I was lost in the moors, alone and hungry. There was no shelter anywhere, I had no weapons, and I didn't have enough power to hunt the Wild Folk way. Finding the body was a godsend. I figured I'd eat enough to keep me going until I found my way back to the conclave, and no one would ever have to know what happened. Only once I took my first bite of him, things changed.'

'If you became lost, why didn't you stay put? Other members of your conclave would have tracked you down

336

in no time.'

Cathwulf snorts. 'They're the reason I was lost in the first place.'

It is my turn to look to her for an explanation.

'You don't know what it was like. I grew up thinking I was human, even if I never saw the world quite the same way as my friends did. Then one day a man dressed in animal skins turned up at our doorstep, claiming to be my father and telling me that it was time I embraced who I truly was. My mum just handed me over without a protest, as if it was no big deal. As if she'd been expecting it. And perhaps she had, or maybe I was just one fewer mouth to feed. I went gladly, thinking it was like being the chosen one. Only, it wasn't.

'I doubt you, a full-blood and someone who grew up in a conclave, could imagine how difficult it was to adjust to a whole different way of life. The other children of my age were a lifetime ahead of me. All I had were years of weird dreams without the context of the Wild Folk lore. I studied as hard as I could, learned as much as I could, but I was always behind the others. When I came to my powers, it was clear that I was much weaker than anyone else. The Elders pitied the taint of human in me, and the younger generations scorned me as a weakling. Every time we ventured out for a big hunt, they told me to either keep up or find my own way back. The last time, I got lost so far away from the heart of the conclave that I never did find the right path. Instead, I ended up here.'

Stunned by her words, I can only stare at her. The casual cruelty of the Wild Folk chills me, but it also rings true. Have I not spoken of half-breeds with scorn myself, horrified by the prospect of giving birth to anything other than a true Wild Folk? Was the pride in our pure blood not one of the

337

first barbs Lord Ellensthorne aimed at me? As soon as Dearon found out Cathwulf was half-human, he dismissed her as a threat to be eliminated rather than a wayward teenager to be helped. Was that my thought too, even subconsciously? I cannot recall and I hate myself for it.

The sound of Karrion's phone ringing is so unexpected, I jolt in surprise. With everything Cathwulf told us still buzzing in my mind, I only half-listen to Karrion directing Jamie and the Paladins to our location. All the anger that animated Cathwulf seems to have drained away, and she curls up on her side on the cold ground. With a stab of pity, I shrug off my coat and drape it over her. The Winter Queen has re-established her hold over me, and I no longer feel the cold. I might as well gain a small benefit from the Fey mark.

Reinforcements arrive soon after, and Karrion helps me to stand. Two Paladins draw their swords and take a position on either side of Cathwulf. The jewels on the hilts and the inscriptions on the blades glitter in the light of the torches. Cathwulf barely reacts to the Paladins' presence until a third approaches her with the magic-nulling chains. Perhaps she has heard stories of them, perhaps her instincts tell her everything she needs to know about their purpose, but her attempts to crawl away are stopped by the swords coming to rest against her chest. She offers no further resistance as the Paladin attaches the chains to her ankles, wrists, and around her neck. The Paladins are firm but gentle as they help her to stand.

Before she is led away, Cathwulf turns to me. 'If you put me in a cage, I'll die.'

Lifting my chin, I meet her gaze. Whatever pity I feel for her vanishes when I recall Cúan's half-eaten body.

'I know.'

35

FIRST AID

Jamie stays with us after Cathwulf and the Paladins have gone. I tell him about the meat cache, and he paces to the far end of the clearing and back while he makes a series of phone calls. My concentration falters when he is asking for a crime scene team, and I turn to Karrion. He is looking like someone has died.

'She ruined my leather jacket.'

'What?'

'Look.' He pushes his fingers through the rips. 'You'd need magic to fix this and I don't know any Mage tailors in Old London. It'll probably be cheaper to buy a new jacket anyway. It's just that this one was my favourite.'

I move to hug him, but the scent of fresh blood pricks up my instincts. Leaning closer, I inspect the tears and see that Cathwulf's claws carved furrows across his chest. Karrion shifts under my inspection, favouring his right leg. I glance down, and he tugs at the hoops on his left ear.

'Yeah… I may have tripped slightly when I climbed the fence.'

Try as I might, I cannot keep the amusement fully from my face. Karrion huffs.

'We aren't all masters of animal athleticism like you,' he says.

'Whether you possess the innate grace of a pigeon or not, we need to make a trip to the hospital. You'll probably need stitches and various jabs to make sure body parts don't fall off as a result of our investigation. Your mum is going to kill me if you go home missing a limb.'

'As unpleasant as amputation sounds, I'd pay good money to see that.' Karrion grins, but it slips off his face straight away. 'But if anyone needs a doctor, it's you. Could you, even just once, leave the fighting to the Paladins? It is their job, after all.'

'In my defence, she attacked me,' I say, but he makes a disbelieving noise.

'I'm sure you'll have an excuse for everything. At least you didn't trip on the fence.'

'Like I'm that clumsy.' I hesitate. 'In animal form, anyway.'

Jamie returns and looks both of us up and down. 'You two look like shit. It's a shame the hospitals in Old London don't offer a loyalty scheme. You could earn bandage miles or something.'

'What a thought.'

'Are you going to tell me what happened?' Jamie prompts, when Karrion and I remain silent.

'Of course. But don't we have a more pressing matter at hand?'

'What's that?'

'I doubt Cathwulf took Thina. There's no sign of her here, and I don't think Cathwulf would have lied about Thina when she readily admitted everything else. Which means we still have a missing child somewhere out there.'

'The preliminary reports from Richmond Park indicate that she's not there.'

'If Cathwulf didn't kidnap Thina, there doesn't seem to be much point in continuing to search the parks,' Karrion says. 'That whole plan was based on the premise that Cathwulf would prefer as natural an environment as possible in Old London.'

'Karrion's right.' I glance between them. 'But if Cathwulf didn't take Thina, who did?'

Jamie rubs his chin, scratching the stubble that has darkened since this afternoon. 'I was so sure she was behind the kidnapping.' When I remain silent, he tilts his head. 'I take it that you weren't?'

'It seemed like the most logical conclusion, but the behaviour of the kidnapper doesn't fit with the Wild Folk mindset. Thina's disappearance shows too many signs of premeditation for me to believe she was chosen at random.'

'Christ, Yannia. Why didn't you say this earlier?'

'Because Cathwulf was the only lead we could pursue straight away. Everything else is dependent on the speed with which evidence is processed.'

'Here's something else that seems odd,' Karrion says. 'If the massive paw prints in the garden were planted there to make us think Cathwulf was behind the kidnapping, then whoever took Thina knew about our investigation.'

Jamie swears as the implications of Karrion's words sink in. Despite not feeling cold, I shiver. We all look around us reflexively, but there is nothing to see but trees and shadows.

'Are you sure you're not seeing conspiracies where none exist?' Jamie asks, but he lowers his voice.

'We could be wrong,' I reply for Karrion. 'In fact, I hope we are wrong. Ask the Paladins to use whatever truth

341

zones they can conjure on Cathwulf. If the forensics connect her to Thina's home, you'll know she fooled us. In that case, she'll lead us to Thina sooner or later.'

'And if she doesn't?'

'Then we need to figure out who else would have had a reason to take the girl.'

Nodding, Jamie checks the time on his phone, illuminating his worried features for an instant. 'Standing here isn't going to help. As soon as the SOCO people and the Paladin guards arrive, I'll drive you to the hospital.'

At his words, all the aches and pains seem to double in volume. I wince, trying not to imagine the tally of my injuries.

'Good idea,' I say.

'My appearance is always a good idea,' a voice calls out from the shadows.

The three of us turn in unison to see Mery strolling towards us. She is dressed in tight-fitting black leather trousers, a matching jacket, and leather boots with heels so tall I am amazed she can walk at all. Both the jacket and the trousers are decorated with silver studs and chains. It is not her usual attire, and Jamie seems to share the view.

'Nice outfit.'

'Did you think I'd wear a trouser suit to go clubbing?' Mery's make-up emphasises her mismatched eyes.

'If you've been to a club, you shouldn't be here,' Jamie says. 'There are rules about drinking on the job.'

Mery grins. 'It wasn't that sort of a club, honey.'

Even in the darkness, I notice the flush creeping across Jamie and Karrion's cheeks, and I duck my head to hide a smile. Mery turns her attention to me.

'What the fuck happened here? There's enough magic residue to make my teeth ache, and you look like you were mauled by a C-list celebrity rushing to a group of paparazzi.'

'A minor Wild Folk altercation, nothing more.'

'If this was a minor altercation, I'd love to see you people when you're properly pissed off.' Mery dismisses us all with a wave. 'Now, shut up and let me work.'

She turns her back as her magic slides around us. More footsteps approach from the direction of the path, and soon the clearing is filled with people. While the SOCO team don their barrier suits, I explain to a police sergeant exactly where the meat is and what else Karrion and I noticed. By the time we are ready to leave, Mery has finished her initial assessment and is typing notes on her phone with enviable speed. She waves after us.

'Don't forget to write, kids!'

It is the early hours of the morning when a taxi drops me off outside my flat. I delivered Karrion home first, with strict instructions to get as much sleep as he can. The best I can hope for is that Aderyn will not kill me when she discovers her son's injuries. I did tell Karrion to keep his distance, but I am not sure whether such an argument will fly with Aderyn.

Sinta rushes to the door when I enter the lounge, her whole body wiggling in pleasure. I scoop her up, nuzzling the top of her head, and let her outside. Dearon rises to his elbows on the bed, his nostrils flaring.

'You are hurt.'

'A little. I've been to the hospital, and they've patched me up. No big deal.'

'I was worried.'

'Since you don't own a mobile, I had no way of contacting you.'

The words come out sharper than I had intended, and I wince. Dearon nods, but the tightness of his jaw shows he took offence.

'I asked the Hearth Spirits to guard you,' he says, directing his words at the fireplace, where the last embers of a fire still glow orange and red. 'A man appeared within the flames. He claimed he was your Hearth Spirit and that he always looks after you.'

'Wishearth,' I mutter. Only now do I recall the pretend offering in the park and the scent of wood smoke giving me the courage I lacked. 'He's a friend.'

'How can a spirit befriend a mortal?'

'How indeed? If I knew the answer to that question, I'd be wiser than most.'

Dearon does not seem to know how to respond, while I walk around the mattress to kneel on the hearth stones. Kindling and twigs coax the fire back to life. I add several logs, despite the oppressive press of the heat upon me, and reach for the bowl of offerings.

'Hearth Spirit, the guardian of all who reside within these walls, we thank you for the heat and protection you provide.' I lower my voice, knowing full well that Dearon can still hear me. 'Thank you, Wishearth, for being by my side when I needed you the most.'

The flames flare high, and the heat from them caresses my face, as if two hands are cupping my cheeks. My eyes flutter closed in anticipation – of what, I am not certain – but the feeling fades away. Unsure whether to feel relieved or disappointed, I remain rooted to the spot for a moment longer.

When I turn away from the fire, Dearon is watching me, eyes hard with dark emotions. Yet I get the impression that they are not directed at me, and I offer him a faltering smile. Sinta lets out a bark to signal she is ready to come inside. I move to stand, but wince when my fractured rib catches. Dearon grabs hold of my elbow to both steady and stop me.

'I'll go. Why don't you lie down and I'll make us some tea?'

Grateful for the suggestion, I try to make myself comfortable on the pillows. Sinta clambers on to the bed, her paws wet from the dew, and I pull her to the crook of my elbow. With a sigh of contentment, she closes her eyes. I too have almost drifted off by the time Dearon returns with two mugs. Both contain Lady Bergamon's pain-relieving tea, and I take a grateful sip.

'We caught her,' I say, trying to figure out where to begin the tale.

'I assumed as much.'

'Spirits of the wild, Dearon. We've been idiots!'

My outburst catches him by surprise, and he frowns at me.

'What right have we to consider someone less worthy because of the blood running through their veins? No one can choose their parentage, nor fight biology. Does it really make us feel bigger, better, to deem others beneath us? Have you ever paused to consider how much pain that attitude causes others?'

The stream of questions is clearly not what he expected, and he considers my words while we drink our tea. When our mugs are empty, he sets them both on the hearth stones.

'Start from the beginning.'

I get no further than our arrival in Hyde Park before my words slur and I slip into a dreamless sleep.

WEDNESDAY

36

OUT OF ANSWERS

When I wake, the sun is high in the sky. My phone rings, and Dearon places his pillow on the floor, muffling the sound. Blinking the sleep from my eyes, I try to make sense of his actions.

'Are you trying to suffocate my phone?'

Dearon looks up, a little guiltily, and moves the pillow aside. 'I didn't want the phone to wake you.'

'It didn't. Can I have it?'

The call cuts off before I have a chance to answer. I have three missed calls from Karrion, another two from Jamie. Dearon must have been guarding my sleep for some time. I return both calls, and we agree to meet at my place in an hour.

While the sleep has done me good, moving flares up the ache in my side. Dearon is gentle as he helps me stand. Together we hobble downstairs and shower as well as we can without getting the various bandages wet. In different circumstances, the moment could be romantic, but everything is so awkward I end up laughing as much as my injuries permit. Even Dearon cracks a smile while he rinses shampoo from my hair.

Karrion promised to bring breakfast for everyone, but Dearon and I both eat a bowl of porridge to take the edge off our hunger. I swallow a handful of painkillers and antibiotics, a little self-conscious under Dearon's intense scrutiny. But he says nothing about the pills, just as he says nothing when I hand him his antibiotic and a glass of water.

We both grow still. In the silence of the kitchen, it is difficult to remember why our interactions at the conclave have been so full of anger and resentment. The life waiting for us both there feels far removed from Old London, as if we have stepped into an alternative dimension. Perhaps we have. But while I may call the city my home, Dearon can only ever be an infrequent visitor. The only way we will be together is if I return to the conclave.

As if sensing my thoughts, Dearon ghosts his fingertips along my jaw and tilts my chin up. His lips on mine are gentle, sending a shiver of electricity along my skin. The kiss holds no demand, merely an acknowledgement of how things are. It is that certainty that allows me to surrender to it fully: I make no promise for the future, merely savour his presence here with me.

My ribs protest when I rise on my tiptoes and clutch the back of his T-shirt for support. Dearon leans back against the kitchen counter, and I follow the movement to press against him. He rumbles an exhale of desire as he nips my neck, slipping his fingers under my shirt and drawing them up along my spine. Heat pools in my stomach, more delicious than the warmth of a new fire, as I feel the effect the kiss is having on him.

I am trying to figure out whether my ribs can handle sex up against the counter when the doorbell rings. Dearon drops his head on my shoulder, but it is me who growls in frustration. He tilts his head so our eyes meet, and we laugh. A wet lock of his long hair tickles my collarbone.

'It can't have been an hour, can it?' Dearon asks.

Checking the time, I huff. 'One or both of them is punctual to the minute.'

With a final kiss on the corner of my mouth, Dearon stalks to the lounge and picks up the fleece Karrion bought for him. 'While you talk to Karrion and Jamie, I'm going to take Sinta for a walk.'

'Really? Why?'

'They won't appreciate the way I thank them for the interruption unless I cool off first.'

Jamie and Karrion have arrived at the same time, and neither comments on Dearon brushing past them without a word, Sinta held in the crook of his arm. Karrion raises an eyebrow at me, but I shake my head and put the kettle on. While I brew us a pot of coffee, Jamie spreads a selection of takeaway containers on the small table in the lounge and Karrion fetches plates and cutlery for all of us. I help myself to pancakes, bacon, and sausages, heedless of whether they go together or not. Despite the porridge, I find I am starving.

'Any news about Thina?' I ask between mouthfuls.

'No.' Jamie sips his coffee with a grim expression. 'The preliminary forensics from her home haven't found any link to Cathwulf. We have people looking into family history and checking all the sex offenders in Old London and the closest New London boroughs. Hopefully something will yield viable leads.'

'I'd still like to speak to the family's cat, if I may,' I say. 'Or rather, ask a contact to do so.'

'While the Met may not be keen on too many outside consultants, I'm willing to try pretty much anything to find Thina. Let me know a time and I'll arrange it with the family.'

'Have you heard anything further about Cathwulf?' Karrion asks.

'The Paladins treated her injuries and she's imprisoned at the Brotherhood while she waits to appear before a Herald. But there's no question about her guilt, given that she openly admits to killing and eating several people.'

'I'll need to speak to the Paladin General about Cathwulf,' I say. 'Dearon will have to come with me as the representative of the Wild Folk Eldermen.'

'Why?' asks Karrion, piling a hash brown with baked beans and mushrooms.

'It's customary for the Wild Folk to police our own. In this instance, the situation is complicated because she committed most of her crimes outside of the Wild Folk territory, but there's a universality to the taboo of eating people. The council of the Eldermen will want to summon her to be held accountable.'

'What's the punishment for eating children?'

'Death.'

'Even if it was a simple case of jurisdiction, the Paladins and the Crown Prosecution Service are not going to let you take her back north,' Jamie says. 'Her victims and their families deserve justice, and they should know that it's been carried out. It would be a PR nightmare if Cathwulf disappeared to the Wild Folk lands, never to be seen again.'

Setting my fork down, I sip my coffee. 'I'm not disputing any of that. All I'm saying is that we need to have a conversation about it with the Paladin General.'

Jamie mops up his remaining beans with a slice of toast. 'I have time for another cup of coffee before I have to get back to work. Why don't I caffeinate myself while you tell me what happened last night in Hyde Park?'

'I thought you would have read our statements by now,' I say.

With a weary chuckle, Jamie pours himself the coffee and tops up our mugs. 'I had about four hours of sleep in the early hours and I've been working ever since. This brunch has been my first opportunity to take a break today.'

I experience a flash of guilt over my lie-in and hurry to recount the events of the night before. Karrion adds details here and there, but we both omit to mention how he hit me with the branch to stop me from tearing open Cathwulf's throat. The awe and wariness in Jamie's eyes are enough as it is.

After our mugs are empty and the tale finished, we say goodbye to Jamie and tidy away the remains of the break-fast. I set aside the leftover food for Dearon, certain he will be hungry when he returns from the walk. Karrion tells me about his siblings' Christmas-themed school play while I wash up, but when I dry my hands, he falls silent. I turn to find him staring out of the lounge window.

I rest my hand on Karrion's shoulder. 'Are you okay?'

'I can't stop thinking about what Cathwulf said about her mother giving her away like that. No matter how difficult things have been for Mum and me, we'd never have considered giving up one of the brood. The whole idea is inconceivable.'

Without meaning to, I allow my thoughts to be drawn to what Dearon told me about his biological parents. His father gave him up to help himself as much as to strengthen the bloodlines of our conclave. How is that any different from what Cathwulf's mother did? As diffi-cult as my relationship with my father has been, I have always known that my mother loved me. How painful must it be to grow up with the knowledge that your parents did not want you?

Realising that Karrion is waiting for a reply, I smile. 'Perhaps there are certain things Bird Shamans do better than humans, or even Wild Folk. Family is definitely one of them.'

Karrion's pleasure shines on his face as he draws me gently against his side. 'Hairstyles are another, right?'

The sound of the door opening below us causes Karrion to step away from me. He paces to the bookcase and back.

'What's our next move?' he asks.

It's a question I have also been pondering. 'I think you should take the day off.'

'But what about Thina?'

'Technically, our assignment was to find Cathwulf, and that case is closed. We're also consulting on the Lloid case, but until something new comes up either from the forensics or through Jamie, there aren't many leads for us to follow. Thina's disappearance has nothing to do with us now we know it's not connected to Cathwulf.' I hold up my hand before Karrion can voice his objections. 'But that doesn't mean I don't want to help. I'll try to arrange a meeting with Fria as soon as possible. There, too, we need more information.'

Dearon comes in and sets Sinta on the floor. With barely a flicker of a glance our way, he walks to the kitchen. I hear the sound of the kettle being filled.

'I feel so helpless, not doing anything.'

'Understandable, especially given how busy we've been over the past few days. But quite frankly, I'm in a lot of pain and I need to recover from last night. I'd be a fool not to do so while we're waiting for information.'

Concern clouds Karrion's eyes. He moves to take my elbow, glances towards Dearon in the kitchen, and lets his hand drop.

'You're right. Maybe you should lie down. Can I bring you meds? Or I could stop by Lady B's to ask for more of her tea for you?'

'Thanks for the offer, but I've got plenty of it. Go home and take it easy for the rest of the day.'

'Sure, you too.'

Hesitating by the door, Karrion calls, 'See you later,' to Dearon, who ignores him. With a shrug, Karrion leaves.

'You could have said goodbye.' I move past Dearon to put his plate in the microwave.

'He doesn't like me.'

'And you don't like him. But that alone isn't a reason to be rude.'

Dearon cocks his head. 'I don't dislike him.'

'Then why do you treat him like he's not worth your attention?'

Turning away, Dearon changes Sinta's water. He gathers her toys, with plenty of disruption from her, and puts them in her toy box. He is avoiding the question.

'Well?'

'It bothers me that there's a whole side of you that belongs to him and which I don't understand at all. He's so... comfortable around you, and you around him. You two never argue and always seem to have fun. Whereas half the time, you can't stand the sight of me.'

Stunned by his words, I struggle to find a suitable response. I never thought Dearon would be jealous of someone in my life and even less that he would admit it.

'Karrion and I argue plenty, we just tend to prefer to do so in private. But for the record, I don't belong to Karrion any more than I belong to you. I'm a person, not a... prize you two can fight over.' When he looks chastened, I soften my tone. 'You should try talking to Karrion and getting to know him. He's a good man and a great friend. I think you would find plenty of common ground.'

Dearon nods. The microwave pings, and I reach for his plate with a tea towel. We settle in the lounge, and while Dearon eats, I finally recount the events of the previous night and this morning.

'We need to speak to the Paladin General about Cathwulf,' I say, concluding my tale. 'I presume as the acting Elderman of our conclave, you have the power to speak for the Wild Folk in this matter.'

Instead of responding, Dearon takes his plate to the kitchen and brews us both a mug of tea. My impatience flares at his silence, but memories of our teenage years suggest that I need to give him space to think. He always had more patience than me.

'If Cathwulf appears before a Herald, will she be found guilty?' he asks at last.

'Assuming she really did kill and eat those people, then yes.'

'And the punishment will be death?'

'I'm pretty sure shape-shifting into a monster and killing people to increase your power falls under the heading of murder committed with the aid of magic. In which case, yes, she will be executed.'

'Then it's best to leave things as they are,' he says.

'You want to leave her to the Paladins?' I ask, surprised.

'One of the greatest assets we have in keeping the conclaves and our lands safe from the suspicions of humans is our ability to stay away from the public eye. If I start an argument, or even just a discourse between the authorities of Old London and the Eldermen, I will draw attention to us. No Wild Folk will thank me for that.'

'What are you going to tell the Eldermen?'

Dearon swirls the tea in his mug. 'That she died in Old London. That is the truth, isn't it?'

'In time, it will be.'

'That's good enough for me.'

I study him over the rim of my mug, wondering about the man before me. The past week has shown that I have misjudged him in more ways than one. As yet, I am not certain what that means for either of us. When Dearon's eyes meet mine, I realise I am scared to find it out.

SATURDAY

37

SHADOW OF DOUBT

Three days later, I'm standing outside the grey block of flats where the Marshells live. A dull ache around my chest is a constant reminder of my injuries, but they have provided a good excuse to take it easy for the past few days. Dearon and I have slept a lot, cooked simple meals, given Sinta sedate walks, and I have restricted myself to short periods of paperwork in my office. Our life would be a picture of domesticity, were it not for the knowledge hanging over our heads that Dearon will soon return to the conclave.

There have been times when the pain has woken me up in the middle of the night, and Dearon's steady breathing next to me has soothed me back to sleep. Soon I will be alone again, and I am yet to figure out how I feel about it.

My thoughts are interrupted when Fria steps out on to the road between two parked cars and jogs towards me. I search the road behind her for the tortoiseshell cat that always seems to accompany her, but she is nowhere to be seen. Fria appears to be thinking along the same lines when she foregoes a typical greeting.

'Did you fire the emo pigeon wizard?'

It takes me a moment to figure out what she means, but when I do, a snort of laughter causes my ribs to twinge. Resting a hand gently over the injured area, I grin.

'Never, ever, call Karrion that to his face. But no, I haven't fired him. We just decided that it would be best if I met up with you alone.'

'You mean you decided.'

'Does it make a difference?'

Fria shrugs and turns to survey the building. 'This looks like a classy establishment.'

'Not everyone can afford to live like the Mage aristo-crats.'

'Thank Bast for that. Imagine the attitude problems and inflated egos.' This is the first time Fria has offered any kind of social or political opinion, but she delivers it with the unconcerned disregard of a feline.

'Hopefully the family pet can shed some light on the disappearance of the little Horse Shaman.'

'It's unusual for Horse Shamans to have a pet cat.'

'They couldn't afford a pony. Thina, the missing girl, named the cat Black Beauty.'

'Of course she did,' Fria says with the tiniest roll of her eyes.

Without waiting for her to elaborate on her disap-proval, I usher her through the front door and down the corridor. Phillep Marshell opens the flat's door. There are dark circles under his eyes, and they, together with his dishevelled hair, give him a gaunt look. We shake hands and I introduce Fria.

'Come in,' he says. 'I'll see if I can persuade Black Beauty to come out from under Thina's bed. He's been spending all his time there since... you know.'

'Why don't you let me do it?' Fria offers straight away. 'I'm quite adept at coaxing cats out from under things.

Sometimes, I feel like that's all I get to do at my cat shelter.'

Fria's friendly tone catches me by surprise. This is a new side to her, and I am intrigued to see more of it. Phillep nods.

'Sure. Thina's room is the first on the right.' Phillep turns to me. 'We can wait in the lounge.'

Phillep takes a seat on the armchair in the corner, and I perch on the edge of the sofa. An awkward silence fills the room while I try to figure out where to begin.

'I'm sorry if I'm going over old ground, but have you thought of anyone in your life who'd want to take Thina?'

'No, there's no one.'

'How about anyone bearing a grudge? Anyone from your or your wife's past?'

'I can't think of anyone. We're nobodies, just an unemployed Shaman and his teacher wife. We've got no money for ransom, neither of us knows any state secrets, and we don't even have any political influence anymore.'

This gets my attention. 'But you did?'

'Only nominally. I was an Elder of the Circle of Shamans until recently.'

'What happened?'

Phillep shrugs with a sad twist of his lips. 'I was no longer able to raise my seat and was therefore not worthy of my place in the Circle.'

Unlike the High Council of Mages, who inherit their seats based on bloodlines and political alliances, the Elders of the Circle of Shamans hold their sessions in the square outside the Guildhall. Using the strength of their spirit, they wrench the seats from the geometric stones of the square and raise them high into the air. Anyone capable of it automatically receives a seat in the Circle.

'How long has it been since that happened?'

'About six weeks. Our financial situation had been strained for some time due to care home fees for elderly parents, but the loss of my position was the straw that broke the pony's back. The Circle had provided us with accommodation, as it does for all its low-income members, but we had to move to this place just over a week ago.'

I barely hear anything Phillep says after six weeks, trying instead to recall the list of the Elders Mr Whyte asked me to vet. Phillep Marshell's name was not on that list, of that I am certain. But I have been working for Lord Ellensthorne for two months. The timing is close enough that it could be a coincidence, but what if it is not? What if Phillep's name was omitted from the list because Lord Ellensthorne knew there was no need to vet him? But how could that be? And why?

'This may sound like a strange question, but was there anything unusual about the circumstance of your losing your seat on the Circle?'

'Unusual how?' Phillep asks.

'I'm not sure. Did anything happen that day that seemed odd? Had you struggled to raise your seat for some time, or was it completely unexpected?'

'Everything had been fine until that day. I felt unwell as I was travelling to the Guildhall, but I just assumed that I was coming down with a cold. Something like that should have no impact on my power. But when I arrived there, it was as though all the strength had left me. The ground barely shuddered when I tried to raise my seat. And that was the end of it.'

A tingle runs down my arms and legs. Surely it couldn't be?

'This is going to sound strange again, but did you notice anyone following you on your way to the Guildhall? Especially when you first began feeling ill? Was anyone going the same way that seemed to be watching you?'

'I'm sorry, but I didn't pay much attention to my surroundings. The Circle meeting preoccupied all my thoughts.'

Flashing Phillip a small smile, I try to rein in my disappointment. He would have had no reason to keep a close watch over his surroundings. Even if he had, there was no guarantee he would have spotted anything out of the ordinary. I know at first hand how Leeches can drain power from afar.

'Didn't you ever try to regain your seat?' I ask.

'It took a long time for my power to recover from whatever bug I had. By the time I felt better, I'd grown convinced that it would be impossible to rejoin the Circle, and thus it became impossible, if that makes sense?'

'Yes, it does. By thinking it was impossible, you made it so.'

'Exactly. I accepted that my career as an Elder was over, though it would be easier to move on if I could find another job.'

'Did you have a specific role within the Circle?'

'We all performed fairly minor roles compared to the High Council. I was in charge of assessing how much of the basic services in Old London was funded by charities rather than the city itself.'

'Have you ever had any dealings with the Lifelines charity?' I ask, chasing another hunch.

'I've heard of it, though it never formed a part of my

calculations. Don't they raise money for terminally ill children? And support the core services hospitals and hospices provide?'

'Yes, that's right. Did you ever have any reason to suspect the charity of any wrongdoing?'

'Certainly not.' Phillep frowns at me. 'But I'm not an auditor, nor have I examined the charity's accounts with that in mind.'

'Don't worry about it,' I say, wondering whether I've strayed on to the wrong path. Reaoul Pearson may have used Lifelines to pay a bribe, but that does not mean there is anything untoward going on with the charity's trustees.

As if sensing that my line of questioning has run its course, Fria appears in the doorway, Black Beauty cradled in her arms. He is purring loudly, eyes closed as his claws appear and retract in a rhythm of his choosing. Phillip looks at them both, mouth half open.

'He's not usually this friendly,' he says.

'I have a special gift.' Fria smiles at Black Beauty.

'When you're ready, could you ask him to tell us about the last time he saw Thina?' I ask.

Phillip grows still in his seat. A connection extends from Fria to Black Beauty, as fine as a cat's whisker, as precise as a tom's claw, as soft as a kitten's dream. The purring ceases. Fria does not speak in any way I can discern, and yet I am in no doubt that the two are communicating.

'There was a patch of sunlight in the room,' Fria says, her voice distant, 'this room. The human with small hands and a soft voice rubbed his belly for a time. A feathered mouse flitted across the floor. He caught it, but there were no bones to crunch, no warm flesh to devour. Food comes in a metal bowl, and it is wrong.'

Across the room, Phillep shifts, clearly uncomfortable with the secrets laid bare before us. He looks like he wants to say something, but I silence him with a small shake of my head.

'He slept in the warmth, dreaming of a time when he stalked through woods and meadows in search of his prey, denned within a fallen tree, and lapped dew from deep leaves. In the humid jungles and the wind-swept tundra, there he was, forever free to roam the wilderness. It was him and not him, the memories of his ancestors entwining with his. He was wild and he was tame and everything in between. But he likes the human with the soft voice, for she pets him, grooms him, and feeds him. To him, she is like a kitten to be guarded.'

Fria's expression darkens. 'But then the shadow stole away the warmth and fear crept into the den. The kitten was taken away, as has happened countless times during his many lives. That is how it must be with humans, though he does not like it.'

My nails dig into my palms as I struggle to keep my expression neutral. Fria's choice of words has struck a chord within me, and fear resonates outwards. Is the reference to shadows literal or something far worse?

'Did he see who took her?' I ask, and marvel how steady my voice sounds.

'They were people, that's all he can say.'

'They?' Phillep asks the question that was on the tip of my tongue.

'There were two of them. Male.'

I lean forward, my heart thumping. 'Can he describe them?'

'Can you describe the clouds you saw on a summer's day?' Fria shrugs. 'Human characteristics have no meaning

367

to cats. We're lucky Black Beauty noticed the kidnappers were male.'

Here, at least, is proof that Cathwulf had nothing to do with Thina's disappearance. But who took her and why? Speaking to Black Beauty has only increased the number of unanswered questions whirling around my mind.

'Did he notice anything else?' I ask before the cat gets bored.

There is a pause while Fria and Black Beauty look at each other. He rights himself in her arms, and they rub heads as two cats would.

'Thina was taken as he might carry an unruly kitten.'

I take a moment to try to figure out what she means and shake my head. 'In what way?'

'As far as I could figure out, he meant that she was carried out, limp and unresisting.' Seeing the colour drain from Phillep's face, Fria hurries to continue, 'But I think she was still alive.'

'So she was drugged? Or under a spell?' I ask.

'Either would do the trick, I think. Black Beauty is not sure which.'

Phillep twists his hands together, his left leg bouncing in an anxious pattern. I turn to him.

'It may not seem like it, but it's good news. If the men bothered to subdue Thina, it means they wanted her alive. That gives us hope.'

'But who would want to take her in the first place?'

'We'll figure it out,' I say, but cannot help feeling like it is an empty promise. We have too few leads to follow.

'Anything else?' Fria asks, and strokes Black Beauty's back.

'No. Thank you.'

Black Beauty stretches and leaps off Fria's lap. He weaves between her legs a few times before sauntering to the door. There he pauses to look over his shoulder. Our eyes meet, and in his gaze, I see a solemn request to return the girl with the soft voice to him. I dip my chin, and he leaves the room.

Outside the building, I dial Jamie's number and watch Fria's retreating back. He answers after six rings, just before I give up.

'What can I do for you?'

'We spoke to the cat.'

His chair creaks in the background. I imagine him leaning forward, flanked by tall piles of case files. I have never been to his office at New Scotland Yard, but my mind conjures images of coffee-stained papers, a coat stand with a black fedora, and a row of sharpshooting certificates on a beige wall. The reality is most likely quite different.

'Did you find out anything?' he asks.

I tell him what Black Beauty said. Someone enters Jamie's office part of the way through my story, and he asks them to come back later.

'Do you think we can rely on the cat?'

As much as I want to offer reassurance, truth wins out. 'I'm not sure. Animals don't perceive time the same way as we do, and therefore thinking about a specific event is difficult for them. Or that's what Karrion has told me in any case. But Black Beauty was genuinely distressed about Thina's disappearance, which makes me think that what he described relates to her kidnapping.'

'Which means we're looking for two men,' Jamie finishes the thought for me.

'Not just that, but I don't think we can discount the possibility that at least one of them was a Shadow Mage.'

'Do you think Lord Ellensthorne is involved?'

While I think it is interesting that he's jumped to the same conclusion as I did, I keep the thought to myself.

'There are plenty of Shadow Mages in the city, and some of them are bound to be as unpleasant as Lord Ellensthorne. It would be just as logical to suspect Leina's flatmate, Jhoel.'

'You're right. I suppose I was thinking about Lord Ellensthorne's possible involvement in Lloid's disappearance... and carelessly tarnished all Shadow Mages with the same brush.'

'We can try to verify the information Black Beauty gave us. Was Mery able to identify any spells and their school of magic at the crime scene?'

'I'd have to check whether she has submitted her report. But that might help narrow down other potential suspects.'

'That's what I thought.' I ease myself into the driver's seat of my car and lean my head back. 'Speaking of Lloid, has he appeared anywhere?'

'We've kept tabs on his accounts and phone. There has been no activity since last Friday.'

I cannot help thinking that Lloid is somewhere out there, not hiding from the Paladins, but a victim of crime. But how do I find him and prove that?

'Were you able to find out whose print was on the warding token?' I ask.

'We got no hits from the usual databases. I've also had people trying to figure out where it was bought from, but it's too generic. There are dozens of shops in Old London alone that sell tokens, not to mention the rest of the country.'

'Given how common warding tokens are, that may be another dead end, unless we find prints to compare. That said...' Something that's been bothering me finally takes shape. 'If the flat was warded for silence and there was a temporary silence ward in place as well, how could the neighbours have heard screams coming from the flat?'

'Bloody hell, Yannia. Do you think it was a set-up?'

'I don't know. Were the silence wards in place when the Paladins broke in?'

Papers rustle in the background. Jamie swears. 'Mery said that one ward was active and one wasn't. We need to speak to the neighbours.'

'Can you trace the call that alerted the Paladins?'

'The number was blocked, not necessarily that surprising in that part of Old London, but the call came from the general area of Lloid's flat. We also managed to track down Curt Wegner. He had nothing to do with Leina's death.'

'Did he have an alibi?'

'And then some. He was competing in an amateur wrestling tournament in Amsterdam last weekend. All the matches were streamed online and he's in plenty of photos taken in between.'

'There goes that lead. All roads seem to point the finger of guilt at Lloid. Do we have anything else to go on?' I ask.

'Possibly. I asked a colleague to dig deeper into Lloid's background. It turns out that he did some volunteering with the Lifelines charity last year.'

There it is again, the same charity that was used to persuade Brother Valeron to fool a Herald.

'Back to Gideor Braeman again.'

'It looks that way,' Jamie says.

'The charity might be a way for us to track down other Leeches hiding in Old London. There must be others, at least if the trust accounts in Lloid's flat are anything to go by.'

'I agree, though we may struggle to persuade the charity trustees to hand over the volunteer lists.'

'Without a court order, I doubt they will. But there may be another way to approach the problem,' I say.

'What's that?'

'They must have social media coordinators and records of their publicity. We could get Karrion to pose as a student working on a public relations case study. If members of the High Council volunteered with the charity, there must be photos or articles somewhere. All we need to do is find them and see who else volunteered there at the same time.'

'You're assuming that any Leech is going to have a public image that allows you to identify them,' Jamie says.

'That's true, but if we're right about the other Leeches being part of Braeman's scheming, then they'll all be in positions of power. Maybe they didn't volunteer at the same time as Lloid did, or maybe they didn't do that at all, but it's a place to start. More than that, it's something Karrion and I can look into without needing to jump through police procedure hoops.'

'Keep me posted, as always.'

I promise to do so, and we end the call. Before I have a chance to start the car, my phone rings. It is an unknown number, and I brace myself for yet another conversation about whether I have been in a car accident that was not my fault.

'Hello?'

'Ms Wilde, you're a hard woman to get hold of.'

Lord Ellensthorne's arrogant drawl causes the hairs at the back of my neck to rise. I glance around me, thinking that he is watching me from the shadows of a nearby building, but the streets are empty. If he was here, why would he call me?

'What can I do for you?'

'I wanted to inform you that we have paid you a bonus following the discovery you made last week. Your charges are steep, but I feel it is worth rewarding efficiency in the hopes that it will encourage an upward trend.'

'Mr Whyte told you about Lloid, I take it?'

'He did. What a shame Lloid seems to have slithered away before the Paladins had a chance to apprehend him. And in terrible circumstances too.' I can almost hear the mournful shake of Lord Ellensthorne's head.

'So you were going to send the Paladins after him?' I ask, trying to keep the scepticism out of my voice.

'Of course. What else was I to do with someone endangering our political system? Have him assassinated?'

'No... I mean...' I can think of no suitable lie.

'You did think that. How curious.' A smirk colours Lord Ellensthorne's haughty tone. 'I'm afraid that's a tad too Machiavellian even for me.'

'I haven't found any more Leeches,' I say in an attempt to steer the conversation away from my suspicions.

'That is what I assumed. You would have been in touch with Mr Whyte if you had.'

The certainty in his tone causes my hackles to rise, but I rein in my anger. Dealing with Lord Ellensthorne is easier when he cannot see my expressions, but I still need to stay on my guard.

'Tell me about Phillep Marshell,' I say before the silence goes on for too long.

'Phillep Marshell? What about him?'

I seem to have piqued his curiosity, but he is not one to volunteer information.

'He wasn't on the list of Elders Mr Whyte sent to me for vetting.'

'If I am not mistaken, he had lost his seat on the Circle a day or two earlier.'

'Your list was very up to date, then.'

'Naturally. Information is worth nothing if it has been superseded.' Lord Ellensthorne's chair creaks. 'His daughter was kidnapped a few days ago.'

'I didn't know you knew that,' I say, taken aback.

'This is my city, Ms Wilde. It is my job to know what happens within our borders.'

'If that knowledge extends to the identity of her kidnappers, I'd dearly like to know.'

'That's a job for the Paladins.'

'Not the Met?'

'What good are humans in solving magical crimes?'

My temper flares, but I swallow back the angry retort that flies to my lips. 'Detective Inspector Manning was instrumental in us catching Baneacre.'

'I'm not certain I would call firing five bullets into someone catching them, but perhaps I am being overly pedantic.'

'Thanks to us, you're still here to argue pedantics,' I say through gritted teeth.

'Touché, Ms Wilde.'

'If there wasn't anything else you wanted to talk about, I have a lot of work to do.'

'Of course. Watch your step out there. One Wild Folk

killer caught in the city is more than your kind can afford. Otherwise people might start saying that all Wild Folk are savages to be locked up. That would be bad for business.'

'I'll bear that in mind,' I say, and hang up.

My hands grip the steering wheel as I wait for my breathing to even out and my anger to subside. I play the conversation in my mind, examining Lord Ellensthorne's words from every angle. He knows more than he lets on, of that I am certain. But how far does his influence extend? How will I beat him at his own game?

Perhaps the answer is simple: by having allies. I dial Karrion's number. He sounds a little breathless when he answers.

'Are you bored of resting yet? I have two projects for you...'

SUNDAY

38

FREEDOM

I lead Dearon up the narrow path to a familiar door. The sting of failure hovers over me like a shadow. It's not the same failure I felt after the Marsh case, but it has haunted me since we caught Cathwulf. We had three mysteries to pursue, but only solved one of them. While neither Karrion nor I have given up, I fear that the more time passes, the less likely we are to find Thina and figure out what happened to Lloid.

While I have been lost in my thoughts, Dearon has stared at the array of pots and plants in the front garden. The sound of the lock disengaging causes us both to turn. Lady Bergamon opens the door and smiles. A colourful shawl is draped loosely around her thin shoulders.

'Yannia, how lovely to see you.' Her eyes drift past me. 'And it's a pleasure to meet you, Dearon.'

Dearon takes the offered hand and bows over it. 'Nature's blessings to you, Daughter of Trees.'

'And to you, Spirit Man,' she says with a delighted smile. 'Come in.'

'We came to thank you for the healing you gave us,' I say once we are all in the kitchen. 'It was of great help.'

'The pleasure is always mine. Would you like some tea?'

I glance at Dearon, who nods.

'Please,' I reply.

'Why don't you wait in the garden?'

It's the invitation I was expecting, and I lead the way out through the back door. As Dearon steps over the threshold, he sways. I take his hand to steady him and lead him to the edge of the lawn. His eyes are wide as he takes in the garden.

'Extraordinary,' he murmurs.

Winter has come to Lady Bergamon's domain, and the nearest fruit trees are weighed down by a blanket of snow. Yet in the distance, the trees are pale green with the new growth of spring. The air is heavy with the scent of earth, snow, and winter jasmine. Were I anywhere else, the sight of the frozen landscape would send a sliver of icy fear through me, but here I feel protected.

Dearon's aura expands outward as he explores the magic of the garden. The threads of power running through the landscape rejuvenate him, and the mantle of power around him grows stronger. It slides along the edge of my aura, and the thought of it mingling with mine sends a shiver through me that has nothing to do with the cold.

'Perhaps you'd like to explore the garden first?' Lady Bergamon asks from behind us.

I turn around to find her standing on the steps, watching us with a knowing smile. Dearon flushes, as if caught doing something forbidden. Yet his gaze strays back to the distant forest, and he nods.

'Go ahead. Tea can wait.' With that, Lady Bergamon returns inside.

'She is extraordinary,' says Dearon. 'Like her garden.'

I am still looking at the back door. 'Yes, she is.'

'You are lucky to have made such a friend, though it would appear the pleasure is mutual.'

'Yes,' I say.

'Unless I am mistaken, however, she's not a Plant Shaman.'

I experience a flash of something, irritation or admiration perhaps, that it took Dearon no more than a few minutes to figure out Lady Bergamon's secret. She had me fooled a lot longer, though perhaps I was too blinded by the preconceived ideas of Old Londoners to see the obvious.

'No, she's not.'

'Yet you know her true nature.'

'I do,' I say, choosing not to elaborate. My friendship with Lady Bergamon is mine to treasure and I feel reluctant to share our intimacy with Dearon.

He accepts this without argument and offers me his hand. 'Run with me.'

'I can't.'

'Our injuries have almost healed and shouldn't hinder us. Run with me.'

'Dearon, I can't!'

'Take some of my power. Here, we can run free. Here, we can be freer than even at the conclave.'

'That's not why.' I swallow. 'I'm afraid of losing control again.'

He steps closer and brushes my cheek with his fingertips. I expect him to tell me everything will be fine, but yet again, he surprises me.

'I worry about that each time I assume a wild form.'

'You do?'

'Of course. It is our nature to fear what we cannot control.'

'Yet you still change forms. How do you deal with that fear?'

'By surrendering to the wild instincts. Animals don't hunt for sport, or kill unless seriously threatened. It's the human in us that causes someone like Cathwulf to accidentally fall upon a human carcass and feast. Even among our kind, human blood will fight our environment, while the animal in us will exist in perfect harmony with everything around us.'

'I've never thought about it that way.'

Dearon offers me a half smile. 'Living here in the city, you are reliant on a whole different set of instincts. Here, the human blood gives you an edge over an animal.'

I think back to the way I shot Baneacre and how a small part of me enjoyed it. But I am not one of the Winter Queen's hounds any more than I am a reckless killer like Cathwulf. I seek to live in balance with the world around me rather than hoarding power. Therein lies the difference, or so I tell myself.

'Okay,' I say, and give Dearon's hand a quick squeeze.

'Will you take some of my power?' he asks.

'No.' I smile at his look of surprise. 'I can manage by myself.'

Stepping off the patio, I open myself to the garden. The soil greets me, the trees whisper my name, and the wind moves in time with my breathing. I am part of it all; as welcome here as in my own home. When I reach for the magic of the wilderness, all my fears evaporate like morning dew in the sun.

Next to me, Dearon's power surges around him. I follow his example and close my eyes as the sensations of a transformation wash over me. When it is done, I stretch on all four paws before looking around. Dearon is watching me. He too has chosen a wolf as his new form, and there seems to be a hidden significance in that. An understanding passes between us. A part of me wants to tell him that this means nothing, that the old scars run too deep to be healed by a week spent together, but expressing such complex information in a wolf form is impossible. I do the next best thing and turn my attention to the garden.

The snow is wet and heavy on my nose, and I sneeze. Dearon huffs his amusement and walks forward. I trot past him, tail held high, and soon we are both loping. We cross the border from winter to spring, and the forest looms ahead of us. The faster we run, the more I am filled with the thrill of the speed and the joy of sharing this moment with someone like me.

Our paws swallow mile after mile of game trails with an ease that suggests we could go on forever. With the wind ruffling my fur and the magic of the garden feeding my aura, I believe we could, and the thought spurs me to run faster. All the while, Dearon is by my side, his pleasure as evident as mine. And if at times a grey horse keeps apace with us, it is with less hostility than before.

ACKNOWLEDGEMENTS

Even after five years of working together on the Wilde Investigations series, I remain eternally grateful to Louise Walters for believing in me, my writing, and the Wilde Investigations stories. Thank you also to Jennie Rawlings, Alison Jack and Leigh Forbes for turning my words into a beautiful book.

Thank you always to Andrew Rogers for being my rock, my guiding light, and my co-conspirator. Your advice and encouragement continue making me a better writer. This path is easier to walk knowing we travel along it together, albeit from afar.

To my family and friends, thank you for indulging a slightly batty writer and plying me with cake while I plot my next novel. A special thanks to my mum for buying me a weighted blanket so I can't get up from the sofa and thus have to finish writing all the books.

I'm grateful to Paul and Steve Craddock for our many talks about Hertfordshire nature, birds, and tracking. In writing this book, I took a few liberties and any mistakes regarding the birds in particular are mine alone.

Thank you to Asha for the gift of the emo pigeon wizard.

A shout out to Moon for providing much needed inspiration in the form of Mexican hot chocolate, deity-filled bread, and pinatas!

Finally, as always, thank you to my two shadows, Halla and Usva.

Louise Walters Books is the home of intelligent and beautifully written works of fiction. We are proud of our impressive list of authors and titles. We publish in most genres, but all our titles have one aspect in common: the high quality of the writing.

Further information about all LWB books and authors can be found on our website:

louisewaltersbooks.co.uk

Fallible Justice
Laura Laakso

*"I am running through the wilderness and the
wilderness runs through me."*

IN OLD LONDON, WHERE
paranormal races co-exist
with ordinary humans,
criminal verdicts delivered
by the all-seeing Heralds of
Justice are infallible. After a
man is declared guilty of
murder and sentenced to
death, his daughter turns to
private investigator Yannia
Wilde to do the impossible
and prove the Heralds
wrong.

Yannia has escaped a
restrictive life in the Wild
Folk conclave where she was raised, but her origins mark
her as an outsider in the city. Those origins lend her the
sensory abilities of all of nature. Yet Yannia is lonely and
struggling to adapt to life in the city. The case could be

the break she needs. She enlists the help of her only friend, a Bird Shaman named Karrion, and together they accept the challenge of proving a guilty man innocent.

So begins a breathless race against time and against all conceivable odds. Can Yannia and Karrion save a man who has been judged infallibly guilty?

This is fantasy at its literary, thrilling best, and is the first title in Laura Laakso's paranormal crime series Wilde Investigations. There is a wonderfully human element to Laura's writing, and her work is fantasy for readers who don't like fantasy (or think they don't!) and it's perfect, of course, for those who do.

Available in paperback, e-book, and audio.

Echo Murder
Laura Laakso

> *"I'm part of every bird I meet,*
> *and they are all within me."*

YANNIA WILDE RETURNS to the Wild Folk conclave where she grew up, and to the deathbed of her father, the conclave's Elderman. She is soon drawn back into the Wild Folk way of life and into a turbulent relationship with Dearon, to whom she is betrothed.

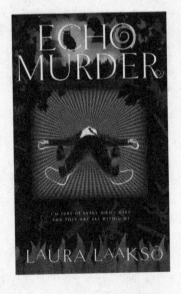

Back in London, unassuming office worker Tim Wedgebury is surprised when police appear on his doorstep with a story about how he was stabbed in the West End. His body disappeared before the paramedics' eyes. Given that Tim is alive and well, the police chalk the first death up to a Mage prank. But when Tim "dies" a second time, Detective Inspector Jamie Manning calls Yannia and, torn between returning to the life she has built in Old London and remaining loyal to the conclave and to Dearon, she strikes a compromise with the Elderman that allows her to return temporarily to the city.

There she sets about solving the mystery of Tim's many deaths with the help of her apprentice, Karrion. They come to realise that with every death, more of the echo becomes reality, and Yannia and Karrion find themselves in increasing danger as they try to save Tim. Who is the echo murderer? What sinister game are they playing? And what do they truly want?

The second in Laura's Wilde Investigations picks up where *Fallible Justice* left off, transporting us once again to Laura's vividly re-imagined London... and for the first time to the Wild Folk conclave which has such an emotional pull on Yannia... a fabulous second-in-the-series novel.

Available in paperback, e-book, and audio.

Roots of Corruption
Laura Laakso

*"What could Lady Bergamon have to fear
in a garden of her own making?"*

ON THE NIGHT of Samhain, the veil between worlds is at its thinnest, and ancient magic runs wild in Old London.

When Lady Bergamon is attacked in her Ivy Street garden, Wishearth turns to Yannia for help. Who could have the power to harm Lady Bergamon in her own domain? While Yannia searches for the answer, nature herself appears to be killing Mages in Old London. Yannia and Karrion join forces with New Scotland Yard to solve the baffling Mage deaths. But wherever they turn, all the clues point back towards Ivy Street.

Yannia's abilities are put to the test as she races to save Lady Bergamon's life, and prevent further murders. But with the lines between friends and enemies blurring, she must decide who to trust and how much she's willing to sacrifice for Old London and its inhabitants.

Available in paperback, e-book, and audio

Longlisted in the inaugural Barbellion Prize 2020

The Doves in the Dining Room
Laura Laakso

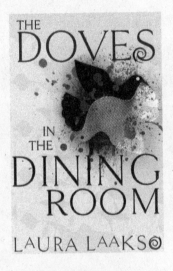

YANNIA WILDE ARRIVES in rural Sussex to attend her friend Jessika's aristocratic Mage wedding. When two butchered doves are left in the hotel dining room, Yannia volunteers to take charge of the investigation. More disturbing events follow, leaving Yannia convinced that somebody is trying to sabotage the wedding.

Yannia teams up with the groom, Robbert, a wheelchair-using fan of detective fiction, and Wishearth, her ever-loyal Hearth Spirit, who surprises her by taking an active role in the investigation. But as the clock ticks towards the big day, the sabotage continues and the contradictions mount. The case turns sinister when Yannia herself is targeted, and Wishearth has to act quickly to rescue her. But can they solve the mystery and save the wedding before somebody loses their life?

This is number 3.5 in the Wilde Investigations series: a "sideways" novella that provides light relief from the darker novels in the series – enjoy Yannia and Wishearth flirting A LOT at a country wedding. What's not to like?

Available in e-book, audio (with Wildest Hunger), and paperback

**All the people listed here took out subscriptions
and in doing so helped LWB enormously.
All my thanks and gratitide to:**

Claire Allen
Edie Anderson
Karen Ankers
Francesca Bailey-Karel
Tricia Beckett
JEJ Bray
Melanie Brennan
Tom & Sue Carmichael
Liz Carr
Penny Carter-Francis
Pippa Chappell
Eric Clarke
Karen Cocking
Louise Cook
Deborah Cooper
Tina deBellegarde
Giselle Delsol
James Downs
Jill Doyle
Kathryn Eastman
Melissa Everleigh
Rowena Fishwick

Harriet Freeman
Diane Gardner
Ian Hagues
Andrea Harman
Stephanie Heimer
Debra Hills
Henrike Hirsch
Claire Hitch
Amanda Huggins
Cath Humphris
Christine Ince
Julie Irwin
Merith Jones
Seamus Keaveny
Moon Kestrel
Ania Kierczyńska
Anne Lindsay
Michael Lynes
Karen Mace
Anne Maguire
Marie-Anne Mancio
Karen May
Cheryl Mayo
Jennifer McNicol
MoMoBookDiary
Rosemary Morgan
Jackie Morrison
Louise Mumford
Trevor Newton
Aveline Perez de Vera
Mary Picken
Helen Poore

Helen Poyer
Clare Rhoden
Rebecca Shaw
Gillian Stern
John Taylor
Julie Teckman
Sarah Thomas
Sue Thomas
Mark Thornton
Penny Tofiluk
Mary Turner
Ian Walters
Steve Walters
Charles Waterhouse
Elizabeth Waugh
Alexis Wolfe
Finola Woodhouse
Louise Wykes